BORN OF ILLUSION

BORN OF

ILLUSION

TERI BROWN

Balzer + Bray
An Imprint of HarperCollins*Publishers*

Library of Congress Cataloging-in-Publication Data

Brown, Teri J.

Born of illusion / Teri Brown. — 1st ed.

   p.   cm.

Summary: "Set in 1920s New York City, this is the story of budding magician
Anna Van Housen, who has spent her whole life playing sidekick to her faux-medium
mother—and trying to hide the fact the she actually possesses the very abilities her
mother fakes"— Provided by publisher.

   ISBN 978-0-06-218754-3 (hardcover bdg.) — ISBN 978-0-06-227720-6
(international ed.)

   [1. Psychic ability—Fiction.   2. Identity—Fiction.   3. Magicians—
Fiction.   4. Mothers and daughters—Fiction.   5. Houdini, Harry,
1874–1926—Fiction.   6. New York (N.Y.)—History—20th century—
Fiction.]   I. Title.

PZ7.B81797Bor 2013   2012038109

[Fic]—dc23

Typography by Ray Shappell

13 14 15 16 17   LP/RRDH   10 9 8 7 6 5 4 3 2 1

❖

First Edition

This book is fully and completely dedicated to my husband,

Alan L. Brown.

No one could possibly take care of me better.

Love you forever.

ONE

The hair on the back of my neck prickles even before I spot him rounding the corner ahead. He saunters toward me, swinging his billy stick, tipping his blue cap here and there to passersby. My spine stiffens automatically and my pulse races. My fear of policemen is as much a part of me as the deep brown color of my hair, and for good reason.

Fortune-telling laws are getting stricter and stricter, so all it takes is one disgruntled client ratting us out to the authorities and we're in deep trouble. They allow us to hold our magic and mentalist shows because they're considered harmless entertainment. It's the private séances the authorities object to, but the amount of money we get is worth the risk.

The officer nods at me and I return his gesture casually, my eyes sliding away from his as he passes. Sometimes I forget how respectable I look now. My green Chanel-style suit, with its boxy jacket and calf-length pleated skirt, doesn't raise suspicion (or eyebrows) like the gaudier costumes I used to have to wear when money was tight. After several moments, I take a deep breath of relief and slow my pace, enjoying the bustling activity around me.

I've only been in New York for a month but have already noticed that everyone acts as if they're frantically busy. Even the little girls and boys in their bloomer dresses and sailor suits look harried. Office girls, with their modern bobs and tight cloche hats, hurry off to work, and the sidewalk newsstand vendors scream out headlines as if they're going to change at any moment. I stop and buy a paper for my mother, who has become obsessed with the new crossword-puzzle craze. I'm briefly tempted by the mouthwatering scent of meat pies coming from a nearby pushcart.

But before I can decide, I spot a young man striding toward me. He too must have just bought a newspaper because he's studying the front page, a studious frown across his solemn features. But it's the way he walks that captures my interest: confident and self-assured, each foot firmly and properly placed in front of the other. I'm so caught up in watching him that I don't notice we're on a collision course until it's almost too late. I swerve to avoid him at the last moment, the sleeves of our coats brushing as we pass.

"Excuse me," he says without looking up.

My face reddens. At least he didn't catch me staring. What's wrong with me, gawking at a stranger in the street like that! At sixteen, you'd think I'd be more experienced, especially considering how much time I spend around theaters. But most of the men I've known have hardly been the marrying type. I snort, thinking of Swineguard the Magnificent, One-Eyed Billy, and Lionel the Lobster Boy. Not the marrying type is an understatement.

A tingling in my stomach distracts me from my thoughts. It grows more and more insistent, spreading to my chest and legs, and that's when I know.

It's happening again.

In public.

Painful red stars erupt in front of my eyes and the world around me dims. I reach for a lamppost to steady myself, hoping no one on the busy street notices. The strong aroma of burned sugar plays around my nostrils. As always, the horror of my visions is served up with the sweet smell of a candy shop.

My heart pounds in terrified expectation of what's to come. The visions are never pretty images of happy endings. When I'm asleep, I can brush these episodes off as nightmares, even though I know better. When awake, I'm treated to the full, excruciating experience.

I clutch at the lamppost as electric flashes, like a distant lightning storm, illuminate a series of pictures. Some are clear; others are obscured behind an impenetrable mist. A burst of light reveals a picture of me running down a dark street. I see empty warehouses flashing by as I run past. It's so real; I feel the rasp of my breath and the sticky, crawly sensation of blood trickling down my cheek. The next image is of my mother's face, her eyes wide with fear, her bow-shaped lips pinched with an effort not to scream. . . .

"Excuse me, miss. Do you know you have a nickel sticking out of your ear?"

The words break through the hammering in my head, and the darkness in my sight recedes as I whirl around. The vision is interrupted, but the horror at what I saw still swirls in my stomach. Then again, fear has been a part of my life as long as I can remember. Visions of the future aren't the only psychical ability I've been "gifted" with.

Nausea rises up in my throat. It takes several blinks before my eyesight returns to normal. My oblivious savior is a short, round man with a handlebar mustache and dark bowler hat. He is patiently awaiting my response. I swallow a couple of times before I can speak. "Pardon?" I tighten my grip on my shopping basket full of the produce and groceries I bought this morning. You can never be too careful.

Around us, pedestrians go about their day with barely a glance. It takes something special to capture their attention, especially in this aspiring working class neighborhood of brownstone apartments and shops.

Flashing a nubby-toothed smile, my companion reaches up and pulls a nickel out of my ear. A few steps away, a small boy in frayed knee pants, holding a sheaf of flyers, hoots with laughter.

Understanding dawns, and the tension along my neck and shoulders loosens—I've been around stage promoters my whole life, and though they're a shifty lot, they generally pose no immediate threat. Whatever the vision was about, it had nothing to do with this stubby bit of a man.

"Thank you!" I tell him, taking the coin with my left hand. I make a show of switching my basket to the other hand and, with one fluid motion, reach my empty right hand up to the side of his head. "And do you realize you have an onion in yours?"

I smile at the boy, whose mouth forms an O as I pull a long, thin green onion out of the man's ear.

The man's eyes widen, then he grins in appreciation. I relax. Most male magicians resent girls who practice magic. Obviously, this little man isn't one of them.

"Wait! There's more!" Not to be outdone, he reaches up and begins pulling brightly colored scarves out of my other ear. Around us, a small crowd forms, and excitement kicks my pulse up a notch. My mother says I'm a show-off, but I prefer to think of myself as a performer. Plus, it's been weeks since I've done any street magic. It doesn't go with the shiny new image of respectability we're trying to cultivate.

"Wonderful," I tell him, taking the scarves and crumpling them into a tight ball. I wink at the people gathering around us. "I was looking for those."

They laugh appreciatively. With a snap of my wrist, I flick my fingers open toward the man's face. There's a small gasp and scattered applause as they realize that the scarves have disappeared.

"Hey!" the man protests good-naturedly. "Those were mine."

"I'm sorry." I set the basket by my feet to free up both hands. Now I *am* showing off, but performing in front of an audience is so much fun, I can't resist. "Perhaps you would take these in trade?" I whisk three silver bangles off my left wrist. They were made especially for me by a silversmith in Boston, and, along with my deck of cards and the balisong in my handbag, I never leave home without them. Working them expertly between my fingers, I juggle them a bit to show everyone they're three separate circlets. Then I catch them one at a time with the same hand and clutch them together. Moments later, I hold them up and the onlookers gasp. The bracelets are now connected like a chain.

The man throws up his hands, laughing. "I give up; you win!"

The boy adroitly maneuvers through the dispersing crowd, passing out flyers.

I replace my bangles and pull the ball of scarves out of the basket where I'd secreted them. "Looking for these?" I ask.

He takes the scarves and shoves them into the pocket of his baggy trousers. "You're quite good—for a girl."

"Thank you," I tell him, ignoring the girl remark. If I argued with every male magician who made a snide comment about my gender, I'd never have time to do magic. I prefer to outperform them onstage, where it really matters. "My mother and I are opening tomorrow night at the Newmark Theater."

"Swanky! A magic show, I take it?"

My stomach sinks a bit. I wish it *were* just a magic show.

"I do a bit of magic in the show, but Mother's a mentalist. I mostly assist her. If you'd like to come, I'll leave you tickets at the box office. Just tell them Anna Van Housen sent you." I nod toward the boy. "I'll leave one for him, too."

"That would be grand! My name is Ezio Trieste." He holds out a grubby hand and I shake it firmly. "You and your mother might be interested in this show Sunday night. Dante!" he yells at the little boy still handing out flyers to anyone who will take one. "Give the lady one of those."

I take the proffered paper with a smile, then hand the man back his coin.

I glance down at the flyer and everything around me dims as I read the headline.

DO SPIRITS EXIST?
HOUDINI SAYS NO AND PROVES IT!

"Thank you," I whisper, and turn away, forcing my heavy limbs to move. The ringing in my ears drowns out the sound of the automobiles on the street as I hurry down the sidewalk. After half a block, I slow and crumple the paper in my hand. Tossing it into the gutter, I stop and take a measured breath. My mother's sharp eyes see everything, and the last thing I need is for her to find out that Houdini's in town.

TWO

I stare at the paper in the gutter and bite my lip. Glancing around, I retrieve the flyer from the street and smooth it out as best I can with my hands. Then I fold it up and slip it into the bottom of my basket, where Mother won't see it.

Why am I so shocked? I wonder as I head toward home. Though he tours most of the year, New York is his home. I should have known our paths would cross at some point.

I shake my head as I reach the steps to my building, resolving not to give Houdini another thought. At least until my mother catches wind of his arrival.

Taking a deep breath to clear my mind, I stare up at my new home. Once a private residence, it was recently remodeled into two apartments. Our new talent manager was courteous enough to find the apartment for us and make all the arrangements. I'm still waiting to find out what price this "courtesy" will entail. I trust managers almost as much as I trust lawmen, perhaps less. At least with lawmen you know where you stand. But managers say one thing and do another. Every one we've ever had has either cheated us out of money or used the contract to take advantage of my mother's obvious charms.

But I do love this home. The sandy-colored exterior and wrought-iron railings gleam in the sun, and the wide stoop welcomes me. It doesn't matter that there are a dozen other identical buildings lining my street; this one is special, the first real house I've ever lived in. I used to dream of living in a house like this instead of traveling all the time.

Though living on the top floor of this beautiful old home instead of in a shoddy hotel thrills me to no end, I'm also left with a nagging sense of unworthiness. This house is all sedate respectability. As the friend of pickpockets and circus freaks, the same cannot be said of me. My only hope is that with our first steady job, I can put the past behind me and be worthy of such a home. My face heats with shame remembering the street performance I just gave. Respectable girls don't do magic on the street. Normal girls also don't have horrifying visions of the future. My stomach clenches as an image of my mother's face swims before my eyes.

I have a sudden need to see for myself that she is fine. I rush up the stone steps two at a time and fling the door open.

"Oof!"

Just inside, a young man dressed in a black suit and derby hat clutches his arm.

"I'm so sorry! Are you all right?" He's so tall I have to crane my neck to see his face, and his shoulders seem to fill the room. His brows rise over eyes so rich and dark they're almost black, like the innermost heart of a licorice drop. My breath catches and my cheeks heat when I recognize who it is. The young man from the street.

To my surprise, his cheeks redden as well, showing his discomfort. "I should be asking if you're all right. You ran inside as if the hounds of hell were chasing you."

I cock my head at the odd words, as well as at the crisp way he said them. It's not an accent, exactly. More like he relishes the English language and takes care to pronounce each word fully.

I shake my head, unsettled. "I'm fine. You're the one I slammed into." I glance behind him at the empty hallway. "Were you looking for me?" If possible, my face burns even brighter. "I mean, were you looking for someone?"

The stranger shakes his head. His dark eyes regard me steadily for a moment but then slide away as if embarrassed before returning to meet mine once again.

I'm used to being stared at, but the men at the theater leer at me in a knowing way that makes my skin crawl. The appreciative gaze of this young man, with his straight mouth and intelligent features, sends a pleasing tingle across my skin. Embarrassed, I look away.

The door next to us opens, causing us both to jump. Mr. Darby, our crotchety neighbor, sticks his head out. "What's the ruckus about?" He sees me and his mouth creases downward, but then he spots the young man and his face softens. He steps into the hall, his arms crossed. "I might have known you'd find a way to meet the pretty young lady upstairs. In my day, we didn't even speak to a girl without a proper introduction."

The young man pushes the derby back on his head and a dark curl escapes. My fingers suddenly itch to nudge it back into place.

"Then please introduce us," he says, and I notice how young he actually is. Maybe seventeen or eighteen—just a bit older than I am. He's clean shaven and doesn't yet sport a mustache, as most men these days do. I like it. Men with mustaches always look like they're hiding a harelip.

The old man harrumphs. "Miss Van Housen, Colin Emerson Archer the third." He shakes his head as if perplexed by such a fancy name. "Colin is a friend of my second cousin and came to stay with me just after you and your mother moved in upstairs. No doubt a spy sent by meddling relatives worried about an old man living by himself. Colin, this is Miss Van Housen. She and her mother live in the apartment above us."

Colin Emerson Archer *the third* whisks off his hat and bows with excessive courtesy. "Miss Van Housen."

I incline my head. "Mr. Archer."

He clears his throat. "Please, call me Cole."

There's an awkward moment of silence as they wait for me to offer my first name. I don't. In our business, all strangers are to be regarded with suspicion.

Mr. Darby clears his throat. "Next time you go out, missy, you might want to stop and ask if I need anything.

11

A cup of that tea would be good in the morning."

He nods toward my basket, which is still full in spite of the collision. My mouth drops open. Is this the same neighbor who has done little more than grunt at me these past few weeks? He's a strange old bird. I hear all sorts of odd banging noises coming out of his apartment day and night, but I have no idea what they could be. He stares back at me fiercely.

Cole gives an unexpected laugh that fills the hallway and breaks the tension. He may look like an English schoolmaster, but his laugh is wonderful.

"And you just reproached me for my etiquette!" he says to Mr. Darby.

"I'm an old man. I can get away with it."

"I'll bring you a package the very next time I go out," I promise, moving toward the stairs. It suddenly dawns on me that respectable girls probably don't hang about in hallways with strange young men. Of course, because of my work, there have been many strange men in my life, but my new neighbors don't need to know that.

"It was a pleasure to make your acquaintance, Miss Van Housen." Cole holds out his hand.

I swallow. I usually try to avoid touching people—it's the easiest way to avoid being bombarded with someone else's emotions. And unlike my visions, this is a "gift" I can actually control, though occasionally, like now, it's unavoidable. "Likewise," I say in my most proper voice.

The moment our fingers meet, a spark flashes between us, so powerful I feel my heart stutter. We stand frozen as the first shock subsides into frothy, electrical pulses that travel between our palms and tickle my flesh like effervescent bubbles. I yank my hand from his.

Surprise widens his eyes, but he recovers quickly and nods his head in that same overly polite way.

Mr. Darby looks at us, puzzlement written across his wrinkled features.

I nod back. Usually when I touch someone, I just get a sense of how they're feeling, not an electrical shock, but if he can pretend nothing happened, then I can too. Still trembling, I make my way up the stairs to my apartment.

I sneak a quick sideways glance as I open our door. Cole's staring up at me, the light from the still-open front door casting an incandescent glow around him. He gives me another nod and I enter the apartment, my pulse thudding wildly. I huff, leaning my back against the door.

An unusual vision, Harry Houdini in town, and a strange young man moving in downstairs. And it's not even noon yet. Perhaps living a quiet, respectable life is going to be more of a challenge than I thought.

The first thing I do upon entering the apartment is to listen for my mother. The memory of the vision and my mother's terrified face is still swirling in my mind. I hear voices coming from the sitting room, and my relief at the sound of her voice is quickly replaced with annoyance when I also recognize our new manager's French accent.

I give myself a shake and put away the groceries and wipe down the counters, hoping the domestic routine I've established since I moved here will calm my nerves. I've never had my own kitchen before, and even though it's more like a galley than a room, it's sunny and bright, and I love the normalcy of it.

But in spite of my busy hands, my mind can't help going back to our new neighbor. Surely that wasn't a normal interaction with a young man? Then again, what do I know about normal social interactions?

But things are different now. My mother and I are supposed to be entering polite society. By being somewhat respectable, we can expand our after-hours business to include the cream of New York society and, as such, charge an ever-increasing amount of money.

Frowning, I place the teapot and cups on a tray and take it down the hall.

"Good morning, darling," Mother says as I enter the room, unsure of how my presence will be received. But last night's tension is nowhere in evidence as she thanks me for her tea.

Jacques rises and relieves me of the tray. He sets it on the table, then helps himself to my cup.

"Good morning, Anna. I trust you slept well, *oui?*"

The words ring with chilly civility and I answer in kind. "Yes, sir. Thank you."

"Please, Anna. Call me Jacques."

I smile but don't say anything. Monsieur Mauvais and I have been circling each other warily since we first met in Chicago several months ago. He's doing wonders for our career, but that doesn't make me like him any more. As far as I'm concerned, he's just one more in a long line of smarmy, cheating managers who have taken advantage of us. I raise an eyebrow at my mother.

She knows I'm curious about what he's doing here but refuses to tell me. Cigarette smoke encircles her dark head like a halo. Gone are the flowing tresses I once played with as a child. Fashion now dictates that women cut their hair as short as possible, though few women pull it off as successfully as she does. I miss her long hair. It made her seem more motherly.

"Yes, Anna, how did you sleep? You seemed a bit overwrought when you went to bed."

Uneasiness flutters in my stomach. So she hasn't forgotten last night. "I said I slept fine!"

Thankfully, Jacques interrupts. "I almost forgot the reason I came over. I want to add two more acts before yours to increase your headline value in the eyes of the public. It would give you a certain prestige."

Grateful for the interruption, I settle into the deep leather club chair across from them, my mind going back to our argument.

It started when I'd asked her why she wouldn't let me expand my magical repertoire to include more complicated tricks. I stood in the hallway, watching her get ready for bed. She was sitting at her vanity table, rubbing Pond's Cold Cream on her face.

Her mouth tightened. "Because it's unnecessary. Your magic just leads up to the main event, which is *my*

15

performance. Really, darling, we've been over this before. Why do we have to revisit it?"

Because just once, I would like her to admit that I'm very, very good and my magic is an important part of the show. But she wouldn't grant me that, so I changed tactics. "If we expand my magic, the show would appeal to more people and would become so successful we wouldn't have to do séances anymore."

"Your resistance to the séances is becoming a bore. Jacques and I have a business strategy, and the séances are an important part of that. Honestly, I don't know why it bothers you so much."

Maybe because I'm tired of her being hauled off to jail for breaking the fortune-telling laws? Because I finally have a real home, and a scandal could cost us our regular show? Because I have a shot at a normal life and I don't want her thirst for fame to ruin it? All thoughts I don't dare articulate to my mother, so I just lapsed into resentful silence. As usual.

Mother claps her hands, startling me back into the present.

"Adding more opening acts is a fabulous idea!" she says.

It *is* a good idea, but I'm not about to tell Jacques that. "Isn't this a bit last minute?" I goad. "We've spent the past month doing teaser shows all over the city in preparation for our debut tomorrow night. Shouldn't this have been set ages ago?"

I hide a smile as Jacques flushes. His dark eyes are expressive but give nothing away, and his black hair is slicked back and curling over the collar of his well-tailored suit. He moved to the United States several years ago to better promote his French acts and get a toehold in the burgeoning American entertainment industry.

"Don't be difficult, darling." Mother dismisses me with a wave of her hand, turning her attention back to Jacques. "Now, what kind of act should we add? Hmm?"

I settle back and fume, watching him sip my tea. My fingers twitch and I reach for the deck of cards on the table. Shuffling them calms me.

"We don't want another medium or mentalist," she continues, not waiting for an answer. "Perhaps a magician? Or no, why don't we go with something completely different?" She's wearing her red, embroidered kimono robe and house slippers regally, as if she were already dressed for the day. I note that her makeup is flawless. She must have known Jacques was coming by this morning.

Jacques nods his approval. "Brilliant. I don't want a magician either. We don't want anyone to compete with Anna, though I've seen few magicians who can." My mother frowns, but Jacques doesn't notice. He should have said he doesn't want anyone to compete with *her*. My mother jealously guards her headliner status, and I can tell by the sudden furrows on her forehead that Jacques just made my part in the show more valuable than she's comfortable with.

"Perhaps we should have a young singer come in?" he continues, oblivious to his faux pas. "And then follow it up with some dancers? Give the society people a little thrill.

But not for too long. We don't want them restless."

"Do you have anyone in mind?" I ask, trying to distract my mother from his comment, though I'm secretly gratified by his high regard for my magic.

He nods decisively. Of course he does. Irritation ripples across my skin. He's adept at making my mother think everything is her idea, when it's already planned. This has probably been set for weeks.

"I recently signed a young singer, and I know of a dance troupe looking for a job."

"Wonderful." Mother reclines regally on the couch, her eyes alight as she and Jacques discuss our opening, his earlier blunder forgiven.

I have to hand it to her; Madame Marguerite Estella Van Housen has come a long way from little Maggie Moshe of Eger, Hungary. Our fortunes have gone up and down over the years, but my mother has never lost her ruthless poise. Whether she's in a cheap boardinghouse in the Midwest or in the drawing rooms of the rich, she is always the same—regal, mysterious, and completely at ease.

I might admire her if she wasn't my mother.

Jacques helps himself to another cup of tea and gives us a benevolent smile. "I will make the arrangements today. Are you and Anna ready for the big time?"

Mother's lips tilt upward. "Of course, I've always been ready."

Jacques turns to me. "And you, Anna?"

"Anna was born ready."

My mouth tightens when my mother answers for me. As if I can't speak for myself.

She places another cigarette in a long black holder and leans forward for Jacques to light it. When the flames flicker, her eyes zero in on me. "Anna and I had the most interesting discussion last night."

I shift, my neck and shoulders tightening. I'm the one she's going to punish for Jacques's thoughtless comment.

"Did you?" Jacques looks from me to my mother as if sensing the tension.

"Yes. It seems our Anna is getting a bit bored with our private séances."

Bored? Bored doesn't even begin to describe how I feel about them. I *hate* bilking money out of grief-stricken, innocent people. But the moment I try letting my mother know how I feel—that perhaps we should give up the séances and just do the shows—this is what I get.

Jacques frowns, his silky mustache drooping downward. "But I thought we'd all agreed that giving a few exclusive séances a month will give you extra cachet?" He turns to me and his frown deepens. "Between the shows and the séances, you stand to make a fortune."

We haven't held a séance since we've come to New York, and I've cherished the break. Our first one is tomorrow night after our opening. The thought of it turns my stomach.

"That's what I told her, but children can be so ungrateful," my mother says, staring at me.

I lower my eyes.

Jacques crosses his long legs and I focus on his striped trousers rather than meet my mother's gaze. "Perhaps Anna is ready for a bigger piece of the profits?"

I feel rather than hear Mother's hiss of anger. My eyes jerk up to meet Jacques's. "My mother knows better than that and if she doesn't—she should."

Our eyes clash and a long, tense moment spins out between us.

Then Mother breaks the silence. "Of course not. I share everything with her. Besides, Anna has been in charge of our finances since she was twelve. I trust her completely."

She doesn't and we both know it. I don't think my mother has ever fully trusted anyone.

Jacques clears his throat. "Then perhaps Anna wants a bigger part in the show? That wouldn't be surprising, considering . . ."

He raises a brow and I shake my head, glaring. Considering who my father is, he meant. Or at least who my mother claims my father is. In spite of wanting to perform better tricks, I don't want a bigger part in Mother's show. I want . . . Well, I'm not sure what I want, but spending the rest of my life performing tired old magic tricks—the only ones she'll allow—and being her assistant can't be all there is.

My mother's smile doesn't quite reach her eyes. "Yes, well." She gives another delicate shrug and my stomach hollows.

I'm going to have to watch myself, but then again, being careful around my mother is a way of life.

THREE

I stay in the next morning, sticking close to my mother . . .
despite my lingering irritation with her. I've never had
a vision about my own life before—they've always been
about horrific events around the world. I don't know what
it means, but the memory of my mother's terror is enough
to interrupt my usual routine to keep a watchful eye on her.

We spend the afternoon preparing. My mother likes to
bathe and get ready in quiet, so I'm careful not to disturb
her. By the time Jacques sends a sleek Lincoln Limousine
to collect us for the show, we're completely prepared. She's
dressed in an Egyptian-inspired beaded evening frock with
short sleeves while I'm wearing a lovely silk drop-waist shift
with caftan sleeves. As I do most of the real magic, long, loose
sleeves are essential, as the sleeves not only cover up various
props, they're also distracting. Tonight, my mother insisted
we both wear feathered headbands, and she kohl-lined our
eyes to make them look larger and more mysterious.

The fine leather seats of the car wrap around me and I

ignore the nerves pinging in my stomach. Once I'm onstage, I'll be fine, but tonight's opening is important for us.

When I first began working as Mother's assistant, it was out of necessity more than anything else. We simply didn't have the money to pay a real assistant. Plus, I'd been watching second-rate magicians practice for years, and sleight of hand came easily to me. More proof, my mother insisted, of my father's identity. It couldn't just be that I was talented. Good Lord, no. It *always* has something to do with my paternity.

I shift in my seat and look out the window. The Newmark Theater is just off Broadway on Forty-second Street, and my excitement builds as we pass the flashing marquees. Mother sits silently beside me, primed and motionless, like a cat ready to spring.

I'm not sure when I realized my mother wasn't like other mothers. It's hard to know what normal is when you travel all the time. But when I was nine, we stayed in Seattle just long enough for me to make a friend. Lizzie's mother didn't spend her evenings performing or going out for late dinners with strangers. Instead, she stayed in nights and made good things to eat. She hugged her children frequently and had a loud, hearty laugh.

My mother, with her volatile moods and sharp tongue, was, and is, terrifying.

The car stops, and I wait for my mother to get out before following her. She walks smoothly toward the theater, ignoring the line of people waiting for tickets. I can't believe all these people are here to see us. Jacques has done his job promoting us well, I'll give him that. The theater is a large sedate brick building, with white columns marking the front entrance. The marquee over the door has my mother's name in giant letters:

MADAME VAN HOUSEN, MEDIUM AND MENTALIST EXTRAORDINAIRE

My name, of course, is absent.

I have little of my mother's poise and can't help but gawk at the crowd, excitement rising in the center of my stomach. Couples stand in line, arm in arm, chatting, laughing, and smoking. The men in their black swallow-tailed coats seem somber, almost grim, compared to the brightly colored flappers in their sassy, short fur coats and their chiffon, net, and silk fringed dresses.

Usually, none of the red velvet opulence of the front of the theater makes it backstage, and dressing rooms are notoriously dark and cramped. I'd been pleasantly surprised by the spaciousness of the room Jacques had led us to before our dress rehearsal. Once inside, an attendant brings me a basket of papers. Each of the papers contains a question from one of the audience members already seated in the theater. I glance at my mother, taking my cues from her.

She removes her wrap and drapes it on a velvet settee. "Let's do eight tonight. It's our opening night."

I nod and go through the papers, marking a red X on the

questions easiest for her to answer. Later, during the show, my mother will select a few "at random" and amaze the audience with her perception. The trick is so simple, it's hard to believe people fall for it. But as Mother always says, the audience believes what they want to believe.

Mother checks her makeup as I work. She's always silent before a performance. My own anticipation is thrumming in my chest, but I try not to show it. I've never told her how much I love performing illusions, even tired old magic tricks. It's a secret I hold close to my heart, half afraid it'll be taken away from me if revealed. Sometimes I pretend that I'm headlining my own show. That the people in the audience are waiting in anticipation just to see me. I thrill at the thought of it but wonder what that has to do with living the quiet, stable life I also long for. I sigh. Sometimes I don't know what I want.

There's a knock on the door and I answer it. It's another attendant with a giant bouquet of red roses for my mother and a smaller white one for me. They're from Jacques, which dims my enthusiasm measurably.

Mother fusses over the flowers until another knock sounds, alerting us that it's time to go on. She turns to me with a disarming smile. "Are we ready?" she asks.

She always asks this.

I smile back. "As ready as we'll ever be," I answer.

Whether we're in a cheap, ugly hotel in a no-name town or in a ritzy theater, our preperformance routine is always the same.

"Are we going to astonish them?"

"We always do."

She reaches out and clasps my hand and together we follow the attendant down a narrow hall to the stage. I scan the darkened stage quickly, making sure our props are in place. The setup has already been checked by the stage hands and Jacques, but I always like to double, triple, quadruple check.

For a long, breathless moment we wait, time spinning into an eternity, while the excitement in my chest bursts. As the red curtain rises, my mother releases my hand and steps forward.

Make no mistake: There is only room for one star on this stage.

Because of the stage lights, my mother's silhouette is all I see as the velvet curtain makes its silent ascent into the darkness. The blinding spotlight looks like a sun rising on the horizon, and though I can't see the people in the audience, the scent of perfume and expensive cigar smoke assures me of their presence, as does the excessively polite, well-bred clapping.

That's fine. By the end of the night they'll be my mother's devoted fans. Unlike other mediums and mentalists, she uses a mischievous humor during her performance that puts the audience off guard. While others rely on darkness, drama, and deception, Madame Van Housen does everything with a wink that asks "Can you believe this?" The audience loves it.

"Thank you so much, ladies and gentlemen!" Though

her voice is projecting to every corner of the auditorium, it still sounds sweetly feminine. She stands until her eyes adjust to the glare of the spotlight, then glides forward so the audience can see her better. Her dark, delicate beauty unfurls like a blossom. "I hope you enjoy this evening's show, but more, I hope you learn something about the spirit world. It can be a dark and dangerous place."

Mother pauses as the audience digests this and then an impish smile wrinkles her nose. You can almost hear the audience relax. Then she continues.

"I've been gifted with the ability to read minds and fore-tell the future, as some of you will discover personally." She pauses again and sways on her feet. My cue. I rush out of the darkness to steady her. She pats my shoulder and gives the audience a tremulous smile. "I'm sorry. I just had an overwhelming feeling that someone here is going to join the spirit world very soon."

Someone screams and rushes out of the theater. A plant.

Mother waits until the slamming door reverberates through the auditorium. "Anyone else is more than welcome to leave if they feel uncomfortable." She presses her hands together, eyes cast downward, looking like a grave madonna.

No one ever moves a muscle. In all our years of doing shows, no one has ever left.

She turns to me. "This is my daughter and assistant, Anna. She is going to entertain you with some magic while we wait for the spirits to respond to my presence."

Though she introduces me as her assistant, in reality,

she is more my assistant than I am hers during this part of the show, which makes us both edgy and uncomfortable, though neither of us has ever said it out loud. Mother hates me being the center of attention, and I hate having to depend on her. I learned early on that my mother isn't exactly the dependable type.

I begin with easy magic tricks—making a cage of disgruntled doves disappear and reappear in different places, cutting a rope and making it whole again, plucking a scarf from a ball of flame. Mother is adept at keeping audience eyes elsewhere while I do the sleight of hand the tricks require.

We communicate by gestures and eye contact. A wink means keep it up. A twist of the wrist means to skip the next trick and move on.

The audience oohs and aahs in all the right places, and my movements get more dramatic as I warm up. Enthralling the audience is the best part, the part I love. I hate when people call magic trickery. What my mother does is trickery. What I do is *entertainment*.

As I work, my senses go on high alert and a million details run through my mind: the location of the audience in relation to where and how I'm standing, my mother's movements, even the collective mood of the people in the first row.

Tonight the show goes well. My mind lights up with excitement. The audience has never been so attentive, the stage lights never so bright. When I finally stop, I'm breathing hard and my heart is pounding in my ears. The clapping is deafening as my mother steps beside me with a brittle smile.

"As you can see, my daughter, Anna, is a very unusual girl."

The audience fades as reality settles in. My mother is furious. I can see it in the tautness of her jaw and the tense line of her back.

Why? Is she angry with me for being good at what I do?

"She reads muscles as easily as I read minds," Mother continues. "Right now, we're going to blindfold her and choose someone in the audience to hide a needle. Just by touching the person's arm, my daughter will be able to find the needle."

The stagehand brings out a blindfold and my mother ties it, pulling far harder than necessary to show her displeasure.

I hear whispering as the volunteer hides the needle.

My mother always has a sense of humor when choosing the volunteer. Sometimes it's a handsome young man who makes me blush. Other times it's a fat, red-faced gentleman with bad breath. Ten to one it'll be bad breath tonight.

We began doing this trick last year, after seeing it in a rival's act. My mother tried and tried but couldn't do it, and it gives me childish satisfaction that I can pull it off each and every time. It's called muscle reading, and the perceptive person is supposed to be able to find the needle through the tension in the person's arm as they lead you around the theater. My mother, as skilled as she is, just can't seem to pick up the signs.

I, on the other hand, have a one-hundred-percent success rate. Of course, my mother doesn't know why.

My mother leads me off the stage, then lays my hand on someone's arm. I clutch it, letting all the sounds and scents of the theater fall away, reaching to connect with the person beside me. In my mind, it's like a silver cord or thread stretching from me to the other person. For years, I thought everyone experienced the same thing when they touched—that everyone communicated on a level deeper than just words or actions. I figured that was why people shook hands when they greeted each other. But things didn't add up. Why couldn't my mother tell when our manager was going to skip out on us? Or that the nice woman at the boardinghouse was only gathering information for the sheriff? It all seemed so obvious to me. After a time, I realized that she couldn't feel what I could—and that no one else could either. By then, I already knew enough to keep my mouth shut. My ambitious mother would happily turn me into a circus sideshow to further her own career. Or maybe in a fit of jealousy take me out of the show altogether. There's no way to tell.

Usually, the first emotion I sense while doing this particular trick is excitement at being chosen, quickly followed by doubt that I can really do it. This man—for it is a man's arm I feel under my fingers—is different. He's intensely curious about me. I sense a barely concealed anticipation. There's also a low buzz of suppressed energy coming from him, as if he's thrown up a dam that is barely holding. I've never felt anything like it. Puzzled, I let him lead me through the theater, trying to pick up on his other emotions. Normally, the guide becomes a bit agitated as we near the needle, but that doesn't happen tonight. He seems calm, patient. But there's also something else. An emotion I can't quite identify. Panic assaults me and my heart accelerates. Surely it's been too long! Will I just wander around the plush aisles of the theater until the audience realizes I've failed?

I probe again, my hand tightening on his arm, and beads of sweat break out on my upper lip. Then it flashes over me as clearly as if he's whispered it. I stop short, a sly smile coming to my lips. "Tricky!" I say, projecting so everyone can hear me. "The gentleman hid *two* pins! One over there"—I point vaguely toward the center of the theater—"and one in his pocket. The one in his pocket is the one I was looking for. The other is a decoy!"

Laughing, I whip off my blindfold.

And stare straight into Colin Archer's handsome face.

His eyes search mine for a moment before he bends to formally kiss my hand. "Well, done, Miss Van Housen," he says in a low voice. "Truly impressive. You passed that test with flying colors."

Surprise at his words silences me on our way back to the stage as the audience claps wildly. *Test? Did Mother know about this test?* I wonder as I join her onstage. And what kind of test was it anyway?

Woodenly, I curtsy and wave at the crowd. I have no time to ponder what Colin meant, however, as we move quickly into the next portion of the show. Now it's time for my mother to amaze and awe.

I bring her the basket of audience questions and blend into the background while she answers the ones I've pre-chosen for her. Then the lights dim as she calls up audience members, purporting to read their minds. They, too, were all pre-chosen. One of the bellhops was assigned to talk with the audience as they came in. Then he reported back to Mother. Jacques has also helped. He knows everything about everyone in New York society and sent out special invitations for the grand opening. Once he saw who would be in the audience, he fed us tidbits of gossip, which have now become a part of the act.

I hide a smile as the amazing Madame Van Housen shares some new insight with a stout lady whose turban glitters with rhinestones as she moves. The audience gasps in shock and admiration at my mother's perception.

The truth is, my mother isn't really a mentalist, a medium, or a magician. She's just an actress with the ability to make people believe what she wants them to. And at the end of the show, as we take our bows to thunderous applause, we have several hundred new believers.

FOUR

After the show, the evening becomes a blur of congratulations, best wishes, and interviews with the press. I respond to their questions with well-rehearsed answers.

"Yes, of course, I love performing with my mother."

"No, I didn't miss a normal childhood. I love traveling!"

"I've always loved magic so it just seemed natural to add it to my mother's show. . . ."

Then posing for pictures with my mother. *Click*, *snap*, *poof.*

By the time we finally get back to our apartment, I'm exhausted.

"Make some coffee," Mother snaps after my third yawn. Her charm disappeared with the newspaper men. She flips on the electric light. "I need you awake."

Of course she does. It's time for the evening's big finale, an "honest-to-god" séance, performed for some of the city's swankiest sophisticates.

I wonder what she'd do if I refused to participate.

On second thought, I don't want to find out. Her temper is monstrous, and though she's never hit me, I've seen her bring grown men to their knees with one small, well-placed fist.

We have about an hour until midnight, when the "guests" will arrive. I make a pot of coffee and pour my mother a cup to take back to her room as she prepares for the next "act." She usually changes into something more mysterious for the séances. I can wear whatever I want.

She takes a step into the hall and then turns. "How did you know about the two needles?" Her forehead knots with puzzlement.

The coffeepot in my hand jerks as I'm pouring myself a cup. I set it down with a clatter and grab a rag to mop up the spill. *So she didn't know.* I babble away, not meeting her eyes. "What do you mean? The same way I always do. It's not that hard. And this fellow was really easy. . . ."

"Hmm" is all she says.

Silence.

Then the measured clicking of her heels as she moves down the hall.

I take a deep breath. I don't need any special powers of perception to know that this isn't the end of the discussion.

My mother stays in her room for the next hour, leaving me to set up alone and giving me plenty of time to wonder about Colin Archer. Does mother know he lives downstairs from us? Why else would she pick him out of an audience of hundreds? I don't believe in coincidences, but on the other hand she really didn't seem to know about the two pins.

By the time the first knock sounds on the door, I'm wide awake and as ready as I ever am. Tension creeps down my spine as several guests enter our drawing room. There are so many bad memories associated with these séances—I'll never be able to take them for granted. Once, after one of our séances was busted up by the law and my mother was led off to jail, a well-meaning townswoman bundled me up and took me home with her. I was only seven years old, but nothing she said could induce me to move from her front window. I even slept on the window seat, my cheek pressed against the pane. I think some part of me was terrified my mother would just move on without me. Three days later, I had my first and only fit of hysterics when I saw her coming up the walk with our bags.

Even now, habit compels me to continually evaluate our guests with one vital question in mind: *Are we safe?*

I glance furtively around the room at the high-society crowd who've come to enjoy my mother's unique set of talents. The bored gentleman wearing a small bejeweled blonde on his arm like the latest accessory—he looks like a high hat who's never worked a day in his life and probably wouldn't take the time or trouble to complain to the authorities, even if he thought he had cause. And the bosomy woman whose pince-nez glasses keep slipping down her nose seems far too kind to turn us in.

Jacques is lurking in the background, but I'm still puzzled by the low number of attendees. I know we were going to be exclusive, but three people are hardly worth setting up for. As if on cue, a knock on the door sounds and Mother indicates I should answer it.

Colin Archer.

Shock freezes me in the doorway and I stare, speechless. What is Mother up to?

"Miss Van Housen."

He greets me quietly, and for some reason a shiver runs down my back. Who is this fellow? Why is he always turning up? Is he a cop? I finally find my voice. "Are you here for . . ."

"The séance. Yes."

And here I was hoping he'd come to borrow a cup of sugar. My heart speeds up, but I just give him a nod. "Please come in."

I lead him down the hall and into the sitting room, where the others are talking. Mother's face registers a moment of confusion before Jacques steps forward, his hand outstretched.

"Mr. Archer. Thank you so much for joining us this evening."

I stand aside as Jacques introduces him to Mother. So she didn't know he was coming.

But Jacques did. He whispers something in my mother's ear. Her eyebrows arch and she gives a small smile and nod. What are they up to?

I watch Cole carefully as I go about my hostess duties. His quick scrutiny of everything and everyone makes him seem as wary as I am, but he's wearing the wrong shoes to be a police officer. They're shiny, flat on the bottom, and look as if they pinch. Policemen wear comfortable shoes and always walk as if their feet hurt. Plus, he's a bit too young. And handsome. But if he's not a cop, why is he here?

"Anna," Mother calls. "Could you light the candles, please?"

As I keep a sharp eye on our guests, my mother fiddles with a deck of tarot cards, her long fingers expertly shuffling and cutting the deck as she waits for her clients to tell her what they want. She taps the deck three times on the table and glances at me for the answer.

I tuck my hair behind my right ear, letting her know that the spirit cabinet is prepared if that's the direction tonight's séance goes. The tenor of each séance differs depending on the needs and desires of the clients involved. It's my job to be prepared for every possible variation. Considering the fact that I don't trust our new neighbor, I pray she won't want to use it.

The flickering lights transform our lovely, warm sitting room into an eerie cave marked by long, ghostly silhouettes. The apartment came fully furnished, but we've rearranged the furniture to maximize the shadows spilling across our guests.

I notice the couple darting curious looks my way and my face flames with embarrassment. Mother must have "accidentally" let my supposed father's identity slip. Once again, I'm reduced to being a celebrity's bastard daughter. I widen my eyes and stare fixedly at the blonde, sending all the scorn and anger I can muster through my gaze. To my surprise, instead of turning away in embarrassment, she gives me a sly wink.

Cole coughs and I turn to face him. He's also staring at me, but rather than delight over a possible scandal, his dark eyes hold curiosity. He probably hasn't heard the rumors. No matter, it's my duty to blend into the background during this part of the evening, so I keep busy, dumping ashtrays, serving finger foods, and freshening drinks from the illegal bottle of gin my mother keeps locked away with the rest of her prohibited liquor.

As I perform these mundane tasks, my stomach twists itself into painful knots waiting for the inevitable moment when their stories will emerge, brought out by my mother's skillful questioning. Every time I touch them, which happens quite a bit, I'll hear their pain and feel their loss as acutely as if it were my own. It's one of the many hazards of this job.

Cole's presence isn't helping; it's making me even jumpier than usual. I catch him staring every time I turn around, but he pretends he's looking at something over my shoulder.

As my mother talks quietly to the older woman in one corner of the room, Jacques, Cole, and the society couple, Jack and Cynthia Gaylord, are discussing spiritualism in the other.

"I just find it fascinating that people can actually talk to the dead. Think of all the things we could learn!" Mrs. Gaylord says earnestly. She looks up to her husband for confirmation, but he's staring, disinterested, at his drink.

"Like what?" Cole asks.

My lips twitch at the amusement in his voice.

For a moment Mrs. Gaylord looks blank. "Well, all sorts of things. There are some very important studies going on right now. One organization in London is doing some groundbreaking scientific work in the field of psychic phenomena. There are even rumors that they have a secret laboratory where they test real psychics and mentalists. It's all very hush-hush." She turns to me. "I'm surprised you haven't heard of it. It's called the Society for Psychical Research."

Next to me, Cole starts, his drink sloshing over the rim of the glass and onto the floor. "I'm so sorry. Clumsy of me, that."

Surprised, I hurry into the kitchen to get a rag, and when I return, the others have joined my mother at the table. Cole's still standing there looking tense and miserable.

"I really am sorry," he says. "I'm a bit of a bungler, actually."

"I wouldn't have guessed that," I say without thinking. "You move like an athlete." My cheeks redden. *Now he knows I've been watching him.*

"Oh. Er, yes. Indeed," he replies pointlessly.

Wonderful. Now I've embarrassed both of us.

I stand and smile brightly. "We should join the others."

He nods and moves away, and, after tossing the rag on a nearby table, I follow.

"I just want to know if you can really talk to my dear son, Walter," the woman with the glasses sniffs. "He died in the war, you know."

My mother stops shuffling and lays her slim hand over the woman's fat one. "I'm so sorry for your pain, Mrs. Carmichael. How old was Walter when he passed?"

Cole snorts. "Why don't you ask Walter?"

This seems so out of character that a surprised giggle escapes my lips. I turn it into a cough and watch as he fights the smile curling the corners of his mouth.

My mother stiffens and then relaxes her shoulders. "The young are always more difficult to reach. I need to know this before we begin."

Cole lapses back into silence. Not many men can resist my mother's smile.

"He was eighteen," Mrs. Carmichael says softly.

My chest hollows. Not much older than I am.

"Oh, dear."

"Yes." The lines of the older woman's face crinkle in sorrow and my breath catches at her anguish. "He died of dysentery soon after he landed in Europe."

"I will do my best," my mother promises. She turns to the Gaylords. Mr. Gaylord takes a case out of the pocket of his vest and lights a cigarette. His young wife hunches forward, eager, excited.

"And what do you wish to gain from tonight's séance?" Mother asks.

"Oh, I don't know!" The blonde twitches her fashionably bony shoulders. "I've just always been interested . . . I got tired of my old medium, and when I told old Jack here about you, well, here we are!" She giggles, and I feel my mother's contempt. Cynthia Gaylord is a dabbler, a dilettante. She's probably as bored with her marriage as her husband is with life and is on the constant lookout for something to fill the emptiness.

But the Cynthia Gaylords of the world are my mother's best clients.

"Yes, well, here you are," my mother says. I'm the only one who detects the underlying scorn.

Cole's eyes dart about, keeping a close watch on everyone. I frown, my spine tightening. Why is he here?

I clear my throat to catch my mother's eye and then scratch my nose, glancing at our neighbor. The signal that we might have a skeptic, come to catch us out. My mother ignores it. She's already chosen the grief-stricken mother as her target and nothing can stop her now. Mrs. Carmichael has both money and sorrow, two things that make her the perfect mark. The other three clients are superfluous. The society couple may bring their friends back for a lark, but the old woman will be returning, her pocketbook wide open—my mother will see to it.

I finish lighting the candles and await her instructions.

"Bring me the Ouija board, darling."

I relax slightly. Good. Maybe she won't use the spirit cabinet tonight. It's our most impressive act, but also the most dangerous, as those who know how the cabinet works can easily expose it by uncovering the hidden compartments. The Ouija board, on the other hand, is simple. My mother is so skilled that no one ever figures out that she's the one manipulating the planchette.

Jack Gaylord is finally roused out of his indifference. "Is this what we paid good money for? Parlor games? What kind of tricks are you up to, Madame Van Housen?"

My mother draws herself up and glares at him. "If you would like to run the séance, Mr. Gaylord, please, be my guest. I often start with the board in order to lure out the spirits, who are shy, especially among skeptics." Gone is her mournful voice, replaced with a commandeering tone worthy of a queen. Mother is the master of a thousand voices, and she uses each one with the skill of a butcher wielding a knife.

There's a moment's silence before Mrs. Gaylord stirs fretfully by his side. "Oh, Jack, really. Just let her get on with it. You're ruining all my fun."

His upper lip curls as he waves a hand, and, with a hidden roll of my eyes, I continue setting up the board my mother had imported from London. The teak wood gleams in the candlelight, and the bone pointer feels hard and smooth. It buzzes lightly in my fingers, as it never does for my mother. I know because I asked her once as a child what made it vibrate. Her confusion made my stomach hurt, and I remember laughing it off. I never mentioned it again.

I place the planchette on the board with a slight grimace. Though my mother has often asked me to participate in the game, I've always refused.

I walk over to the hall and switch off the last lamp, marveling once again that we now live in a home with electricity, even if it is courtesy of my mother's smarmy manager.

"First, we join hands."

"Isn't your daughter going to join us?" Cole asks, his eyes on me.

"No. Her job is to keep me safe as I open myself up to the spirits."

The corner of his lips twitch, and I shiver at the perceptive glance he sends me. Why do I get the feeling that he knows more about me than I want him to?

"But my dear madam, I insist. It will help calm my mind that there is no deception involved." Though he only looks a bit older than me, his manner of speaking is so old-world that it makes me wonder where he's from.

Mother looks as if she's going to explode, but then she catches the eye of Mrs. Carmichael, who's staring with open curiosity. I can almost see the gears switching as my mother tries another tactic. She tilts her head, causing her jet earrings to dangle flirtatiously. "My dear Mr. Archer, if you're such a nonbeliever, what are you doing here?"

"Please, call me Cole. And I never said I was a nonbeliever. I'm open to all sorts of mystical experiences, but I was quite impressed with your daughter's magic tonight. She's very talented. I think I'd prefer to have her where I can see her."

Cole pats the empty chair next to him and my heart rises up in my throat. I've always avoided the Ouija board like the plague. Stupid to be frightened of a mere game, but then again, I've never had mah-jongg tiles or checkers buzz in my hands.

Please don't make me join, I entreat my mother silently.

But as my mother glances again at her mark, I know I'm doomed.

"Sit, Anna."

"But, Mother . . ."

"Sit."

Cole's stiff formality slips and he flashes me a knowing look, sure he's called my mother's bluff.

I plop down into the chair and wipe my palms off on my dress before joining hands with the others. Cole's fingers curl slowly around mine. To my relief there is no accompanying spark like there was last time, though the feel of his hand in mine still sends heat rushing to my face. I glance over at him and am surprised to find that he looks as uncomfortable as I feel. I wonder if he came here on his own or if one of the other mediums, jealous of my mother's growing reputation, sent him. I also wonder what his connection to Jacques is. Jacques, on my other side, also takes my hand, but his emotions are always muddled. Some people are like that—a jumble of undecipherable impressions. Jacques is one of those unreadables, part of the reason why I don't trust him. Cole, on the other hand, isn't even a jumble—just nothing. Strange.

My mother, voice dark and mysterious, begins her chant.

"Oh spirits, hear our plea. Join us. Speak to us. Teach us. Oh spirits, I implore you. We respectfully ask that you join us, speak to us, teach us."

She instructs us to repeat the words after her. We follow her lead and wait again.

The blonde giggles nervously, but the older woman, leaning forward in hopeful anticipation, hushes her. Tension, as thick and smoky as burning incense, fills the air as the clients breathlessly wait for something to happen. Even Jacques, who knows better, seems strained and quiet.

"Mrs. Carmichael, please place your hand on the planchette first, as I am going to try to contact Walter. The rest of us will follow suit," my mother instructs.

As soon as our hands unclasp, I wipe them again on my dress.

I force my breath to an even, measured rate. In and out, calm and slow. *Don't be silly*, I tell myself. *You know more than anyone just what a farce this all is.*

Hesitating, Mrs. Carmichael lays her fingers on the pointer. Everyone else follows suit except me. I bite my lip.

"Anna?" My mother's voice holds a faint note of warning, undetectable to the others.

Trembling, I reach out my fingers but can't make them connect. Taking a deep breath, I shut my eyes and gingerly place my fingertips on the piece. It's no longer cool but warm to the touch, and the slight buzzing has increased. I cast a quick glance around the table, but no one else seems to be aware of it. Lucky me.

Touching Mrs. Carmichael's fingers opens me up to her feelings. I try to close myself off as her hope, shining and tremulous, reveals itself to me. The truth is, it isn't the grief of my mother's clients that rips me apart; it's the hope.

My mother's beautiful face is composed, her bow-shaped mouth relaxed. Her large, normally expressive eyes are flat, unreadable.

"What's supposed to happen?" Mrs. Gaylord whispers.

"Hell if I know," her husband answers.

My mother ignores them, waiting. "Spirits! Use me as your mouthpiece. I am open, yours!" she bursts out. Mrs. Gaylord gives another nervous titter, but everyone else is silent. "Walter, your mother is here and would very much like to converse with you," my mother continues in a softer tone.

Mrs. Carmichael sniffles, and my heart twists painfully.

Feeling the emotions of others is both a godsend and a curse. If I knew how to turn it off completely, I would, but I don't know how, and God knows there isn't anyone to ask.

"Do you have a question for your son?" Mother's voice is quiet. If I didn't know better, I'd think she really cared about Mrs. Carmichael's grief. Maybe she does. It's hard to tell with my mother.

"Ask him if he's all right, if he's happy," Mrs. Carmichael's voice thickens. Her anguish is relentless and I suck in a tight breath as the heavy mass of her grief crushes me.

Suddenly the temperature drops and I stare, shocked as an icy tendril of air snakes its way across the room. As if it has a purpose it heads right for me. Then it's inside and I feel it moving, shifting, taking over. Terror overcomes me and I want to scream, but I'm frozen in place. A painful current shoots through my fingertips and the planchette quivers. My mother and the Gaylords jerk their fingers from the piece. Cole's eyes widen as the planchette begins to move. *MOTHER*, it spells out under my numb fingertips, *GOD IS GOOD.*

FIVE

"That's my Walter!" Mrs. Carmichael cries out. "He was such a good boy; he was going to go to divinity school."

But the planchette isn't done and neither, presumably, is Walter.

A piercing squeal rings inside my ears and my skin is both painfully hot and glacially cold. Walter's spirit crams itself more fully inside my body and I'm suddenly stuffed, as if I've eaten too much Thanksgiving dinner. I clamp my teeth together, holding back a panicked cry as the pointer slowly, inexorably moves from letter to letter.

BE AT PEACE.

Mrs. Carmichael is sobbing openly now, and I gasp as Cole snatches up my free hand and squeezes it. A spark flares between us, just as it did the first time we touched, and I shudder as Walter vacates my body as suddenly as he arrived. Released, I yank my fingers back from the planchette, breathing hard. My mother's eyes narrow, but I evade them.

I'd been right to avoid the board.

Another icy breath blows out the candles and the door to the sitting room slams shut. The blonde screams.

"Bloody hell," Cole mutters next to me, releasing my hand.

There's a moment of silence as everyone holds their breath.

"Don't be afraid; the spirits have gone." My mother's voice shakes slightly as she moves to flick on the electric lamp.

Mrs. Carmichael clutches her chest. "That was my Walter, telling me to search no more. He is at peace and wants me to be at peace as well."

My mother throws me a venomous look. Jacques is looking from me to my mother, confused. Mrs. Gaylord clings to her not-so-bored husband, her frightened blue eyes trained on me. Cole scrutinizes my face, questions in his dark eyes. I stare back, my heart thudding in my chest. I feel a magnetic pull, compelled to look deeper into his eyes to see what lies beyond such silky darkness. I jerk back, alarmed.

"My dear Madame Van Housen," he says, rising. "I would hazard a guess that you're not the only medium in the family. Well done."

The hair across my neck prickles. Have I just been tested again? Does Cole know something about my abilities? I'm torn. Part of me wants to confront him to find out what he knows and part of me wants to hide under my covers.

The Gaylords gather their things.

"You're not leaving, are you?" my mother asks.

"Er, yes," the husband murmurs, wrapping his wife's fur

around her shoulders. "We're heading out to the Island to visit the Gardiners for a long weekend. Our car is waiting."

Mrs. Gaylord turns to my mother. "My friends will be so excited to hear all about you and your daughter! I've never seen . . ." She shakes her head and turns to me. "You are the cat's pajamas, sweetheart!" She shakes her head again and they leave the sitting room.

Cole inclines his head toward me and follows them out. Moments later the front door slams.

"Would you like a cup of tea?" Mother asks Mrs. Carmichael, her voice pleading.

The older woman shakes her head decisively. "I'm at peace. Walter told me to search no more and I'm going to respect his wishes."

"Hold on, Mrs. Carmichael, and I will walk you to your car." Jacques turns to Mother and kisses her hand. "I will see you soon. *Oui?*"

Mrs. Carmichael wipes a tear from her eye and clasps my frozen hand. "Thank you so much, dearie. You have helped me so much."

I smile at her, forgetting for a moment that I will soon be facing a furious mother. As terrifying as the whole experience was, for the first time during a séance, I *helped* someone. Then I turn to face my mother and I swallow nervously. *But who is going to help me?*

Taking a deep breath, I avoid her eyes and begin to clear the dishes. My mother can put the stupid board away. I am never, ever touching it again.

She picks up her own glass and downs the gin in one gulp. "Just what the hell was that?"

I hesitate. I can't tell her the truth—and if I tell her I did it on purpose, she'll want to know why I've chased her clients away. I'm damned if I do and damned if I don't.

"A séance," I reply, avoiding her eyes. "I thought it went rather well."

"You should have left it to me. Mrs. Carmichael would have been back."

"But the Gaylords said they'd tell their friends. That's good." Desperately, I try to keep her focus on the clients. That way she won't focus on me.

"Yes, but I would have preferred to string them along a bit. I don't like you taking control of my performances." She's silent for a moment. "Why did you?"

"Why did I what?" I ask, stalling.

"Don't be obtuse. You know what I'm talking about," she says, suddenly petulant. Without her audience, she has no reason to act, and all the charm is gone.

I keep my face carefully blank, in spite of my racing pulse. "I was tired. I wanted them all to go home." That, at least, is the truth.

My mother frowns but says nothing. She has done the same thing, but I've never before rushed a séance along, and she doesn't like it. Not one bit.

"But how did you do it?" Her voice is more puzzled than angry now, but it still holds a skeptical note that makes me uneasy. She must not, ever, know about my abilities. The same instinct that kept me silent about them as a child sends me scrambling for an explanation that will appease her.

"I opened the window before I sat down."

She glances at the window.

"And closed it while the lights were still out," I add quickly. "The wind blew out the candles."

Even to my ears, it sounds like a flimsy explanation. On the other hand, what other explanation can there be? My mother doesn't believe in spirits.

"And the planchette? How did you know what to say to Mrs. Carmichael?"

This is harder to explain away. I look her right in the eye, heart in my throat. "I've been watching you do it for years. Perhaps it's rubbed off?"

She meets my gaze dead-on. Suspicion eddies between us for one agonizing moment before she backs down. "Well, please let me know next time you decide to take over one of my séances. It might have gone very badly. And we did lose a client."

She's still suspicious but is choosing to let it go—for now.

"But on the bright side, the Gaylords will definitely be back."

"True," she says. "And Jacques says Jack Gaylord's family is almost as rich as the Vanderbilts. Where did he get his wife, though? Can you believe her?"

I run the evening through my mind but can't think that she'd done anything out of the ordinary. "What do you mean?"

"She can put on all the airs and graces she wants to, but she doesn't fool me. That girl's so rough around the edges, she could be a ripsaw. I bet she's only one or two generations away from the boat." My mother gives a delicate sniff as if she hadn't come over on a boat herself. I say nothing.

Still shaking, I take the rest of the dishes and place them in the sink. I'll wash them in the morning. I want to ask my mother if she knows that Cole lives with old Mr. Darby downstairs, but I hold my tongue. I don't want to start another conversation. Right now, I just want to go to bed and wrap myself in blankets—anything to warm the bone-deep chill seeping into my whole being.

"Good night, Mother," I call, and hurry down the hall.

My stomach churns as the events of the evening sink in. Evidently, my talents extend far beyond just sensing people's feelings and having the occasional vision of the future. I shut my eyes and tremble as the truth settles more deeply into my soul. My body had been used by a boy who had died during the Great War. He'd used the Ouija board to send a message from beyond the grave.

I can do what so many say is impossible—I can communicate with the dead. My stomach rolls and I hurry to my room.

Once there, I shut the door and wedge a chair under the handle. With that done, I kneel and pull out several large hatboxes from under my bed. The first one contains a dozen or so handcuffs and a ring of keys and picklocks. I have several Giant Bean handcuffs from the 1880s that all open with the same key. Silly. Then a pair of Iver Johnson cuffs with their funny round keys, and a pair of Lovell cuffs. I can get out of all of them with the picklock, no matter how I'm cuffed. I also have a special pair for Mother that have been gaffed, so they're easy for her to open. They're used to fasten her to the chair in the spirit cabinet. She doesn't know about the rest of them and I want to keep it that way. It would give her too much satisfaction to know that I share the same obsession as my father.

Of course, it's lucky for her that I do. I was thirteen the first time I broke my mother out of jail. After that it got easier, though I have to admit, even I had trouble getting the door unlocked while hanging off the back of a paddy wagon. It's not an experience I wish to repeat.

I don't even recall which small town it was, but I do remember how terrified I was as I hid behind a truck and waited for the paddy wagon to pass. They hadn't placed a guard with my mother, figuring that one pretty little woman wouldn't give them any trouble. As soon as the timing was right, I leaped, as quiet and quick as a cat, onto the back. I'd clung to the bars, and remember thinking that my mother, in her champagne-colored lace dress, was too beautiful to be stuck in the back of a police wagon.

"Mama," I'd called softly, to let her know it was time to go.

"What took you so long?" was all she said as she removed her shoes to make the jump to the street easier.

I was already working on the padlock and didn't answer.

It took two tries but I soon pulled the lock out and the door opened.

I pray that's the last time I'll have to do that.

I sigh and move on to the next box, which contains the straitjacket I bought from a homeless man in Kansas City. I shudder to think where he got it and remember how long it took me to learn to escape from it. Swineguard the Magnificent helped me in and out of it for weeks before I finally had it down pat. Mother doesn't know about that either.

Then, slowly, I remove the cover from a box filled with newspaper clippings on my father's many exploits. A familiar sadness takes over, the same childlike yearning that has been with me since I first realized my father couldn't possibly want me. If he did, I would be with him, right?

I stare down at a handbill I'd picked up in San Francisco when the circus was doing a California tour. Harry Houdini's fierce eyes stare back at me. "Did I get this curse from you?" I whisper to the most famous magician and escape artist in the world.

Because I don't want it. Any of it. Not the visions of the future, not feeling the emotions of others, and certainly not the ability to talk to the dead. All I've ever wanted was to be a regular girl with a regular life. Talking to the dead or seeing the future cannot, in any way, be considered normal.

As I tuck the handbill back in the box and shove it all back under my bed, a band of pain tightens around my chest like a straitjacket.

My father wouldn't know me if he passed me on the street.

He has never claimed me for his own.

He doesn't even know I exist.

But I can't help but wonder, as I ready myself for bed, if my abilities are the curse I must bear as Harry Houdini's illegitimate daughter.

SIX

In spite of my exhaustion, it takes forever for me to fall asleep, and when I do, I'm restless. I keep waking up, half fearful of a repeat performance from Walter. But slowly I feel myself relaxing as sleep finally overtakes me.

Electrical flashes. Image after image. Inky black water surrounds me. Disoriented and confused, I can't find the surface. My arms are useless, bound tight behind my back, and my lungs burn for air. Death circles me like an approaching shark, but it's not myself I'm terrified for. My mother's lovely face flashes in front of me, nostrils flared, eyes wide with fear, and I hear her screaming my name over and over.

I sit up in bed, gasping, my heart racing. The scent of burned sugar still lingers in my nose. Trembling, I toss off the covers and tiptoe down the hall. Only after I see my mother still sleeping peacefully and hear her quiet breathing does the pounding of my heart begin to subside.

Was it just a nightmare? Or a premonition of things to

come? What is happening to me? I've never had recurring visions like these before and certainly none about me and my mother. Visions of the Great War, the Spanish influenza, and the *Titanic* were horrific enough, but these are frightening in a whole new way. Maybe they're not really visions? But what else could they be?

Of course, I've never talked to a dead boy before either.

I blink heavily and rub my hands across my face, trying to dispel the dull ache in my head. Perhaps Walter's brief sojourn in my body has left more than just a bad memory. How many times have my mother and I found disgusting traces of the previous tenant in the hotels we've stayed in? Perhaps, at this very moment, my insides are smeared with some kind of spirit scum.

Shuddering, I wash, don a blue and white sailor dress, and quickly run a comb through my dark hair. It's certainly easier to care for now that it's bobbed. Mother fought against the cut, claiming that the long hair made more of a contrast between us onstage, but I think it has more to do with her reluctance to see me as an adult. Because if I'm a young woman, what does that make her?

I slip on my shoes and my blue wool wraparound coat before grabbing the shopping basket and heading out the door. I make sure to check the lock twice before running down the stairs. I'm usually a cautious person—you have to be in my line of business— but now, I'm out-and-out spooked.

I hear the door below me open as I come down the stairs. "Good morning, Mr. Darby," I call.

Mr. Darby grunts and shuts the door. So far he hasn't been very open to my friendly advances, but I'm nothing if not persistent. I'm dying to get a peek inside to find out what causes all the banging in his apartment, though I'm not sure I'm ready to face Cole again. I have too many questions, and I'm afraid of the answers.

A blast of frigid October air greets me as soon as I open the door. I clutch my coat tighter, wishing I were still wearing my warm woolen stockings instead of these new silk ones. Growing up isn't all it's reputed to be.

At the newsstand around the corner, I pick up the *Daily News*, the *Times*, and the *Sun* and tuck them into my basket. My mother will be eager to see if there are any reviews of last night's show. Then I turn and head toward Broadway. I'd spotted the bookstore yesterday on our way to the theater, tucked in between a millinery shop and a café. In the brief glimpse I got, it looked to be just the type of shop I like most—old and musty and chock-full of books. The kind of books that one day may give me some answers about my abilities.

Books on spiritualism, psychic phenomena, and witchcraft are usually twaddle, but sometimes I find interesting tidbits of information that add to the tapestry of knowledge I'm trying to weave. And right now, with the visions I've been having, finding answers seems more urgent than ever.

I hurry down the busy sidewalk, clutching my coat tight against the chill of the wind. If I remember right, the bookstore should be just before Columbus Circle. It's a lot farther by foot than I thought, and my toes are numb by the time I spot the sign for the milliner's.

It's a relief to step into the warmth of the bookshop, and I stand for a moment, letting my eyes adjust to the dim interior. Instead of being stacked in pretty rows across the shelves, the books are piled haphazardly on every available space. Of course, this means it will be harder to find anything useful, but the chaos pleases me.

An elderly woman behind the counter observes me sternly over the top of her glasses.

"If you're looking for gossip magazines, you're in the wrong place."

I shake my head. "I'm not," I assure her. "Do you have anything on . . ." I'm all set to say the occult, but something about her pursed mouth changes my mind. "Um, history?"

With a skeptical sniff, she leads me to a section toward the back of the store. I wait until she leaves before browsing the shelves. Maybe I can find something on my own. There are worse ways to spend a Saturday morning. Once, quite by accident, I discovered a fascinating book written more than fifty years ago by Robert Hare called *Experimental Investigation of the Spirit Manifestations, Demonstrating the Existence of Spirits and Their Communion with Mortals*. It was the first time I've ever come across a book where the science of spiritualism was being explored rather than just anecdotal evidence. Of course, until yesterday I was a lot more skeptical about communing with the dead.

Thinking of last night reminds me of my conversation

with Cynthia Gaylord. What exactly is the Society for Psychical Research? An organization that studies psychic phenomena? I decide to ask her more about it next time I see her. I stare at the old history books in dismay. It'll be impossible to find anything in this mess. Girding my loins, I march back to the clerk. She has a large book open on the counter and refuses to look up as I approach. Behind me, the bell over the door rings and still the clerk remains motionless.

"Excuse me," I finally say. She places her finger at the end of a sentence and looks up with a frown.

"May I help you?"

"Yes. Do you have any books on the occult? Or on the Society for Psychical Research?"

Her frown deepens. "I've never heard of the Society for Psychical Research, but we do have a small section on the occult. Are you looking for anything in particular?"

"Do you have anything on Mrs. Emma Hardinge Britten or Nellie Brigham?" Both women were spiritualists during the late 1800s, and some of the supernatural activities that occurred during their séances had never been explained.

She sniffs. "You will have to look for yourself." Her heels click impatiently across the wooden floor and I follow, wondering if she hates her job or if she's just taken an irrational dislike to me. She indicates a shelf about two feet above our heads, then turns on her heel and stalks off. I spot a step stool at the end of the aisle and head down to grab it.

"Can I help you?" I hear her snap to the other customer.

So it isn't just me.

I climb up on the stool and run my fingers along the titles. Some I've read; others don't look helpful at all. I pause for a moment on *Spells and Incantations* but then move past it. My mother and I often used incantations during our séances to add authenticity, but I'm no longer interested in helping to make our séances better. It's enough for me to keep us from getting caught.

"Excuse me. I couldn't help but overhear you asking about mediums and the occult," a rich English accent comes from behind me. "Have you read anything on D. D. Home?"

Startled, I grip the shelf and turn to find an older gentleman looking up at me.

"Excuse me?"

"My apologies for eavesdropping, but spiritualism is a hobby of mine."

"Oh. No, I haven't."

"If you like Nellie Brigham, you might find him interesting."

He looks past me and pulls out a book, *Unexplained Mysteries of the Nineteenth Century.* "This one devotes a whole chapter to him."

As he hands the book to me, our fingers brush and I receive a rush of emotional messages. Curiosity, amusement, and some other emotion I can't identify. It makes me shiver a bit.

"Thank you." I quickly turn back to the shelf and squeeze my eyes shut, hoping he'll just move on. After a moment he does, and I breathe a sigh of relief.

I wait until I hear the door open and close before hurrying to pay for my book. It's getting late and I still need to do the day's marketing.

The household upkeep is my job and has been since I was a little girl. My mother's too spent from work to do much in whatever home we happen to be in. Usually I enjoy it, but this morning, the frigid weather and my anxiety over last night compels me to rush through my shopping as soon as I make it back to our neighborhood.

The hair on the back of my arms rises just as I enter Wu's Tea Shop. The feeling isn't overpowering, like the time my mother and I were attacked by a purse snatcher on our way home after a show. Then, the foreboding was so strong it almost drove me to my knees. This is just unsettling, like something around me is just a bit off.

Swallowing, I glance around the shop, but the only people inside are the clerk—an elderly Chinese man with a long braid and perfect English—and a round woman, who's probably some family's capable housekeeper.

So if the threat isn't in here it must have come from outside. Am I being followed? And if so, why?

I walk through the store slowly, feigning preoccupation with the staggering assortment of teas and the odd Oriental knickknacks. The bell over the door rings and I startle, but it's only the housekeeper on her way out.

"Can I help you, miss?" the clerk asks.

I nod. "Yes, I'll take this one." On impulse, I pick up another packet of tea for Mr. Darby. "And this, as well."

The storekeeper places my tea in a paper bag and rings up the purchase. I linger at the counter as long as possible chatting with the clerk, who turns out to be Mr. Wu himself.

When I can't possibly procrastinate any longer, I take my leave and pause just outside the door. The neighborhood is busier now, the streets packed with harried mothers doing their shopping, children playing raucous games to keep warm, and elderly men and women exchanging neighborhood gossip.

I take a deep breath and open myself up. Over the years, I've realized that my clairvoyance has separate facets—emotions that come to me when I touch other people, uncontrollable visions that pop up out of nowhere, and those rare occasions when I get the eerie sense that something bad is about to happen.

For survival's sake, I've had to hone my observation skills to a razor-sharp point because the truth is that what people *say* isn't always how they *feel*.

Though I don't see or sense anything out of the ordinary, I still hurry through the rest of my shopping, not even lingering to visit with the shopkeepers as I usually do. Thanks to my time with the circus I'm pretty good at defending myself, but I don't want to risk it. Plus, I want to get back home to make sure my mother is all right.

As always, the thought of the circus brings to mind all the wonderful people I knew there. "Circus" was actually an optimistic term for a ragtag collection of freaks who couldn't get employment with the bigger, more successful shows, but I'd only been nine years old when we joined and, after spending two years with them, those freaks became my family. Swineguard, the knife thrower, taught me how to use a blade and to hold so still that even my heartbeat slowed. Hairy Harold played checkers with me every night after the show, and Komatchu, the Last of the Zulu Princesses (actually a former maid from Atlanta), loaned me books from the trunkful she hauled with her everywhere she went. I loved it there. Mother hated it. She felt the whole thing, especially the people, were beneath her. She's a terrible snob for someone who swindles people for a living. The only reason we stayed so long was a contract she couldn't get out of. As soon as the contract was up, she left without a backward glance.

I was heartbroken. Traveling with no one but my mother for company can be incredibly lonely.

I turn the corner onto our block and slow as I see someone come out of our building. I know it's Cole not only by his height and broad shoulders but also by his distinctive walk. I hold my breath but instead of coming in my direction, he crosses the street and turns at the next corner. I hesitate, but only for a moment. Something about Cole makes me uneasy, and my cranky neighbor may have the answers. Considering the visions I've been having, I can't afford to leave any stone unturned. It's time Mr. Darby and I had a little chat about his mysterious houseguest.

SEVEN

Once back in my building, I do a quick check on my mother to make sure she's still happily sleeping before heading back downstairs. I waver before knocking on Mr. Darby's door. But then I take a deep breath and knock softly. He answers within seconds.

"That's the problem with neighbors," he says in greeting. "You're nice to them once and you never get rid of them."

I hide a smile, refusing to let him intimidate me. I've always wanted to live in a place long enough to have neighbors, and a crotchety neighbor is better than none at all. Besides, Mr. Darby's grumpiness is nothing compared to some of the stage managers I've worked with. I put one hand on my hip and raise an eyebrow. "Just when were you ever nice to me? And you should be nice. I brought you some of that tea you said you wanted."

He eyes my basket. "I see that. And croissants, too?" He opens the door wider. "Well, come on in, girl. It's cold out here in the hall."

Hesitating only a moment, I follow him into his apartment, not bothering to correct his mistake. If my mother can give my tea to Jacques, I can give her croissant to Mr. Darby.

I glance around as I follow Mr. Darby into the kitchen. The rooms are neater than I'd expected for a bachelor apartment, and I wonder which of its residents is the tidy one.

I slow as I pass a desk with an envelope on it. It is addressed to Cole in a flowery, feminine script. The return address says London.

"Well, come along." Mr. Darby waves his hand at me and I blush, hoping he doesn't think I'm snooping. Even if I am.

"You might as well sit down and make yourself comfortable."

I sit at a small table and watch as he puts the water on the stove and adds more coal to the fire. Like the sitting room, the kitchen is clean and comfortable. The furniture looks worn and less expensive than our brand-new set but far more homey. As if someone actually lives here. Sometimes I wish our apartment looked a little more lived in. Of course, lived in isn't really good for business. Not now that we're trying to attract a ritzier clientele.

Mr. Darby places a cup and saucer in front of me and then adds a plate. "You'll probably want to be served, too." He furrows his forehead in disapproval.

"Well, I did bring the tea and the croissants," I say, sarcasm seeping through my smile.

The corner of his mouth twitches as he sets the tea down in front of me. "You don't fool me, missy. You're just hoping to run into Cole."

My head jerks up. "I am not!"

He snorts and takes the seat across from me. "Anyway, you're out of luck. He's gone already."

I shift in my seat, my face flaming. If Mr. Darby thinks I'm interested in Cole, maybe he'll be a bit more forthcoming with information. All I have to do is swallow my pride.

"When did Cole move in with you? I didn't see him when we first came here." I widen my eyes, trying for fake innocence.

He flashes me a knowing glance. "So that's why I got the croissant! No, don't try to deny it." He holds up a hand to stop my protest. "I knew a young miss wouldn't go to all this trouble for an old man like myself. He moved in just before you did, but he pretty much keeps to himself and is gone for a good deal of the day."

"Does he go to work?"

Mr. Darby shrugs. "Not that I know of. He just got out of some fancy school in Europe somewhere."

Europe. That explains the letter and his formal way of speaking. "Then where does he go all day?"

"To the library to study. He says he can't think with all my racket going on. Now enough questions. If you want more information, you'll have to ask him yourself."

I want to find out more but decide against prying further. Instead, I move to the next topic of interest. "And what would all that noise be? My mother and I have heard you down here banging away."

"Ah, wouldn't you like to know! Tell you what, you tell

me what you and your ma do with your late-night company and I'll tell you what I do that's so loud."

So Cole didn't tell him about our séance. Mr. Darby's blue eyes gleam and I can't help but smile back at him. "You drive a hard bargain, but it's a deal."

He nods and bites into a croissant. "Mmmmm. Would you like one?" he asks, innocence written all over his gnomelike features.

I glare and the corners of his mouth twitch upward.

He hands me a croissant. "Thanks," I say, equally ungrateful, and receive an actual grin as reward. I bite into the buttery, flaky crust and take a sip of tea. The croissants are the best I've ever tasted.

We drink our tea and eat in silence until the last delicious flake is licked from our fingertips.

"Well, at least you know how to eat well," he commends. "Most women talk, talk, talk all through the meal while a man is trying to enjoy his food."

"Good food deserves concentration," I answer solemnly.

He nods. "Very sensible. Now, on to our bargain."

"What bargain was that?" I tease.

"Cheeky girl. You know very well what bargain. Now tell me, and no more of your stalling."

"Very well." I lean forward and drop my voice to a whisper. "We hold séances."

He smacks the table with his palms. "No."

I nod. "Yes."

"I knew it was something like that, the way your mother

dresses. So mysterious. A real looker, she is." He tilts his head to the side. "You're not so bad looking yourself, though a bit too soon to say for sure."

I roll my eyes. "Thanks."

"You're welcome. Now tell me something. Are those séances of yours for real, or are there tricks involved?"

My stomach knots and I shake my head, giving him as big a smile as I can muster. "We had a bargain and now it's your turn."

"Well, now, I don't know . . ."

"Mr. Darby! Are you saying you won't keep your word to a lady?"

"Of course not. I'm not saying that at all. Now you have me all confused. Very well, I'll tell you." He draws himself up with pride. "I'm an inventor!"

I sit back in my chair. That isn't what I was expecting, but I can tell he's looking for a reaction, so I clap my hands together and try to look properly surprised. "Really? What do you invent?"

Mr. Darby smiles smugly. Evidently, my reaction pleased him. "Now that's for me to know and you to find out."

"Can't you show me one thing?"

He considers my request for a moment, then gets up from the table. Taking a square metal box out of a cupboard, he unwraps a long cloth cord and plugs the pronged end into an electrical outlet in the wall. He then cuts a slice of bread and bids me to join him. When I do, he spears the piece of bread with a fork and carefully jostles it into the box. Closing the small door on the side, he looks at me expectantly.

"Er, now what?"

"Now we wait." He pauses dramatically. "For the bread to toast and then pop up!"

My eyes widen. "Oh my! A pop-up bread toaster. I've heard of those."

His face falls and he heaves a deep sigh. "That's the problem. Every time I think I have a winner, I find out it's already been invented. But this one is much improved."

"I'm sure it is and I'm positive you'll think of something," I say to reassure him. "What else have you invented?"

"Oh, wouldn't you like to know! But you'll have to tell me something first. Aren't those séances just a hoax?"

His eyes fix on mine, glinting with shrewd curiosity. My first instinct is to lie. The truth might get us arrested. But an image of the planchette moving on its own under my fingers and Walter moving through my body makes me shudder. "Not always," I say softly.

"So then your mother is more of a magician than a medium?"

I consider that. Though my mother knows a bit of sleight of hand, her abilities are the result of my showmanship. "Not really. She's more like a really good actress."

I shift uneasily in my seat. That's more than I've ever told anyone about what my mother and I do. How odd that I should trust a gruff old man with clever blue eyes.

Suddenly a burning smell fills the kitchen and thick

black smoke pours from the bread-toasting machine. I back up hastily and Mr. Darby yanks the plug from the wall. Then he grabs a wet towel from the sink and pulls the scorched bread from the machine. I clap my hand over my mouth and he casts me a look as he tosses the burned offering into the sink.

"Don't you laugh at me, missy!"

I shake my head but don't dare answer.

"Good God! What have you done this time?"

I jump as Cole rushes through the doorway behind me. He skids to a stop when he spots the machine sitting on the counter. "Oh. Burned toast for breakfast again, I see." He notices me and nods politely. "If you've come to dine, I think you should reconsider."

His voice is thick with irony and he gives me a smile—a real smile that lights up his whole face and makes him look more like a boy than a schoolteacher. My breath hitches.

"We've already had breakfast," Mr. Darby answers crossly. "I was just showing her my machine."

"You should be flattered. He doesn't show his machines to just anyone."

Cole glances at me and then away. Casually, I move back to the table and brush up against him, sending out a pulse strand as I do so. But before the strand can connect, it's deflected, like it hit a wall of some kind. I frown. I've never felt anything like that before.

"And just who else would I be showing it to?" Mr. Darby asks belligerently.

I edge toward the sitting room, unsettled. "I should be going. My mother will wonder where I've gotten to."

I gather up my things, and Cole takes the basket from me.

"Allow me," he says politely.

"It's only upstairs," I protest.

"I don't often get to act like a gentleman. Indulge me." He inclines his head and sounds so formal, it's hard to believe that he was teasing Mr. Darby just a few minutes ago.

I follow him through the sitting room, Mr. Darby right on our heels. "You come back anytime, girl. I haven't even shown you my workshop yet."

I nod. "I will. I'd love that."

Cole and I walk out into the stairwell. I reach for my basket and he hands it to me with a slight smile that softens his stern lips. I find myself staring at his lips and look quickly away, embarrassed.

"Thank you for coming to visit. Mr. Darby can be a bit crabby, but that's only a front."

"I like him," I say truthfully.

As I stand there, looking into his dark eyes, the strangest feeling comes over me. As if we are somehow connected. The space between us is almost alive with a dawning awareness of the other person. This new sensation is as intriguing as it is alarming and I fight my temptation to just give in to it.

Swallowing, I turn to go upstairs, but he reaches out and catches my coat. "May I ask you something?"

His voice is casual, so different from his normal, stilted

71

tone that I'm instantly on alert. I bite the inside of my lip and give a slight nod.

"What happened last night—does it happen often?"

His eyes lock onto mine. I feel as if he's plucking the answer right out of my mind, so I shake my head. "No. No, never."

He lets go of my arm and I hurry up the stairs on shaking legs.

"Anna!"

I pause halfway to my door and turn.

His face is solemn. "Be careful with that."

I don't have to ask what he's talking about. With another quick nod, I run the rest of the way up the stairs.

I awake the next morning, as relieved by not having another vision as I am disappointed by it. At least with a vision I may get clues as to what's happening. Or might happen. I rub my temples, confused. I check on my mother, which is becoming sort of a nervous habit, and, of course, she's fine. After washing up and getting dressed, I hesitate, looking at my shopping basket. I know it's silly, but I don't want to leave her alone.

Instead I procrastinate by cleaning the flat until I hear her stirring in her bedroom. I pour her a cup of coffee and take it back to her.

Her eyebrows raise. "What's the occasion?"

I shrug, trying to look nonchalant. "Nothing. Just thought you might like some."

Her brow furrows. It speaks volumes about our relationship that bringing her coffee when she wakes up is viewed with suspicion.

"What are your plans for the day?" I ask, picking up her red Oriental silk wrap and handing it to her.

"Jacques will be here in a bit. He is taking me shopping and then to lunch with potential clients."

I frown. I don't trust Jacques for a moment, but on the other hand, the show is making him money, so surely he wouldn't hurt my mother, would he? "What clients?"

"I don't know! I haven't met them yet." She laughs, but I sense her exasperation. "Now run me a bath, will you, darling?"

Wisely, I hold my tongue and do as I'm asked. Once she's safely in the tub I slip on my coat and gloves and pull a dark blue woolen cloche down over my ears. If I lock the door behind me, she should be perfectly safe.

I pick up my shopping basket, but just as I step onto the landing, I hear Mr. Darby's door opening. Peering down the stairwell, I see Cole's broad shoulders as he opens the outside door. Silent as a cat, I step back into my doorway. It only takes moments before I decide to follow him and see if he really spends his day at the library.

Setting my basket at the top of the landing, I slip down the stairs and count to five before opening the door and peeking out. I spot him rounding the corner and run to catch up. Darting through the crowded sidewalks, I slow when I'm the perfect following distance behind him. There are enough people on the street that I shouldn't be too noticeable, as long as he doesn't head to a quieter area.

I stick to the shadows and am grateful for my dark blue coat and dress. Even the group of girls I'm keeping between myself and Cole don't know I'm following so close behind them.

Growing up, I learned that collecting information on potential clients was easier if I made myself inconspicuous, and because I'm so small and quiet, I can be darn near invisible when I want to be. I'm thankful Jacques has his lackeys do the client research now. I'm tired of being the lackey myself.

The girls in front of me go into a hat shop and my heart stops in my throat when Cole pauses. Rather than risk it, I dart kitty-corner across the street, keeping one eye on traffic and the other on Cole. I don't think he'd appreciate being dogged.

I slow down, waiting for him to move on. I'm so busy watching him that I don't see the woman carrying a bag full of potatoes until it's too late. Potatoes roll everywhere, and by the time I help her gather them all up, Cole is long gone.

My shoulders slump. I can't help feeling that Cole isn't being completely open with me. Could he have something to do with all the odd things that have been happening? The feeling that I was being watched outside the tea shop the other day? My visions? Walter? But how could he? I remember him smiling and teasing Mr.

Darby, and I suddenly hope with all my heart that he isn't somehow linked to my visions.

Turning back toward my own neighborhood, my feet reluctantly take me to the ancient theater I'd been avoiding ever since I spotted the title on the marquee last week.

A group of young boys crowd around the ticket box. After much jostling and stealing of caps, they finally pay for their tickets and disappear through the wide front doors. If I go in, I'll probably be the only person in there over thirteen. Sunday matinees are the province of the young. I bite my lip, that age-old pain hovering around my heart as I stare at the marquee:

HALDANE OF THE SECRET SERVICE
STARRING HARRY HOUDINI

Mother doesn't know it, but I've been to all his movies. I missed this one the first time it came out and I'm torn, wondering if I should even go inside. For me, watching a Houdini movie is like fouling up a trick onstage: It starts out great, then suddenly it's not, and you end up with a pit in your stomach, wishing you hadn't tried it at all. Considering my relationship with Houdini, I should probably just walk away.

But I don't. I take a deep breath and march up to the glass ticket box. Just as I'm compelled to perform magic, I'm compelled to see Houdini whenever I can.

I give the man behind the glass my dime. He tears a ticket off the roll and hands it to me.

"I thought you were never going to go in," a familiar voice says from behind me.

I whirl around to find Cole standing close, very close, behind me. "You startled me!" My eyes narrow. Did he know I was following him? He must. He had to backtrack to get to the theater. My cheeks flame. What would he say?

"I'm sorry." He pays for his ticket and then turns to me. His herringbone overcoat sits well on his broad shoulders, and a Homburg hat is slightly tilted on his head, lending a rakish air to his dignified features. "Do you mind if I accompany you?"

I've never shared this part of my life with anyone, but then again, I don't think Cole knows that Houdini is my father, so it wouldn't be like sharing. His neck reddens under his collar as he awaits my answer. *He's afraid I'll say no,* I think in surprise. "That would be nice," I say, and then curse myself for sounding so prim.

He holds the door open for me and we go inside. The theater itself is lovely, though a little worse for wear. The red carpeting is worn in spots, and several lights in the lobby chandelier are missing. I can tell by the decor that it used to be a proper playhouse and has been converted into a movie theater. Usually, I enjoy going to the movies, but today, the combination of seeing Houdini on-screen and proximity to Cole sets my stomach churning, so I decline refreshments.

Our seats are uncomfortable, but sitting so close to Cole, it doesn't really matter. Boisterous kids in the balcony above hoot and holler while the lower part is almost empty. I try to think of something to say but can't, so instead I study the other theater patrons. There's a pair of young women about my age close to the front and a woman holding a baby across the aisle. I glance away and then back, caught by something I don't understand. The old coat she's wearing looks like it might have been a man's, and the blankets swaddling the baby are tattered. But that isn't what is catching my attention. I've seen many poor people in my life, some much worse off than she is.

It's the pulses of worry and despair coming at me from across the aisle that command my attention. I stare, my heart thudding in my chest. I shut my eyes, but her emotions continue to batter me like breakers against the shore. Why is this happening? I grip the armrests until my fingers hurt. It's bad enough feeling other people's emotions when I touch them, but being assaulted by them through thin air is unbearable.

Then as suddenly as it began, it stops. I take a deep, shuddering breath and glance at Cole, who seems unaware of my strange attack of anxiety. I look back at the woman, who is rocking the baby in her arms. I feel nothing. Was it my imagination?

Just when the silence between Cole and me becomes unbearable, he says, "So how long have you been in New York?" His voice is strained as if he, too, was having a hard time thinking of something to say.

"For a little over a month. You?"

"About six weeks. But I've been in the States for almost three months. I went to Baltimore first."

"Oh, are you doing the tour?"

"Something like that."

We lapse back into silence. So much for that topic. We're saved when the lights go off and the newsreel starts. We watch in quiet as the famous boxer Jack Dempsey participates in an automobile race, one hundred hot-air balloons take off in Brussels, and officials break up an opium ring in Shanghai. When the flickering images of a movie-star dog doing tricks comes on, Cole actually laughs out loud. The sound sends a tingling warmth from my toes to the top of my head. He looks at me, the light from the screen dancing against the darkness of his eyes, and my breath catches in my throat. Once again, I feel that strange awareness that I felt in the stairwell, that warm connection that I've only ever sensed with him. For a moment, we're caught in each other's gaze and then the organist starts to play. We both jump, and I laugh self-consciously.

Then I turn back to the flickering images and Cole is forgotten as Houdini fills the screen.

The feature is on.

Dread and anticipation battle inside me as the opening credits roll. Watching his movies raises the age-old question in my mind: Is he really my father?

His charisma, alluring and potent, emanates from the screen in waves. The story line and the printed dialogue that goes with it are simple, but I'm not following it. I'm watching the man who may be my father. His hair is wild, thick, and unruly like always. His eyes are fierce, magnetic. It's easy to believe that he could have the same abilities that I do—his power is palpable. I watch the escapes with a professional eye. Could I do that? The vision of me under-water flashes in front of my eyes and I shiver. Could I break free of something like that? Will I have to?

Next to me, Cole is completely involved in the movie. The organist is quite good, the music swelling and subsid-ing with the action. He smiles at the funny bits and tenses at the suspenseful parts.

Across from us, the baby fusses and the woman tries to calm it, jouncing it up and down. Then her anguish washes over me so clearly, I begin to tremble. I clasp my hands together in my lap and look down at the floor, but the sor-row and fear continue to lash at me like a hurricane. My shoulders hunch and I draw inward, trying to protect my heart, which feels as if it's about to break.

Unable to bear it any longer, I leap out of my seat and scoot past a surprised Cole. Pausing only for a second, I take my emergency ten-dollar coin from my purse and toss it into the woman's lap. She looks up, startled, but I turn away and race up the aisle.

I run through the lobby and burst out the doors in front. Only then do I pause long enough to take a breath. Moments later, Cole comes through the same door.

"Are you all right?" Worry creases his forehead.

My cheeks flush. "I'm fine. I just forgot I had to do something."

I turn and start walking away, tears of humiliation forming in my eyes.

"Are you sure you feel well? Do you want me to come with you?"

I hear the concern in his tone but can't face him. "Everything's fine. I have to go," I call over my shoulder. I hurry away through the crowd, frantic to leave Cole, Houdini, and that poor, desperate woman behind me. Then I do what the Van Housen women always do when things go wrong. I run.

EIGHT

The eight of spades. The eight of spades.

My legs shake as we walk down the hall to our dressing room. Mother opens the door and waves me in as if nothing has happened.

But it has. *The eight of spades.*

Of course, she doesn't care. She wouldn't have been the laughingstock of the show. My fists clench. She'd done it on purpose. Coldly, consciously, and deliberately.

The séance obviously provoked her more than she'd let on.

On her table is a bottle of the chilled French wine she likes to finish her evenings with. By the time she pours herself a glass and takes a sip, I've had enough.

I snatch my coat off the coat rack and wrap it around me. Facing her image in the mirror, I glare as she checks her hair and powders her nose. She avoids my eyes even though she knows I'm watching her.

"Why did you do that, Mother? To show me who's boss?"

"Don't be sulky, darling. I was just having a bit of fun."

"Your fun humiliated me," I say through clenched teeth.

"Oh, please." Her tone is sharp. "The audience hardly even knew there was a mistake."

It was supposed to be an easy card trick. I would "force" a card onto a volunteer, make it disappear and then reappear in the pocket of a different "random" member of the audience. It was Mother's job to plant the correct card earlier in the show. Only tonight it didn't work out that way.

I'm so mad, I shove aside the caution I usually use in dealing with my mother. "I gave you the eight of spades to plant, but strangely enough, I pulled out the jack of hearts. Now why is that?"

My mother's mouth tightens. She's not used to me calling her on the carpet. "Keep your voice down! Like I said, I was just having a bit of fun. You covered it up and it's over."

I place both hands on my hips as hurt and angry tears swell in my throat. "It wasn't fun for me, Mother, and I don't want it to happen again. Ever."

Her face stills into an impassive mask as she finally meets my eyes. "Excuse me?"

"You heard me." Before I leave, I slap a card faceup on her vanity table—the eight of spades, which was still in the pocket of her dress when we came down the hall.

Stomping out, I slam the door behind me for good measure. Then I take a second to catch my breath. It's coming out in short gasps. I've never given her an order like that before.

I'm not sure whether to jump up and down in glee or be sick.

Had she really been so angry about the séance that she was willing to jeopardize the show for it? Attack and counterattack. Strategy and schemes. Why is my relationship with my mother more like a chess game than a family bond?

No matter how badly I want to take a taxi home and leave her to stew all by herself, I know I can't. I lean back against the wall, shaking, and close my eyes. No matter how angry she makes me she's still my mother, and I have to protect her if I can.

I hear voices and take a deep, shuddering breath, trying to compose myself.

Jacques is approaching me, accompanied by a handsome young stranger with strikingly blond hair. "Are you leaving?"

I nod. "I have a headache." This isn't far from the truth.

"I'm so sorry." Jacques's words slip from his mouth as if they've been lubricated. "I was hoping you would join us for dinner. We have a guest tonight." He turns toward the young man. "Owen, this is Anna Van Housen. You saw her lively performance earlier. Anna, this is my nephew, Owen Winchester. He surprised me at the show this evening."

"Enchanted, Miss Van Housen." Owen takes my hand and kisses it. His blue eyes rove over me, lighting up with appreciation. My stomach gives a little responding flutter. Turns out being looked over like that is much more agreeable when the man in question is young and handsome. I feel a jumble of emotions coming from him—including nervousness and admiration. Could he be nervous about meeting me?

Owen glances at his uncle. "I've been in New York for several months now. I've been meaning to get in touch with you, but it's taken me a bit to get settled in. Besides, you're the one who didn't keep in touch with the family."

I can't help but notice the slight dimples framing his crooked smile. He's wearing a dapper black evening suit and his blond hair's longer on the top and slicked back in the latest fashion. My mind jumps to Cole's neat, close-cropped curls. "Nice to meet you," I murmur, a warm blush staining my cheeks. Whether it's because of Owen's obvious approval or the thought of Cole is hard to tell. I'd blushed on and off ever since my humiliating behavior at the movie theater. I wonder what Cole must think of me.

"I was thinking we could all go out for dinner," Jacques says, interrupting my thoughts. "But if you aren't feeling well . . ."

I hesitate, but only for a heartbeat. This young man, no matter how attractive, isn't enough to tempt me into enduring an evening with my mother. Not after what she pulled tonight.

"That's all right, Uncle J. I have an early morning anyway. Perhaps I could escort Miss Van Housen safely home? That way, you and her lovely mother could go directly to dinner."

Jacques frowns. "Perhaps we should . . ."

"That would be very kind, thank you," I say firmly, taking Owen by the arm. I'm being very forward, but I don't care. This is Jacques's nephew, after all. Surely Mother won't have any objections. If she does, that's just too bad.

Owen leads me down the dark hall and out into the night. The sidewalk in front of the theater is still packed with audience members waiting for taxis or simply chattering about the show. Usually I love this sight, but I'm not in the mood tonight.

"My car is this way," Owen says. I follow him down the street.

He glances at me. "That was pretty bold, the way you insisted on leaving. Aren't you afraid your mother will have kittens? We're practically strangers."

"My mother won't care. I've been handling myself in adverse situations all my life."

He laughs. "I certainly hope you aren't calling me an adverse situation."

I blush, praying it's too dark outside for him to see the color in my cheeks. "Of course not."

"I knew what you meant. But well done for not letting etiquette stand in your way. The old folks don't understand that life is much different now than when they were young. Our generation has grown up faster. We're much more mature than they were at our age."

I thrill at his sophisticated, worldly tone.

"Your mother doesn't really strike me as the old-fashioned type, though," he continues, opening the door to a neat Model T. The scent of gin, leather, and something sweet tickles my nose as I climb in. He starts the car and I give him my address.

"No, my mother is a modern woman," I say, going back to our conversation. "And for the most part, she's always treated me as an adult. She's had to." When she's not laying traps for me.

"What a screwy life you must have led!"

I think back to our years of travel and all the people we'd met. "Yes, but . . ." I hesitate.

"Pretty lonely, too, I bet."

My eyes widen. "How did you know?"

"I guessed."

We fall silent for a moment. No one else has ever noticed my loneliness, but then, no one else has been paying much attention.

"You're sitting pretty now, though, with your new show."

We drive in silence for a few blocks. "I have a confession to make," he finally says.

"What's that?"

"I told my uncle I wanted to meet the amazing Madame Marguerite Van Housen, but I was much more interested in meeting you."

I frown. What a line.

"I wanted to know how such a beautiful young woman could also be such a talented magician."

"Oh." My cheeks flush a darker shade of red.

He laughs, and I've never felt less sophisticated.

"What kind of work do you do that you have to get up so early?" I ask, changing the subject. I don't feel up to telling him the story of my life.

"I work in a bank on Wall Street. It's not very exciting, but the pay is good."

It sounds exciting to me. Well, not exactly exciting. More like solid and comfortable. Which, given the harum-scarum life I've led, sounds pretty wonderful.

"So how about you? You happy being in the show?"

I think about it. "Sort of. But I'd rather just do magic and skip the mentalist act."

Owen smiles. "The show is nifty, it really is, but I think it would be even better if there were more magic and less of the other stuff. I've always enjoyed magic."

I snort. "Try telling my mother that."

"Why doesn't she want you to have a bigger part in the show? You're good enough to do bigger illusions."

"Thank you," I tell him. "But Mother *is* the headliner."

"Ah." His voice is leading, but I don't take the bait.

"So are you really Harry Houdini's daughter?"

My breath hitches and my fists clench. I stare at them in the darkness. Counting to three, I slowly uncurl them before replying. "Where did you hear that?"

"I said something to my uncle about how talented you are, and he said you should be, since you were Houdini's daughter."

I stare out the windows at the dark streets, a solid mass of emotion pressing against my chest. Wherever I go, the rumors follow. I suspect Mother starts most of them herself.

"Hey," he says, reaching across to touch my arm lightly. "I didn't mean to upset you. I think it's pretty great."

"It's just not something I talk about." I shake my head. He must think I'm a real flat tire, a bore even.

He pulls up in front of my building. "That's okay. I can think of better things to talk to a pretty girl about."

"And what would that be?"

"'Of shoes and ships and sealing wax . . .'"

"'Of cabbages and kings,'" I finish, laughing. I've read *Through the Looking-Glass* at least a dozen times.

I reach for the car door.

"No, wait. Allow me!"

He hops out and rushes around the car, while I settle back, a small smile playing about my lips. Living a nice, respectable life definitely has its benefits. This is the second time in less than a week that a handsome young man has treated me like a lady instead of some sort of stage hussy. It makes me feel . . . *special*. Just before he reaches the door, however, Owen stumbles and falls, landing in the gutter. One moment he's there, and the next he's sprawled, spread eagle, on the street. I wrench on the handle and jump out, careful not to step on him.

"Are you all right?"

He springs to his feet, brushing off his suit. "Yes. But what do they say about pride going before a fall?"

I stifle a laugh. "I never understood that, myself. I always thought pride went after the fall."

He gives me an embarrassed grin. "I can assure you, that is indeed the case."

I smile back. "Well, thank you for the ride."

He wipes off his hand on his trousers before taking mine and kissing it. "My pleasure, Miss Van Housen.

Especially the bang-up finish."

There's a smudge of dirt under one of his cheekbones and I have to smile. Then he catches both my hands in his. They're warm and gentle and to my relief, sending me no overt emotional messages. My breath hitches as his laughing blue eyes grow serious. "Would you like to go dancing with me sometime?"

"Why?" I ask, and then want to kick myself again. I can pick a lock or pocket with ease, make cards appear and disappear like a jack-in-the-box, and break in and out of small-town jails without being detected, but put me in the presence of a nice young man and I become the village idiot.

"Because I like you."

I lower my eyes to hide my confusion. He likes me? Isn't this all happening a little fast? I look back to his face. His dimples deepen as a smile curves his lips, and a lock of hair has fallen over his forehead. But then, maybe this is how it works. I shove the Harry Houdini comment out of my mind and answer his smile with one of my own.

"Perhaps."

He laughs. "Perhaps?"

I nod, too embarrassed to speak.

He gives my hand a squeeze. "That's swell, Anna. See you soon."

I turn away to unlock the door to my building and wait until Owen's car chugs away before letting myself look back over my shoulder. The events of the evening are catching up to me. I'm always tired after a show, but tonight, after the fight with my mother, even my bones feel fragile.

Suddenly the hair on my neck and arms prickles and fore-boding brushes across my skin like a blood-dipped feather. My fingers, so adept at picking locks, fumble with the key. Like a child afraid to look under the bed, I'm terrified to peek behind me, afraid of what I might see. A thief or worse? The door falls open, and I shoot through it, giving the stoop one sweeping glance before shutting the door behind me.

Nothing.

But I can still feel something out there, lurking. And whatever it is, it isn't going anywhere soon.

"Quit your sulking and help me choose a hat."

I'm lying on the sofa reading an old copy of the *Sphinx* magazine, trying to ignore my mother, who has been hovering all morning. Being ignored is her worst nightmare and my best line of defense.

I raise an eyebrow and give her a cursory glance. She's dressed for the day in a soft maroon worsted-wool suit that reaches just below her knees. The color sets off her creamy complexion—my mother's proud of her skin and deplores the fashion that makes women powder their faces white. She only does it at night or for shows.

She sets two hatboxes down on the coffee table and pulls out a jade-green cloche and then a black one.

As always, I'm torn by my desire to please my mother and my survival instincts. After a brief struggle, I sigh and lay down my magazine. "The black one. It'll go with the dress once you take your coat off."

"Hmm. I think perhaps the green."

Of course she does. I pick up my cards and begin shuffling. She pins on the hat and twirls for me. "How do I look?"

"Lovely as always. Where are you going?"

"Lunch with Jacques."

Worry pulses through me and I rub my temples. "And then what?"

She frowns. "I don't know. Why?"

"Are we working tonight?" What I'm asking is whether we are doing a séance or not. The theater is closed Sunday nights to appease the churchgoers.

Mother shakes her head. "No. Jacques thinks we should only do a few séances a month. That way they're more exclusive and we can charge more."

I breathe out a sigh of relief and she frowns. "Have a lovely time and don't spend too much money," I say before she can chide me about my attitude. It works.

"Don't worry so much about money, darling." She gathers up her purse and gloves and I get up and follow her to the door. "We're going to have plenty from now on." She pats my shoulder patronizingly. "And don't wait around for me. I'm not sure when I'll be home. Now I really must go; Jacques is probably already downstairs. Oh, and I ordered some material for a new spirit manifestation. It's even gauzier than what we're using and will be perfect. Can you pick it up for me?"

I give her a small, defeated nod.

She writes the directions on a piece of paper and hands it to me before opening the door. I turn toward the window so I can watch her get into Jacques's car.

Then her scream shatters the air.

I whirl around, expecting to see her being hauled away by an unknown enemy. Instead she is standing frozen in the doorway. I'm by her side in a heartbeat, my hands raised, wishing I had my balisong, anything, to use as a weapon. But there is no one there. Then I notice her extended finger and suck in my breath when I see what she's pointing at. A sewer rat the size of a small cat is lying on our doorstep.

"What is that?" my mother asks, her voice raw.

I swallow, my pulse starting to slow. "It's just a rat."

"How did it get here and what do we do with it?" As usual, she's completely at a loss. I touch her shoulder.

"Go on with Jacques," I tell her. "I'll take care of it."

The gratitude in Mother's eyes is real, and she leans forward and kisses my cheek. "Thank you," she whispers. She skirts the dead animal carefully and hurries down the stairwell.

I rush back into the apartment and over to the window just in time to see her climbing into Jacques's sleek Packard. Then, with a heavy sigh, I grab a rag from under the kitchen sink and use it to pick up the rat by the tail. Staring at its dull brown eyes and long yellow teeth, I can't help but wonder what killed it. I toss it down the incinerator, shuddering.

As soon as I shut and lock my apartment door, I lean

against it, breathing heavily. I've lived in the building for more than a month and have never seen traces of rodents. So how does one end up dead in the hall smack dab in front of our doorway? Coincidence? Or did someone leave it there for us to find? And if so, why? I take a deep breath, willing myself to calm down. My mind spins with all the other things that have happened in the last week. The visions. Walter. Feeling the emotions of people without even touching them. Are they all connected? If so, how?

Something niggles at the edge of my mind and I take a deep breath, letting it come to me.

Cole.

Everything started changing when I first met Cole.

I walk into the sitting room and stand in front of the window, not seeing the street below. Hugging my arms around me, I think hard, one thought racing after another. The very first vision I had about my mother was right after I ran into Cole in the street. The first time I ever channeled a dead person, Cole was there. The first time I felt someone's feelings without touching them, Cole was there. But that's *insane*. How could Cole possibly have an effect on my abilities? And how can I find out without giving myself away?

One thing is certain. If I want to keep my mother safe, I'd better figure it out.

NINE

I spend the rest of the morning and part of the afternoon cleaning our flat, allowing the menial work to soothe the turmoil in my mind.

No matter what I think of him, Jacques has secured us a wonderful apartment. It boasts a modern kitchen—the first I've ever had—with a gas stove, a sink with hot and cold running water, and tiny black and white tiles on the floor. A work area runs the length of one wall, and a small wooden table stands in front of a sunny window. Just off the kitchen, I have the unheard-of luxury of my own bedroom—the first time in my life I don't have to share with my mother.

After I finish cleaning, I glance at the clock. It's still too early to leave. Mother's errand will have to wait because I have other plans for this afternoon. Plans that have me twitchy as a cat's tail. Biting my lip, I'm drawn back to my bedroom and pull out my hatboxes. I take out my handcuffs, lock them, and then pick them open several times. The action calms me. I replace them and take out an old handbill showing Houdini locked inside a chest. I study the chest as if it were real instead of a drawing. I'm pretty sure I know how he's able to escape, leaving the chest locked and bound with chains. All it would take is someone to replace the longer bolts with shorter ones. Of course, he would need a tool of some sort to pound them out. Not sure where he would hide it, though. Perhaps his hair?

I stare at the publicity still, remembering the first time my mother told me Houdini was my father. I must have been four or five, and it was one of those rare occasions when she wasn't working or going out with a gentleman caller. I don't remember which city we were in but I remember it being nice, with clean sidewalks and shiny shops. She had bought me a lollipop for a treat and I slowly licked its sugary sweetness while we strolled along hand in hand. The sun felt nice on my back, and she was showing me the difference between a hat that would look good forever and one that would be outdated in a year. I remember being more interested in the lollipop than in what she was saying, but it still felt good that she was talking to me so seriously. Then she suddenly stopped, staring at a giant poster in the window.

"What's that, Mommy?" I had asked.

For a moment, I thought she wasn't going to answer, but then she reached down and picked me up. I remember squirming at being held like a baby in public but her arms tightened and I stilled. "Look, *kis szerelem*," she said softly, slipping into the old language she used less and less. "There's your father."

I looked around in confusion until my mother pointed at the poster. Then I made out the image of a man whose eyes seem to be staring directly into mine.

"That man is my father?" It must have been a trick of the light, because for a moment it looked as if we were standing together, the three of us. But it was just our reflection in the window. That night my mother told me for the first time how she met Houdini and how I came to be.

Now I wonder if any of it was true.

Replacing the handbill, I take out the flyer that the promoter gave me. The Hippodrome is on Sixth Avenue. It shouldn't take me too long to get there.

After hiding my collection, I eat a quick lunch and shrug on my coat. The afternoon sun is thin in the waning October afternoon and gives little warmth. Before heading to the show, I explore the neighborhood. Some of the buildings, like ours, have been cut up into flats, while others remain stately single-family homes, with wide steps and wrought-iron railings. It isn't a ritzy neighborhood, but it is an established one, and it wraps me in a firmly middle-class hug.

Everywhere I go, I see regular people—mothers taking their babies out for some fresh air and children playing games on the street. The young women look as if they were all cut from the same fashionable cloth, with their identical calf-length bias-cut dresses, cloche or helmet-style hats, and dangling bracelets. They stroll together with their arms linked, exchanging confidences. I feel a pang as I realize I'm the only one walking alone. But then, I've always been alone.

Most of the girls I've met have been put off by the scandalous life I lead and because my mother looks the way she does. While I've been picking locks, defrauding war widows, and performing onstage, other girls my age are attending high school, helping their mothers around the home, and maybe sneaking off to a dance or two on the weekends. The few friends I've had have been adults connected with the theater, and since we were always moving around, they never lasted long anyway.

I look right and left as I cross the street, remembering the foreboding I felt last night, but the only anxiety I feel right now is over what I will find at Houdini's show.

I catch a streetcar going downtown, smiling at the toothless driver as I pay my fare. There are plenty of seats on this Sunday afternoon, and I take one close to the front.

Glancing around, I slip the flyer out of my purse and read the headline:

A MAGICIAN AMONG THE SPIRITS

What does that mean?

Knowing Houdini's skepticism, I'm almost afraid to find out. Like most performers just beginning their careers, Houdini barely scratched out an existence and became adept with card tricks, the pea game, and other carnival cons in order to survive. He also claimed to talk to the dead and performed all kinds of amazing tricks to prove his authenticity. When his magic began to pay off, he left all that behind him, except the knowledge he gained from doing it.

For years he worked on his own career and never gave a thought to mediums defrauding the public of money, but all that changed when his beloved mother died. He had been desperate to get in touch with her and offered a substantial amount of money to anyone who could contact her spirit. Many tried, but Houdini exposed them all as frauds. He became bitter and increasingly convinced it could not be done. After a time, it became his mission in life to expose spiritualism as a sham.

I get off the streetcar and walk half a block to the Hippodrome. With its stately spires, flags, and ornate detailing, it looks like a castle, out of place among New York's businesslike streets. A throng of people are already gathered outside, and I join the line.

Just one of the crowd.

It's as one of the crowd that I pay for my ticket. It's as one of the crowd that I buy a hot pretzel wrapped in brown paper, and it's as one of the crowd that I take my seat in the mammoth auditorium.

But it's as Houdini's daughter that I pull out a notebook and pencil to take notes on what I see. The people around me are tense, excited, and I'm reminded again of just how famous he actually is.

I hold my breath as Houdini is introduced. I've seen him perform before, of course. I was on the pier when he jumped into the Hudson River when I was a child. I saw him hanging, eight stories up, when he escaped from a straitjacket in Chicago. But those events were attended with my mother, who took me just before the escape occurred and hurried me away soon after. This is different. This time I can study him at my leisure.

Houdini steps out onstage and I lean forward, tension coiling my stomach like a rope. He's shorter than I remember, all compact muscles and strength. But it's his voice that really surprises me. His persona is all masculine bravado. But his voice, high-pitched, almost effeminate—doesn't seem to match.

"I declare that nothing has been revealed to me in my twenty-five years of research to convince me that intercommunication exists between the spirits of the departed and those still in the flesh."

My skin crawls, remembering the Ouija board. I wonder what Houdini, the great skeptic, would make of Walter.

Houdini goes on to explain that he's not attacking spiritualism as a religion, but only those mediums taking advantage of the grief of others to defraud them of their money.

I shift uncomfortably. He means people like my mother and me.

I struggle to remain calm and to follow the thread of his lecture. "Imagine the medium's horror when halfway through the séance, I throw off my disguise and cry out,

'I am Houdini and you are a fraud!'"

My blood chills. *Oh, I can imagine.*

He expounds on how the mediums research their clients before they give each séance, and I remember how many small-town graveyards I visited before my mother and I set up shop. How often I would eavesdrop at the general store, blending into the background, listening for tidbits of information that could be used.

After Houdini finishes discussing the forethought and care that goes into each séance, his assistants join him onstage.

"Now, I will show you some of the more common tricks used by mediums to make you, the unsuspecting public, believe in their treachery."

He begins with the slate-writing trick, during which the spirit writes a message to one of the clients from "beyond the grave." Houdini shows the small ring on his finger that contains a piece of chalk. He demonstrates how the slate is held by both the medium and the client and how the medium can write on the bottom side without the client's knowledge. One diversion later (usually created by an accomplice) the slate is momentarily pulled from the client's fingers and flipped over, without the client even knowing.

My heart sinks. One of my mother's better tricks is now worthless. We'll have to come up with a whole new variety of Houdini-proof tricks.

My pencil flies as he goes through a repertoire of techniques—many of which my mother and I have utilized on countless occasions. The eating of burning coals, which in reality are merely cotton balls set in burning alcohol; the mysterious rapping, which is done with a cleverly designed mechanism in the heel of one of my shoes; and table levitation, which is merely the medium's or her accomplice's foot.

My horror grows with every sentence he utters, every trick he exposes. Our livelihood is being destroyed—by the same man my mother tells me is my father.

My legs twitch from wanting to run and hide. I put the notebook in my bag and clench the velveteen armrests. I came to meet Houdini and meet him I will.

He concludes the show with some of his most beloved escapes. This is what people are clamoring for, and I occupy my mind by running through the steps to each trick as they occur. I note the dramatic inflection of his voice and his striking gestures as he works the crowd.

At the final curtain, it's announced that Houdini's book, *A Magician Among the Spirits*, will be for sale in the atrium and that Houdini will be autographing them.

This is the opportunity I've been waiting for, and I slip from my seat so I can beat the rush.

No such luck. By the time I purchase the book, I'm stuck in a line that stretches almost out the front door. The mingled scent of body odor and perfume wrinkles my nose. Everyone wants to tell Houdini his or her story. He cocks his head and makes the right noises, but I know he's barely paying attention. No doubt his quick mind has already jumped to the next scheduled event in his incredibly busy life.

Then it's my turn.

I look into his face, holding my breath, waiting for something to happen. Perhaps a sense of confusion or unconscious recognition. But his expression is the same as it was for the person ahead of me—polite, pleasant, public.

I wonder how his expression would change if he knew what I do for a living.

The book feels lethal in my hands as I give it to him, as if the covers could swallow me whole.

"Would you like me to inscribe it?"

I avoid his eyes, as if he can read my guilt. "Yes, please."

He waits, impatience crossing his face. "The name?"

I clear my throat. "Anna."

"Just Anna?"

I nod. Words fail me.

He signs it as I watch, *Best wishes, Harry Houdini.*

Best wishes.

Resentment and anger flare up inside as a small brunette woman moves to his side and whispers in his ear. His wife. He pats her hand and hands me the book with a distracted smile.

I'm expected to move now, but I don't. My feet remain firmly planted.

He looks up at me, his brows raised. "Yes?"

I hold up the book. "You should have titled the book *What Not to Do.*"

Houdini cocks his head to one side. "And why is that?"

"Because no medium will ever use these tricks again . . . but we both know they'll just devise new ones, won't they?" I give him a cold little smile and walk away.

"Wait a moment," he calls, but I keep moving and lose myself in the crowd heading for the door.

Once outside, I pull in a couple of deep breaths of the frigid air.

My father, a man I have only known through newsreels, movies, and clippings, is now all too real to me. And he's my enemy.

TEN

Keep moving. Keep moving.
    I hurry past my streetcar stop, clutching Houdini's book in my hand.

Knowing that he'd been working with the American Scientific Society to debunk mediums and writing long diatribes in the newspapers didn't prepare me for this level of exposure.

Everything my mother and I have worked so hard for is at risk because of Harry Houdini. While I hate doing the séances and yearn for a time we can stop, they've always been an important part of our survival. Sometimes a successful séance means the difference between having a roof over our heads or not, between going to bed with a full stomach or an empty one.

Harry Houdini is out to expose mediums, but I wonder what he would say if he met a real one. Someone who had really communicated with the dead or saw the future in terrifying visions or felt the emotions of others coming off them in waves.

Someone like me.

I bump into somebody on the busy sidewalk and cut across the street to avoid the crowd. I don't need to feel anyone else's emotions right now. My own thoughts are racing, one after another, each more alarming than the one before. My mother and I are so close to putting our nomadic life behind us. I shudder, wondering how many zealous skeptics this latest attack is going to inspire. What if they go after our show? Part of me wants to toss the book in the gutter, but I can't. I need to see what tricks he's ruined for us. I slip it into my bag and keep walking down one dimly lit street after another.

"Excuse me, miss, can you spare an old man some change?"

Startled, I glance up at the wizened beggar in front of me. The filthy rags he wears attests to his circumstances, and I automatically reach for my purse. I press a bill into his hand and ignore his muttered thank-you as I glance around, frowning.

Nothing looks familiar.

Did I walk east or west? I'm no longer in the theater district, that's for sure. Gone are the beckoning restaurants and busy shops. The buildings here are rough, ramshackle. Families taking leisurely Sunday strolls have been replaced by coarse men slipping into unmarked buildings. A few of them give me sidelong, curious looks and I realize how out of place I look in my blue woolen surplice coat and black

Mary Janes. The few women on the street are wearing shabby, shapeless dresses that reach their ankles and heavy shawls that are their only protection against the weather.

I hurry for the nearest corner to see if the street name will give me some clue as to which direction I should go. The salty, tar-drenched stink of the river is stronger here and the streets are narrower. I must be near the docks. Chewing on my lip, I clutch my purse closer and try to look more confident than I feel.

As I pass a dilapidated building with blacked-out windows, the front door opens. Music and light fill the street, and a burly man, holding another man by his suit jacket, steps outside.

"And don't come back unless you have the money, ya piker!" he says, tossing the man into the gutter.

I freeze, my heart beating in my ears.

The man stares at me. "You coming inside?"

I shake my head. Shrugging, he steps back and slams the door.

The man in the gutter moans and I'm half tempted to help him, but fear paralyzes me. For the first time it dawns on me that I'm in very real danger. Giving him wide berth, I quicken my step. The few street lights flicker on and I see a corner ahead. I hurry toward it, trying not to run. I'm at West End Avenue and Fiftieth Street. We live on West Seventy-Fourth. I rack my brain trying to remember how New York is laid out.

I start walking again, hoping I'm going in the right

direction. There are fewer people on the street now and the wind picks up, scattering trash across the cracked sidewalk. I hear something behind me. Heart in my throat, I slow, and the sound stops. I begin walking and the noise resumes. Footfalls. My breath quickens as I struggle not to run. Kam Lee, an acrobat from San Francisco, once told me that criminals are attracted by fear and repelled by confidence. He refused to teach me kung fu, as it wasn't proper for girls, but he did teach me how to walk aggressively.

I stretch myself taller and square my shoulders. Lengthening my strides, I change my gait from uncertain to arrogant.

Casually, I glance behind me. Is it my imagination or did something just disappear into the shadows? Am I being followed?

I speed up and the footfalls behind me resume. Swallowing, I feel for the fan knife I've kept in my purse ever since my mother and I were mugged in Kansas City several years ago.

I try to remain calm, but my senses switch to high alert. At first, I only get a general sense of menace, then malevolence, deep and smoky, oozes out in pulsing waves and surrounds me. My breath hitches and I jerk the knife out of my purse. Gripping it tight, I forget all of Kam Lee's teaching and break into a dead run.

The footsteps behind me keep pace, never coming closer but never falling behind, either. Tears leak from my eyes and soon I can't hear anything over my own labored breathing. My heart pounds and dizziness overwhelms me. If I don't do something soon, I'll collapse with exhaustion and be overtaken.

Instinctively, I skid to a stop and whirl around, knife in hand. Kam Lee told me it's better to face off with an opponent than to run. If my pursuer thinks I'm an easy mark, he's got another thing coming. *Come and get me*, I think, snapping the blade open.

"Anna! Anna!"

Suddenly, someone catches me up in their arms from behind and I scream. With a lightning flick of my wrist, I slash downward toward the arm that's holding me. I hear a muffled curse just before I'm shoved away. My knife clatters to the ground.

"Anna! It's all right; it's me!"

Shocked, I stare up into Cole Archer's alarmed brown eyes.

Acting on instinct, I grab for the knife, but Cole is faster and kicks it away before I can reach it. I crouch on the ground, staring up at him, wild-eyed and panting.

"Anna, it's okay." His voice is soothing, and I relax in spite of being disoriented.

Why is he here? Could he be the one . . . but as soon as the thought pops into my mind, I discard it. Cole isn't breathing hard and his clothes aren't mussed. He holds out a hand. With one eye on me, he bends and picks up the knife. "Would you like to tell me what happened?"

With a shuddering breath, I open my mouth to speak and instead burst into tears.

Cole reaches for me and I allow myself to be gathered

up, shaking, into his arms. His warmth and strength engulf me and I take another deep breath. I can feel concern emanating from him in waves. It's the only time I have ever gotten a good read on him.

"Someone was following me."

He looks behind me, his eyes scanning the street. "No one's there."

I look, too, through eyes blurred with tears, but the street is nearly empty. "Someone was there," I say positively.

But strangely enough, I suddenly feel it again, more distant this time but with the same menace, lurking out there in the dark. I still, concentrating, and the pulsing feeling fades, bit by bit, as if the threat was moving away from me.

"It's leaving," I murmur softly. I feel him nod, accepting my words, even though I hardly know what I mean. My abilities, as familiar to me as my own skin, seem to be changing, growing, and becoming something I hardly recognize.

I remember my earlier revelation and wonder if these changes are indeed due to Cole's presence in my life. Uneasy, I turn back, only to realize that his eyes are inches from mine, so close I can see little flecks of mahogany and gold amid the brown. Embarrassment heats my cheeks and I step awkwardly out of his arms. Cole clears his throat and hands me a handkerchief. I turn away and wipe my face, as mortified by my reaction to his proximity as I am by my tears. I hand the sodden handkerchief back without meeting his eyes. "Thank you."

"Are you okay? Did he . . . ?"

I shake my head. "I never even saw who it was."

"Good."

I stare in horror at the rip in his sleeve. "Did I get you?"

"No. You came close, though." He looks at the open knife in his hand and raises an eyebrow. "What type of weapon is this?"

I look down, embarrassed. "It's a balisong—a fan knife." Not something a real lady would carry in her purse.

He frowns at it in his palm. The knife has swung open into three hinged pieces: the delicately etched bone covers and the blade itself. "And you have it, why?" His voice is slightly amused but also puzzled, no doubt wondering why a respectable young woman would need such a wicked weapon.

Perhaps because I could never be classified as respectable?

"For protection." Sensing his curiosity, I take the knife and expertly swing it around in my hands, the ominous clicking of the blade as it hits the handles making Cole's eyes widen. I give it another twirl before latching it and sticking it back in my purse.

"Where did you get it?"

"Swineguard the Magnificent." Disbelief creeps over his strong features and I'm suddenly annoyed. "A sword swallower. He gave it to me and taught me how to use it."

"A sword swallower?" His voice rises, incredulous.

Shame and disappointment sink my stomach and I turn my face away. I remember Swineguard giving me his dessert at the food tent every night, how he worried when I roamed around strange towns by myself, and how he tried not to laugh at my knife-throwing attempts.

I loved Swineguard. Why should I be ashamed of that? Because he wasn't respectable? Because he worked in a circus and had tattoos covering both arms?

"Shouldn't we be getting home?" I ask, purposely sidestepping the topic. Someone as proper and formal as Cole wouldn't understand my circus family.

"Of course." Cole offers his arm, and once again I find his emotions curiously blocked. Not a jumble like so many others I've felt, but simply not there.

"What on earth are you doing out here anyway? This isn't a safe neighborhood, especially at night."

Anger prickles across my skin at his words. "I took a walk and got lost," I tell him.

He frowns. "You shouldn't be walking around by yourself at night. What was your mother thinking?"

I stop walking and yank my arm out of his. "I was perfectly safe! Until I got lost," I amended. "Besides, what are *you* doing here if it's such a bad neighborhood?"

"I had an appointment," he says shortly.

What kind of appointment could he possibly have in this neighborhood on a Sunday night? But I say nothing.

I put my arm back in his and we resume walking.

Cole clears his throat uncomfortably, and it occurs to me that perhaps I confuse him as much as he does me. "Do you have family in the city?" he asks as if we're picking up the brief conversation we had in the movie theater.

I shake my head. "I don't have family, period. It's just my mother and I." I wait for the inevitable question and it comes almost immediately.

"What about your father?"

I shrug. "I never knew my father." Let him think what he wants. I'm certainly not telling him I'm Harry Houdini's bastard daughter.

"When did you start performing?"

Is he really interested or is he just being polite? I sneak a sideways glance at him. The moonlight softens the planes of his face, making him look younger, less guarded. Suddenly, I want him to understand that being the friend of a sword swallower doesn't mean I'm a circus sideshow, and that some of those so-called freaks were the nicest people I have ever met.

"I guess I was eight or nine when I first started performing. Before that, I just helped my mother with her séances. In a traveling circus everybody helps out with everything."

"And how did you help out?" His voice is bemused, and I lift my chin.

"I was the knife girl," I answer with dignity.

"The knife girl?"

I bristle, annoyed by his amused skepticism. "Yes! The original one ran off with a cowboy in Kansas City, and Swineguard needed someone to throw knives at for the second part of his act."

"And what was the first part of the act?"

"He swallowed swords for the first part. He was

talented and wonderful and I adored him." I throw this last part out defiantly.

"Except when he was throwing knives at you."

I laugh in spite of my annoyance. "Even then," I insist. For a moment, I'm tempted to tell him about the time I was shot out of a cannon but decide against it. He probably already thinks the worst of me. I'm used to being judged for my unorthodox life and I try not to let it bother me much, but somehow, the thought of Cole judging me rankles.

We walk for a few moments in silence before he finally says, "Anna, you have lived a most exciting life."

My eyes widen. That's definitely not the reaction I expected. Maybe it was exciting. But I'd give up all the excitement for one day of not worrying about bad managers, law-enforcement officials, and where our next meal was coming from.

"What about you?" Perhaps I could get some answers straight from the horse's mouth.

"My family lives in Europe."

"What did they think about you moving here?"

"They know I won't be here permanently."

As interested as he was in my life, Cole gives answers about his own grudgingly, offering no extraneous information.

"You know, Europe is a pretty big place. Think you could be more specific?" My nerves are jangling like coins in a tin cup. He now knows more about me than almost anyone besides my mother. He owes me at least the basics about himself. It's only fair.

To my surprise, he laughs out loud. "I guess that's fair."

What is he, a mind reader? "I certainly think so."

"Very well then. My parents are British, but my father worked for the government, so we traveled a lot. Italy, France, Greece. When I was old enough to go to school, I was placed in a boarding school."

My mind conjures visions of *Jane Eyre*. "Was it horrible?"

"Not really. At least not until the war. You see, the school was in a little town in western Germany. I heard very little from my parents for four years."

"That's terrible!"

He shrugs. "It wasn't too bad. It was a small boarding school, in a tiny, unimportant town. The war missed us, really. The teachers' greatest fear was that we older boys would be forced to fight for Germany. I was twelve by the time the war ended and big for my age. The staff would hide us whenever there were rumors of soldiers nearby. The worst part was not knowing how my parents were."

Something compels me to ask, "And how were they?"

"My mother was fine. My father didn't survive the war."

"I'm so sorry." I glance at him sideways. While his voice is casual, tension firms the already Spartan planes of his face, making him look more reserved than ever. The laughing young man of a few minutes ago is completely gone.

"Were you close?"

He gives a half smile. "As close as you can be when you

are sent off to boarding school at a young age. He was a good father. He had integrity and truly believed in his work. I hope to be half the man he was."

I want to tell him that he seems to be on the right track, but I don't. Although it feels so intimate walking and talking in the dark, I barely know him. I decide a change of subject is in order. "How do you know Jacques? It wasn't a coincidence that you were chosen for our show, was it?"

I can see the flush of his cheeks by the light of the streetlamp.

"Er, no. Mr. Darby introduced me to Jacques. After running you down in the hallway, I wanted to meet you properly and asked him to introduce us. I'd expected a formal meeting, not a part in your show. Then I was invited to the séance."

If not for his obvious discomfort, I might have laughed out loud.

I want to ask about the two pins he deceived me with but don't want to risk him asking how I usually do the trick, so I switch subjects again. "So what are you doing in America?"

For a time, it seems as if he might not answer, but then he says quietly, as if speaking to himself, "I think I was supposed to find you."

We reach the bottom of our stoop and I stop. "What do you mean by that?"

Cole's licorice eyes are mysterious. Why could I read him so easily before and not at all now?

"I wanted to tell you . . ." He clears his throat as if embarrassed. I wait. "You are bewitching onstage."

My breath catches and he looks down at the ground.

"I mean, you're really good."

Warmth spreads across my chest. "Thank you."

His head rises and he draws closer.

"Your mother is a fraud, but you aren't, are you, Anna?"

ELEVEN

I pull my arm out of his, alarm racing through my body. What am I supposed to say to that? The answer condemns both me and my mother. A thought strikes me. "That's why you didn't second-guess me earlier, isn't it? When I said I could still feel someone there?"

I take his silence for affirmation and my heart skips a beat. How much does he know? And more important, how does he know it?

My breath catches in my throat and a long moment plays between us. There are so many things I want to ask, but I'm afraid anything I say will reveal more about me than I'll learn in return.

Just as I turn to open the door, Jacques's car stops in front of us. My mother steps out. She's dressed up, which means she stopped by the house while I was out.

"Where have you been? We've been trying to reach you all evening."

"I went for a walk and got lost." No need to mention Houdini, though his book, tucked away in my purse, weighs on me like one of Houdini's own mammoth chains.

My mother's perfectly painted lips purse. "Really, darling, how careless of you." An eyebrow arches as she realizes I'm not alone. "Mr. Archer?"

His name is a question and Cole hurries to explain. "I ran across Anna when she was lost and escorted her home."

I throw him a grateful glance, glad that he didn't mention that I'd been running, terrified, through the slums when he found me.

"How fortuitous for Anna," my mother murmurs.

Cole gives a courtly little nod. "I was glad to be of service."

The formality, which had dropped away during our walk, is back, and I wonder if my mother makes him uncomfortable.

I try to see my mother as a stranger would. Her quilted lamé evening wrap is banded with black satin and encrusted with crystal beads. Her arms drip with costume jewelry, and she's wearing more than her usual amount of makeup. She looks rich and intimidating.

Or maybe Cole's uncomfortable because he knows she's a fraud and a cheat.

The back door to the car opens and Owen gets out. I feel Cole stiffen beside me. Owen looks like a dashing man about town in his fashionably cuffed trousers and tightly fitted jacket. His sophistication is only slightly marred by the wide smile that lights up his face when he sees me. In contrast,

Cole, glowering in his plain dark suit, looks like a grumpy undertaker. I have to hide a smile.

"Your carriage awaits, milady!" Owen sweeps an arm toward Jacques's dark red Packard Phaeton. "Willest thou goest?"

I cross my arms and, aware of Cole's disapproval next to me, try not to smile at Owen's antics. "Depends on where we're going."

"To the moon, sweets, to the moon!" Owen gives me a wink and I laugh out loud.

"Oh, stop your silliness," Mother says. "We're going to The Colony for a late supper."

She shoos me upstairs to change, but I pause to glance at Cole, who's still frowning at Owen. "Good-bye, Cole, and thanks . . . for walking me home."

He nods curtly.

I open the door and the last thing I hear is Owen introducing himself. "Hello there, old boy. I'm Owen."

I snort as I follow my mother upstairs, wondering what Cole thinks of being called an "old boy."

"Look what I bought for you today!" my mother says once we reach my bedroom.

I'm about to chastise her for spending money when I see the peach georgette evening dress trimmed with silver seed beads and glittering rhinestones. It's unbelievably stunning. Without a word, I let her help me change and then stare into the mirror, unable to believe the transformation. The filmy material clings subtly to my body before falling in graceful folds to just below my knees. The rich, glowing color complements my dark hair and warms my skin. For the very first time I feel almost as beautiful as my mother. I turn to her with shining eyes. "It's lovely. Thank you so much."

She turns to the vanity table. "Just don't spill anything on it at the restaurant. Now we need to hurry. We've kept the boys waiting long enough."

She helps me with my cosmetics—deepening my eyes with kohl and spit block and painting a bow shape onto my lips with rouge. Once she deems me ready, we rush down to the car in record time.

I climb in beside Owen, delighted by the admiration in his eyes. He's so handsome with his silky blond hair and dimples that it's hard to believe I'm going out on the town with him. The feeling is only partially spoiled by the fact that my mother and manager are sitting in the front seat. In spite of Owen's silliness, it's clear that he's far more sophisticated than I am. The male counterpart to the glamorous flappers I've seen attending some of our shows. I look down at my beautiful dress and the costume jewelry Mother slipped on my wrist and thrill at the thought that I could be mistaken for a flapper myself.

"You look stunning," Owen tells me, shifting a bit closer.

"Thank you." I smile and look down at my hands. Then, not knowing what else to say, I pretend to be interested in Mother and Jacques's lively discussion about people I don't know. My mother is quickly becoming a New Yorker, which gives me hope that we'll stay on here, in spite of Harry Houdini's witch hunts.

"A penny for your thoughts," Owen says, leaning closer.

My heart speeds up at his nearness. He smells like pomade, gin, and something sweet that I can't quite identify. "Only a penny?"

"Depends on the thoughts, doesn't it?" he whispers softly, and I catch my breath. Then the car makes a sharp turn and he's suddenly in my lap, his hat tumbling to the floor.

I yelp and throw my hands in the air. He pops back up, his face mortified.

"I really must stop making such a fool of myself in front of you," he says, clapping his hat back on his head. "It's not at all good for my ego."

I laugh, envious of Owen's unassailable confidence. He moves through the world with such ease. I wish I could be more like that.

"I bet you have many interesting thoughts," he says, going right back to our conversation.

"I'm actually thinking about how nice it would be to stay in New York permanently."

"Are you sure you don't want to see Europe? You're a talented magician; you could do a world tour. I love New York, but I'd kill to be able to travel from city to city, performing."

"Really? I thought you worked at a bank."

"I do. But I dabble in magic a bit too." He glances down at his hands, trying and failing to look modest.

My eyebrows shoot up. "I didn't know that." I knew he enjoyed magic, but I didn't know he practiced it.

"I started when I was in school. I'm not nearly as talented as you or your father, though."

Thankfully, we reach our destination before I have to reply.

The Colony is the place sophisticated New Yorkers go to see and be seen, Owen informs me, and I can see why. The wildly striped walls catch my attention immediately, but it's the glittering chandeliers and well-dressed patrons that hold it. The head waiter seems to know Jacques, and we're led to a table near the center of the room. A tall man with curly hair and a black silk suit walks up to our table soon after we're seated and introduces himself as Cornelius Vanderbilt. His eyes rove over my mother in spite of the presence of a pretty, if mousy, blonde hovering nearby.

"My wife and I attended your opening night," he says. "You and your daughter have a wonderful act."

Mother inclines her head and gives a brilliant smile that leaves both Jacques and Mr. Vanderbilt blinking. "Thank you so much, Mr. Vanderbilt."

"Please, call me Cornelius. And this is my wife, Rachel."

His wife gives a tight smile. "Nice to meet you. Really, darling, we must get back to the Goulds."

Little sparks of jealousy come off her like darts when she gives my hand a reluctant shake. I'm relieved when Cornelius casts my mother one last, lingering look before leaving with his possessive wife.

Owen leans toward me. "The Vanderbilts are filthy rich. I heard they had a five-hundred-pound cake for their wedding reception."

I try to envision what that might look like but can't.

"I want to see the oven that could bake a five-hundred-pound cake," I whisper back.

Owen laughs and I relax. Jacques orders us four Colony Specials.

"What are those?" I ask, and Owen leans in close.

"Gin drinks. They're pretty good if the hooch isn't too bad."

I look around and notice that almost everyone is holding a cocktail. "How do they get away with it at such a high-profile restaurant?"

"Marco Hattem is the bartender here. He keeps all the booze in a freight elevator in the back. If the feds pay a call, he sends it all up to the top floor of the building."

I laugh, picturing a wily bartender pushing the up button whenever trouble threatened.

"Plus, how many feds do you think have the guts to make a raid on a restaurant that regularly serves Vanderbilts, Goulds, and Carnegies?" Owen waggles his eyebrows at me and I grin.

The waiter delivers our drinks and we all take a careful sip. It's strong with a hint of anise and orange. "It's good," I say with some surprise.

"Let's drink to a superior shipment!" Owen raises his glass and Mother, Jacques, and I join him in a toast.

"I've never been able to resist a celebration!" Cynthia Gaylord trills from behind us. "What are we celebrating?"

"Success," Jacques puts in quickly, raising a glass to my mother. She tilts her head slightly and smiles in response, pleased with his answer.

The Gaylords grab chairs and squeeze in at the table while the waiter brings another round. Cynthia is at her glittering, giggling best as she, Jacques, and my mother gossip. You would never know of my mother's contempt for her. Her husband looks on indulgently.

Couples, glamorous in their evening finery, stop by the table to meet my mother. Word of mouth is making her a new sensation in the city. It feels strange after being run out of so many towns by the law and angry citizens. She accepts the homage as if it were her due, inclining her head and bestowing dazzling smiles. The rest of us just bask in her glow as we stuff ourselves on oysters, caviar, and blue cheese, along with rounds of The Colony's famous toast.

All the while, Owen continues whispering gossip in my ear, some true and some so outrageous that I know he must be making it up to entertain me. It works.

"There's Lois Long," he says, indicating a gorgeous and daringly dressed brunette. "She writes scandalous columns for *The New Yorker* under the pseudonym Lipstick. It's said she spends her nights drinking and dancing with New York's finest before weaving her way to the offices at four in the morning. She writes an entire gossip column about the people she just spent the night with and then passes out at her desk."

I stare wide-eyed, imagining a life like that. She's surrounded by a sparkling clique, hanging on to her every word. Then I notice a well-dressed gentleman standing on the edge of the crowd, part of the group but separate.

"Who's that man, the one who doesn't look like he's having a good time?"

"That's Vincent Astor. He inherited millions when his father went down on the *Titanic*."

Titanic. The word echoes in my mind, evoking the memory of my first vision—even though I was so little at the time, I didn't know that's what it was. I'd been walking through a late-spring snow with my mother, looking for a cheap boardinghouse. Fortune had frowned on us in Denver and my worn shoes were soaked through. When the first pain erupted behind my eyes, I stopped, clutching my hands to my head. My mother, oblivious, walked on for a moment before noticing. Though she asked me repeatedly what was wrong, I couldn't answer, petrified by the images playing out in my mind. A broken ship. People running, screaming, drowning in the dark, icy water. Just before blacking out, I remember the overpowering scent of burned sugar. Though that moment was terrifying, it was nothing compared to the horror I felt when I first saw the newspaper headlines bringing my vision to life.

"Are you all right, sweetheart?"

I jump as Cynthia, on my right, lays her hand on my arm. Through her fingers I feel snippets of concern laced with a giddy, uncomplicated happiness. Though the emotion warms me, my heart gives a wistful little tug. I don't know if I've ever felt that carefree.

"I'm sorry. I guess I was daydreaming."

"Oh good. For a second there you looked like you'd seen a

ghost." She winks at her little joke and I give her a wan smile.

But the word *ghost* reminds me that I wanted to ask her about that ghost society. "Why don't you tell me more about the Society for Psychical Research?"

"Oh, honey, it's the most amazing thing. At least, that's what I've heard. I've never actually attended a meeting, but we have an English guest lecturing at our church who used to belong. It just sounds fascinating. Very scientific."

I snort. "What kind of church do you go to that has guest speakers on ghosts?"

She laughs. "A very modern one with very old roots. It's a Swedenborgian church called The New Church. You and your mother must come with us sometime. As mediums, you would be very welcome."

My mother's mouth tightens and I know it's because Cynthia called me a medium. "I think it's time that we were going," she says, rising from the table.

Everyone gets up to leave and I grab Cynthia's arm while Jacques helps my mother into her coat. I'm not about to let this opportunity slip through my fingers. If other people like me exist, I'm determined to find them. "I would love to visit your church sometime."

She claps her hands. "Wonderful. It's on East Thirty-Fifth Street between Lexington and Park Avenue. We meet at eleven on Sundays, though the lectures are usually in the evenings. I'll let you know."

"I'll be there," I promise.

I don't know if it was the Colony Specials or the events

of the day, but I'm numb with exhaustion by the time we gather our things. I lean heavily on Owen's arm on our way out to the car, once again relieved I don't have to worry about how he's feeling.

"You look like you were born to this way of life, doll," he whispers.

I give him a sleepy smile and settle back against the seat.

My head bobs twice before he moves close. "Go ahead and put your head against my shoulder. I promise I won't bite."

The offer is too good to refuse and I lay my head on his shoulder with a weary sigh.

We don't get home until almost one. My mother, still drunk with her success, gaily asks the men if they want to come up for a nightcap. Thankfully, both decline. Jacques cites Mother's need for sleep as his reason and she smiles and waves a hand.

I follow her upstairs, my feet dragging. Mr. Darby sticks his head out of his doorway and scowls as we pass by. "All this gallivanting around at night is going to make you sick, missy; mark my words!" He slams the door.

My mother yawns. "What a strange man."

I give a sleepy smile. What he really meant was "Be careful, missy; I don't want to see you sick." It's nice knowing someone cares about my welfare. But I don't try explaining that to my mother.

TWELVE

I rub my tired, gritty eyes, cursing my inability to sleep in. Even though I'd been exhausted after getting home the night before, I read Houdini's book until my eyes crossed. At least it kept me from wondering who'd been following me and why. Three times in the past week, I've felt someone watching me, and I'm pretty sure it's not because I'm irresistible. But that isn't the only reason I can't sleep.

I'm afraid of having another vision.

Why am I suddenly having visions about my own life? They've always been about other people or events—never about me or my mother. Perhaps they really are just dreams? I shift uneasily. But if they aren't, shouldn't I try to do something? Find out more? But how? My mind blanks. Perhaps the answer lies with that research society. But as much as I would like to find other people who have abilities like mine, my whole being rebels at the thought of telling anyone about my secret. How do you reveal something that you've guarded your entire life? Especially when you know, instinctively, that your entire survival depends on keeping it hidden?

But what is the worst thing that could happen if it became common knowledge that I have these abilities? The question touches something raw and primal inside, setting my pulse to racing, but I force myself to think it through.

I would never be able to live a respectable, normal life. People would want things from me; they would hound me, and all my privacy would be gone. Even my magic would be affected—people wouldn't come to see Anna the magician; they would come to see Anna the freak. No matter that they think my mother has all these special powers, I don't want to be the girl who can talk to the dead or have visions of the future. I don't want to be a medium. And my mother—my breath hitches—my mother would never allow me to be the center of attention.

I realize I'm trembling and take several deep breaths. But does any of that matter? If my mother is in some kind of danger, I have to risk it. I resolve to go to that lecture with Cynthia and find out more.

Putting it out of my mind, I move on to the next problem: Houdini and his vendetta against mediums.

Could our livelihood really be at risk? We've always had to watch for skeptics, but Houdini is making medium hunting fashionable. Being exposed has become more and more of a possibility. Can I trust Jacques to personally vouch for all the people he brings to our séances? I've always dreamed of giving them up and living a normal life, but can we afford to stop?

I go over our bank book again, my heart sinking. As always, Mother lives right up to the edge of disaster and then waits for me to pull money out of a hat.

I'm a good magician, but I'm not that good.

According to the book, we have enough money to keep us in food and little more than that. I frown. Mother has been shopping much more than the bank statements indicate. My new dress hasn't even been entered. Where is she getting the money? I hope she isn't getting credit from the stores. That kind of headache I do not need.

I slip the book back into the desk drawer and take a deep breath. With another glance toward the bedrooms, I recount my own carefully hidden stash of money. Still thirty-eight dollars. Enough to keep us from going hungry or being homeless for a little while, but not much more than that. I add a ten from our last séance and put the rest in an envelope to deposit at the bank. Hesitantly, I take out another ten and add it to my stash. Fifty-eight dollars, now. Still not enough.

Knowing what I do about Houdini's vendetta, I can't share Mother's financial optimism.

Which means one thing: Not only do I have to continue doing our séances, but I have to make them spectacular enough to charge even more money. Something different. Something so amazing that we have people clamoring to get in, and we can charge an exorbitant amount of money.

What that something is exactly, I'm not sure. But once we have more of a cushion we can quit. And hopefully, we can do it before Houdini or one of the other vigilante skeptics ruins our credibility. Because if we are publicly denounced as frauds, the Newmark Theater will cancel our contract and everything will be ruined.

But is it right for me to continue doing something I know is wrong for my own gain? Harry Houdini's words reverberate in my mind: *It is not difficult to convince people who have recently suffered bereavement of the possibility of communicating with their loved ones. To me, the poor suffering followers, eagerly searching for relief from the heart-pain that follows the passing on of a dear one, are a sacrifice to the scavengers who make money from them.*

He's talking about me and my mother. Scavengers.

With a sharp sigh, I hide the money and get ready to visit Mr. Darby. Again I check the locks carefully before leaving.

Still skittish from being chased last night, I decide to stick close to home and end up just darting into the corner bakery for sugar buns before heading back.

Mr. Darby opens the door before I can even knock.

"It's about time," he grouses. "I was getting hungry. It's almost eleven."

"What did you do for breakfast before I moved here? I'm fairly certain you didn't starve." I eye his paunchy stomach and grin.

"Don't be impertinent, missy. The kettle is already on."

We move into the kitchen, but surprise stops me short when I see a strange girl sweeping the floor.

She glances at me and then away. "I'm almost done in here, sir. Would you like me to take the trash to the basement?"

"No!" he barks. "You stay out of my basement, you hear? Now, be off with you. You've done enough for today and I don't want you bothering my guest."

Her eyes dart about, indicating her nervousness, and I note how soft and well cared for her hands seem for a cleaning woman. She hurries out of the room with another glance at me and I set the basket on the table.

Mr. Darby peers into the paper bag. "No croissants this morning?"

"No, I wanted to try something different." I hesitate. "Who's the girl?" I ask. Something about her felt off. Though happily, it's in a normal, run-of-the-mill, I'm-not-sure-I-like-you kind of way instead of a premonition due to my abilities.

He shrugs and pours our tea. "She came by yesterday looking for work, and Cole took pity and hired her to come in for a bit every day to clean. I think she's a spy."

"A spy?"

"Yes. A spy for a rival inventor."

I laugh. "More like a spy for Cole. He's probably going to report to your relatives what you do when he's gone all day."

He snorts. "I'm more interested in what *he* does all day!"

That makes two of us.

Mr. Darby gives the sugar bun a sniff, then takes a bite.

His face wrinkles in concentration as he chews. "These are good. Though not as good as croissants, mind you."

I'm curious about the girl, but more curious about what's in Mr. Darby's basement. "Would today be a good day to see your workshop?" I ask, keeping my voice nonchalant.

"Perhaps. Perhaps not."

The old tease, I think, eating my own roll. But I say nothing. If I show too much interest, he'll just dangle it in front of me like a carrot.

I keep my silence until we both finish our breakfast and tea.

"Well, come along. I know you're dying to get a peek."

As I follow him through the kitchen and down a long hallway I hear stirring above us and know my mother is up.

Mr. Darby opens a door and pulls a string hanging from the top of the stairs. "Watch your step," he cautions.

The scent of grease, mildew, and burned coffee becomes stronger and stronger as we descend. When we finally reach the bottom, I take a look around and gasp. I don't know what I was expecting, but certainly not this conglomeration of copper, steel, and wiring. My eyes don't know where to look first. The room runs the length and width of the house and is brightly lit with bare bulbs hanging every third or fourth beam. Workbenches line one wall and hold a glorious mess of oddly shaped instruments, boxes, and spheres. In one corner stands a giant, cylindrical welder and a lathe. In the next is a huge machine I can't identify. Mr. Darby is either a bona-fide genius or a madman.

"This is swell! What is all this stuff?" I breathe.

He claps his hands in glee. "This, missy, is my life's work. Isn't it magnificent?"

His arms spread out, taking in the whole room, and I nod in admiration as I carefully step over a giant coil of barbed wire. "It's wonderful."

"I knew you'd appreciate it. I know a kindred spirit when I see one."

"What does everything do?"

He crosses his arms. "First off, you have to show me one of your tricks."

I look around the room. "Okay. Um, can you tie me up?" I give him a mischievous smile.

His eyebrows rise. "Pardon me? What kind of trick is that?"

"Tie me up to a chair and I bet I can get out of it."

"Are you sure?"

I nod. "I can get out of almost anything."

I see disbelief on his face as he pulls a long, dirty rope from a toolbox. That doesn't stop him from making a good job of it, though, as he binds me tightly to a chair. "I'm not hurting you, am I?"

I scoff. "I've been bound with chains before."

His face scrunches. "You've led a very odd life, missy."

I laugh. Escape tricks were a practical addition to my repertoire, considering how often I had to break my mother out of jail. They add an air of credibility to our séances when clients want to make sure I'm not the spirit manifestation. Of course, they don't know that I can escape, manifest, and bind myself back up before they even bat an eye. I think my mother encouraged my efforts so I would be more like my father. I just like the challenge.

"Now turn around."

"Why?" he asks belligerently.

"Because a good magician never gives up her tricks," I tell him. "I told you I would show you a trick, not give you my secrets."

The look on his face makes it clear that he thinks he's been had, but he does what I ask. The truth is, it doesn't really matter if he does watch, but I like to keep an air of mystery around my act. "Now count to ten. Slowly."

He sighs but does what I say, not knowing I'm already through half the textbook sailor knots he tied. Very few people understand that using lots of rope doesn't necessarily mean a tight bind.

"Turn around," I say before he gets to eight.

He turns, and I giggle at the bug-eyed astonishment on his face. "Well, now! That *is* quite a trick. Can I try it again?" he asks.

I shake my head. "No, a deal is a deal. You promised to show me one of your inventions."

He nods, looking none too happy. "You're right there." He eyes the room, considering, then he motions me to follow him. To my disappointment, he doesn't head toward the huge machine in the corner but rather to a much smaller brass one.

"This one is my pride and joy," he says, stroking it.

"I haven't gotten all the kinks worked out, but when I do I'll make a fortune, just you wait and see."

I eye the machine skeptically. "But what is it?"

"I call it my ODD—it's an Object Displacement Device."

"Well, it is definitely odd," I say. "But what does it do?"

He waves a hand impatiently. "It moves objects."

"What kind of objects?"

He picks up a small gray button. "I'll show you. Step back."

He looks around and then grabs a broom. He tapes the button to it and sets it in the corner. He then unwraps a long cord. "I used to use clockwork machinery for everything," he says, nodding toward the machine. "But that was before I fully understood the potential of electricity."

He plugs in the machine, and it makes an almost inaudible whirring noise.

At first nothing happens, but then my jaw drops as the broom begins wiggling back and forth in a circle all by itself. I move closer to look for transparent strings, but I see nothing. The broom dances more wildly and I jump back just as the handle dips toward my face, missing me by inches. Mr. Darby quickly turns off the machine.

"That's the downside," he admits. "It's still in the experimental stage. But once I figure out a way to control it, the sky's the limit. Housewives everywhere can lounge about while the machine does their work for them."

I pick up the broom and study the button with admiration. "How does it work?"

"Magnetics. I found a way to harness the electricity to

make the magnets more powerful." He points up to the ceiling and I see another gray button affixed to a beam.

"That's incredible!"

He nods, beaming.

I suddenly gasp, my mind whirling with possibilities. There is nothing in Houdini's blasted book about anything like this. It is almost certainly undetectable. "Would this work anywhere?"

He shrugs. "I don't see why not. Why?"

I smile at him. "Because I have an idea. How would you like to be part of a séance, Mr. Darby?"

THIRTEEN

I reach back and rub the tightrope-taut muscles in my neck. Next to me, in the backseat of her luxurious, deep-red Isotta Fraschini automobile, Cynthia Gaylord prattles away while I try to pinpoint why I'm so edgy.

When Cynthia rang me up this afternoon, I'd jumped at the chance to attend a lecture at her church. A church that mixes science with spiritualism? Connections to a society that actually studies the supernatural? Maybe some answers to my questions regarding my abilities, my visions about my mother, and—I shudder slightly—Walter's unexpected visit. I might even discover why my abilities are changing and how I can use them to find out who's following me. There's no way I could decline.

So why so nervous? Could it be I'm not as eager to find out about my abilities as I think I am? More likely, I'm terrified of being exposed.

I frown, staring at the driver in the front seat. He's different from most of the drivers I've seen carting the rich about. His neck is thick and meaty and his nose is broken, and, if I'm not mistaken, he's missing part of the little finger on his left hand.

I twist a stray curl around my finger and turn to Cynthia to distract myself. "So tell me more about this guest lecturer."

She stops in midsentence, and I realize I'd interrupted her. I can almost see the switching of gears in her pretty blue eyes. "Oh. Well, he's British and very smart. I just love the Brits, don't you?" An image of Cole pops into my head and I quickly push it out of my mind. I nod as she continues. "He's a doctor of some sort. I forget what kind. Jack always tells me I'm as forgetful as a child. Anyhoo, he's worked with all the premier psychical scientists in the world and will be discussing some of the studies of the Society for Psychical Research on how the dead are around us all the time, just waiting to guide us on our journey. They do experiments with electricity and things." She waves her hand vaguely and I know I've come to the end of her knowledge on the subject.

"It sounds very interesting," I assure her.

"You're going to simply love it. I can't believe your mother didn't want to come. She's such a good medium, though I'm pretty sure you have the gift too. What you did at that séance—"

"No," I put in quickly. "It was my mother's presence the spirit was attracted to."

Cynthia wrinkles her nose, and for the first time I'm

aware of just how young she is. Probably in her early twenties. What must it be like to be so young and so very rich? I don't care if Mother thinks she's rough around the edges; I bet she's never had to worry about scraping together enough money to keep off the street at night. Tonight, she's wearing a tailored winter ermine fur coat with a huge white fox collar that probably could have paid for a year's worth of lodging.

"Well, maybe you're just now getting the gift? Maybe it runs in families."

I don't mention that I've wondered the very same thing.

I'm saved from having to answer her, though, as the car pulls up to a lovely Renaissance-style building constructed of light gray stone. The wide bay windows give the façade a welcoming look, conflicting with the tall, forbidding iron fence guarding the front. Somehow, I don't feel welcomed.

Cynthia whisks me through the gate and up the steps, her trim silhouette a modern contrast to the classic structure. I hesitate at the door, my nerves bouncing.

"Come on, silly." Cynthia reaches out and catches my hand. "We want to get good seats."

She pulls me down the aisle, nodding here and there like a young queen to those already in the pews. Now I think I know the secret to being a socialite—make every occasion a festival.

The walls are done in a soft, creamy plaster that gives the room a warm glow, and the graceful Italian styling continues with decorative arches and ornamental urns. In fact, the whole atmosphere of the sanctuary is so tranquil and serene that it's hard to believe that people regularly try to conjure the dead here.

The room continues to fill, and I'm surprised at just how many people are interested in supernatural science. There are a few men scattered here and there, but the majority are well groomed, fashionably dressed women.

Cynthia nudges me and discreetly points to a corner of the room. "That's the Reverend Herbert Cullen. And the man he's with is the guest speaker."

The reverend is short and round and almost completely eclipsed by the tall man in front of him. I can't see the visitor's face, as his back is turned, but the reverend's expression is deferential.

The reverend nods pleasantly to the man and steps behind the pulpit. He clears his throat and the congregation falls silent.

"Many of you heard the stunning lecture our guest gave last week on spiritualism, science, and Christianity," the pastor says in a nasal voice. "We are blessed enough to have him return for another illuminating talk entitled 'The Science Behind Psychical Research.' It is my pleasure to introduce you to Dr. Finneas Bennett."

I clap politely with the rest of the congregation and then freeze as I see who the guest speaker is.

The man from the bookstore.

I watch, curiously, as Dr. Bennett takes his place behind the pulpit. At the bookstore, he'd said that spiritualism was a hobby of his. I'd say this is more than a hobby.

"Thank you, Dr. Cullen," Dr. Bennett says, taking over the pulpit and the room with ease.

Next to me, Cynthia Gaylord leans forward, her eyes alight. Maybe her interest in the speaker has as much to do with the man as the subject. Dr. Bennett, with his ruddy complexion and thick, wavy hair, looks more like an English country squire than a psychical investigator, and his accent is much more pronounced than Cole's. Of course, Cole traveled quite a bit with his parents when he was younger. Maybe he has a more European way of speaking.

"Ladies, gentlemen, and fellow spiritualists, thank you again for inviting me to this illustrious church to share with you what little wisdom I have gleaned from my years of studying telepathy, apparitions, extrasensory perception, and the physical aspects of spiritualism."

His theatrical mannerisms are so different from the man I briefly met at the bookshop that I'm instantly on alert. I recognize in Dr. Finneas Bennett a snake-oil salesman of the highest caliber.

Of course, it takes one to know one.

His voice is almost as spellbinding as my mother's as he explains the differences between angels and demons and spirit guides. So far, he isn't telling me anything I haven't come across in my own haphazard research, but then he mentions some preliminary investigations on extrasensory perception and precognition—the ability to tell what others are thinking or know something is going to occur before it actually does.

I listen intently.

"We vet our subjects first with simple card tests. If they pass those, we then go on to more challenging analysis. The research is not yet conclusive but looks very promising. I hope to publish my findings on the subjects in the next year or so."

I slump back down in my seat. Well, that was less than helpful. Aside from suggesting that there are others out there who may have gifts like mine, I got nothing new. Maybe if I speak to him personally I can learn more, though something inside me hesitates at becoming more involved with Dr. Bennett.

Beside me, Cynthia sways slightly from side to side, like a slender reed in the breeze. I frown and glance around at the others in the congregation, all of whom seem utterly transfixed by Dr. Bennett.

"So, my good people, you all understand the importance of my work. I'm very excited to announce that I am looking into buying a piece of property in New York with the intent of building an American branch of the Society for Psychical Research and Laboratory."

He holds up his hand as if to forestall clapping. "But, my dear fellow believers, such a project takes money, and I . . ." His voice drops. ". . . am but a poor man of science."

The congregation sits motionless, scarcely breathing. Narrowing my eyes, I scrutinize the faces of those nearest to me. Most are relaxed, pleasant, bemused. Some, like Cynthia, are swaying slightly.

Dr. Bennett continues. "Your good pastor has generously offered to pass around the proverbial hat to give the new laboratory a good start."

My mouth falls open as the plate is passed around. I have no doubt it'll be brimming with cash by the time it returns to the front. I've seen trances performed on large groups by stage hypnotists, but in those instances, the members of the audience have been willing participants. Somehow I don't think that's the case here.

Dr. Bennett's eyes scan the crowd, a smile playing about his lips. They sweep past me and then back, the smile slipping. I cross my arms and raise my brows at him. He gives me a slight nod, and the corners of his lips curl slightly. If he's at all nervous at being caught out, he doesn't show it. Maybe I'm wrong. Then I see Cynthia slip a one-hundred-dollar bill out of her purse and onto the plate.

Or maybe not.

After the plate is passed, we gather for coffee and dessert. The crowd shakes the remaining cobwebs from their minds and hurries off to claim their oatmeal-drop cookies and ginger creams. Cynthia volunteers to serve coffee, and, after getting a cup and refusing the cookies, I edge up to a small crowd surrounding Dr. Bennett.

Though I didn't actually see Dr. Bennett hypnotize the crowd, I recognized some of the signs, which could mean the congregation had been previously entranced and Dr. Bennett used a key word. People in a trancelike state are very open to suggestions—like filling up collection plates.

"I think automatic writing is a clear view into the spirit world, but there are very few people who can actually do it," Dr. Bennett is saying.

"Are you a medium yourself, Doctor?" A man with a thick mustache and equally thick German accent asks.

Dr. Bennett laughs. "I'm afraid not, Mr. Huber. My talents lie elsewhere."

"Indeed," I murmur.

His head turns in my direction. "And you are?"

"Anna Van Housen."

"And you are interested in spiritualism and mediums, Miss Van Housen?"

So he does recognize me from the bookstore. "Yes, among other things." I give him an innocent smile. "Such as hypnotism."

Dr. Bennett clears his throat. "Ah yes, hypnotism. A fascinating subject, that."

"I find it so. Especially Gustave Le Bon's studies on crowd psychology and suggestibility." That'll teach him to try to charm a charmer.

Surprise flickers across Dr. Bennett's face but is soon replaced by a wry grin. "You're very well read, Miss Van Housen."

I smile. "As I said, I am interested in the supernatural. I'm afraid I've missed your previous lectures. Could you tell me a little more about the Society for Psychical Research?"

"Of course. The Society for Psychical Research is comprised of researchers, writers, and others who are interested in the supernatural. At first we only studied spirit manifestations and appearances, but then we made some remarkable discoveries with regard to other psychical powers."

I take a casual sip of my coffee. "And what other psychical powers would you be speaking of?"

He smiles. "I'm afraid I'm not at liberty to divulge that in a public setting, but I wouldn't mind going over some of this privately. You are a fellow aficionado, after all. Perhaps you and your acquaintance—it is Cynthia, isn't it?—would like to meet with me sometime."

Cynthia appears beside me and I can practically see dollar signs in his eyes.

I stiffen. *Please don't let her tell this man what my mother and I do*, I think. The first rule in getting information from someone is to not give them too much information about yourself in return.

She links her arm in mine. "Thank you for the invitation. Anna is quite young, you know. I do think it would be better if I attended this meeting with her. I'm sure it would ease her mother's mind."

Truthfully, I'm happy to have her tag along. Dr. Bennett may be a psychical researcher, but he may also be a swindler. I can't judge him, but I *can* be careful. And maybe I'll be able to encourage Cynthia to keep a tighter grip on her purse strings.

"That would be a delight. Just let me check my schedule. You can get in touch with me through the church later this week." He gives Cynthia a patronizing pat on her arm and moves away.

"Isn't he handsome?" Cynthia asks, watching Dr. Bennett conversing with Mr. Huber. "Not as handsome as Jack, of course, but still distinguished."

Cynthia and I walk toward the door, my mind spinning with possibilities. After years with no information about my abilities, could I really be close to getting some answers? It's too bad I didn't get a chance to touch his hand. I would like to have known how he was feeling. Before walking out the door, I glance back through the crowded room one more time, only to find Dr. Bennett staring back at me.

FOURTEEN

As I set up for a séance the next evening, I realize I'm more nervous than I've ever been for a performance. Between my heightened fear of being caught by a skeptic and adding Mr. Darby's ODD device to our repertoire, I'm as edgy as a tightrope walker. *Just a few more*, I promise myself. *Just a few more, then we can quit.*

Earlier, a messenger boy had delivered a note that read:

I would risk ghoulies and ghosties, and long-legged beasties and things that go bump in the night to spend more time with you . . . see you tonight.

I have it tucked away in my pocket. The note makes me smile, just like Owen. Sure he's a bit theatrical, but with a mother like mine, who am I to judge? Everyone in my life is a bit overblown and theatrical.

Except for Cole, a little voice whispers. No, Cole isn't

either of those things. Next to Owen, Cole seems a bit stern, except for those rare times when he lets down his guard. Then he seems almost like a different person.

I shake my head, embarrassed by my thoughts. Why am I standing around daydreaming when I have a séance to prepare for?

After Mother left for the afternoon, Mr. Darby and I spent our day setting up the Object Displacement Device, making sure it worked from downstairs. He was no doubt below me right now, fiddling with it.

"Are you sure about this?" I'd asked him.

He'd rubbed his hands together gleefully. "I just wish I could see the looks on their faces."

He, at least, has no moral reservations about what we're doing. He looks at it as a giant practical joke.

The trick, of course, lies in not letting our guests see the small buttons that control the device and making sure no one hears me tapping my foot on the floor three times, which is our signal. We put one button in the light above our table and hid the other inside a cheap clock I've bought especially for tonight. Even if the clock does break into smithereens during its flight across the room, I figure the guests will just think the button is part of the works.

We'll only do it a few times, I promise, trying to ease my conscience. Once word gets out that objects sometimes hurtle around our rooms, people will beg to attend one of our séances. We've already raised our rates, and tonight's séance will bring in more than two hundred dollars. As we charge more money, I'll be able to save enough to keep us from destitution. Then we can finally stop.

Mother waltzes out in a long, flowing Oriental silk dress with a high waist and caftan sleeves. In one sleeve, she has the key to the handcuffs that will be placed on her when she enters the cabinet. Also secreted away in her dress is the paper-and-flour spirit face she'll use for the manifestation. It's one of our most shocking tricks, as it appears ghostly and convincing in the candlelight.

Unless one of our guests has been to Harry Houdini's latest lecture.

"So who is coming again?" I put the kettle on for tea.

"The Gaylords, a Hungarian couple that Jacques sent to us—I can't remember their names—and a mother and daughter from Cleveland, Joanna and Lisette Lindsay. They're all believers in spiritualism, so no skeptics this time."

Mother's eyes are ringed with kohl against a stark white face and she's wearing a beaded Egyptian bandeau. She looks just like Theda Bara in *Cleopatra*—exotic, beautiful, and mysterious. I'm dressed more simply in a dark blue georgette silk with white piping. Mother thinks the contrast we make is simply delicious. Whatever that means. Personally, I think she's just ensuring that all eyes are upon her tonight.

"Oh, and Owen called today while you were gone and practically invited himself." She casts me a glance from the corner of her eye and I turn away.

I make myself a cup of tea and then set out a plate of tiny sandwiches for our guests. While my mother is busy pillaging the liquor cabinet, I check the light on the ceiling again to make sure the button isn't visible.

"Oh, stop it," Mother complains, sipping her sherry. "You're making me nervous. Don't fret. Jacques checked almost everyone out and gave me some juicy tidbits on the Gaylords."

Almost everyone?

A knock on the door sounds and I let the first of our guests in: the mother-daughter pair from Cleveland. With their frizzy blond hair and prominent blue eyes, they look more like sisters than mother and child. I'll never be able to keep them straight.

"Would you like something to eat?" I hold out the plate of sandwiches. Both shake their heads curtly. The daughter avoids all eye contact, while the mother stares at me boldly.

"I would like something to drink, though. Any spirits?" She gives a loud, barking laugh at her pun.

"Gin? Sherry?"

"Gin would be fine, thank you."

"I'll just take water," the daughter says with a glance at her mother.

I get their drinks and hand the glasses to them, but the mother downs hers before I turn away to offer something to the Hungarian couple who've just arrived.

"Another, please."

My eyes widen. "Of course." I pretend not to notice as the daughter sends her mother another warning glance. On impulse, I reach out and gently touch the daughter's arm. "Are you sure you wouldn't like a sandwich?" My mouth gets dry as her agitation transmits itself to me. Why is she so nervous?

The night is *not* starting off well.

After that, the Lindsays, in their Wards-catalog dresses, stand silently in the corner. This is unusual. Most of our guests love being invited to our exclusive "parties" and chummy up to us right away.

I have no time to worry about it, though, as within minutes, the rest of our guests arrive and I'm kept busy chatting and refilling glasses and cups. The Hungarian couple gobble up most of the sandwiches and seem too jolly to truly be into spiritualism. Mr. Gaylord looks bored, but I have a feeling that's just the way he always looks. Cynthia is like the frisky puppy he couldn't resist. Owen hasn't arrived yet. I notice that the sandwich plate is empty and give my mother a signal that it's time to begin.

She claps her hands together. "Well, now, I know you all didn't come here for the food. Shall we start?"

Just then another knock sounds. Even though I've been expecting it, I still jump. Owen.

Taking a deep breath, I hurry down the hall and open the door.

Owen is leaning against the doorjamb, his head at a jaunty angle. "Did I miss the ghosties?"

I laugh in spite of my nerves.

"No, we're just starting."

Just then a door clicks shut downstairs and my heart plummets. What now?

Even before he appears, I know it's Cole by the firm, measured steps on the stairs. He gives Owen a once-over and turns to me. "I hope you don't mind if I join you?"

"Suit yourself, old chap. But it might be a bit crowded," Owen says in a cheerfully fake English accent.

Cole acknowledges the dig with a raised brow.

"Please come in." I move aside to let them both in.

"You look wonderful tonight," Owen says as he walks past.

I give him a distracted smile and shut the door. "The rest of our guests have arrived, Mother," I call down the hall. Owen joins the others, but Cole catches my elbow to hold me back in the hall.

"I'm glad we're alone for a moment." His voice is low, insistent. "It's important I speak to you tonight about your abilities."

I swallow, my heart racing like an old-fashioned pair of grays in a buggy race.

"Excuse me?"

His voice becomes more urgent. "You know what I mean, Anna. We need to talk."

My mind spins. I can't admit or deny anything, not when I don't know who he is or what he wants. I take a deep breath. "I am a magician, Cole," I say softly. "My mother is the medium. Now, we really should join the others."

I turn toward the sitting room but before I can move, Cole leans in close behind me. "I'm going to need you to trust me on this, Anna. Please."

I shiver as his breath whispers over my ear and across my

neck. Swallowing hard, I walk away, not knowing what else to do. He follows me into the sitting room and my stomach twists itself into knots tighter than I've ever been tied with.

I take a seat next to Owen, and Cole sits across from me, next to the Lindsays. To the others he says, "I'm sorry I'm late. Thank you for inviting me, Madame Van Housen. I'm honored."

I frown at my mother, who gives me a cat's-got-the-cream smile and then closes her eyes. "Let's all join hands as we welcome the spirit world to join us."

I seethe as she asks everyone to close their eyes and leads them in the customary chant. Why couldn't she just tell me she invited Cole? Why does everything have to be a game?

With effort, I bring my mind back to the séance. My mother uses her voice like an illusionist to cast a spell over the others. I glance around the table, gauging their reactions. Excitement lights up Cynthia's pretty features, though her husband looks a bit nervous. I don't blame him, considering what happened at the last séance they attended. The couple from Hungary is practically erupting with anticipation. Owen's brows are knotted in concentration, while Cole's face is still. Then I catch the mother and daughter exchanging glances. I close my eyes when they look my way and watch through my lashes as the daughter slowly leans over and peers under the table. The mother scans the room, her mouth set. My chest squeezes closed like an accordion. Something is very, very wrong.

Shifting in my seat, I stretch my leg across the table

toward the mother. The moment my foot connects with her calf, I get an electrical shock of deep animosity. Not skepticism, exactly—something worse. Right behind the animosity is backbiting, stomach-twisting jealousy. Then it dawns on me.

She's not a skeptic; she's a rival.

I yank my foot back, but the pulsing grows, creeping across my skin like a slug, and suddenly it hits me so hard I gasp. This is the same feeling I had after Owen dropped me off. *She* is the one who watched me from the shadows that night.

My stomach clenches. I open my mouth to ask Mother if she wants a drink of water, but before I can form the words, she rises gracefully from her chair.

"The spirits demand I enter the cabinet."

Desperately, I ask, "Would you like a drink of water before you tax yourself so?"

Mother's eyes fly open, but she shakes her head. "It's too late," she said, her voice hollow. "The spirits already have me."

I nearly scream in frustration. Why is she ignoring me? Is she so intent on showing me who's boss that she's willing to risk everything?

I help her into her handcuffs while keeping an eye on the two women as best I can. What are they up to? Do they mean my mother harm? Are they here to learn her tricks or to discredit her? In England, one medium hired a rube to throw acid on the face of a rival during a manifestation.

I try to signal to my mother with my eyes, but she's playing her part of empty vessel so thoroughly that she either doesn't notice or is ignoring me.

Breathing in and out, I invite Cynthia and her husband to check her handcuffs. Usually, I ask that all the guests check, but I don't want Mrs. Lindsay anywhere near my mother.

I shut and lock the cabinet. Hesitating only briefly, I snuff out all the candles, leaving only a small one in the middle of the table. All I can do now is help create the illusion. I keep an eye on the women as I begin to chant. My voice isn't nearly as effective as my mother's, but it does the job. It's only meant to give my mother time to slip off the handcuffs and caftan dress and out the hidden panel.

Halfway through the chant, Cole's eyes fly open in the dim light and his head jerks toward the two women on my right. He looks back at me, his face dark with worry.

He knows something's wrong.

He can feel it.

The hairs across my arms prickle as I feel for the first time someone trying to get a read on *me*. It's almost as if he has cast a silver strand in my direction and is trying to connect with me. My voice stumbles for a moment before I regain my composure. My mother is counting on me. Panicked, I look back at the women; both are still in their seats, watchful.

A cloud of smoke explodes near the cabinet. The others gasp as the vapor hangs in the air for a moment, shimmering in the candlelight.

Cynthia and the Hungarian woman scream as a ghostly apparition floats in the darkness near the cabinet. The mask covers my mother's face and hair, and because of the dark suit she wears underneath the caftan, the face seems disembodied.

Without warning, the temperature of the room drops and fear prickles across my skin. My head swivels from side to side as I search the darkness, dread tightening my chest. The last time I felt this . . . There's another flash, and then a figure appears behind my mother. I freeze and stare, my eyes burning from the smoke as the image wavers, then grows stronger. My fingers clench around the edge of the table so tightly I'm surprised they don't snap off. A young man, dressed in army green, stands at rigid attention, his dark eyes trained directly on me.

My head turns to see if anyone else can see it, but it's hard to tell because everyone's face is already shocked. Only Cole's eyes seem to be looking beyond my mother, his brow furrowed in concentration.

I turn back to the figure only to find his hand stretched out.

"I need to speak to you."

Fear snakes its way up my spine.

Walter.

Ribbons of light reach toward me and a roaring sounds in my ears.

"No!" I scream, waiting for Walter to inhabit my body.

"Anna!" I hear Cole's voice, but it comes to me as if through a layer of frost.

Out of the corner of my eye, I see Mrs. Lindsay rise from her chair. She's muttering something incoherently under her breath. Desperately, I cry out, *"Go sabhála Dìa muid ar fad!"*—Gaelic for "God save us all!" The use of another language impresses the clients. While I'm yelling, I stomp my foot against the floor three times. My signal to Mr. Darby.

A smile plays across Walter's face.

"I could always speak to your mother."

I leap to my feet, fists by my side.

Mrs. Lindsay moves toward my mother, but Cole lays a restraining hand on her arm. He shoots me a look of alarm, but I don't have time to puzzle out what he means. I'm still focusing on Walter, whose fingers rest lightly on my mother's shoulder.

"Go sabhála Dìa muid ar fad!" I scream out again, stomping harder, a short, staccato burst of sound. Walter hesitates. Cole's hand tightens on Mrs. Lindsay's arm, who's now mumbling a strange, unintelligible chant. Her daughter is clinging to her other arm and whispering fiercely in her ear. Owen must have caught my desperation because he stands as well. Suddenly, I hear the slight whir of the machine from downstairs and nearly collapse. It has to work. In the chaos that follows the clock moving, my mother will be able to return to her cabinet.

If Walter lets her.

The Hungarian woman lets out a soul-splitting scream, pointing at the clock hanging suspended over the mantel.

Cynthia clings to her husband and stares transfixed. The mother and daughter turn toward the clock and I see the women look up, as if expecting to see strings.

Suddenly, the clock shoots across the room and smashes into our beautiful rose cut-glass lamp. The Hungarian woman screams hysterically, and even the rival medium pales in the candlelight.

Mother disappears and, to my horror, so does Walter.

Did he go after her? Is he at this very moment taking over her body?

I pound on the door of the cabinet. "Mama! Are you okay?" Nothing.

"Walter!" I scream, and then clap my hand over my mouth. No one except me even knows he's here.

"Right here," a voice to my left murmurs.

I whirl toward it, breathing hard. I can't see much in the darkness but an outline. I turn back toward the spirit cabinet, tremors running through my body.

"I'm sorry for playing tricks. I don't have much time. But you helped me, now I can help you."

I want to ask him a million things but I'm frozen. Frozen because I'm speaking to a dead person and frozen with worry that the others will know I'm speaking to a dead person. I stare fixedly at the cabinet.

"You don't want them to know I'm here, do you?" He sounds disappointed.

I give the slightest shake of my head. I can hear Cynthia tending to the Hungarian woman, who is still moaning, and Mrs. Lindsay whispering angrily to her daughter.

"I'm here to warn you, Anna. You helped my poor, sweet mama and I want to help you. There's danger all around you and your mother."

I turn toward him, not caring if the others think I'm crazy. "What kind of danger?" I whisper.

Walter shakes his head. *"I don't know. But there are people here who would do you ill. Take care."*

His image begins to shimmer in the darkness.

"Wait!"

But Walter is gone.

I turn back to the cabinet. Has he invaded my mother's body after all? "Mama!"

There's a few moments' silence and then my mother begins sobbing, which is exactly what she's supposed to be doing.

My knees buckle.

Cole is there in an instant, steadying me.

Everyone gathers around the cabinet to see my mother.

"Stand back!" I order. Part of me is dying inside, wanting to make sure she's all right, but I also have to give her time—there are so many things that can go wrong when she's appearing as an apparition, and she has to look exactly the same as when we left her.

Please God, let her be the same and not possessed by a dead boy.

"I have to make sure the spirits are gone." Slowly, I fumble with the locks and then hold my breath as the door inches open.

FIFTEEN

My sigh of relief as I see my mother sitting exactly as she should be is audible. In spite of everything, we haven't been caught and my mother is safe.

For the moment.

Now I just want to get those women out of our house. If there is danger surrounding me, as Walter said, it's probably from them.

"What was that?" Cynthia twists her beads around and around, her blue eyes wide.

"I think, my dear, we were just treated to a visit from the nether world," Mr. Gaylord drawls. Animation lights his face for the first time.

I unbind my mother and lead her back to the table. She's still weeping softly, real tears streaming down her cheeks. Had my mother wanted to pursue a career as a stage actress, there's no doubt she could have been the best.

"She always has this reaction after manifesting a spirit,"

I tell the others. "It's very taxing. Please sit down. She'll be all right in a moment."

Everyone sits, except Cole, who asks if I would like him to clean up the glass.

I nod as I tend to my mother. "The broom's in the hall closet."

My mother takes a deep, shuddering breath and glances around the table as if just coming out of a trancelike state. "What happened?" she asks in her little-girl voice. But I hear something different as her eyes zero in on me. *What the hell happened?*

Cynthia and the Hungarian woman get up and fuss over her as I turn on the overhead electric light. I shoot a quick glance around the room to make certain that everything is in its place. All is as it should be.

"That was quite amazing," the Hungarian man tells me. "I've never seen such a talented medium. I hope you don't mind if we tell our friends about your mother, do you?"

"Of course not," I tell him wearily. That's what I want, right?

"I think it's time everyone left," I say, raising my voice. "My mother needs her rest." My mother assumes her pathetic face, but I'm not fooled. I'm sure she's keyed up from her performance and ready to grill me about the broken lamp. The Hungarian couple leaves right away, but Cynthia grabs my arm and walks with me to the door.

"I got in touch with Doctor Bennett. He's holding the very first meeting of the American branch of the Society for

Psychical Research tomorrow night and especially asked us to be there." She clasps her hands together in excitement. I can't help but smile at her in spite of my own agitation over the séance. Her enthusiasm is infectious.

"I have a show tomorrow night," I tell her.

"I told him that, so I'm going to attend the show, and we can go after. He said he would wait for us."

I smile and agree to go, in spite of the nervous butterflies fluttering in my stomach. As afraid as I am of being exposed, I'm more worried about protecting my mother. What had Walter said? We were in danger from someone at the séance. I turn back to the sitting room. My bet is on Mrs. Lindsay. But I would like to know for sure. I want some real answers, and if Dr. Bennett has them, I need to get them, no matter how much I distrust him.

The Gaylords and the Hungarian couple are gone, but for some reason, the Lindsays are lingering. Mrs. Lindsay sidles over to my mother and I stiffen.

"That was really quite impressive." Her eyes poke and prod the room, looking for signs of trickery. "You'll have to show me how it's done."

My mother arches an eyebrow, then sits weakly in the nearest chair. "The spirit world is a mystery, even to me."

"Oh, posh!" the woman says scornfully. "You and I both know that this was an illusion of some sort. It was. No one can do what I—"

"Mother!" The daughter's pale skin grows red and she lays a restraining hand on her mother's shoulder.

I quickly slip beside my own mother, who draws herself up. "I can assure you, Mrs. Lindsay, this was no illusion. The spirits work—"

Mrs. Lindsay smiles thinly. "In mysterious ways," she finishes. "So you've said. Come, Lisette. I think we're finished here."

Owen raises a brow as the women leave. "Well, you two certainly do know how to have a good time."

My mother snorts and goes into the kitchen, no doubt to pour herself a good strong drink. I hear voices and know she's talking to Cole, who is throwing away the last of the glass remnants. I take Owen's arm and lead him toward the door. "Thank you so much for coming."

He laughs. "I can take a hint, but you know I didn't really come to attend the séance, don't you? I came to ask if you would like to go out with me Friday night after your performance. Some friends and I are going to a little speakeasy up in Harlem. I think you'd like it."

My stomach falls at the sudden silence in the kitchen. "I'm not sure my mother . . ."

"Go ahead!" My mother's voice comes from the kitchen. "You should get out more with people your own age."

My face burns, then I get angry with myself. What do I care if Cole is listening? "Well, I'd love to, then."

Owen reaches out and squeezes my hand. "I look forward to it."

His touch kicks my pulse up several notches. His hair, which was slicked back formally when he first arrived, has fallen down over his forehead. With his slightly crooked nose, sparkling blue eyes, and impish smile, he looks like a naughty child. I smile as I shut the door behind him.

Owen is definitely interested in me, but am I interested in him? Why shouldn't I be? He's handsome, funny, sophisticated, and the life of the party, and even more important, he has a stable job and a stable life. Of course I'm interested. Any normal girl would be.

Cole comes into the hallway. His mouth is set. His eyes swirl with anger and something else. . . . Could it be jealousy? The thought rocks me back on my heels and I look up at him with surprise. He seems so much older than I am most of the time, so proper and solemn, it never occurred to me that he thought of me that way.

Yes it did, whispers a small, traitorous voice.

"I guess I should be going as well. It's getting late," he says with a stiff little nod.

He tries to brush past me, but I step in front of him and plant my hands on my hips. Now that I want to talk to him, he's in a hurry to leave? We'll see about that. "Wait, I thought we were going to . . ."

He presses a finger to my lips and I freeze, all my nerve endings suddenly focused on the heat being generated from that simple touch. Our eyes meet. The anger in his gaze ebbs and the corners of his mouth tilt up ever so slightly. He motions with his head toward the silent kitchen.

"Tomorrow," he mouths, taking his finger from my lips. I press them together, missing the heat.

"Good night, Anna," he says simply, and walks out the doorway.

I give myself a mental shake. Fine, but tomorrow I want answers.

"So what do you think of Mrs. Lindsay?" Mother asks as I enter into the kitchen. "The nerve of that woman! I detest skeptics. They're such sneaky liars."

I hide a smile. That's the pot calling the kettle black. "I don't think she was a skeptic, Mother. I think she was another medium."

My mother narrows her eyes. "That makes sense. I'll have a word with Jacques. We're going to need better information on our clients from here on out. It's getting too risky." She pulls the mask out of her sleeve and lays the key to the handcuffs on the table. "So what happened out here anyway?"

I'm ready for the question and answer without hesitation. "I tripped the cord. Mrs. Lindsay looked like she was going to attack you, so I kicked it with my foot. Sorry to make such a mess, but at least you were able to get back into the cabinet safely."

I see her mental guesswork as she tries to remember where I was when it happened, but I know the mask grants limited visibility and it was very dark in the room.

"Sorry about the lamp," I say sincerely.

She shakes her head. "Don't worry about it. Jacques will buy me a new one if I ask."

I frown. I hate being dependent on someone I don't trust.

Mother turns toward me, her face so innocent that I stiffen in preparation.

"So, you and Owen?"

I sigh. "Me and Owen, what?"

"Well, you're going dancing with him Friday, aren't you? Do you like him?"

I shrug, thinking it's a little late for coy mother-daughter talks. When you make your daughter help you cheat people out of money for a living, you forfeit your right to teach her life lessons.

"You'll have fun," she says.

"Why did you invite Cole tonight?" I keep my voice casual.

She busies herself with wiping down an already clean counter. "I wanted you to have choices."

I sense she wants to discuss it further and hesitate. Do I really want to know what's on her mind? Part of my survival has always included not dwelling too deeply on my mother's motivations. So I give the pretense of a giant yawn and edge toward my bedroom. "I'm really tired. I think I'm going to call it a night."

For a moment, I think I see a look of disappointment flash across her face but then she smiles. "Good night then, darling. Sleep tight."

She leans toward me and I dutifully kiss her cheek.

"Good night, Mother."

I wonder about that look as I head off for bed. Is she really disappointed that I won't confide my thoughts and dreams to her? Did I just miss an opportunity to get closer to my mother? Or was it an act? It's impossible to tell.

The weight of my clothes is dragging me down. I can't breathe. Mama. I have to help her. My lungs are burning for air. She's screaming my name. I can't breathe. I'm so sorry.

I awake soaked with sweat, my legs caught up in a tangle of blankets. I kick them off and listen. Nothing. I check on my mother, my heartbeat slowly returning to normal. After getting a drink of water from the kitchen, I return to my bedroom, my mind racing. Why is this happening? Is it real? I slip back into bed and pull the blankets up to my chin.

Fear sits on my chest like a heavy cat, staring me in the eye. Walter, the visions, someone stalking me . . . I wish there were someone I could talk to. Someone who understands. Someone who could help. I curl up in a tight fetal position and pull the blankets over my head.

I've never felt so alone in my life.

I wake hours later, gratified to see the sun shining through the window. Fear has little toehold on sunny days. This morning, I talk to Cole.

I wash quickly, taking more care than usual with my appearance. The memory of Cole's finger on my lips has me changing my hat three times, even though I call myself all sorts of silly names for doing it. Nerves bounce around in my stomach like a juggler with bowling pins—as much from the prospect of seeing Cole again as from what I might learn from him. Because I know what I felt last night when the tendrils of his emotions wove their way across the table to me. He can do what I do.

I rouge my lips and then, dissatisfied, wipe off the makeup. I'm not flashy or mysterious. Staring at myself in the mirror, I wonder what other people see. "A beautiful young woman," Owen had called me. Does Cole think I'm beautiful, too? Living with my mother, who turns heads as she walks down the street, it's difficult to know.

Unlike my mother, who transforms herself, depending on her mood, I always look the same—serious and thoughtful—no matter what I'm wearing or how I do my makeup. Today, I'm wearing black silk stockings, a dark blue wool dress, and my dark surplice coat. The hat I finally decide on is a new black cloche with a beaded flower on one side. I look smart and modern, but in no way bewitching. Impatiently, I turn away from my reflection and gather up my things.

I head downstairs and pause before the door. Should I knock? Just ask Mr. Darby if I could talk to Cole? What would a respectable girl do?

I'm saved from having to figure it out when the door opens and Cole slips out.

"Good morning."

"Good morning."

We stare at each other for a moment before he gestures toward the door. The sun may be shining, but the air is crackling with cold and I pull on my soft leather gloves.

"Would you like to go to Child's for waffles?" he asks, offering me his arm.

I nod, and we walk in silence to the elevated train stop. Men in their dark suits and bowler hats are hurrying to and fro. Women, mostly office workers, are rushing to get to the office in order to make the first pot of coffee.

The El is crowded, but Cole and I push our way on like true New Yorkers. We can't talk here, but he gives me a reassuring smile as I cling to the strap hanging from the roof. He's pressed so close against me that I can smell the clean scent of his soap underneath the stench of body odor, perfume, and cigarettes coming from the other passengers. My head reaches his chest and my gaze travels up to where the collar of his white shirt meets the dip in his throat. I stare at it, transfixed, wondering what it would be like to press my lips precisely there. My face flushes hot and my throat gets dry. I've never felt so shaky or confused in my entire life.

So I pick his pocket.

I don't mean to do it. I haven't done it in ages—not since I was eleven or twelve and we needed cash for a fast train out of town. But standing so close to him and feeling so strange, I can't help myself. I figure I'll just pass it off as a joke and hand him back his wallet or keys or whatever it is I come up with. A quip about the dangers of a crowded train and it would be over. But the minute my fingers curl around an envelope, my mind flashes to that loopy, feminine writing on the letter addressed to Cole on Mr. Darby's desk and I know I won't be giving it back. I slip the envelope into my pocket, my cheeks burning.

Cole looks down, his expression puzzled. I give him a half smile and drop my eyes, sure guilt is written on my face. I'd forgotten that he may be able to read me as well as I read others.

At Child's, the cheery blue awning and the waffle maker in the window welcome us, but I'm too impatient for answers to appreciate any of it. I bite my tongue and wait for Cole to speak, but he seems in no hurry, so I watch as he butters his waffles, then pours a great deal of syrup over the top. He digs in and I wait for a moment before cutting into mine. Though they smell delicious, my stomach is too knotted for me to eat.

"Are the waffles not to your liking?"

That damned formal tone again. Taking a deep breath, I put down my fork and simply stare at him. He stares right back at me.

"I wish . . ." He stops and his mouth draws into a straight line.

I lean forward, my heart swelling. "What do you wish?"

His lips curve slightly at the corners. "I wish we had met under different circumstances. That I didn't have to try to explain." He shakes his head as if impatient with himself.

"But you haven't explained anything!"

"I know. I'm terrible at this. I just never imagined it would be you."

He's talking in circles and looks as if he wishes a hole

would open and swallow him up. "I don't understand."

"I wish we were just out having breakfast together, without all the rest of it." The words come out in a rush.

I gape for a moment before sitting up straight. "You're shy!"

Cole glances away. "I guess. A bit. At least around women. In my defense, it *was* an all-boys boarding school."

It makes so much sense now. The formality. Being uncomfortable around my mother. My chest tightens as my heart grows tender and bruised for him. Then I remember my reason for being here.

Answers.

"I think I know what you're trying to say," I say carefully, as if navigating through shards of glass. "But I really need to know what's going on. I need you to explain the rest of it."

Cole looks down at his hands. They're strong hands with tapered fingers and short fingernails. I remember the way his finger felt on my lips.

"I know what you are."

My eyes jerk back up to his face.

"At least what I think you are."

I bite my lip and drop my eyes. "What? A girl? A magician?" I don't say a fraud, but the word hangs between us, bright and deadly.

"No, a Sensitive."

The word *fraud* falls, with a plop, into the syrup.

"A what?"

"A Sensitive. Someone with psychical powers."

I bite my lip and glance away, afraid of what he might see in my eyes. "Really?" I say faintly. "And what kind of powers do you think I have?"

"I know you feel other people's emotions. I also know you can speak to the dead, though whether that's something you can do on your own or just with me, I'm not sure. You said you've never done it before?"

I shake my head before what he's said sinks in. "Wait. What do you mean, just with you?"

He glances away. "I'm a Sensitive too. Well, not really. I'm more like a conduit. My abilities make yours stronger. I can even mimic them as long as I'm with you."

My mind whirls and my heart thuds painfully against my chest. The restaurant tilts and wavers before righting itself and I cling to the edge of the table. "So that explains Walter."

He nods and looks down at his hands. "I'm not sure if it would have happened anyway or if my presence made your abilities that much stronger. That's why I wanted to talk to you so badly last night. I'm sorry I waited so long."

I close my eyes for a moment, the feeling of Walter using my body so strong that I almost gag.

"Anna, I know. I didn't mean for that to happen. And I did stop it, once I realized . . ."

"When you grabbed my hand."

He nods. "I have the ability to block, or stop, the powers. Remember at the movie theater? When you felt that poor woman's emotions? As soon as I knew what was happening,

I stopped it, but then I got interested in the movie and it slipped past me again."

So I was right. It was Cole's presence that was changing my abilities. My stomach churns and I take a sip of hot coffee to settle it. The mug is thick and comforting. I wrap my hands around it and take another sip. All around us is the buzz of conversation but nothing can drown out the buzz of anxiety and hope ringing in my ears.

"You can, um, control it?"

"Yes, but it takes time. It takes longer for some people to learn than it does for others."

My heart stops. For a moment, I can't breathe or move. Finally, I look into Cole's eyes, which are edged with worry and something else I can't identify.

"There are others?" I whisper.

He looks away. "Yes."

I'm not alone.

Relief, sweet and liberating, overwhelms me and I slump back in my chair. There were times growing up when I thought I was a lunatic, imagining things. But all along, there were others. It's not that I haven't suspected it. There are too many books on the subject of psychical phenomena to be a coincidence, but to have it actually confirmed. . . .

"Who?" My voice comes from a lost, lonely place deep inside.

Cole hands me his handkerchief. "I can't tell you," he says softly.

I stop dabbing at my eyes. "Why?"

"I can't tell you that either. Not right now." And even

though his voice is laced with regret, I know he means what he says.

"When can you tell me?"

He shrugs, his mouth tight. Hurt edged with desperation radiates through my chest. I snatch up his hand, concentrating hard, trying to get a read on him. It's blocked.

I don't know why I feel so betrayed. I barely know Cole. I just . . . A sudden thought comes to mind. "When I asked you why you came to the States, you said it was to meet me. What did you mean?"

"That I can tell you. I came to find other Sensitives. You're the first real one I've located." His eyes, dark with concern, search my face.

My head spins trying to connect all the dots. "That's what you do when you leave the house all day? Look for Sensitives?"

He nods.

"And that's what you were doing in the slums the night I was lost?"

He nods again. "I go to see fortune-tellers, mediums, et cetera. There are a lot of charlatans in the business, but you never can tell."

"That's why you introduced yourself to Jacques. To get an invitation to our séance."

"After I met you in the hallway, I knew."

My heart dips in disappointment. And here I thought it was because he wanted to get to know me. But he wasn't interested in me, just my abilities. "Why are you looking for people like me?"

He closes his eyes and shakes his head for a moment.

"Look, this isn't really my secret to tell. There are other people . . ."

I clench my hands in frustration. "Why say anything at all if you can't explain yourself?"

He shakes his head. "I told them I would make a mess of this."

"Told who?" At the look on his face I stand up. "No, don't say it. You can't tell me."

I turn on my heel and walk away.

"Anna, wait. Please, you have to trust me." I hear the pleading in his voice, but I have nothing to say. I just want to get as far away from him as possible. He gets up to follow and I put my hand out. "Not. Right. Now."

He looks in my eyes and gives a short nod.

My jaw clenched, I walk out into the frigid morning, not quite sure whether the tumult of emotions inside stems from anger, disappointment, or heartbreak.

SIXTEEN

The anger roiling inside keeps me warm as I march past the El stop and on down the street.

How dare he tell me things about myself that I've always wanted to know, and then refuse to give me any details. To leave me hanging with little bits and pieces of information and nothing more?

"Trust me," I mutter, dodging people on the busy sidewalk. How can I trust him? I don't trust anyone. I stop.

Maybe I'm more like my mother than I ever imagined.

I continue walking, trying to sort all the thoughts whirling in my mind like confetti caught in a whirlwind. There are others like me. Others who can control their abilities. Turn them off, maybe? Live a normal life? I yearn for that. To be able to turn off my "gifts" and be like everyone else.

And Cole is the only one who can teach me. Cole, who vacillates between aloof and caring faster than a magician can say "Abracadabra."

I stop for a moment as another thought strikes me. My vision. If his presence makes my abilities stronger, that may explain why I'm suddenly having multiple visions concerning my own life.

My anger dissolves, leaving me alone like a child who, having found her way to the center of a maze, realizes she has no way out.

I consider jumping on a streetcar but decide the crisp air will help clear my mind and chase away the last vestiges of anger. I have hours before I have to get ready to go to the theater. Besides, it's a beautiful day in spite of the cold. The sun makes the pristine marble facades of the older buildings gleam as I walk past them.

I continue walking along Sixth Avenue, through the sky-high buildings that make me feel as if I'm at the bottom of a steep canyon. The walking calms me as I try to put my conversation with Cole out of my mind.

I must have walked for more than an hour when I suddenly stop, stunned by a large sign hanging on a storefront across the street.

THE MARTINKA-HORNMANN MAGIC CO.

I gaze at the sign, excitement replacing confusion. Who cares about my personal life when the most famous magic shop in the entire world lies before me? Like any other magician worth her salt, I know that the Martinka brothers started their shop in the 1860s and ran it for forty years before selling it to Carter the Great, who then sold it to

Harry Houdini. After several years, Houdini sold it to another famous magician, Otto Hornmann.

And it's right there in front of me. I glance around. Is it serendipity that brought me here right after my talk with Cole? Or something else? I pause but feel nothing but the hammering of my own heart.

I barely miss being run down by a taxi as I rush across the busy street. Just before opening the door, I pause and take a deep breath. At this moment, I'm not a girl with an overbearing mother. I'm not a girl who likes a boy who's only interested in her strange abilities. At this moment, I am a magician.

It takes a moment for my eyes to adjust to the dim indoor lighting, but once I do I gasp. The store is stocked with floor-to-ceiling shelves and filled with so much clutter that it makes Mr. Darby's workshop look orderly.

No one is at the front counter and the shop looks empty, but the murmur of voices from the back room assures me I'm not alone. My eyes are drawn to the merchandise stacked haphazardly on every available surface. On one shelf, decks of cards perch precariously. On another, scarves stream down in brightly colored waterfalls. In the back of the shop, I spot magic cupboards and boxes of all kinds. Every bit of wall not covered with shelves is decorated with posters and handbills of famous magicians. I pick out several of Houdini right away.

I sniff deeply at the musty scent of wood, old books, and card-fanning powder.

My hands are drawn to a deck of cards lying open close

to me, and I shuffle and reshuffle. The deck is beautiful, with wands and swords intricately drawn on the back. With the cards in hand, I wander over to a display of burnished wood boxes with undetectable false bottoms.

"May I help you?"

Startled, I turn to find an older gentleman with thick glasses poking his head out the doorway to the back room.

"I'm just looking, thank you."

His eyebrows draw together curiously, but then he nods and his head disappears again.

"It's just some girl, looking around," I hear him say.

Just some girl. I shuffle a single card through my fingers several times, pop it in the air, and catch it in the middle of the deck. Then I do a one-handed cut, a flip back, and then, for flourish, a long spring.

Some girl indeed.

"Very nice."

My heart shoots up to my throat as I find myself looking into Harry Houdini's cool gaze. I glance down at the floor. This is the most famous magic shop in the world. Of course he would be here.

Maybe deep down I hoped he would be?

"Thank you," I murmur, heat rising in my face. Maybe he doesn't remember me. He must have signed hundreds of books the other day.

"You like cards, Anna?"

I shiver at the way he says my name. With his Hungarian accent, he pronounces it with exactly the same intonation as my mother. *Ahnah.*

I bite my lip. "Yes. I like magic."

His brows rise. "Ah, an aficionado."

I look him right in the eye. "No, a magician."

His brows rise again.

"Do you perform?"

I want to bite back the words. Why don't I just paint a target on my mother's back? Instead of answering, I start doing flips with my cards. In response, he picks up another deck of cards and begins manipulating them. He's good, but there's no question that I'm better.

"I had a feeling I would see you again," he says, his eyes on his cards.

My blood chills. Does he mean that in a normal, I-had-a-feeling way or in an I-can-see-the-future way? Many people, Sherlock Holmes author Sir Arthur Conan Doyle among them, believe Houdini has psychical powers—a claim Houdini aggressively denies.

"And here I thought you weren't a mentalist," I say boldly, setting down my cards.

Houdini follows suit. "I'm not. It was purely instinctive."

"Good instincts."

He smiles slightly. "So tell me, Anna the magician, is our meeting accidental or on purpose?"

Nervous now, I move over to another display. "You mean, am I following you?" I pick up a box and open the false bottom, not meeting his eyes. I hadn't been following him, so why do I feel so guilty?

Out of the corner of my eye, I see him shrug. "It's happened before."

Of course it has. With his fame, it would be surprising if it hadn't. "Well, I'm not." I replace the box and move to the juggling balls. Picking up a set, I give them a few experimental spins in the air.

He folds his arms, crinkling the sleeves of his suit jacket, making him look even shorter than he is. "You juggle and do card flourishes quite well, but those are circus antics. Not magic."

"Not like your escape tricks, you mean?" Defensiveness creeps into my voice. *Show him*, the magician in me urges. *Get out!* my survival instincts scream back.

"*Trick* is the operative word there." His mouth twists wryly. "Now Adrian Mons and Robert Houdin, they did real magic."

"Real magic?" I grin, and he returns the smile. Emboldened, I push on. "But you dedicated an entire book to exposing Robert Houdin."

He shrugs. "I was young and impetuous." He cocks his head to one side, his eyes narrowing as if considering something before reaching into his pocket and drawing out a card.

"My personal business card. I think the world could use more talented female magicians. My own wife is quite adept. You're more than welcome to come and show me your act. Perhaps I can give you some pointers?"

I juggle the balls a few more times before sitting them down. Taking the card slowly as if it might explode in my face, I drop it into my pocket. The temptation to show him what I can do is stronger than my common sense. "Perhaps I can show you something now?"

His pointy eyebrows shoot up in amusement.

I covertly palm a picklock from my handbag. "Have any handcuffs?"

"And what would you know about handcuffs?"

My pulse quickens and I give him an impudent smile. "Try me."

His own smile deepens as he moves behind the cluttered counter. Bending, he rummages around and comes up holding a pair of Lovell handcuffs.

I don't show my relief. For a moment, I was afraid he was going to trick me with a pair of Giant Bean handcuffs. I don't have an extender on my pick and would have had to admit defeat. But these, these I can get out of.

He locks me firmly into the cuffs, not seeing the picklock in the sleeve of my coat. Then he spins me around to face him.

"Turn around."

Unlike Mr. Darby, he doesn't ask why. Houdini does most of his escapes behind a curtain.

For a moment, I just stare at the set of his neck and the way his shoulders fill out his jacket. He and I are the exact same height.

"So what did you mean when you said that mediums would figure out new ways to trick their clients?"

I startle, almost dropping the picklock. "I meant that they will design bigger and better illusions, just as magicians do."

My fingers fumble for a moment before I quiet my mind and allow my body to take over. My muscles remember what to do.

"How would you know anything about that?"

Instead of answering, I counter, "How do you get out of your locked trunks?"

He gives a low chuckle. "Touché."

Moving closer to him, I whisper, "I think the secret is shorter bolts." Then I drop the handcuffs on the counter in front of him and hightail it out the door.

As promised, Cynthia is waiting in front of the theater after the show that night. Inside, excitement wars with nerves for top billing. Part of me wants to learn all I can about the Society for Psychical Research. The other part is afraid of what I'll find out. Namely, that premonitions can't be stopped and the visions I'm having are going to come to pass, no matter how closely I try to watch my mother.

Anticipation lights up Cynthia's face and she's stunning in a lustrous coral cardigan sweater that she'd paired with a beige pleated skirt. A felt, gigolo-style beige hat sits upon her shining blond head. She looks strangely demure, much different from her usually sparkling self. I'm still in my stage clothes and feel overdressed and glittery in my bright Oriental silk dress.

"Are you excited? I'm so excited!"

I smile in assent and climb into the automobile.

The ride to the church is a quick one, with Cynthia

jabbering happily next to me. It's reassuring that she's still the same in spite of her new look. Keeping up with her chatter distracts me from the pit in my stomach.

Instead of meeting in the sanctuary, we go to a back room that looks more like an office than an Italian villa. A dilapidated desk sits in one corner and the dark brown carpeting is worn and stained. In the center of the room, eight straight-back wooden chairs are set up in a circle.

Several people stand near the middle of the room talking when Cynthia and I come in. After the introductions are over, I sit in one of the chairs, while Cynthia continues chatting. There's no way I can make small talk in my frame of mind. I don't know what I expect out of this meeting, but I'm hoping for some answers. It's not as if Cole is going to give me any.

My brow furrows. He said there were others with my abilities. Though he'd never mentioned it, I wonder if he was talking about the Society for Psychical Research? I turn the idea over in my mind. Perhaps, but spiritualist societies abound. Or maybe he was talking about a far more sinister kind of society? Like the kind Aleister Crowley or other occultists belong to. Since he won't tell me, I have no way of knowing.

Even though I'm facing away from the door, I know the second Dr. Bennett walks into the room. His energy reaches me before he even says a chipper hello to the others. My abilities are getting stronger and sharper, just as Cole said they would. The vision leaps into my mind and I shudder.

Why do I feel like I'm running out of time?

"I'm glad you could make it, Miss Van Housen."

Startled, I look up into Dr. Bennett's florid features. "Er, yes. Thank you for inviting me."

"What are you hoping to learn from this meeting?"

I'd expected a question like that and have a pat answer already in my pocket. I flash him a Cynthia Gaylord smile. "Oh, I'm just interested in any and all psychical phenomena."

He tilts his head and considers me. I smile until my cheeks hurt. Just because I want answers doesn't mean I trust him. Not yet.

"You have come to the right place," he says finally. "He clasps his hands. "Shall we all take a seat?"

With his fingers interlaced over his vest, he tells a bit of the history of the Society for Psychical Research. "It's the longest-running psychical investigation group in the world and has included luminaries such as Dickens, Yeats, and currently, Sir Arthur Conan Doyle."

"What do they investigate?" asked Mr. Huber, the German man I met at the lecture.

"Extrasensory perception, clairvoyance, dream theory, and of course, channeling the dead in its many forms, such as spirit writing or telekinetic activity."

I watch Dr. Bennett carefully as he speaks. He doesn't hesitate over his answers and speaks with authority. But then again, so does my mother.

"Has the Society for Psychical Research found incontrovertible proof that this type of activity exists?" Cynthia asks.

I look at her in surprise.

Dr. Bennett smiles. "That, my dear lady, is what the wider scientific community wishes to know. Thus far, the Society for Psychical Research has been vague about its findings so as not to alarm the general public. But I can tell you that I have been present at some of their investigations, and I have seen the proof for myself."

There's a rustling and murmuring among the other attendees.

"What kind of proof have you seen?" I finally ask.

"I have seen apparitions, telekinetic activity, and spirit writing. I also personally know people with a high degree of extrasensory perception."

I cross my arms and frown. I've seen all those things too. Ha! I've created all those things.

"You look suspicious, Miss Van Housen." He smiles as he says this, but I think he's pegged Cynthia and me as troublemakers.

"I'm a cautious person, Doctor Bennett. Can you tell me more about the extrasensory perception?" That seems the closest to what I have. I don't even want to think about Walter.

"Extrasensory perception is the ability to read thoughts or emotions, or foretell the future. Some of the tests I've seen use cards, while others are more complex and use electroencephalograms, which is a device used for reading the electrical waves within the brain and was first developed by a friend of mine, Richard Caton."

I tentatively raise my hand again and he nods. "You mentioned clairvoyance. Have you known anyone who has visions of the future? And if so, are the visions set in stone or have you seen people actually alter the events foretold in the visions?" I'm skating on thin ice with such a specific question, but I see no other way to get answers.

He raises a brow. "From what I have learned, the clairvoyant is actually seeing what will happen, not what might happen. I've been told that seeing the future is much like seeing the past; it's unchangeable." He smiles and looks around the room. "Next question?"

My heart races and I clench my hands together in my lap. *Unchangeable*. I take a shaky breath, trying not to attract attention. Focus.

Mr. Huber raises his hand. "So you are trying to start a North American branch of the Society for Psychical Research?"

Dr. Bennett's face wrinkles into a deep frown. "That was my mission when I first arrived in the States, but I have to be honest and tell you that the Society for Psychical Research and I have had, how shall I say it, a parting of the ways? Yes, that is a good way to put it."

His voice is leading and an older woman in a feather boa asks, "May I ask what happened?"

Dr. Bennett heaves a sigh. "I do not wish to malign an organization I used to have so much respect for. I had issues with their methodologies and I reverently believe that all humans should be treated as equals. Unfortunately, I feel that the scientists in the Society for Psychical Research lost sight of that and treated their valuable subjects no better than mice in a laboratory. But enough of that. Suffice it to say that I plan on forming my own organization, where science is valued, but not more than the people it serves."

He stands as he delivers that last line and one nice lady claps. Oh, he is a showman.

"Now, let's get right down to the tests, shall we? Though some of them may seem strange, rest assured they are all very scientific. Think of it! Some of you may have actual psychical abilities!"

I wipe my hands on my dress nervously. Will he really be able to tell? I suddenly don't want him to know. Not yet. So far he hasn't given me any reason to trust him.

He runs us through a series of quizzes that include guessing the picture on a number of cards with symbols on them, and though the answers float into my mind, I give him the wrong response every time. I've never been able to read people's thoughts before and wonder if this is more of Cole's effect on my abilities or if I've always been able to do things like this and just never tried it.

After he finishes, he announces that he wishes to interview everyone privately. "I have a sign-up sheet I would like you all to fill out. Please put your name and address on the sheet and I can send you more information on meetings and such. There are also cookies and coffee. Chat amongst yourselves while I talk to each of you. Miss Van Housen?" He nods his head toward a couple of chairs set up in the corner of the room.

We have a seat, but before we get started, Mr. Huber

walks over. "I'm sorry to interrupt, but I can't seem to find a pen."

"Oh, I'm sorry." Dr. Bennett takes one out of his vest pocket and hands it to him.

The pen has a fancy engraved silver barrel and jet black top. Mr. Huber looks at it and frowns. "Where did you find this? Mr. Parker lost one the other day that's similar to this one."

Dr. Bennett smiles easily. "I actually bought that at Harrods before I left London. It's a beauty, isn't it?"

Mr. Huber nods his assent and walks back to the desk where the others are eating cookies and talking.

Dr. Bennett's dishonesty hits me in the chest like a brick. "You're lying," I blurt out, then cover my mouth with my hand.

Dr. Bennett narrows his eyes and sits back in his chair. "And you know that how?"

I swallow, my mind scrambling. "I'm sorry, I don't, of course."

"Oh, I think you do, Miss Van Housen. Don't try to cover it up. You are a very gifted young woman."

I stiffen in my chair, but inside I'm trembling.

He knows.

I don't trust him at all, and yet part of me desperately wants to. Wants to be able to just spill everything out to someone who obviously knows a lot more about extrasensory perception than I do. But unlike my mother, I am not a risk taker and it's far too soon to put my trust in a man who is clearly a scientific con man.

He waits for me to answer, his face practically bursting with suppressed excitement.

No. I do not trust him yet. I try to look confused. "I have no idea what you mean. Are you talking about my magic show?"

He laughs. "Actually, no. I'm talking about your psychical abilities. You're the only person I've ever tested who got every single answer wrong. The laws of chance alone are against that happening. So you see, your slipup over the pen didn't give you away, my dear. I already knew. My question is, Why are you hiding it?"

I curse my own stupidity and am completely at a loss as to what to do or say that won't give me away further. I finally shake my head. "I think this interview is over for now, Dr. Bennett, but I am very interested in your research and organization."

He stands as well. "Very well, Miss Van Housen, I understand your position. You're not the first person who has wanted to hide their abilities. I will keep you informed. I do hope you will at some point be able to trust me. There are further tests I would like to do, and I believe I can help you immensely."

His gray eyes are clear and completely candid, but they don't mesh with the mixed messages I feel coming off him.

"Are you ready to go?" I ask Cynthia when she's finished her interview. I want to get out of here and mull over what I've learned.

His eyes track me as I leave, and I have a hunch that Dr. Bennett will be getting in touch with me very soon.

SEVENTEEN

Several days later, I'm surprised to find Mother up and dressed after my morning's shopping is done. She's been on her best behavior the past few days—our shows have gone off seamlessly and she's made no more references to our last séance. It makes me wonder what she's up to.

So far, I've managed to avoid Cole, but perhaps he's been avoiding me, too. Truthfully, I'm a bit miffed he hasn't sought me out to see how I've been. Maybe he's waiting for me to come to him. I probably will eventually, but I'm in no hurry.

I haven't had the vision again and I am praying it was just some sort of strange anomaly, but Dr. Bennett's words keep going around and around in my brain. What if he's right? What if I can't stop it?

"Where have you been, darling?"

I shake my basket at her. "Shopping."

"All you ever shop for is food. I want to go buy you some new clothes. You have nothing to wear tomorrow night."

My mind blanks. "Tomorrow night? I thought I'd just wear what I always wear for the show."

"No, I meant with Owen, afterward. You want to look smart, don't you?"

I let out a breath. "Oh. I forgot." What's wrong with me? Here I am a mere day before going out dancing with a handsome young man and I've completely forgotten about it. Sometimes I despair of ever being normal.

She throws up her hands in mock hopelessness. "What am I going to do with you? Come on. I'll call Jacques and he can send a car over for us. Let's go to Bonwit Teller and find something."

I shake my head. "No, I have plenty of clothes. Or I can borrow something of yours."

"But don't you want something new?"

"Mother, I don't need it. And what's more, we can't afford it."

She sits at the table, her mouth pursed with disappointment. "Sometimes it's hard for me to believe you're my daughter."

"That makes two of us," I say dryly.

"Now, none of your sass. And what do you mean, we can't afford it? We're making good money, aren't we? The apartment is practically rent free and electricity is cheap. I don't know why you're so worried all the time."

Because someone needs to be, I think. "We're almost the same size, and you have lots of clothes. I might as well take advantage of it. Come on; let's go see what you have."

The thought of looking through her clothes mollifies

Mother and I spend the next hour choosing what I'll wear. We decide on a short-sleeved beige shift with silver beads dressing up the front. It has a daring handkerchief hemline and I'll wear it with a long silk scarf tied about my neck. It's fussier than I want and half as fussy as my mother would prefer.

After picking out my clothes, a knock on the door sounds and I answer, hoping it's not Jacques again. He's taken to coming over almost every day now.

To my surprise it's Cole, holding a huge bouquet of flowers. Two blotches of color stain his cheeks and he looks so uncomfortable and boyish, I immediately forgive him.

Wordlessly, he holds out the flowers. It's a mix of lilies, roses, daisies, and orchids.

"For me?" I ask, thrilled to my very toes.

He nods. "I didn't know which flowers were your favorites so I had her put several different types in. I hope you like them."

"They're beautiful," I say, burying my face in the flowers and breathing in their sweet fragrance.

"I just wanted to apologize . . ." He clears his throat and looks over my shoulder.

I get his meaning and step out into the hall, quietly shutting the door behind me. I look up into his handsome face. His dark eyes are pensive, as if he's unsure of what his reception will be. I get the strongest urge to touch his cheek and reassure him. I resist. I want to hear what he has to say.

He tries again, his voice stiff. "I just wanted to apologize for making such a mess out of our talk the other day. I was going to wait until I knew exactly how much I could tell you, but I had an urgent sense that you needed to know right away."

He pauses and the vision of my mother pops into my head. He has no idea just how urgent it is.

He continues, "If it were up to me, I would tell you everything, but there is a lot more at stake here than just you and me, and they're not really my secrets to tell freely."

His jaw is working and his uncertainty and self-doubt transmit themselves to me as if he'd whispered them in my ear. I stare transfixed by the apprehension in his dark eyes. My heart swells with such an aching tenderness for him that I impulsively stand on my tiptoes and brush his cheek with my lips. "I understand," I tell him softly. I'm not sure which one of us is more surprised, but I can tell he's pleased by the smile in his eyes.

"Thank you," he says simply.

We stare at each other for a moment before I clear my throat. "I should get these into water. Do you want to come in?"

He looks at the door, his cheeks still faintly flushed. "No, I actually have an appointment, but maybe later?"

"Sure," I tell him, opening the door to my apartment as he moves toward the stairs. "Later. And Cole?" He turns. "I need to talk to you about something that's been happening with my . . ." I hesitate, knowing Mother is somewhere in the flat. I need to tell him about the visions. Maybe he can at least give me some insight into those. "My abilities," I whisper.

He gives me a nod and heads down the stairs while I go into the apartment with my flowers, practically dancing.

When I awake the next morning, I receive a note from Dr. Bennett asking if I can meet with him at a little café a few blocks from my home. With the memory of my last vision still pirouetting in my head, I agree, but as I watch the minutes tick away on the big clock over the lunch counter, I'm starting to second-guess myself. The lunch crowd has descended upon the café and the noise is giving me a headache. Or maybe it's my nerves.

The waitress refills my cup. Her black and white uniform hangs limp, as if she's at the end of a long shift, and there are stains on her white apron. "Are you sure you don't want to see a menu?" she asks.

I shake my head. "I'm still waiting for someone."

She gives me a weary smile and I almost smell the anxiety coming off her in exhausted waves. She must have trouble at home, I think miserably. This has to stop. Maybe it's time to be honest with Dr. Bennett. He said he could help me, and I'm tired of having to deal with everything alone. And in spite of the flowers, I'm not sure I can count on Cole.

As if I'd conjured him, Dr. Bennett comes through the doorway, at his charming, English-squire best, wearing a dapper houndstooth suit and gray overcoat. Though he's late, he takes his time, smiling and chatting with the waitresses and nodding to the other diners. He beams when he sees me and saunters back to the corner table I'd chosen for its privacy.

"Good afternoon, Miss Van Housen. Thank you for meeting with me on such short notice. I trust you had a good morning." He removes his bowler and takes a seat in the chair across from me.

"Very good," I tell him stiffly. I can't seem to help it. One moment, I'm telling myself to accept his offer of help and the next I'm in full-blown retreat. I try again. "I hope yours was, as well?"

"It was interesting. Very interesting."

I'm about to ask him what made it so very interesting when the waitress returns with a bit more spring in her step. Dr. Bennett orders coffee and the waitress practically simpers over his jovial manner and crisp English accent.

I'm already on edge and his theatrics annoy me. "So why did you want to meet with me, Dr. Bennett?" I ask as soon as the waitress leaves.

He smiles. "The direct approach. I would expect nothing less from a young lady of your caliber."

I frown. "And yet you refuse to give me the same courtesy."

His smile slips a bit and he inclines his head in agreement. "Very well put, Miss Van Housen. I am here because I know you're interested in my new organization and I would like you to be a part of it." He holds up his hand to stop me from speaking. "No, I'm being honest. I did a little checking on you. I know you and your mother are doing very well with your show, but I also know you can't be making a potful of money doing it. I don't want any money from you. It's your psychical talents I'm interested in."

My chest tightens, as much from the fact that he checked up on me as from his words. I look down at our table, following the grain of the wood with my finger. The itch to run is strong, but my desire for help is stronger. I have to know if he can actually do that. I raise my eyes. "Why?"

"The group I have in mind is very special. I need smart, talented people to help me get it started. My objectives are twofold: I wish to study psychical phenomena and bring their gifts to the world, and I wish to help those who are being crushed by the responsibility of those very gifts."

Uneasiness prickles down my neck and arms. Am I supposed to believe that his motivations are purely noble? There has to be a way to find out what he really wants from me. Then an idea pops into my head. Just how honest is he willing to be with me? I set both my hands on the table and lean forward. "Did you mesmerize the crowd into giving you money?"

Our eyes lock. Right now, he has no idea what kind of talent I possess, except that it's some kind of extrasensory perception. I see the struggle on his face. Should he lie and risk getting caught or settle for the truth?

He decides. "Yes."

We stop talking when the waitress brings his coffee.

Then I face him again, my heart beating in my throat. "So you're a con man?"

"I'm a scientist."

I glare. "Wrong answer."

One side of his mouth creeps up. "I'm a scientific con man," he concedes. "When a scientist needs money to further his research, he does what he can. What I can do just happens to be a little unorthodox."

"Why did you really leave the Society for Psychical Research?"

He shakes his head. "My turn. What you and your mother do . . . it's a sham, isn't it?"

I maintain eye contact, even though my first impulse is to look away. I swallow. "Wrong question," I say faintly. There's no way I'm giving him ammunition to use against me or my mother.

He nods, a smile playing around his lips. My stomach sinks. Why do I get the feeling I just showed him a chink in my armor?

"Protecting your mother, I see. Very commendable. So what kind of abilities do you have?"

I cross my arms. "You couldn't tell from your tests?"

His face stills and he leans forward. "My time is very valuable, Miss Van Housen. Don't waste it." His voice is quiet, but the meaning is clear.

I lean away in spite of myself and he relaxes, knowing he made his point. I understand. He will give me nothing else until I give him something. "I can talk to spirits."

His eyes narrow. "A claim made by many. How do I know you're telling the truth?"

"How do I know *you're* telling the truth?" I counter. Then I take a deep breath. "Everything is a risk. The trick is to figure out whether that risk is worth it or not. Channeling the dead is only one of my abilities, and unfortunately, it is very, very real. What I'd like to know is what I get in return for allowing you to study me?"

He considers me for a long moment and I sense that he mistrusts me as much as I do him. Oddly, the thought comforts me. At least we both know where we stand.

"The opportunity to work with others like yourself, for one," he finally says. Then he leans across the table, his eyes gleaming. "And the power to control your own abilities."

I stare at him, scarcely breathing. If I didn't know better I'd give in right then and there, but at the core of every successful con is the appearance of giving the marks what they want. In my mother's case, she appears to give her clients a chance to talk to their deceased loved ones. Here, Dr. Bennett seems to be offering me what I most desire. Which only tells me that he is very, very good.

Before I can react, he glances at his watch. "Now, Miss Van Housen, I have a meeting I must attend. Please consider what I've said. I would love for you to be a part of my organization."

He stands, claps his bowler onto his head, and nods.

"Why shouldn't I just contact the Society for Psychical Research and work with them?" I ask quickly.

He freezes. The look he gives me is unreadable, but suspicion emanates from him like incense. "The Society for Psychical Research is very, very hard on people like you, Miss Van Housen. That is why I left. Contrary to your obvious opinion of me, I do have some scruples." He touches his finger to the brim of his hat and tossed some coins on the table. "Good day. I'll wait for you to contact me."

The moment he's gone, I slump and let out a breath. Sweat trickles down my spine. Why am I even considering collaborating with someone I don't trust? Because, in spite of everything, I have to protect my mother.

I turn onto my block and notice Jacques's car parked down the street from our flat. Wonderful. Now I'll have to spend the rest of the afternoon watching him ingratiate himself with my mother. But just then he hurries out of our building and down the street. Leaping into his car, he speeds off, not even noticing me as he passes.

The sound of my own heart thuds in my ears as panic ignites in my blood. I race down the street, tears leaking from my eyes. Something is wrong. If he hurt her . . .

I pound up the stairs and shoot through the unlocked door. The apartment is still and quiet when I burst in.

"Mama," I call as I race from room to room.

She's sitting straight up in bed. "What? What is it?"

I stop and take a deep, shuddering breath. "Nothing. I thought something had happened to you."

She frowns as her sharp eyes take in my disheveled appearance. "I was just lying down to have a rest."

I bite my lip. I want to cry with relief, but then she would want to know why I was so upset. "Did you and Jacques have an argument?"

She lies back down on her pretty ruffled pillows and pulls the quilt over her. "Of course not. I haven't seen him all day."

I still, my pulse spiking again. Then what was he doing here? Why had he run so wildly to his automobile?

My mother gives me a half smile and shuts her eyes. Not ready to leave her alone yet, I curl up with a throw blanket in the wingback chair across from her bed. I listen as her breaths grow soft and regular.

She looks younger when she's sleeping—vulnerable and more approachable. I wonder what happened to her to make her the way she was before I came along. She rarely speaks of her family, and the few things she's let slip suggest a childhood of poverty and deprivation. She ran away when she was fourteen and never looked back. Watching her sleep always makes me feel protective, though in reality, Marguerite Estella Van Housen is perfectly capable of protecting herself. Of course, when your entire existence depends on one person, her survival is pretty important. My mother has always been all I have. And now?

Now I don't know.

Not wanting to sit any longer with my thoughts, I slip out for a quick walk through Central Park, careful to lock the door behind me. The wind picks up as I walk, scattering dead leaves across my path.

My antipathy toward Dr. Bennett is rivaled only by my need for his knowledge. Will I go to him? I don't know. It would just be easier if Cole would be straightforward with me. I may not trust him one hundred percent, but I definitely like him more than I do Dr. Bennett. I smile, remembering the flowers he brought yesterday.

While I'm still upset that Cole won't give me more information about the others, I do understand. He has such high moral standards for himself that I can't see him telling me anything unless he was sure he had the right to.

My cheeks heat, wondering what he'd think if he ever found out just how few moral standards my mother and I actually have. Cheating, lying, stealing, and fraud are all in a day's work for the Van Housens. If I'm honest with myself, I'm not really worthy of his friendship.

But that doesn't mean I don't need answers. If I knew how to control my abilities, I might be able to get more information the next time I have a vision.

Like who wants to hurt my mother and why.

I wrap my muffler more tightly around my throat, thinking hard. Could it be someone we know? Mrs. Lindsay and her daughter are high on the list of possible suspects. Mrs. Lindsay doesn't seem too stable, and I know she's the one who followed me the night I got lost. Her daughter doesn't strike me as the criminal type, but you never can tell. As much as I mistrust Jacques, there's no question he's making money from our shows. I can't see him jeopardizing that. Not only is he a good businessman, he doesn't seem like the violent type. My stomach tightens as I remember how he had run from our building today. What was he doing? I dismiss Mr. Darby and Owen. Mr. Darby doesn't even really know my mother, and Owen has no reason to hurt her. Cole? My chest tightens. Yes, he has secrets. I know he does. But surely they don't have anything to do with my mother.

So I'm back to Mrs. Lindsay and her daughter.

I round a corner and have just decided to head back when I'm overcome by a dark wash of emotions so ominous I stop in my tracks. I concentrate, wishing again that I knew how to control my abilities. Sensing other people's emotions when I was touching them was bad enough, but this is much, much worse.

The feeling grows stronger and I whirl around, looking this way and that.

"Well, if it isn't the charlatan's daughter!"

I freeze as I'm faced with Mrs. Lindsay's hate-filled eyes. I try to give off a confidence I don't feel. "Hello, Mrs. Lindsay. Imagine meeting you here. I thought you lived in Cleveland."

"And I thought your mother wouldn't let you out of her sight."

Mrs. Lindsay's coat is worn and thin, and her blond hair is matted against her head. Dirt smudges one cheek, and I see more caked under her nails. She looks as if she spent the night in the park. I edge away from her, but she steps closer and the scent of alcohol churns my stomach. "I don't know what you mean. Isn't your daughter with you this afternoon?" The daughter seemed to have some control over her mother and I desperately hope she shows up. Soon.

"No, dear. It's just you and me. I used to have séances booked every night—all the best people in New York came to me, because I am the real thing. You hear me? The real thing."

I nod, my heart racing.

"But not anymore."

She draws closer and I go motionless, afraid any sudden movement will set her off.

"Now everyone is talking about your mother!" She spits out the words, her face twisted and ugly. "And your mother, she's a fraud, a trickster! A thief!"

I don't see her hand coming and the blow stings my face before I can react. She hits me hard enough that I reel backward, then looks at her hand as if she can't believe what she just did.

I take advantage of her surprise to back away. "You're off your nuts!" Tears spring to my eyes.

"No, your mother is crazy to think she can get away with this. I know people. All kinds of people."

Her eyes are wild, and as I turn and run she screams after me, "You'd better tell her to watch her step! I'm going to stop her! You tell her that! The dead won't like this one bit!"

I run until a hitch in my side forces me to stop, my ankle throbbing and my breath coming out in short gasps. She's mad, completely batty. I hurry the rest of the way to our apartment to warn Mother.

EIGHTEEN

"I'll kill her," Mother says, applying ice to my cheek. "We'll never be able to hide this."

I stare at her, my mouth open. "Is that all you're worried about?"

A frown line appears between her eyes and it strikes me that my mother is getting older. She's still lovely, but tiny lines of time are beginning to fan out from the corners of her eyes.

"Of course not. But we can't let a crazy woman frighten us." She gives a grim smile. "She doesn't know who she's messing with, does she?"

No. She doesn't.

I ponder that as we leave for the theater. My mother's memory is long and she never forgets someone who does her wrong. She once turned in a bum manager for extortion before we hightailed it out of town. Tonight she is silent, grim, and I wonder what she's thinking.

Or planning.

I press the side of my face against the chill of the window, cooling the heat that still lingers from Mrs. Lindsay's hand. We round the corner and everything in my body stills as I spot a peculiar couple across the street from the park. They're standing under the striped awning of the butcher I frequent, their faces partially obscured in shadows. But it doesn't matter; I know who they are.

Cole and Mrs. Lindsay.

As we pass by them, I instinctively duck my head, but not before I see him press something into her hand.

"What are you doing?" my mother asks next to me.

"Oh. Nothing. I dropped my vanity case." I linger a second more until I'm sure we are safely past before sitting up, my mind racing almost as fast as my pulse.

Why would Cole be speaking to Mrs. Lindsay? He was at the séance. He knew she intended to harm my mother. Hurt ricochets through my chest and my hands clench in my lap. Was Mrs. Lindsay talking about Cole when she said she knew people?

I remember the connection I felt on our walk and then again at Child's. The warmth of his finger on my lips. Him standing with a bouquet of flowers. I blink back tears. Was any of it real?

By the time we go onstage, I've shaken off most of my turmoil and go through the performance by rote, smiling when I need to smile and hitting all my cues with practiced ease. Nothing must harm the show. The house is always packed now and our reputation is growing. By the time my mother and I return to the dressing room, I've resolved to put Cole and Mrs. Lindsay out of my mind and have a wonderful evening out with Owen. Sweet, uncomplicated, handsome Owen.

My hair is already crimped and looks cute with the pale beige cloche I'm wearing. As I change into my dress, my mother has an unusual attack of maternal instincts.

"Now, I don't want you to be out all hours of the night. And I want to talk to Owen before you go anywhere."

"Yes, Mother."

I put some stained balm on my lips and look at myself in the mirror. The bruise is barely visible under the pancake makeup. I look good. Not as beautiful, perhaps, as my mother, but certainly pretty enough. I have her dark hair and our nose is the same, short and slim. But as I look at myself I begin to wonder if the other parts of me, the parts that look nothing like my mother, are from my father. My complexion is rosier than my mother's, my jawline firmer, and my eyes are blue. Am I really Harry Houdini's daughter?

A knock sounds on the door and my mother answers it. Jacques and Owen come in, both looking dapper in their fine suits. I watch Jacques suspiciously from under my lashes. After my run-in with Mrs. Lindsay, I'd almost forgotten him rushing out of our building. What was he doing there if it wasn't to see my mother? My heart stops. Could he have been there to see Cole? But why?

Owen does a dramatic double take when he sees me.

"Someone looks absolutely gorgeous tonight," he says, interrupting my thoughts.

In spite of everything, I'm looking forward to going out. With Owen, I don't think about my abilities, or worry whether he is going to find out that my mother and I are frauds. In fact, I don't worry about anything when I'm with Owen—I just enjoy myself.

I roll my eyes at him and he grins.

"Make that two someones," Jacques says, his voice full of admiration. I glare at him, but he's too busy looking at my mother to notice.

My mother, used to such male admiration, comports herself much better than I. She tilts her head and looks up at him through long, painted eyelashes. "Now Jacques, I bet you say that to all your clients."

"Not all, darling. I'm sure Clyde and his talking horse wouldn't appreciate it much."

"The horse might," Owen quips, and everyone laughs. "I'd love to stick around yukking it up all evening, but Anna and I should go. We're meeting friends."

"Where are you going?" my mother asks as I search for the fake fur stole she's lent me.

"A place called the Cotton Club," Owen says.

My mother hands me the stole. "Darling, may I have a few minutes alone with Owen?"

My eyes narrow and she looks back at me, all wide-eyed innocence. Sighing, I give in. "I'll wait for you in the lobby," I tell Owen.

I hurry down the hall on my Cuban heels, sidestepping

two janitors who are already cleaning. I hope Owen doesn't regret asking me out.

I round a corner and stop short when I spot Cole leaning against the wall.

"Anna."

My heart hurts just to look at him. "Hello, Cole."

"You said we could get together later. It's later." He grins and his face lights up.

Why do I suddenly feel like crying? Then I remember him talking to Mrs. Lindsay and check my emotions. "It's Friday. You knew I was going out on Friday."

"There you are," Owen's voice comes from behind me. "I thought you'd gotten lost."

Cole's eyes sweep past me, his expression still.

Owen nods at Cole. "Hello, old boy. What are you doing here? Are you ready to go cut a rug?"

Cole ignores Owen and gives me a slight bow with his head and moves out of the way. "Please don't let me keep you."

"Oh, we won't," Owen says cheerfully, taking my elbow and guiding me firmly down the hall.

"Perhaps tomorrow?" I glance back over my shoulder, vacillating between anger and regret, but Cole's not looking at me.

He's staring at Owen, his eyes dark with hostility.

My fingers fumble as I fasten the fur stole around my shoulders. Leaving Cole in the hallway feels wrong, but I don't know what he expected, showing up unannounced, not to mention hobnobbing with someone who is clearly out to get me.

Owen claps a black felt fedora on his head and shrugs into his wool overcoat. He looks spiffy in his tight double-breasted jacket and baggy trousers. I wonder what Cole would wear dancing—or if he even goes dancing.

"Your mother is something else." Owen laughs, opening the door for me.

"What did she say?" I ask, once out of the theater.

He shakes his head. "She told me I was to show you the best time of your life but that you had a show tomorrow so I'd better bring you back in one piece."

He holds the door open for me and I get in the car. It's so cold I can see my breath by the light of the streetlamp. Owen trots around the front of the car and jumps in. "Are you ready for a good time, doll?"

I smile. "Only if you stop calling me doll. I am not, nor have I ever been, a doll."

"Would cupcake work better?" He grins to show he's teasing.

"How about just Anna?"

"Of course. So are you ready to have the time of your life, Just Anna?"

I laugh, a weight lifting off my chest. Maybe Owen's got the right idea. Why should life be serious all the time?

The minute we walk into the Cotton Club, I realize that Owen is right about something else, too—this is definitely the place to have a good time. The air is thick and smoky, the music brassy and insistent. Owen leads me around the perimeter of a horseshoe-shaped room, past throngs of tables and clusters of fake palm trees. My head swivels right and left as I take in the women in their brightly colored dresses, wraps, and headgear. Some of the hats are truly marvelous, concoctions of feathers and beads so bright it almost hurts to look at them.

Owen takes me to a long table where six or seven other people are already crowded in. The boys greet him effusively, while several of the girls cast me curious, if not exactly friendly, glances.

"This is Anna, the girl I was telling you about," Owen shouts as we squeeze into a couple of empty chairs that have materialized out of nowhere. "Anna, this is everyone."

I give a quick smile. A drink appears in front of me as if by magic and one of the women offers me a cigarette. I take it, though I don't usually smoke. But I feel silly not doing it when everyone else at the table is.

The girl next to me gives me a light and I suck on the end, choking as the harsh smoke hits my lungs. I take a sip of the drink in front of me and choke again as the liquid burns its way to my stomach.

One of the girls next to me laughs. "The hooch they serve here takes some getting used to." She holds out her hand. "My name's Addy. That there is Prissy, Ella, and Maryann."

I shake her hand and wave at the others, dazzling in their glittering dresses and tight, fitted hats. All have bobs like mine with curls pasted in front of their ears.

"It's hard to believe that Prohibition exists here," I yell above the music.

"That's the whole point!" Prissy says. "It doesn't exist here." The others laugh as if this was the funniest thing they've ever heard.

"How can they get away with this? Why don't the cops shut them down?"

The girls laugh even harder.

"See that fat man over there?" Addy points.

I follow her finger until I spot a chubby man next to an equally chubby woman wearing a headband with a cluster of black feathers sticking out of it. They're sitting with a dark-haired man and a stunning little blonde in a beaded black net evening gown. I nod.

"That there is the chief of police and his wife. He's sitting next to Nico 'the Knife' Guilianni, a big man in the Morello mob. No one hits the Cotton Club."

My eyes widen and Addy laughs again. "You *are* wet behind the ears! Don't worry, little girl, there won't be any raids here tonight."

I shift, embarrassed to be caught out. Now everyone knows that I'm new at all this. I take another careful sip of my drink. It goes down easier this time, which may or may not be a good thing.

Suddenly, Owen stiffens beside me.

"What's she doing here?" I hear him mutter. He turns to me. "I'll be right back."

He scoots out of his chair and disappears, leaving me with a bunch of strangers.

I see Prissy and Addy exchange looks again.

"What?" Maryann cranes her neck. "What did I miss?"

"Lorraine," I see Addy mouth to her.

Maryann's eyes widen. "Oh!"

"And is she ever casting a kitten!"

The girls crane their necks trying to see what's happening, but my view is blocked. Then a tall man steps aside and I see Owen arguing with a blond woman. Her back is to me, so I can't see her face, but Owen's is furious. He grips her arm and gestures wildly. Suddenly the woman pulls out of his grip and stalks out the doorway. Owen straightens his tie and turns back toward the table. I avert my gaze so he won't know I've been watching.

My face heats and I feel more out of place than ever. He sits next to me and drinks deeply from his drink. "Is everything okay?" I ask, pretending to watch the dancers.

"Sure. My old girlfriend showed up to cause a scene. I gave her the gate a few weeks ago." He drapes his arm over my shoulder. "Right after I met you, actually."

His dimples deepen as he smiles down at me, and I feel better until I catch the other girls exchanging yet another volley of glances. Is this what normal girls do? Go to speakeasies and make other people feel bad? I've had enough. I stand up and take his hand. "Didn't we come to dance?" I ask.

He looks surprised for a moment, then laughs. "That's my girl!"

He leads me out onto the crowded dance floor and we begin to move. I'm unsure of myself at first, but the music is snazzy, toe-tapping good, and I'm soon shimmying with the rest of them. The room is almost unbearably hot, but the blind determination to have a good time is contagious. Owen's a good dancer and keeps grinning at me as if he's happy to find that I'm still his partner.

The tempo slows and I turn to step off the dance floor, but Owen catches my hand and swings me back into his arms with a wink.

"Not so fast, Just Anna. I've been waiting for this number all night."

He pulls me close, lifting my right hand in a basic waltz position.

"This is slow foxtrot music, but there's no room on the floor to trot, so we just call it The Slow," he says, his breath whispering across my ear.

I tilt my head back to get a better look at his face. His bright blue eyes, usually so teasing, are warm with admiration.

"You have no idea how beautiful you are, do you?"

I lower my eyes, both flustered and pleased. The heat from his palm, resting lightly on my back, spreads through my body. As usual, the emotions coming off him are all mixed up, but this time the strongest emotion is joy. Happiness is radiating off him like heat from a woodstove, and I move closer to bask in the magic of it all. I sneak a glance back at his face and my breath catches, he's so handsome. I close my eyes and we sway to the music, as the melody curls around us like silken ribbons.

His arm tightens and his cheek presses against mine. "I wish I could dance like this with you forever and let the rest of the world go hang."

My heart swells. At this moment, with the lights glittering like diamonds and his arms wrapped tightly around me, I almost wish the same thing. An image of Cole holding a bouquet of flowers at my door flashes before me and my cheeks flush. What kind of girl am I to have feelings like this for two different men? Besides, I'm still angry with Cole.

The music ends and I make a motion to stop, but before we leave the dance floor, Owen raises my hand to his mouth. "Thank you for the dance," he murmurs. His blue eyes twinkle at me as he brushes his lips across my knuckles.

I swallow, my mouth so dry I can't respond. So I give him a weak smile and he leads me back to our table.

I gulp down my drink, forgetting about the burn, and end up sputtering half of it onto the table. They should use my mother's supplier. I lean toward Owen, still coughing. "What I could really use is a glass of ice water."

"Anything for Just Anna!" He spreads his arm expansively and goes off in search of something cool to drink. The table is empty—everyone must be on the dance floor—and I amuse myself watching as people stagger about, laughing too loud. It looks as if half of New York is going to have hangovers tomorrow. The band takes a break and the rest of the gang comes trooping back. The men, dripping with sweat, are discarding their jackets. The girls fan themselves with their hands. Owen returns, a young black man in tow. "This round is on me," he announces grandly.

"That's the last of the ice, so enjoy," the waiter says, setting the drinks down in front of us.

The waiter leaves and I take a long, grateful drink of the water. Maryann fishes a sliver of ice out of her cocktail and holds it to her forehead.

"It's hotter than Hades in here. Why don't we head over to Connie's Inn? At least we'll cool off on the way down there."

Addy shakes her head petulantly. "Nah, let's go to Paradise Alley."

"We could stay here and watch the show," one of the men suggests. "Next one starts in an hour."

Owen cuts in. "You all do what you want to. We need to get a wiggle on. I promised Anna's mother I wouldn't have her out too late."

Everyone looks at me and I feel about two feet tall with a bib around my neck. Owen catches the look and adds, "No, it's not like that. She has a performance tomorrow night."

Suddenly their faces change from derision to something akin to respect.

"Oh, that's right. Owen told us you were a magician. How on earth did you get into that?" Prissy wants to know.

"My mother is a medium. It kind of runs in the family."

Owen snorts. "I'll say. Her father is Harry Houdini," he adds.

My stomach drops.

"But hasn't Houdini been married forever? He doesn't have kids, does he?" One of the men looks confused.

My face gets itchy and hot. "He and my mother knew each other in Europe, a long time ago," I explain, waving my hand as if that will make it go away.

The truth of the situation dawns on everyone about the same time. "Oh! So you're like his illegitimate daughter? And you're a magician, too? How fantastically odd!" Maryann says.

"How romantic," Addy breathes, linking her arm in mine. "Are you sure you can't go with us?"

They look at me with more warmth and interest than they have all evening.

I could *kill* Owen.

I shake my head. "I'm sorry, I really can't."

The men all pull out their wallets and throw bills on the table. Owen looks through his billfold, frowning.

"What's wrong?" I ask.

"I thought I had another ten in here. That's why I bought the last round."

He checks his pockets, becoming more frantic.

Everyone else gathers their things, oblivious to Owen's discomfort. I reach for my purse. "I think I have some money."

"God, I'm so sorry," he whispers as he takes the money I hand him. Twin roses of embarrassment mottle his cheeks as he flags down our waiter.

"Four-flusher." Addie rolls her eyes.

I want to ask what that means, but Owen seems in a hurry to go.

We take our leave then, and the crowd piles into one car while Owen and I walk down the block to ours.

"Did you have fun?" Owen asks a little anxiously.

I pull my stole closer against the biting cold. "Yes." The whole evening has taken on a sense of unreality, as if someone else lived it. The conversation about Houdini cast a shadow over my whole night. Why did Owen have to ruin it by telling everyone?

Owen's arm snakes around me and I smile in the dark, remembering the magical moment when he'd held me close. The evening wasn't a total loss. Some parts were wonderful.

"I'm glad you had a good time. Nights like this are one of the reasons I left stuffy old Boston."

"You were raised there, weren't you?"

He snorts. "Unfortunately, I was."

"Why unfortunately?" I realize how little I know about him.

He's silent and for a moment I think he's not going to answer. When he does, it's in a voice different from his normal happy-go-lucky tone. "My father comes from an old Boston family. You know, the kind that makes tons of money but never talks about it?"

He looks at me and I nod. I do indeed know. One of the reasons we never hit Boston. Too tightfisted and suspicious.

Owen continues. "They disinherited him when he married my mother. They think of her as some sneaky French dance-hall girl who tricked him into marriage. I think my father believes it, too. At least that's how he treats me."

I catch his sideways glance and understanding dawns. "Ah."

"Oh, they paid my way into all the good schools. It was unthinkable that a Winchester should go to public school. But my father, and all my many cousins, went out of their way to make sure I knew I was a second-class citizen."

I shiver at the bitterness of his words and he's instantly contrite. "I'm sorry. I shouldn't ruin our wonderful night by telling you my troubles. Besides, none of that matters. Someday I'll return triumphant as a rich man."

His arm tightens around my shoulders. "I really do wish tonight could last forever."

My heart constricts in sympathy at the wistfulness of his voice. I know how it feels to be unsure of a parent's love. I turn to him and he wraps both arms around my waist. The light from the streetlamp encircles us. Mrs. Lindsay, Houdini, my mother, and my vision all fade away in the warmth of his gaze.

For a moment, I know exactly what it's like to be a normal girl enjoying the company of a normal man. "I really had a wonderful evening. Thank you so much for everything."

He tilts my face up with his finger. *He's going to kiss me*, I think. But all he says is "You're a wonderful girl, Anna. The pleasure was all mine."

We resume walking, and I don't need my abilities to tell me that he is as happy as I am.

Then a shiver of apprehension races up my spine and I stumble.

Owen laughs and grips my arm. "Too much to drink? I didn't think you'd had that much."

I don't answer him. Instead I pause, my whole body frozen in concentration. Sweat breaks out on my upper lip and I start trembling.

Something is horrifyingly wrong.

NINETEEN

My trembling increases, and Owen puts his hands on my shoulders. "Anna, are you all right?"

Suddenly a milk truck squeals around the corner and races toward us. Before we can react, it screeches to a halt and a man leaps out and punches Owen in the face. Owen falls to the sidewalk in a deflated heap and the man kicks him in the ribs. I scream and back up against a brick wall. The back doors of the milk truck swing open and another man jumps out. He grabs me by my arms and yanks me toward the vehicle. Realizing his intent, I throw myself to the ground. Surprised, he lets go and I scramble backward, looking for a weapon. Any weapon. Not seeing anything, I straighten, ready to run for help if I can, but the man who punched Owen reacts faster than I do and seizes me from behind. He picks me up and tosses me like a bag of potatoes into the back of the milk truck. My head smashes into the side of the door. Stars explode before my eyes, and blood trickles down my face, warm and salty. Desperately, I try wiping it away, but I'm slammed against the floor of the truck.

"Go! Go! Go!" someone screams.

"Anna!" I hear Owen yell, his voice fading as the vehicle careens sideways.

Something dark and suffocating is yanked down over my head and I begin to fight in earnest. I shove my elbow backward and hear an *oof* as it connects with something soft and squishy. Someone grabs me by the hair and slams my head against the wooden floor.

"Tie her up!" a female voice snaps.

The man forces my arms behind me as I struggle to place the woman's voice. The ropes bite into my wrists, but I cease struggling. Rope I can handle. The man, satisfied that I'm properly bound, crawls away from me. I pretend to swoon, which isn't much of a pretense as the dank, smelly hood over my head doesn't allow enough air to get through. I remember how Houdini once said that he concentrates on slowing down his breath and heartbeat when he's doing his escapes. Easier said than done when panic has your pulse racing.

"Did we kill her?" someone asks.

"Nah. Just stunned her."

The woman whispers something and I strain to hear her voice again, but it's too low. Perhaps she's afraid I'll recognize it?

I'm not sure how long we drive. Time slips away as I vacillate between heart-pounding terror and an eerie calm.

I keep my eyes squeezed shut even though my captors can't see me with the hood on. Finally, after an eternity, the milk truck stops.

"What should we do with her?"

"We can't move her right now. People are still out. Someone will see for sure."

"I'd like to just dump her in the river," the woman snarls. My blood freezes. Again, I recognize the voice but can't quite place it. Could it be the Lindsay daughter? I've only heard her voice that one time, so I can't be sure.

"Remember who you're working for. She's just bait."

"Yeah, crab bait."

"Not a hair on her head can be hurt," the man warns.

They've hurt a hell of a lot more than my hair, but I remain silent.

There's movement in the front of the truck and then the sound of doors opening and closing. I make myself count to one hundred before my fingers slowly begin to work on the bindings that hold me. My fingers are numb from shock and cold, and it takes me far longer than it should to undo the rope. Once my hands are free, I reach up and slip off the hood.

I let my eyes adjust to the darkness but can only make out dim outlines.

Quickly now, fearing they'll be back for me, I reach down and undo the ropes around my legs. Inching my way over to a window, I peer out, afraid someone will see me and knock me senseless again.

The milk truck is parked in an alley and there's nothing but brick walls on either side. My first instinct is to throw open the door and make a run for it, but I hold myself back and consider my options. If they catch me now, I won't get another chance. I wonder briefly if Owen has called the police, but they would have no way of finding me.

I see no movement outside and the windows looking out into the alley are dark and still. Slowly, every muscle in my body protesting, I search the back of the milk truck for my purse. At least then I'd have a weapon. But I find nothing. Either they've taken it or I dropped it when they first grabbed me.

I crawl to the front to open the door. Surely they'll be watching the back? I inch the door open, my nerves screaming as the hinge squeaks. When nothing happens, I open it farther, just wide enough to slip through. My head throbs with every heartbeat and I lean against the truck for a moment, fighting off nausea. Then I crouch, moving along the side until I reach the front. Drawing in a deep, ragged breath, I wait for the longest second in history. If they're going to see me, it'll be now. Then in a flash I take off for the street ahead.

Fear clutches my throat as I strain to hear the sound of pursuit behind me. Nothing. I round the corner and keep running, trying to find a place with enough people that I can get lost in the crowd.

My heel swivels on an uneven patch of concrete, twisting my ankle beneath me. I don't slow. One block, then two.

Metal buildings loom on either side, but the few stores are closed. I press on. Shadows assail me from all sides, dark and terrifying. I pant, fighting for air, wondering how long I can run. Coming to a corner, I finally slow down, my heart drumming in my ears.

I double up, gasping. Blazing pain sears my chest with each breath of air I take in. When I finally straighten up, I squint at the street sign, but the words blur into dancing blobs. I reach up to wipe my eyes and my hand comes away with a combination of blood and tears.

I take stock. I'm hurt, lost, and possibly being hunted like an animal at this very moment. Nope, it doesn't get much worse than this. I draw in a deep breath and wipe my face on my scarf. After looking at the street sign, I hurry west, keeping my eye out for a store where I can call my mother. Every time an auto passes I cringe, waiting for the shout that means I've been found.

I finally spot an all-night grocer on the corner. I dart across the street and into the brightly lit store.

The woman inside takes one look at me and screams. I must be worse off than I thought.

The clerk hurries over to me. "What happened? What happened?" he asks with a thick German accent.

"Do you have a telephone?"

He frowns for a moment and then nods. "Yes, yes."

"May I use it?"

The woman, recovered from her fright, clucks over me. "Poor *Liebchen*. Come sit first."

I'm more than happy to move away from the windows toward the back of the store. The woman sits me in a chair next to an old-fashioned potbellied stove and wraps a scratchy wool blanket around my shoulders. I shiver. My stole must have come off in the milk truck or during my run.

A mug of hot coffee is placed in my hand and I sip gratefully. I hear the clerk yelling into the phone but can't make out what he's saying.

The woman keeps patting my head and murmuring words in German. Shelves of cans with names I can't read are stacked around me and bins of vegetables give off a sharp, pungent odor.

The clerk comes back and gives me a look so sympathetic, a lump rises in my throat. "I have called the law. They are on their way."

I start to shake and he puts more coal in the stove. Policemen. Of course they'd call the police. Most people like the police.

The woman reappears with a bowl of steaming water and a clean cloth. She wipes my face, clucking in sympathy. I wince but say nothing. What can I tell them? That I was taken by unknown people for reasons equally unknown?

My heart thumps as I remember my vision. I picture myself being trapped underwater, knowing Mother was in danger. What if they go after her now? Who were my captors and what did they want? And why was the woman's voice so familiar?

An image of Mrs. Lindsay's contorted face comes to

mind. She's crazy, but crazy enough to try to kidnap me? For what purpose?

A little bell in the front of the store rings and I nearly leap out of my chair. The woman lays a comforting hand on my shoulder. "Is okay now. The police have come."

I'm not comforted.

Questions and more questions. First from the police officers, then from the doctor, and then from my mother, Jacques, and Owen, who were all waiting for me at the hospital when the police took me there, just as the sun was coming up.

Now, after hours of sitting and waiting, I'm finally home. I've left them all in the front room and gone directly to the washroom.

Nothing is more important right now than this bath. Steam rises around me like a reassuring shroud, keeping me safe from the outside world. The hot water soothes the aching in my legs and back. I squeeze the sponge over my head, allowing the water to trickle down my face and neck. Even the stinging as it runs over my scrapes feels good, like it's eating away all the bad.

I sink into the water up to my neck.

I draw in a deep breath, until my lungs are almost bursting, then gulp down just a little more. Then I slip my head underwater and begin counting. Houdini can hold his breath for more than four minutes. I'm up to just under three. Usually, I blank out my thoughts while I count, but today that's almost impossible. A sudden image from my nightmare pops into my head. Me, trapped underwater, knowing that my mother's safety depends on my ability to get free.

I bolt straight up, water sloshing violently over the edge of the tub. I remind myself that it's not real, but my bath is ruined. Gingerly, I get out and pull the plug, watching the water swirl down the drain.

After toweling off and climbing into my cotton nightgown, I pad down the hall to my bedroom and slip into bed, reveling in the feel of fresh linens against my skin.

Moments later, my mother appears in the doorway, a steaming mug in her hand. Dark circles ring her eyes, and I realize that she must be as exhausted as I am.

She hands me the cup. "I figured you might need this. Owen and Jacques left a bit ago."

She picks up my silver-plated brush from off the desk.

"Here, let me brush out your hair while you drink."

Her voice is gentle and I relax, leaning my head back. I raise the mug to my lips and sigh as the creamy taste of warm milk, nutmeg, and rum hits my tongue.

"Are you sure you don't know who it was?" my mother asks, her tone velvet over steel.

I struggle to remember the woman's voice, but everything is fuzzy, and a tremor ripples down my back. "No. And I don't want to talk about it."

"Of course."

I take another sip of my drink, the alcohol and exhaustion making the world soft and downy at the corners.

"What would you like to talk about?" she asks.

I lean my head into the rhythmic feel of the brush against my scalp. Warmth radiates through my chest. Tired. I'm so tired. I remember something. "Mama, what's a four-flusher?"

I turn my head to look at her as she answers. The corners of her lips turn down in disapproval. "Someone who acts like they have a lot of money but mooches off other people. Why?"

I frown, trying to think.

Another thought floats through my head. "Why don't you tell me about how you met my father?"

The brush falters for a moment before resuming. "You've already heard that one."

"Tell me again," I demand like a child.

She keeps brushing. "I was working as a magician's assistant. Houdini came backstage after one of the magician's shows. I didn't pay him much attention at the time."

She stops brushing and takes the mug out of my heavy hands. I lay back against the pillows, my body too tired to stay upright.

"Then what?" I prompt.

She smoothes my hair away from my face. Nice. She's being so nice. "Then I looked into his beautiful brown eyes and fell in love," she says simply. "Now sleep, my girl, sleep, *édesem*."

I frown, struggling for a moment against the slumber descending over me like warm, dark fur. Something is wrong. It comes to me just before everything goes black.

Houdini's eyes are blue.

TWENTY

I awaken, groggy and disoriented. My shade is closed, but the light filtering through is the artificial yellow of the streetlight. I must have slept all day. The show! I bolt straight up, every muscle in my body protesting.

"Mother?" I call, but even before I do, I know the apartment is empty. I snatch up my wrap and struggle to get my arms into it as I dart from room to room.

Pain shoots up my foot as I smack it on the doorjamb on my way into the kitchen. "Blast it!" I pull my foot up and, standing on one leg, stare at a small flap of skin hanging from the tip of my big toe. Blood oozes from it and I hop over to the counter to grab the dish towel. As if I weren't hurting enough already.

Then I notice a note propped up against the teapot.

Went to do the show. Will bring back food.

I frown, the pain making me slow and stupid. How can she do the show without me? "Blast it," I repeat. Hopping over to the icebox, I chip out a sliver of ice, then limp over to the table.

I rub the ice across the tip of my toe, remembering how sweet my mother had been to me just that morning. She'd tucked me in, for God's sake, something she hadn't done in years. But now she's off doing the show, leaving me bruised and alone with a potential kidnapper out to get me.

The rational part of me knows she had no choice—the show must go on and all that—but still resentment gnaws at my stomach. One moment I have a real mother and the next she's been snatched away from me, as if she never existed.

I wrap the towel around my foot and tie it before hobbling over and lighting the stove. Teatime. I spot the flowers Cole brought me just the day before sitting on the counter. Something in my chest catches as I remember kissing his cheek, but then I remember him standing with Mrs. Lindsay and I'm more confused than ever.

A sudden knock at the door shoots my heart into my throat and I freeze. What if the kidnappers have come to finish the job? I slide open a drawer and snatch out a knife before silently limping down the hall. Just as I reach the door, the knock sounds again and I jump. Then I'm furious with myself for being afraid. This is my home. I'd like to see someone try to take me now that my guard is up. I grip the knife tighter in my hand, liking the solid weight of it. Just let them try.

"Anna, it's Cole. Are you all right?"

Cole? Relief courses through me at the sound of his voice, sending my pulse skipping. Suddenly, in spite of everything, I want to see him more than anyone else in the world. "Just a minute." I look around wildly for somewhere to put the knife and finally settle on sticking it behind the fake rubber plant sitting next to the door. I tie my robe more firmly in place and open the door.

Cole's standing there, rumpled and tired, looking so different from his normal tidy self that I can't help but gawk. Well, that and the fact that I'd forgotten how he fills up a doorway.

"Can I come in?"

To my complete surprise, I launch myself at him, tears forming in my throat. His arms wrap around me and I feel, rather than hear, his whole body sigh in relief.

"You're all right," he murmurs, his lips against the top of my head. I squeeze my eyes closed and nod. I don't want to think about anything right now. For the first time in a long time, I feel warm and safe. I press my face against his chest so hard that I feel the solid muscles underneath the coarseness of his wool jacket. For once, his feelings are coming through to me loud and clear: concern, worry, caring. The scent of soap and autumn cold tickle my nose and, for a minute, I allow myself just to breathe him in, wishing I could hold on to this moment forever.

But turning off thoughts is not that easy, and the moment Mrs. Lindsay pops into my head, I stiffen with doubt. As if sensing a difference, Cole slowly lets his arms fall away.

I step back, my face heating. What on earth possessed me to throw myself at him? A piercing whistle comes from the kitchen. "Would you like some tea?" I ask, not meeting his eyes.

He follows me down the hall and I wave at him to sit at the table.

"No, you rest," he says, indicating my foot. "Where are the cups?"

I show him where everything is and then sit, watching him make me tea.

I accept the cup from him and he sits across from me. His dark eyes regard me steadily, his features solemn. He's wearing his professor face.

"So," I finally say, unable to take the silence.

"So." He looks down at his cup and then back at me. "How are you really?"

"Sore. Confused." I raise an eyebrow. "Disappointed."

He nods. He knows I'm not just talking about the kidnapping. "You have every right to be."

And I know he's not just talking about the kidnapping either.

"So?" This time it's a question.

"So what would you like to know? I'll tell you what I can."

I take a sip of tea, my mind whirling. What do I want to ask first? Should I just flat out ask him about Mrs. Lindsay? Or see if he tells me? I think about the way I hurled myself od way to start out. You should rest first."

down at the table, struggling to put my thoughts
ls. "I know who snatched me." I give a quick shake
ad at the alarm on his face. "No, I mean, I was
with one of the three people involved in taking me.
I knew that Mrs. Lindsay was the person who'd
ching me."

h his face carefully. All I see is concern.

ou think Mrs. Lindsay was behind the abduction?"
elings of helplessness I'd experienced in the milk
sh over me again. Cole reaches across the table and
and over mine. The moment our fingers touch, his
ansmits itself to me loud and clear. Whatever he
g with Mrs. Lindsay, I don't think it had anything
h hurting me. At least I hope not. "I don't know.
had better control of my abilities, I might have
to figure out who it was." And finding out who
me is the first step in protecting my mother.

e stretches between us until I finally look up to
dark eyes.

an start tomorrow," he says.

roat swells and I glance away. Can he feel my emo-
t now? Can he tell how grateful I am? *How much*
Heat rises in my face. I definitely need some les-
nt to learn how to put up a wall like he does.

my hand away and regain my composure. Some-
ide me, something that has been tied in knots for
ses. "How old were you when you were trained?

into his arms and my cheeks grow hot again. How can I be
so drawn to someone I'm not even sure I trust? "You said
you came to America to find other Sensitives. Why?"

I'm half expecting a dodge, but the answer comes immediately. "I was sent to find other Sensitives to help them in
any way I can."

"Why would they need help?"

Cole hesitates and I stiffen, but he holds up a hand. "It's
hard explaining this in a way that's not offensive."

I snort. "I'm not a wilting daisy."

Cole's lips twitch upward. "Anna, you're not like anyone
I've ever met before." His eyes catch mine and for a moment
I can't breathe. Then his face settles back into serious lines.

"Many Sensitives end up in an asylum. They don't
know what's going on, and unless they somehow learn to
control their power, it drives them mad. So, to be perfectly blunt, finding someone of your age with abilities as
strong as yours is rare."

I look down at my cup, remembering how many times I
felt haunted by the emotions coming off other people, how
many times I had visions I thought would drive me insane.
I draw in a deep breath. "So who are the others?"

"Mrs. Gaylord already told you. I belong to a club called
the Society for Psychical Research. We are a group of scientists and Sensitives. The scientists study us and the
Sensitives help one another control their abilities."

A chill runs through me. The Society for Psychical
Research. The same society Dr. Bennett left because of

their treatment of the people they were studying. The same one he said is hard on people like me. Why would Cole belong to an organization that treats Sensitives so badly? Then I remember what he told me the first time we talked about it—*that he was more like a conduit than a Sensitive*, he'd said. Whose side is he on? I want to ask him but decide to keep my mouth shut. Right now, all I want is information, and I need to get it before he clams up again. "Are all Sensitives' abilities the same?" I ask.

Cole shakes his head. "No. Some can read people's thoughts, while some pick up on people's dreams. A few have visions of the future, but I've never met any who can feel the emotions of others or channel the dead."

I shake my head. "This is so confusing. How is it that I can do things the others can't? What makes me different?"

"No one knows. That's one of the things the Society is trying to answer with their research. There are a bunch of different theories."

"Such as?"

"Some people believe Sensitives are using more of their brain than most people do. Others think such abilities are passed from one generation to the next."

So perhaps I did get my talents from my father. I file that away for later. Right now, there is a more pressing question I've got to ask.

"You said there is a way to control it. How?"

"With training."

I swallow. "Can you teach me?"

Cole takes a deep breath a only sat in on a few sessions w trained, of course—what I c be able to control it—but I'm good. Some within the Societ

Interesting. I wonder if t talking about. "Why is that?"

"They're afraid that too r mess up the research. Give power would. The Sensitives, to be able to live as normal a l don't mind helping with the r able to turn their powers off

Them. So he doesn't think the scientists don't like that? two groups?"

I watch him carefully and r

"There is, but that's one of talk about."

Disappointment almost ch I want to be able to trust him. do I control it? What kind of

"Pretty much just practice I take a deep breath and ma Cole smiles, softening the s Right now?"

I shrug. "Why not?"

"Because being physically

isn't a g

I look into wo of my h familiar Just like been wa

I wat "Do The truck w lays his worry t was doi to do w But if I been ab abducte

Silen meet hi "We My t tions ri *I like hi * sons. I

I pul thing in years, e

I mean, when did you know there was something different about you?"

"Because I'm just a conduit, I only experienced psychical incidents when I was near another Sensitive. It rarely happened when I was little, and because I didn't have the words to describe the experience anyway, my parents had no idea. Then I was sent off to boarding school. Unfortunately, or fortunately, depending on how you look at it"—his lips quirk up—"one of the teachers there happened to be a Sensitive. I was trained during the war and formally became a member of the Society last year."

I frown, my mind skipping ahead. "I'd never thought of it before, but this ability could be really useful during wartime. If someone was so inclined, it could actually be quite dangerous."

A muscle in Cole's jaw jumps. "That's one of the disputes within the Society and one of the reasons I've been so reluctant to tell you more about us."

I catch his meaning. "So there are members . . ."

"We don't trust. Yes. I told you I came to find Sensitives and that's true, but there is another reason I was sent to the United States."

I still. "Why is that?"

"Some of the leaders of the Society for Psychical Research felt I was in danger because of my ability to sense other Sensitives." Cole's mouth tightens. "They worried that if someone found out I'm a conduit, they could use me for their own ends."

Alarm sends my pulse racing. "So you're in danger?"

Cole shrugs. "Not that I know of, but there is some concern that my whereabouts is now public knowledge. I was sent a letter from a trusted friend within the Society, but I misplaced it before I had a chance to read it."

My heart stops. The letter. After meeting Houdini in the magic shop, I had completely forgotten about it. It's still in my coat. Shame heats my cheeks. What if Cole is in danger because of me? I have to tell him.

I swallow. "Cole, I . . ."

Before I can say anything else, the door opens and my mother and Jacques come into the kitchen.

"How about we meet tomorrow to start your training?" Cole asks.

I give a quick nod. Perfect. That would give me a chance to return the letter and apologize for stealing it.

"Oh, you're up, darling. How are you feeling?"

Mother comes over and kisses my cheek. "I'm well, thank you for asking," I say rather coolly. I'm still smarting over being left alone. A raised eyebrow tells me my mother notices my tone.

"Wonderful," she says, handing me a bag. "I picked you up some sandwiches on my way home." She glances at Cole. "Thank you so much for checking on her for me. I had no choice but to leave." She gives me a pointed stare.

Cole rises to leave. "I need to be going, but I'll see you tomorrow, Anna?" With a little bow of his head, he takes his leave.

I pull a sandwich out of the bag and unwrap the waxed paper. I take a deep, appreciative sniff and bite into it ravenously. God only knows how long it's been since I last ate.

Jacques clears his throat. "Your mother and I were very worried about you."

I want to laugh but am too busy eating. Chicken salad on rye never tasted so good.

"How did the show go?" I ask with my mouth full.

"Perfect, darling, absolutely perfect."

Mother pours two glasses of gin and hands one to Jacques.

"I'll admit, it turned out much better than I thought it would. It was touch and go there for a bit," Jacques says.

"I knew he'd be fine." The words drop out of Mother's mouth like smug little pebbles.

I glance up, suspicious. Her eyes are bright. She's dying to tell me something but doesn't want to be too obvious about it. My heart sinks and I hobble over and toss the rest of my sandwich in the garbage. I'm not hungry anymore.

I turn to face Jacques and my mother. "Who would be fine?" I keep the tone of my voice even. Besides watch your back, the number one rule of living with my mother is don't let her know she's hurt you.

"Owen!" Mother bursts out, unable to hold back any longer.

"Owen?" I fumble for my chair and sit with a thud.

"Did someone say my name in vain?" The person in question calls and I hear the slam of the door behind him.

"There's my girl!"

He falls down on his knees in front of me and holds out a rose. "I would have been here sooner, but I didn't want to show up empty-handed. Not after I let them take you like that."

He lays his head in my lap, still holding up the rose. "I will never be able to forgive myself, but I dare to hope that you will, one day, forgive me. . . ."

For a second, I'm speechless, but then I take the rose and rap him on the head with my knuckles. "There's nothing to forgive, you goose. It happened so fast . . ." I swallow hard and shove the memory from my mind. "Now, get up. This is ridiculous."

"Thank you," he says, popping up like a jack-in-the-box. "My knees were killing me."

I start to roll my eyes but then catch sight of the bruise he has along his jaw and cheekbone. "Oh, my God, are you okay?" I reach out to touch his face but then pull my hand back, embarrassed.

"I'm fine. It's you I was worried about. I also brought your purse. You dropped it when you were taken."

I take the purse gratefully. I would have hated to lose my knife. I need it more than ever.

"Shall we move this conversation into the sitting room?" Mother is still gloating.

Owen takes my arm and helps me down the hall, but my toe feels better, and I feel stupid with a towel wrapped around my foot. Owen's excitement sticks out all over him.

"So you took my place in the show?" I ask, sinking gratefully into the closest chair.

Jacques snorts. "Hardly."

Hurt passes over Owens face before it clears and I frown at Jacques.

"Well, no one can take your place," Owen says. "I just filled in."

"You did a wonderful job," my mother says, smiling at me. "Simply wonderful."

The mistress of games is letting me know how easily I can be replaced. She's trying to make me jealous. It works.

But I'll be damned if I let her see that.

I turn to Owen and give him a smile so bright, he blinks. "Did you enjoy it?"

"It was amazing! The people, the lights, the applause. I've never felt anything like it."

"Don't get too used to it. The show needs Anna's talents," Jacques says firmly.

Surprised, I throw Jacques an appreciative glance while my mother's smile becomes fixed.

She busies herself by grabbing a throw and tucking it in around my legs. "Yes, of course, but it's nice to know we have a replacement. Just in case it's ever needed."

Her dark eyes bore into mine, giving lie to the smile still curving her mouth. She looks so different from the mother who brushed my hair this morning that I look away, my heart aching.

Before she can move, I tentatively brush her hand with

my fingers. My mother's emotions have always been easy to read, but I learned early on to ignore them whenever possible. A child only wants to know so much about her mother's resentment toward her. Today her emotions are so mixed that I have trouble separating them out. I'm gratified to find love among the usual mix of resentment, impatience, and single-minded desire, but I'm also picking up fear. Trying to figure out what my mother is afraid of is like trying to read a set of tarot cards. I know it's connected to me, but is she afraid for me or of me?

I can't tell. But one thing is certain. She wants me out of the show.

TWENTY-ONE

I punch my pillow for the hundredth time. If it were a person it would be dead by now. How dare she? I've been more of a mother than she has. I've done the shopping, made the travel arrangements, found us employment, and cheated people—all in my mother's service.

I punch the pillow again, thinking of all the snooping I've done, looking for information on clients she wanted to shill. The menial jobs I've taken so we could eat. And all I've asked for in return is the opportunity to perform my magic.

Now she wants to take that away from me.

But why? What does she have to gain? And what would I do if I couldn't do the show anymore?

I feel tears and furiously wipe them away. Why am I so surprised? I have been afraid of this forever. It's my darkest fear come to life. No. I take a deep breath. My darkest fear was that my mother would abandon me in some cheap hotel room. At least she didn't do that.

I'm angry and scared and mixed up. The story of my relationship with my mother. When I think of how much worrying I have done the past few weeks, the lengths I've gone to make sure she was safe . . .

I shut my eyes, but they pop open again, reminding me that I slept most of the day. Sighing, I lean over and turn on the light, then feel under my mattress until I locate the notebook I keep hidden there. Pulling it out, I flip to the rough sketches I made about a year ago. It's an illusion I was designing.

I follow the simple lines with my finger and then, inspired, I walk to my desk and grab a pencil. I'm a year older now—a year more experienced—and I've got some ideas to make the design better, sharper, easier to follow.

As long as everything is done exactly as I have it drawn, it should work beautifully. Last year, I had no way to make the design a reality. Now, thanks to Mr. Darby, I do. I smile, thinking of Mr. Darby's shop.

My mother wants me out of the show? Fine. But it's going to be one hell of a send-off.

I wake up the next morning exhausted and thankful it's Sunday. I need the day of rest.

Though I assure my mother that I'll be fine, she isn't convinced.

"Are you sure? Do you think we should call a doctor?" Her brows knit together, and for a moment I sense her worry.

I'm not impressed.

I know she loves me. She just loves her career more. It's a lesson I should have learned from her a long time ago. Take care of yourself first.

"I'm fine. Just tired. I think I'm going to run down and visit Mr. Darby. I'm sure he's been worried about me."

Mother waves her hand, and as soon as she's out of sight, I grab my coat and pull out the letter still tucked in the pocket.

I turn it over in my hand, fighting temptation. It's written in the same loopy handwriting as the letter on Mr. Darby's desk, and the postscript says London. I glance at the return address, but it's just a post-office box number. It's still sealed, which makes me think Cole must have just grabbed it on his way out of the house the morning I slipped it out of his pocket.

I really, really want to open it. It is, after all, from someone in the Society Cole trusts. And judging by the beautiful penmanship, that someone is a girl. I hesitate. Maybe this could shed a light on his meeting with Mrs. Lindsay. Of all the things I know about Cole, that is the most baffling. What could he be doing with someone I know is out to hurt me? And exactly what are his ties with the Society for Psychical Research? Is it as bad as Dr. Bennett said it was? Is that what Cole doesn't want to tell me?

Taking a deep breath, I shove the envelope back into my pocket without opening it. After we finish our lesson, I'll give it to him and beg his forgiveness. And I'll ask him about Mrs. Lindsay, too.

Before I head downstairs, I grab the plans for my illusion. I'm pretty sure that Cole is taking me somewhere for my first lesson, but I plan on talking to Mr. Darby before we leave.

Cole lets me in seconds after I knock.

I frown. "Were you waiting for me?"

His smile lights up his face and my breath hitches. "I was indeed, Miss Van Housen."

"Could you"—I look around for Mr. Darby—"sense me coming down?" I whisper.

"No," he whispers back, leaning closer. "I could hear you. You clomp down those stairs like a herd of elephants."

Surprised, I swat him and he jumps back, laughing. Then I blush a bit, wondering if the expression on my face is as goofy as the one on his. I love this carefree side of him. I wonder if I'll ever see it again after I tell him I picked his pocket. When he learns the truth about who I am.

"Morning, missy!" Mr. Darby wraps me in a warm hug. His emotions are as simple, gruff, and caring as he is. "Your face looks like you got the hard end of a baseball bat. And you're empty-handed. Where's my breakfast?"

"Sorry. Anna and I are going out this morning," Cole says quickly.

Mr. Darby sighs and his face wrinkles with mock pity. "Of course you two wouldn't want to spend time with an old man. No thought for the aging. Well, don't worry about me. I'll stay here and wait for the cleaning girl to arrive."

"We'll bring you back some waffles," I promise, before

turning to Cole. "Actually, I could use a few minutes alone with your cousin if you don't mind?"

Cole raises a brow and turns to Mr. Darby with a grin. "I do believe you are trying to make time with my girl."

His girl? I feel another smile taking over my face.

"If I were half as young, you wouldn't have a chance!"

"I don't doubt it." Cole smiles at me. "I'll meet you outside. Don't take too long or I'm liable to freeze to death."

"I won't." I can't stop smiling and my cheeks are still flushed from the exchange. Is that how he really feels or was he just teasing me?

After Cole leaves, I pull my notebook out of my handbag and hand it to Mr. Darby. "Can you make this?"

He frowns, studying my sketches. "Possibly. What is it?"

"A new illusion I'm working on. Something big. I just need to know if you can do it." I turn the page and show him the notes I'd labored over. "I added these so you'd have more information."

He nods. "I'll look these over while you're out and let you know later."

I move toward the door. "Thanks, and let's not mention this to anyone, okay?"

He smiles, his face crinkling into a hundred good-natured wrinkles. "Don't worry about me. My lips are sealed. As long as you bring me those waffles!"

By the time we reach Child's, I've developed a keen appetite, and the savory-sweet aroma of bacon and maple syrup makes my stomach growl. The waffles are light and airy, the bacon crisp. While we eat, we talk of mundane things, but as soon as we finish, we lean back in our chairs.

"Can we begin?" I ask. Excitement wars in my stomach with the waffle I just devoured. The combination is making me a little queasy.

Cole gives me a crooked grin. "Are you sure you wouldn't rather just take a nap?"

I glare and he laughs. "Never mind the nap."

His face clears and he leans closer to me. "The reason I brought you to a public place is that it will give us better access to subjects."

"Subjects?"

"To practice on."

"Oh." I turn my head, observing the other diners: an elderly woman in a gray feathered hat dining alone and a mother and her two identically dressed daughters—probably tourists trying out Child's famous waffles—and the dozens of others who pack the dining area. "You mean we'll be experimenting on them?"

Cole shrugs. "Who else? So do you ever feel other people's emotions without touching them?"

I chew on my lip, wondering how to explain myself. "I've always been more perceptive than most people and I can make a pretty good guess as to what they are feeling when I'm trying to, even when I'm not touching them. But lately . . ." I pause.

Cole leans forward. "Lately, what?"

"Lately my abilities seem to have heightened. Sometimes I feel myself getting messages when I'm not touching people or even paying much attention. And I've been having this recurring vision—I've never had more than one about a certain event." I drop my eyes, fear and worry weighing on me like a ball and chain. The temptation to confide in him is overwhelming. Before I can say anything, however, he continues.

"You're not the only Sensitive to say that after I've been around them for a while. The researchers have all sorts of guesses about why you are able to do the things you do, but no one understands how I do what I do."

Distracted from my thoughts, I look up and meet his warm, dark eyes. My heart flutters in my chest. I don't know how he does what he does either.

He clears his throat. "First, I want you to try it on me, then I'm going to throw a block up so you can get a sense of what that feels like."

I make a face at him. "I already know what it feels like."

He rolls his eyes. "No, I mean what it feels like to have someone block you after you've already made a connection. Maybe that will help you understand how to do what I'm doing."

"All right."

"I want you to explain to me what you're doing while you're doing it. It will give me a better sense of your process. Like when you're doing the muscle-reading trick."

"I'll try. I just never thought about it much before."

"Thinking about it is the first step in controlling it."

I take a deep breath. "First, I clear my mind, though that's a little difficult under the circumstances."

Cole nods his encouragement. I try calming myself, but I keep thinking of him watching me and wonder how his eyes can be so dark and bright at the same time. "I need you to look at something else, all right?"

He grins, as if he knows exactly why I can't concentrate. I resist the urge to stick out my tongue at him. He does what I ask, though, and stares back toward the kitchen area.

I take a deep breath and try to relax. "Then I touch the person, and it's almost as if there's a strand of silver ribbon reaching between us. Sometimes it's really straight. Other times it wavers." I lay my hand across his and my fingers curl around his automatically. A delightful shiver runs down my spine as his warmth transmits itself to me.

"What is it like right now?"

I give myself a good mental shake. Focus! "Clear and strong. Almost like a rod instead of a ribbon."

"Interesting. Then what?"

"Then I wait. When it comes, it feels like a static electrical shock. If it's really strong, it's more like a charge of emotion." I stop talking as I feel a connection being made and Cole's emotions wash over me.

First, I feel his insecurity about what we're doing, as if he's unsure he can really teach me. I also feel the strength of his determination. But under that is a whisper of something else. I grab onto a tendril and am overwhelmed by the warmth and longing directed toward me. It almost feels like . . . My eyes widen and my breathing quickens.

Suddenly a block is thrown up so hard, I gasp. It's like being flung headfirst into a brick wall. "What was that?"

Cole shifts in his chair and his eyes avoid mine. "I told you I was going to block you, so you can feel what it's like."

"Oh. Right." I lick my lips. "Now what?" I pull my hand away from his and it trembles as I raise my coffee cup to my mouth.

He pushes on, his voice exuding a confidence I now know he doesn't really feel. "I want you to practice on someone else without touching them. Feel them out, then shut it off."

"How?"

"Most Sensitives I know use their imaginations to visualize the process. Try sending a silver ribbon across the room. Just imagine it in your mind reaching out to them. Since you already do that when you're touching someone, I think you should continue along those lines and just imagine yourself cutting it with scissors or something."

I hear Cole's words, but I'm distracted. I can't help but wonder if one of the other Sensitives he's talking about is the one who sent the letter sitting in my pocket.

"Are you ready?"

I force the woman from London out of my mind and nod. "Who would you like me to try it on first?"

Cole nods toward the woman and her two daughters, who are now finishing up their breakfast. "How about them?"

I shrug. "Okay."

I look at the woman, now drumming her fingers on

the table as if she's impatient to get going. I notice the shadows under her eyes and the tightness in her mouth before spinning out a thread toward her. The woman's emotions zip back toward me with surprising speed. Then I remember that Cole makes my abilities stronger. I wonder if he feels the tension pulsing down the strand. My own stomach clenches in sympathy. Quickly, I imagine a pair of scissors to snip the line with. They hover for a moment before I force them to cut. For a second nothing happens, but then the feelings coming off the woman in waves simply stop.

My eyes widen as I turn to Cole. "I did it!"

He nods solemnly, but his eyes glint with amusement. "You did."

"So now I can control it?" My heart races. This means freedom. Normalcy.

"I don't know. Some people pick it up rather quickly, because they've been doing it unknowingly for years. Others take months of training. You have more experience than most because of your work with your mother—the muscle reading and the séances and so on."

I wrinkle my nose. "The séances are the worst. The people who come to us are so heartbroken. It's hard . . ." I look down at my hands.

"To offer them hope when there is none?"

My heart beats faster, but I say nothing. Some things cannot be shared.

After an awkward silence he continues. "Grief is a really

intense emotion. It might be harder to control. Maybe that's part of the problem."

I think about it. "That makes sense."

Cole shakes his head, sympathy lighting his eyes. "Maybe you need to start by practicing on people whose feelings are less intense, then move on to people who have really strong emotions? This is all guesswork right now."

I lean back in my seat. Maybe I can learn more about the Society for Psychical Research. How much of what Dr. Bennett said is true? Cole already confirmed some of it, but how bad is it really? I'd like to ask him if he knows Dr. Bennett but don't want to tip my hand, especially if Dr. Bennett parted with the Society on poor terms. "Tell me more about the Society for Psychical Research."

He knits his hands together in front of him as if giving a lecture. "The Ghost Club, as it was originally called, was started in 1862. Past members include Charles Dickens and Sir William Barrett. It disappeared in the 1870s, and then in the 1880s it merged with the Society for Psychical Research. That's the part people know about."

"And the other part?" I ask.

Cole hesitates. "It's rumored that the Society for Psychical Research disappeared because the researchers discovered that Sensitives actually existed and they went underground because they didn't want to alarm the public with the fact that people who have special abilities live among them. Later they merged with the more scientifically based SPR and became public again, without any public announcement about the Sensitives. They keep the existence of Sensitives quiet for their own safety. There have been people who wish to use the Sensitives for their own gain. Secrecy helps protect them from that. For the most part."

I want to ask him what he means by that, but just then Cole places his hand over mine. Our fingers twine together and my breath catches at the warmth in his eyes.

"Honestly, I wish I could tell you everything, but there is so much going on right now. And when I'm with you, everything over there feels so remote. Like it doesn't matter at all."

My skin heats and my heart turns into a swirl of sweet, melting chocolate. Everything I was going to say or wanted to say goes right out of my head.

I know exactly how he feels.

But will he feel that way after I give him the letter?

I pull my hand away and put it in my pocket, feeling the crisp edge of the envelope.

Give him the letter.

Taking a deep breath, I pull it out and place it on the table between us.

"What's that?"

The noise around us dims and my mouth feels cotton stuffed. "A letter."

"I know it's a letter, Anna." He smiles a small half smile and picks it up. His brows knit together, puzzled. "How did you get this?"

I swallow. "I took it. From your pocket." At the look on his face I rush on. "It happened last week. I don't know why I did it; I was confused. I'm so sorry."

"You picked my pocket because you were confused?" Cole's voice is tight and I wince. "Do you have any idea how important this might be?" He rips open the envelope.

I open my mouth, but he holds up one finger and I fall silent. After scanning the letter, he looks up, his lips compressed.

I try again. "You have to know I wouldn't normally . . ." My voice trails off. There is no way to tell him how it felt, so close to him on the train that day. How I needed to make contact with him. "I mean, that's not the kind of girl I am," I finish lamely.

I look down at the table, unable to meet Cole's eyes, but I can feel the anger and hurt coming off him in waves.

"Anna, I don't know what kind of girl you are."

Shame burns through me. "You don't mean that. You know more about me in some ways than anyone ever has."

"Right now all I know is you swindle people for money and pick pockets when you're confused. Who knows? Maybe you rob banks in your spare time?

"I thought I knew you, but I was mistaken." He tosses the letter on the table. "There. You wanted to read it so badly. Read it."

And this time, he walks out on me.

TWENTY-TWO

I should have at least received some credit for not reading the letter, I think miserably a couple of days later. Then I wonder if it even matters. To my surprise, Cole had been waiting outside the restaurant when I finally emerged. I'd hoped that meant he'd relented enough to at least give me a chance to explain, but he didn't want to talk. "I can't leave you to walk home alone" was all he'd said.

I sigh and try to powder away the dark circles under my eyes and the leftover bruises from my abduction. Cynthia Gaylord is coming to pick me up to take me out to dinner with Dr. Bennett. I wonder who set up this meeting, Dr. Bennett or Cynthia? Maybe I'll get more info on the Society. I'm a little uneasy, though.

Maybe I should just go ahead and talk to Cole about Dr. Bennett. They had to have at least heard of each other. Maybe he can give me some information on him. Or maybe I should talk to Dr. Bennett about Cole.

I try not to think about the fact that Cole may never talk to me about anything ever again. My insides hollow at the thought.

I hear a door shut, then a voice, and I know Cynthia must be here. Shaking my head, I snatch my coat off the bed, where I'd tossed it, and hurry down the hall.

My mother is standing in the kitchen with Cynthia, sly curiosity evident in the lift of her brow and the hidden quirk of her lips. "Cynthia tells me you two are going to dinner with a doctor who researches spirit manifestations and spiritualism? How . . . intriguing."

My smile reflects nothing but innocent enthusiasm. "Yes, I think it will be a fascinating evening. Don't you, Cynthia?"

Cynthia nods excitedly, her head a pale flower against the enormous dark fur collar of her coat. I wait for her to invite my mother, but she doesn't. Then I smile. Of course not. Cynthia wouldn't want to compete with my mother for Dr. Bennett's attention. We head down to the car, leaving my mother's eyes filled with questions. In light of everything, it seems only fitting.

The car turns onto Broadway and I stare in wonder at the giant signs advertising everything from Camel cigarettes to the Ziegfeld Follies. It's pure magic to see the sun go down in the west, while all around you thousands of dazzling lights are blinking on. No matter how many times I see it, it still takes my breath away.

"Where are we going?" I ask.

Cynthia lights a cigarette and blows a smoke ring. "Have you ever been to Lindy's?"

I shake my head.

"You'll love it. Good food. Relaxing. Not fancy-pantsy at all. More my kind of place."

I open my mouth to find out what she means by that, but she doesn't let me get a word in.

"So tell me, which one of those two young sheiks are you stuck on?"

I blink. "What?"

Cynthia rolls her eyes. "The young men who were at the séance. Which one do you like? Because sure as I'm sitting here, they both like you. They couldn't keep their eyes off you."

"Oh. Um . . ."

Cynthia laughs. "Just string them both along till you figure out which one you like best. That's what I did until my daddy decided for me. I'm so glad it was Jack. He had scads more money and is so handsome. The other man had a disgusting nose. I don't know if I could have married that nose."

I can't think of anything to say to that, but luckily, she doesn't seem to need an answer. She tosses her cigarette out the window and digs a silver-and-green enamel compact out of her bag. She pats some powder on her nose and reapplies her lipstick. "If I were you," she says, snapping her compact shut, "I would go for the tall, dark-haired one. Like Jack, he has scads more money."

The car slows and pulls over to the sidewalk. Cole? I laugh. "How do you know?" I ask.

"Oh, I just know these things," she answers, sliding out of the car. "The other one might be more fun, though. Depends on what you're looking for."

What I'm looking for? My life would be far simpler if I knew the answer to that.

"Uncle Arnie!" I hear Cynthia squeal, and turn to find her in the arms of an imposing man in a tailored black suit. He's tall, with thin lips and the imperious nose of a hawk. His hairline may be receding, but the fit of his jacket shows a man in his prime. He looks vaguely familiar and I wonder where I've seen him.

"How you doing, baby doll? How's that swanky blue blood treating you?"

"Like a queen, Uncle Arnie, like a queen."

"He'd better. Or I'll have to break his legs." He laughs, but the laughter doesn't quite reach his eyes.

Cynthia swats him. "You be nice. I brought a friend tonight." She grabs my arm and pulls me next to her. "This is Anna Van Housen. She and her mother are famous mediums. They have their own show."

He holds out his hand. "Is that so? I never believed in that stuff myself. No offense, Miss Van Housen."

"None taken," I assure him. The moment he touches my hand, a dark, ambivalent emotion snakes its way up my arm and I shiver. I don't even know what to call it but I know for a fact I've never felt anything like it. The strange thing is that's it's not directed at me or Cynthia, or anyone in particular. It just is. He kisses my hand and releases it and I suppress a sigh of relief.

Another man in a black suit approaches and jerks his head to the side. Arnie nods and turns back to us. "Got to run, girls. Business calls. You take care of yourself and let me know if you need anything, okay, baby doll?" Cynthia nods. "Nice to meet you, Miss Van Housen."

He turns to go and then turns back to me. "Van Housen? Say, you're not that magician girl who's Houdini's daughter, are you?"

My jaw drops and Uncle Arnie laughs. "I know everything that happens in New York, sweetheart. Even if they're just rumors. I used to know your father before he got all famous. We get our handcuffs from the same feller. He's a good man, Houdini."

He gives me another, friendlier nod and disappears with a group of men surrounding him.

Cynthia links her arm in mine. "Come on. Let's go get a table. Dr. Bennett should be here in a few minutes."

She bypasses the line and a waitress seats us right away. Lindy's is a nice place, but not fancy or exciting like The Colony.

"Wait till you try the cheesecake," Cynthia says. "It's to die for."

We take off our coats and open our menus.

"Uncle Arnie is a sweetheart, isn't he? It's hard to believe he's one of the most powerful men in the city. Everyone's so intimidated by him, but he's just a pussycat, really. Well, unless you cross him."

I freeze as I suddenly realize where I've seen him before. Arnold "the Brain" Rothstein is the head of a Jewish mob family and practically a permanent feature in the papers. He's been indicted more times than I can count and was rumored to be involved in the 1919 World Series scandal.

"Arnold Rothstein is your uncle?" I squeak.

Cynthia's shoulders slump. "Oh, please. Don't tell me you're going to go all disapproving. This always happens! As soon as I make a friend, they find out about my family and bam, it's all over. Jack's family will hardly even talk to me."

Tears spring up in her eyes and I reach out to grab her hand. "No, of course not! I'm the last person to judge anyone. I was just surprised, that's all."

She sniffles. "Are you sure?"

"Positive." I watch curiously as she dabs her eyes. "How old are you anyway?"

"I just turned twenty last July."

That explains so much.

She offers me a cigarette and I shake my head, so she lights it and exhales while giving me a sharp look. "So why does your face look like you've been in a boxing match with Jack Dempsey?"

I touch my cheek self-consciously.

"No, you did a good job of hiding it," Cynthia assures me. "I'm just good at seeing that sort of thing."

I bet she is.

The waitress interrupts and asks us if we would like to order or wait for our guest. Cynthia consults her watch. "Let's go ahead and eat, shall we? I'm famished."

We order, and as soon as the waitress leaves I tell Cynthia what happened.

Cynthia's big blue eyes get even bigger. "I can't believe you escaped! I'd have been so scared!"

I shiver as I remember my nightmare run through the streets. "I was scared. Now I'm just angry."

Cynthia nods. "I would be, too. You want me to get Uncle Arnie to look into it? I know he would. He likes you."

"I just met him!"

"He likes your father. That means a lot. And he wasn't kidding when he said he knows everything that happens in New York. I bet he could find out who it was."

The waitress sets down our food as I consider her offer. On one hand, it would be really nice to know who is out to get me. On the other, what would "sweet" old Uncle Arnie do if he found them? Do I want to be responsible for that?

"Ladies, deepest apologies for my tardiness." Dr. Bennett's effusive voice interrupts my thoughts. "I ran into a colleague of mine and I've persuaded her to join us. I do hope you don't mind."

I look up with a smile, grateful for the distraction.

Dr. Bennett removes his greatcoat and turns to draw his companion forward. Everything inside me freezes when I see who it is.

The next few seconds play out in slow motion, my every sense heightened. Mrs. Lindsay's smile is pasted on, but her cheek is twitching as she nods politely to Cynthia. As her eyes swivel toward me, I note that though she's wearing a clean coat, it's covering the same ragged dress she was wearing when she attacked me. I want to run when her eyes lock on to mine, but I'm frozen in my seat, even when her mouth opens in a perfectly shaped O.

It's when the screaming starts that I finally leap to my feet, knocking my chair backward. At first, there are no words, just an unearthly wailing that sounds as if it were ripping her soul apart. Her hands form claws and I snatch up my purse and leap back, running into the person dining at the table behind me. Everything in the restaurant screeches to a halt as the ghastly sound continues.

Then a word rises from the cacophony. "Witch!" she screams. "Wiiiitch!"

"My God, woman!" Dr. Bennett grabs onto Mrs. Lindsay's arm just as she makes a lunge for me, which is a good thing as my knife is already out of my purse and hidden in the palm of my hand.

Cynthia grabs our coats and pulls me out of the restaurant, leaving Dr. Bennett to cope with the still-howling Mrs. Lindsay. In seconds, she has me in the car with the doors shut and locked.

"Hurry up and get us out of here, Al," she tells the driver before turning to me. "What was all that about? I simply can't be involved in any kind of scandal. Both my family *and* my husband's family would kill me, though for different reasons. Wasn't that woman at the last séance I went to?"

I nod, my teeth chattering.

Cynthia hands me my coat and waits till I put it on. "What's wrong with her?"

I shake my head. "I think she's crazy," I say, and tell her about Mrs. Lindsay attacking me in the park.

"You mean you've been attacked twice in the last week? You should carry a gun."

In answer, I take out my knife, the blade flashing as the lights of Broadway reflect off it. "I'm more comfortable with this."

She stares for a moment, then laughs. "You carry a shiv?" She reaches into the pocket of her fur coat and pulls out a small pistol.

We stare at each other silently as the car winds its way through the traffic. Then we burst into laughter, the kind edged with both hysteria and relief.

It looks as if I've finally found a friend.

I sleep in the next morning, letting Mother fix her own breakfast. After the trouble last night, I'm not really hungry anyway. She and Jacques went out earlier, but are back now and talking quietly in the sitting room.

Cynthia and I decided against telling anyone about Mrs. Lindsay's breakdown in the restaurant.

"My uncle is going to hear about it, regardless," she'd

said. "Lindy's is practically his office, but I don't want Jack or his family to get wind of it."

I agree. I don't want my mother to hear about it either.

I pace my bedroom after dressing for the day. Mrs. Lindsay is insane. Why do I keep running into her? Could she have been involved in my abduction?

I have to find out more about that vision. I know it's the key to everything.

I shiver. Owen is taking me to the Metropolitan Museum of Art tomorrow, but last night's fiasco has cast a pall over everything. Tomorrow will be fun because Owen is fun. *He* knows how to have a good time. I viciously jab a pin into my black cloche to hold it in place. Cole isn't exactly a barrel of laughs; he's more . . . I sigh. Wonderful. Cole is more wonderful.

And my actions might have put him in danger.

My eyes are inadvertently drawn to the drawer where I'd hidden the letter. Guilt and confusion kept me from reading it that day in the restaurant, but maybe there's something in it I should know? I bite my lip and, glancing at the door, pull it out. I was right; the big, loopy handwriting definitely belongs to a girl.

Dear C—

Hope this missive finds you well and safe, with special emphasis on the safe. (More on that later.) First, I fear the Society is coming apart at the seams, or will once the vote occurs. Some of our kind will not stand for being barred from club policy any longer, not to mention forbidding women to sit on the board! Our supporters are many, but our enemies are numerous as well, even if their leader has gone missing. Which brings me to the point of this letter—our contacts were correct. We do believe he is in the States. We have discovered one of his former Sensitives in an asylum in Surrey. She has gone quite mad from all the experiments and I'm not sure if we can do anything to help her. We are told the poor girl was not always this unstable. It makes me so angry! Anyway, I'm sure our "friend" won't try to contact you directly—not after the thrashing you gave him last time—but he is quite capable of hiring someone to persuade you to his way of thinking. Which brings up my next thought, How well do you know this girl you keep writing about? How strange that it is the daughter and not the medium who is like us! And how strange that a solemn young man like yourself would write so about a girl! But seriously, can you trust her? I would tell you to be careful, but you are always so.

Please stay safe. H— sends his regards.

L—

My heart aches as I return the letter to its envelope. If Cole did trust me, he certainly doesn't now. Does he think I might have snatched the letter to give to their enemy, whoever he is? And why is Cole still here if he's in danger? What does it all mean, and does Dr. Bennett know about any of this? Why did Dr. Bennett really leave the Society? As always, I have more questions than answers.

TWENTY-THREE

"Are you sure you're feeling up to this?" Jacques asks that evening as we get ready for our performance. Anxiety lines his face—even his mustache looks nervous. I send out a silver ribbon like Cole and I had practiced but come back empty-handed. Even though I've been working on controlling my abilities on my own, I still can't pick up on Jacques's emotions.

"Yes, darling, are you sure you're okay? Owen is out front in the audience. I'm sure he wouldn't mind spelling you for another show."

I snort. Mother's true intentions come through loud and clear—even without using my abilities.

"Owen isn't nearly as talented or experienced as Anna," Jacques snaps. "People look forward to seeing her. We don't want to disappoint them further."

I don't know who is more surprised, me or my mother.

From the look on her face, I'm betting on Mother. Jacques is oblivious to her, however, and leaves after wishing us luck.

"Is this the kind of life you want?" Mother asks suddenly.

I turn from the mirror, where I've been trying to hide my fading bruises.

"What do you mean?"

She gives a slight smile. "You're almost an adult. I don't think I've ever given a thought as to what you might want for your own life." She stands and stares into the mirror, smoothing her already smooth hair. "Now that things are so much better for us, perhaps you want to give up the show—get married, have children. Live a more normal life."

My chest aches. Mother's capacity to surprise never lessens. But is she sincere? Or is she just trying to maneuver me out of the show? I send out a strand, but it wavers and fades before it reaches her. Maybe my own emotions are tangling things up, or maybe I don't really want to know how she feels.

There's a knock on the door—the signal that the show is starting—and I follow her to the stage. I stand in the wings, excitement making my pulse race. No matter how bad things are or how complicated my life is, performing is always a joyous thing for me.

Perhaps it's because my mother and I are both emotional, or maybe it's in the stars, but the show is going well.

Being in front of an audience, listening to their gasps and laughter—it feels so right. Mother's question sits in the back of my mind as I perform. Do I want to settle down? Do I want respectability? Or do I want this?

Why can't you have both? a little voice inside me whispers.

Why can't I be both a wife and a magician? A mother and a performer? Mother did it. But then again, Mother isn't really the best role model.

Toward the end of the show a sense of déjà vu creeps over me. A tingling sensation in my stomach spreads to my chest and I miss a cue as the overpowering scent of burned sugar assails my nose. My breath quickens as I smile, stupidly. Painful red lights flash before my eyes and soon the audience, the stage, and even my mother fade from view. Then, in the dark place where the visions come, the images appear. *My mother, bound and gagged. Bruises mark her face, and her eyes show both terror and defiance. But not for herself. She's afraid for me. I feel the enormity of her despair as if it were my own. A dark, hulking figure moves into the picture and chills run down my spine. He's coming for me.*

For the first time during a vision, I try watching it as if it were a picture show, to separate my mind from the terror running through my body. I stare at the figure moving toward me, desperately trying to see who it is. Who is after me? Who is holding my mother prisoner? But the image shifts and I'm underwater, my lungs burning. Nausea rises up and the image spins away like a top.

The theater snaps into sharp focus; and for a fraction of a second, I see the audience watching, puzzled, as my mother calls out to me. Then the room spins, faster and faster. The last thing I hear before the room goes dark is my mother screaming my name.

I awake sometime later on the couch in our dressing room. A stranger with a large, sandy-colored mustache is bending over me. I let out a strangled noise and push him away.

My mother rushes to my side. "It's all right, darling, he's a doctor."

"I'm just checking your pupils. Bright light," he warns before shining a light into my eyes. "Again."

I blink and he presses lightly on the sides of my throat. "How do you feel?"

I take a mental catalog of all my body parts. I'm still bruised from the abduction, but that's nothing new. "I feel fine."

"Can you sit up?"

I nod and he slips his arm behind me and helps me up to a sitting position. My mother hands me a glass of water. I take a careful sip, remembering the nausea I felt before everything went black.

"What on earth happened?" she demands. "You were fine, and then all of a sudden you weren't responding."

I close my eyes, too disappointed and heartsick to come up with an excuse. My brain is too scattered for coherent thought. "That's pretty much what happened," I tell her. I try to put the vision out of my mind, but it replays itself over and over in my head. What does it mean?

"She's probably having a delayed reaction to her

experience the other night. I bet she's just exhausted," says Owen from the other side of the dressing room.

I shift uncomfortably. What is Owen doing here?

The doctor packs up his black bag. "I would say exhaustion is a very good guess. How many shows do you do a week?"

"Four," my mother answers. "I knew she shouldn't have gone on tonight. She should have just rested."

I lower my eyes so I don't have to look at her. She sounds sincere, maternal, but she doesn't mention that she didn't mind me cleaning our flat this morning or making her tea.

"Can you cut it back to two?" the doctor asks.

My mother glances at Jacques, who shakes his head. "*Non*. We are contracted for four a week, Wednesday through Saturday. I fear we would lose our contract if we cut back."

The doctor frowns, making his mustache even droopier. "I think this young lady should cut back to two a week for the time being. She needs to rest. She's had a serious trauma and it takes longer than a few days to recuperate." He tilts his head to one side, his frown so pronounced he looks like a sad walrus. "She's young. She should be able to resume her regular schedule in a couple of weeks."

After he leaves, the silence is deafening.

Furrows crease my mother's forehead and her mouth purses. I want to tell her I'm fine and it won't happen again. But how can I when I have no idea how to stop the visions? Visualizing imaginary scissors cutting an imaginary strand isn't going to work for those. I wish I had thought to ask Cole about it.

"I'll take her place if you want me to. We don't want to risk making Anna worse by pushing her." Owen glances at me sympathetically.

I glare. What stake does he have in all this? I know I'm being unfair considering how nice he's been. I cross my arms and look away.

Jacques is frowning, and my mother lays a reassuring hand on his arm. "It's only two nights a week for two weeks, darling. Four shows only. Surely that won't make much of a difference in the long run?"

"I certainly hope not. I'll talk to the venue manager."

"Good!" Mother beams as if everything were just ducky. Of course it is. She is getting what she wanted all along. I turn my face miserably to the wall.

"Excellent! That's settled and my poor girl can get the rest she needs."

"I don't want to misspeak here . . . ," Jacques says, hesitating. I look over at him and he is frowning at Owen. "But your tricks are not as sophisticated as Anna's. I worry that the audience will get bored."

My eyes fly open in surprise. I'm flattered to hear that Jacques thinks so highly of my magic.

Mother waves a hand. "That's no problem. Anna can teach him her tricks."

My chest tightens. My tricks? I don't think so. Owen must have seen the look on my face because he rushes in to reassure me.

"No, not your magic tricks, I'll refine my own. I promise you, Uncle, no one will be bored."

I try to sense Owen's emotions, but today he feels like his uncle—all a jumble. Leaning back against the settee, I shut my eyes, tired of all of them. None of this matters if my vision comes true and my mother and I are destined to be imprisoned and killed by a madman. But maybe the doctor is right? Maybe I'm just exhausted and that's affecting my visions.

"We could shorten the show," Jacques says musingly. "But Anna is getting quite a reputation for her magic."

"But it's me they're coming to see," my mother puts in quickly. "And she'll still be doing two shows a week."

"It's settled then," Jacques says.

I try to shut them out and concentrate on the vision, but the swirl of unidentifiable emotions is too thick. I need to talk to Cole so badly it's like a physical ache. Maybe he can help me figure out what the vision means. I have to make him talk to me.

I'm tired and worn-out the next day but decide to go on my outing with Owen in spite of it. I've been looking forward to spending some time with him. I want to find out if that moment we shared while dancing was the beginning of something real or simply an illusion brought on by the lights, music, and excitement of the evening. Last night, he irritated me to no end, but then, everyone was irritating me. That's what happens when you have a horrifying vision of your mother in pain.

Owen is fun and sweet and everything is so simple when

I'm with him. Isn't that the way love is supposed to be? I snatch up my coat and hurry down the hall.

"You look like the Queen of Autumn!" Owen says, referencing the burnt umber color of my wool dress. I roll my eyes and he grins.

"I'm not sure if it's a good idea for you to go out so soon after your collapse. Don't keep her out too long," Jacques frets from behind us.

I raise an eyebrow. I still don't know what he was doing that day he rushed out of here so fast, but I notice myself relaxing more in his presence.

"I just don't want you to overdo it," he explains. "Your first show back is tomorrow."

"You're worse than an old woman," Mother drawls from where she's lounging on the settee.

Jacques flushes and shoots her a disapproving look.

"We should go," I tell Owen, not wanting to witness an argument. The tension that has sprung up between Mother and Jacques these last couple of days makes me uneasy. Whether I like him or not, Jacques has been good for our career. Leave it to Mother to ruin a good thing.

We're almost down the stairs when Cole comes out of his apartment. I swallow hard as he steps aside to let us out the doorway.

"Afternoon, sport." Owen tips his hat. Cole returns the gesture, but his eyes are focused on me. I send out a strand like he taught me and come back with worry before the block goes up. But strangely, even though Cole has a block up, I'm still feeling strong pulses of emotion. They're just a mishmash, really, until one emotion seems to reach out before it disappears again into the mass. A feeling of . . . triumph?

Owen ushers me through the doorway and down the steps. I hear Cole's footsteps behind us and can't help but glance back. I want to warn him to be careful, but he turns and heads in the opposite direction.

Owen offers his arm and I link mine in his. "That limey is one wet blanket."

My chest tightens as I remember the infectious sound of Cole's laugh. "No, he's just quiet. He's actually quite nice."

"If you say so, doll. I'll take your word for it. He freezes me cold."

Irritation ripples across my skin. "Don't call me doll," I snap.

Owen gives my arm a squeeze. "I'm sorry; it's just habit." He turns his blue eyes on me and I see remorse in them. I give his arm an answering squeeze. It's not his fault I'm in a bad humor. I pause to tighten my scarf.

"Anna," a voice behind me says.

I turn to find Dr. Bennett walking toward me. I stiffen and feel Owen start beside me. What is Dr. Bennett doing here at my home?

He takes my hand in his and tilts his head. His gray eyes are sincere. "I hope you don't mind; I called Cynthia to find out where you lived so I could come and apologize personally for Mrs. Lindsay's behavior the other night.

I had no idea she was so unstable. I would not have brought her to meet you had I known."

My stomach clutches as I recall the crazed look in her eyes. "You had no way of knowing. It's not the first time I've had difficulties with her."

"So I gathered. She was raving about how you and your mother had robbed her of all her clients. She kept talking about a rat?"

I shudder. So Mrs. Lindsay *has* been after us since the beginning. I nod but can't speak.

He patted my arm. "Well, no need to worry anymore, my dear. The police carted her away yesterday morning, and unless I miss my guess, she is going to be sent upstate to Willard Asylum for the Insane before too long."

I breathe a sigh of cautious relief. There are still too many unanswered questions for me to be completely satisfied that Mrs. Lindsay was responsible for my abduction and was planning on hurting my mother. But the thought that I won't have to worry about her again is very, very good news. The smile I give Dr. Bennett is heartfelt. "Thank you so much for coming to tell me."

He inclines his head and his eyes flick to Owen, who has remained silent through the exchange.

"I am so sorry. How rude of me. Dr. Bennett, this is my friend, Owen Winchester. Owen, this is Dr. Finneas Bennett, a lecturer at The New Church." They shake hands and I pray Dr. Bennett doesn't mention my abilities.

"You were on your way out. Don't let me keep you. I just

wanted to tell you the news." He bows his head again and saunters back down the street the way he came. I watch him leave for a moment. Relief and worry war in my stomach. Did my mother and I just dodge a bullet?

With Mrs. Lindsay off the streets, could it really be over?

"You didn't tell me about Mrs. Lindsay," Owen says.

We pause before crossing the street and heading toward the park. "No. With everything that has happened, I didn't think of it. Now, thankfully, it's over." I don't want to talk about it. The feeling of reprieve is still too new to share.

The day is cold and gray, which somehow seems fitting, and the park looks lonely and depressed with most of the leaves gone from its trees. We walk slowly along the transverse road and I note that even Croton Reservoir looks dejected. Plans are already being made to fill it in, so perhaps it knows its days are numbered.

Owen catches my mood and the walk through the park is a somber one. He pauses in front of the museum entrance and takes out a flask. "You look cold. Here, have a nip. This will warm you right up."

I shake my head and he takes a long pull from it. "Suit yourself. Let's get inside before we freeze our bums off."

The Great Hall of the museum stretches out in front of us. "Where would you like to start?" I pick up a map.

"Doesn't matter to me. I like mostly modern stuff. You pick."

"Then why did you suggest coming here?" I ask, exasperated.

"Because last time we went out, you got kidnapped. I figured this would at least be safe."

I can't help but laugh. "We could have just gone for a walk around the park."

Owen leads me to a bench near the doors and we sit. "But you were attacked in the park, too, weren't you?"

I shiver, remembering Mrs. Lindsay's craziness. I wonder what Lisette will do without her mother and I almost feel sorry for her. "Yes, but I knew who that was."

Owen puts his arm around me and gives me a gentle squeeze. "Don't worry about all that, Anna. I'll keep you safe."

His voice is tender and I can't help but lean closer into him. With a gentle finger, he turns my face to his and traces the line of my jaw, leaving a pathway of warmth in its wake. My breath catches at how handsome he is, and the sounds of the museum fall away. For a moment I think he's going to kiss me, right here in front of God, the curators, and everyone. My heart races, but then a clear emotion of Owen's reaches out to me. It's an emotion that extinguishes my mood, for it's not one of tenderness or love or even passion.

It's regret.

I pull away and the moment is broken.

Owen clears his throat and continues the conversation as if the moment never happened. "You sure do seem to attract trouble. I wonder if it has anything to do with your father."

I shrug, hoping he gets the hint that I don't want to talk about Houdini.

"It's pretty amazing that you became a magician, just like him. Did you get to see him very often growing up?"

He leans toward me, his eyes gleaming, and I shift away, disappointment tightening my throat. I briefly wonder how much of the flask he "nipped" before picking me up.

"No, actually I didn't."

"That must have been tough on you. Have you seen him since you got to the city?"

I stand. "You know, the walk here tired me out more than I thought it would. I don't think I've fully recovered yet."

Owen isn't the first person to poke and prod me about my father once they heard the rumors that I was Houdini's daughter. I'm just frustrated that he seems as interested in my parentage as he is in me.

Or maybe underneath it all, I'm just too preoccupied by Cole to appreciate Owen's company.

Owen's handsome features fall into lines of disappointment, but then his face brightens. "Well, don't worry. If you're not feeling up to it, I can do the show tomorrow. Your mother seems to think it's working out really well."

I just bet she does. "I'm sure I'll be fine by then," I tell him firmly, and this time I brush past him, ignoring the arm he offers.

By the next morning, I've fully recovered from my collapse and am impatient to get the talk with Cole over with. Mother fusses over me, ignoring my surly attitude. She's feeling generous now that she has what she wants. I'm having none of it. Years of benign neglect lend steel to my spine. Besides, just because I would do anything to protect her doesn't mean *I* don't want to wring her neck.

I flick through one of Mother's magazines, hoping she'll soon tire of playing this particular role and run off to lunch with someone. With Mrs. Lindsay out of the picture, my worries about her have abated somewhat. I haven't had a vision since Mrs. Lindsay was taken away. I hear Mother moving through the back bedrooms, occasionally making a comment about this or that, but I ignore her.

Suddenly, anger slams into me and I turn to see my mother standing in the doorway, a book in her hand. Her mouth is set, and her eyes are shooting dark sparks of fury. "What is this?"

Shock waves run through my body and I bolt upright. "What?"

She holds out the book mutely. *A Magician Among the Spirits.*

I gulp and remain silent. What am I to say?

"You've seen him?" Her tone sounds conversational, almost normal. Unless you've spent a lifetime studying the nuances and timbre of that voice. Then you'd realize just how loaded the question is.

I force my eyes to meet hers and incline my head ever so slightly. She moves closer and I stand. Kam Lee once told me never to meet an opponent sitting down, and, God help me, I feel as if I'm entering into battle. Against my own mother.

She opens the book and I wait. "'To Anna, best wishes, Harry Houdini.'" Her voice drips with caramel and arsenic.

The seeds of anger I've been carrying around sprout. The roots dig deep into soil that has been tilled and ready for more than a decade. Then it shoots upward, spreading through my chest.

I wait, my breath calm and measured. I will not let her see that my heart is racing. That my skin has suddenly grown clammy with dread. I must not show any sign of weakness.

"How dare you."

The words skim across my skin like the quiet breath of a snake ready to strike. I keep my face still, showing just a hint of scorn by widening my eyes ever so slightly and raising one brow.

Actually, it's one of my mother's looks I'm borrowing.

"How dare you," she repeats, louder this time.

I fight to keep my face unmoving, but my expression wavers and then fails. For a moment I look to the floor, unable to meet her eyes. Then my anger flares and I meet her gaze again. "How dare I what?" With effort I keep my voice composed. "Go to see my father? Why shouldn't I?"

Her eyes cloud for a moment before hardening again. "You know why. He could ruin us."

"Ruin us? Or expose you?"

Her eyes never waver. I lick my lips. "Is Harry Houdini really my father?" The moment the words are out of my mouth I want to take them back. It's a question I can't afford to have answered.

Her eyes sweep away and then back. "Of course he is," she snaps.

I want to believe her. Want to believe the only parent I have would never raise her only daughter with an elaborate lie to gain some kind of disreputable fame.

But there it is.

I carefully set down the magazine I'd been strangling in my hand. "You don't even know the color of his eyes," I say quietly. Without another word, I get my coat from the closet and walk out the door, leaving her alone with the monstrosity of her lies.

TWENTY-FOUR

I stare up at the four-story building, the icy wind whipping in my face. I give up trying to keep my cloche on my head and stuff it in my pocket. It'll never be the same.

But then again, neither will I.

When I left the flat, I never thought I would end up in front of Houdini's house. The card he gave me at the magic shop was still in the pocket of my coat, but I didn't need it. I'd already memorized the address. There's no movement inside and I wonder if he's already left on another tour.

I've left my mother behind, in more ways than one, and here I stand in front of my father's house. But in reality, he's as removed from me as my mother is.

I think I had some vague notion of confronting him, but now, faced with the reality of his four-story brownstone mansion, the notion dies a cold death. As far as I know, my mother never told him he had a daughter.

My breath catches as the truth settles more deeply into my heart.

If I were really Houdini's daughter, my mother would have moved heaven and hell to make sure he knew it. She always made sure to let the rumor of my paternity slip wherever we went, so would she really give up the financial and social advantages that such a connection to Houdini would produce?

I remember his wife's sweet, lively face. She's hardly a match for my mother. I can't see her squirreling letters away from her husband. Put that together with the fact that Mother didn't even know what color eyes he had and the truth seems obvious.

My throat tightens. I never realized how badly I wanted him to be my father until the moment I knew he wasn't.

I turn from the house and wipe away the tears before they have a chance to fall. If I'm not Houdini's daughter, who am I?

I hurry down the street into Central Park, which is bleak and deserted. Not many people would choose to brave the sharp November wind. It's a long walk home, but I don't want to take the streetcar.

I don't really want to go home either. Mother's at home. "Anna?"

I startle and turn to find Houdini arm in arm with his wife. Both are dressed against the weather in heavy woolen coats, scarves, and gloves. Her cheeks are rosy from the cold and she looks at me with friendly interest.

Houdini introduces us. "Bess, this is Anna. She is also a magician. Anna, this is my wife, Bess."

If my appearance has shaken him, Houdini gives no sign.

I take the hand Bess offers. She's feeling simple, uncomplicated contentment. "Nice to meet you."

She gives me a smile that takes up her entire face. "Silly men. They can never get introductions right. What is your last name, dear?"

My eyes dart back and forth. If I gave him my last name, how long would it take him to track me down? From me to my mother to our séances to ruin.

But isn't everything ruined already?

My mother may be a liar, but I am certainly not, and the devil rises up inside of me. "Van Housen." I smile. "Anna Van Housen."

Her forehead wrinkles. "That sounds familiar. Are you one of the Philadelphia Van Housens?"

I shake my head, the devil spurring me on. "No. Actually, Van Housen is the name my mother took after moving here from Europe." I smile at Bess, but my eyes are on Houdini. "Her real name is Moshe. Magali Moshe."

For a fraction of a second, his eyes widen. His lips and jaw tighten before smoothing back into a pleasant smile.

My heart races and my fingertips go numb. *He knows that name.* The ramifications of that shoot through me like an arrow. If he knows my mother's name, maybe she hadn't lied about knowing him. Maybe some of what she told me is the truth, and if that's so . . . I get dizzy just thinking about it.

Bess, oblivious, just shakes her head. "No, that isn't familiar at all, but Van Housen . . ."

Houdini takes his wife's arm. "It's time I got you inside, my dear. It's getting too cold for you to be out."

"I'm just getting over a cough," she explains. "Harry is so overprotective."

"You should go home as well, Anna. It's getting dark and the park isn't safe for young girls at night."

His manner is calm, but his agitation ripples and snaps like a flag in the wind.

"It was nice meeting you," Bess calls as Houdini hurries her away.

I wrap my arms around my torso, but my legs are frozen. How had he known my mother's name? Could she have been telling the truth? I press my hands against my eyes, my mind spinning. I don't know how long I stand that way, but slowly I realize that Houdini is right; it's getting dark, and it isn't safe for me to be wandering around on my own. Even if Mrs. Lindsay is no longer a threat.

The streetcar is half empty when I get on, and in no time I'm in front of my house. I linger outside in spite of the fact that I'm freezing. I don't want to see my mother.

I finally drag myself up the stairs just as Jacques steps out the doorway.

"Anna!" His voice is disapproving. "Your mother is worried sick about you. You know the doctor said you are to rest. And it isn't safe for you to be out alone."

"I'm fine," I tell him.

He shakes his head. "That isn't what your mother says."

I look up at him, my heart sinking. "What do you mean?"

"Your mother told me she isn't at all pleased with your progress. I think twelve weeks of rest sounds a bit extreme, but she seems quite concerned."

For the second time that day I freeze. "Twelve weeks?"

Jacques tilts his head and gives me an odd look. "That's what your mother says. I don't like it, though, not at all. You are a big part of the success of the show and I'm just not sure Owen can carry it."

I swallow back my anger. "Mother's just being a worry-wart. I'll only do two shows a week, just like the doctor advised, and I promise to see him before I come back full-time. I'm fine, see?" I hold my arms open, trying to look as healthy—and as innocent—as possible.

His forehead wrinkles as his professional instincts struggle with the part of him that wants to please my mother. The manager within him wins and he nods. "As you say."

He steps past me, but I latch onto the arm of his coat. "And also, I have a new illusion to try out. Don't tell Mother yet; I want to surprise her during rehearsal. I think it will really bring the house down."

"Excellent. I look forward to seeing it. I've often thought you could beef up the magic portion of the show, but your mother said you weren't interested."

I clench my teeth but manage a pleasant smile as Jacques goes on his way. I pause before opening my door. If Mother thinks she can get rid of me this easily, she'll need to think again.

★ ★ ★

"We need to talk."

"You said that already."

Cole's dark eyes regard me steadily. They aren't exactly angry, but they're not friendly either. Mr. Darby made himself scarce after ushering me through the doorway. So here I stand in the middle of his living room, my hands pressed together in front of me, more nervous than I've ever been before a performance.

"I read the letter."

Cole inclines his head and waits. He's not making it easy on me, but then, I didn't expect him to. I press on.

"I don't know what's going on and I'm not sure it's any of my business. I just wanted to apologize again. Taking the letter . . ." I swallow hard against the mass of tears in my throat. "Well, it had nothing to do with anyone else but me."

He sits silently, his eyes never wavering, and I know I have to tell him why I picked his pocket in the first place. How can I explain without sounding inexperienced and awkward? That I couldn't breathe, couldn't think, and could hardly move because of how close he was. My cheeks burn as I continue. "I picked your pocket because I've never felt the way I felt on the train that morning. About you, I mean."

I look down at the worn gray carpet, humiliated. It isn't much of an explanation, but it's the best I can do.

"How did you feel?"

I raise my eyes to look at him and suck in my breath. The same way I feel right now—like I want him to kiss me more than I've ever wanted anything.

Waves of embarrassment rush over me and I collapse in the nearest chair, covering my face with my hands. "I knew you were going to ask that!" I moan. "I don't know!"

A long moment passes before he says quietly, "That makes two of us."

My hands come down and I take a good look at him. His face is still, his eyes cool. What does that mean? That he doesn't know how I felt or that he doesn't know how he felt?

"Anna, I never believed that you taking the letter had anything to do with the problems we're having within the Society. I just wanted to know why you did it." He clears his throat. "I don't understand it any more than I did before, but I do accept your apology."

"Thank you," I tell him simply.

An awkward silence follows before Cole rises to his feet and moves toward the door.

I'm being dismissed.

I follow him and then pause, unable to hold back any longer. "Tell me one thing, though. Are you in danger?"

Cole lifts a shoulder. "Perhaps. Or perhaps not. You were right about one thing."

"Only one?" I make a lame attempt to joke, but there's no answering humor in his eyes.

"It's really not your business."

I shiver at the coldness of his voice. He opens the door and I step outside. He doesn't offer to see me up the stairs and my heart aches. I wish we could just go back to the way things were before.

I turn. "If you're in danger, why haven't you just gone back to England?"

He looks at me. "Don't you know?"

And before I can answer, he closes the door quietly.

I pace up and down the theater hall, my chest tight. Mr. Darby promised to have the illusion set delivered an hour before the show. I told Mother I would see her at the theater and then left the flat, which didn't raise any suspicion as we haven't spoken more than a handful of words to each other in the week since our fight. She tried to stop me from performing tonight, but I insisted and eventually, she acquiesced. She gave in a bit more easily than I would have expected, which makes me wonder what she has up her sleeve. I shove that thought out of my mind. She isn't the only one with plans.

"Miss Anna?"

I jump at the tap on my shoulder. It's only Bart, the stagehand, who will help me cart in the props. I give myself a mental shake. If I don't calm down, I'll never pull this off.

He leans forward conspiratorially and I keep myself from stepping back from his garlicky breath. "The old man is out back," he says in a loud stage whisper.

I glance around, half afraid I'll find Jacques lurking nearby. He wasn't happy when I told him the props wouldn't be delivered until just before the show. Then I implied that Mother and I had already practiced the new routine. God help me, I'm getting as good at lying as she is.

I follow Bart to the back door, where Mr. Darby is waiting.

"Do we still have time to set it up?"

"I have everything ready to go."

I give him a big hug. "You'll be out front, won't you?"

His eyes twinkle at me. "Of course! I wouldn't miss this for the world." He shakes his head. "I built the damn thing and know how it works and I still couldn't believe my eyes."

"You're a genius," I tell him. "Thank you so much." I pause. "Is Cole here?"

He gives my hand a squeeze. "Of course."

Cole has been distant and reserved ever since my big apology. I really want to talk to him about my vision, but there never seems to be a good time. I wonder if there ever will be. But he did come to see the show. Maybe that's a good sign.

Bart lugs the table up the stairs and then waits patiently while Mr. Darby puts the wheels on it. It's absolutely perfect—it looks like an ordinary table. Once it's set up, it'll be covered in black velvet and no one will see underneath.

I sigh in relief when we finally get it onto the stage. Mr. Darby instructs Bart on what to do and keeps careful watch as everything gets set up.

"Do you have the time?" I ask Mr. Darby.

He pulls out a pocket watch. "Quarter to five, missy."

"Can you finish this up?"

He looks around at the dim stage. "I'm almost done here."

"Good, I'll be right back."

I dash down the hall toward the side door. Most theaters are a labyrinth of rooms and halls and this one is no exception. I'm counting on that to keep my secret safe until the moment I choose to reveal it.

Doubt churns in my stomach. This could very well be the end of my relationship with my mother. She might forgive me for seeing Houdini behind her back, but she will never forgive me for stealing the show.

But maybe that's the point? Maybe I've always known this day would come. The day when I show her once and for all that I'm not hers—that I don't belong to her. I love her and would do anything to protect her, but I won't allow her to play me like she does her clients. If she wants a relationship with me, it's going to have to be one of equality.

My pulse races as I reach the door. The dancers are filtering in, chattering like brightly colored birds. The show is going to start soon. "Please God, let him be here," I pray under my breath. Then I spot him, almost blending into the shadows. "Dante," I call, waving him in.

The boy comes toward me, a wide smile on his face. "Da told me to wait and not to muss my clothes."

The boy in the black velvet knee breeches hardly resembles the waif passing out flyers all those weeks ago. I was half afraid they'd absconded with the money I gave them for clothes, but I was counting on his father's business instincts to come through. A chance for his son to be a permanent magician's assistant would be a better opportunity in the long run than the ten dollars I'd given them earlier this week.

"That's the swankiest car I've ever ridden in," he exclaims.

I look out across the street. Cynthia waves to me and points, indicating that she'll be in the audience. I wave thank-you and turn back to Dante.

I lead him by the hand to the theater. We pass the musicians setting up in the orchestra pit. Mr. Darby is waiting for me just offstage.

"All finished here."

I give him a hug. "Thank you so much."

"My pleasure, missy." He gives Dante a conspirator's wink. The two of them are already fast friends, having met when we practiced the illusions.

I kneel, face to face with my new assistant. "You remember everything we went over yesterday?"

Dante's eyes are as wide as his smile and he looks like he's been scrubbed within an inch of his life.

"Yes. I remember everything."

"Good. Do you have to go to the bathroom? Get a drink of water?"

He shakes his head solemnly.

"Perfect." I lead him back to the wings to where the set has been hidden. "I need you to hide under here until you hear your cue. Remember, there's going to be a singer coming out and then dancers, so it will seem like a very long time."

"Don't worry, miss. I know what to do." He gives me a confident nod.

I grin in spite of my nerves. He's like a little old man in a seven-year-old body. I pull up the black coverlet and he scoots underneath.

I hold out my hand and he shakes it. "Good luck," I tell him.

"Good luck," he says.

I'm going to need it.

Tension ricochets through the dressing room like a bouncing ball. Mother sits straight backed at her vanity, pretending to fix her flawless makeup. I can't help but pace, going over every detail of the new act in my mind. I'm counting on Mother's showmanship to cover up her surprise. Then she will have nothing to do but watch as her daughter steps from the shadows into the light. My turn at last.

I just wish I felt less guilty about what I'm about to do.

A knock on the door signals that it is time for us to go on. My mother rises and we walk silently into the hallway.

Then she holds out her hand. I look at her open palm extended toward me and I take it, hurt forming in my throat at our old tradition.

"Are we ready?" she asks.

I look into her eyes. They're flat. Cold. Emotionless. The urge to cry disappears as my pain and anger once again take hold.

"As ready as I'll ever be," I answer.

"Are we going to astonish them?"

I look at her and I feel a strange, triumphant smile curl my lips—one my mother has no doubt given many times. "You have no idea."

She falters for a moment, but I grip her hand more firmly and keep moving.

This time when the curtain opens I stay in the spotlight, my pulse racing. I hit every line and cue until my mother introduces me. Then I step forward and wait until the audience settles, pausing a few beats more for effect. I've watched my mother captivate audiences for years. Now it's my turn.

Tonight I'm wearing a black silk chemise dress, heavily beaded with white pearls that shimmer as I move. It's perfect for the dreamy mood I want to set.

I hold out my hands to show a deck of cards, then I begin manipulating them. Card flourishes aren't really magic unless you show the audience things they aren't expecting to see, such as cards disappearing and reappearing in different places. The tricks are lovely to watch, with their delicate fans and arches, but difficult for an audience as big as this one to see. I exaggerate my movements just a bit and a cello below me in the orchestra pit begins playing, a soft melodic tone. I've always wanted to add music to the act and now I match my movements to the melody.

"What is magic?" I ask the audience, projecting loudly. I spent most of last night trying to figure out what I would say—this performance is, after all, my swan song. "I've spent my life among magicians and performers and I've always wondered what true magic is. Is it what my mother does? Is it what Harry Houdini does? Is it real?" At this point I show the audience the eight of spades. Turning toward my mother, I show her the card. "Or is it trickery?" I place the eight of spades between my teeth and turn sideways. Then I hold a large fan in one hand, diverting their attention for a fraction of second. Waving my free hand over the fan, I pull out the eight of spades from the end of the deck. No one saw it move from my mouth.

The audience claps and I give a little bow. Then I turn toward my mother, whose smile is frozen on her face, waiting for a cue that isn't going to come. I flash my audience, my mother, and the whole world a smile. "Tonight, you be the judge!"

At that, a violinist joins the cello and the music swells. Dante rolls out the long table, just as smoothly as we'd practiced. I almost laugh at the confident set of his head and the haughty look on his face. He exudes professionalism and I follow suit. The table is loaded with the props I'll need. First, I hand Dante the deck I'm holding and move into the routine we've practiced in Mr. Darby's basement. The theme of the performance is freedom, and the audience gasps as I set various items—a card, a ball, and finally, a large hoop—free, levitating them magically around the stage.

Excitement flows through my veins, and at the end of each trick, I bow my head slightly toward my mother.

Look, Mother, no hands!

When it's time for the finale, I stop and face the audience, breathing hard. This is my pièce de résistance. A few members of the audience are clapping uncertainly, not sure if this is the end or not. The applause fades as the music quiets, the delicate notes of Debussy's "Clair de Lune" filling the theater. I turn and hold my hand out to Dante. He comes to me, so small, trusting, and innocent. The audience sighs. The kid should be an actor.

I lead him to the table that's been cleared of all props. Helping him onto the top, I hold his hand for a second before releasing it. The success of this trick, any trick really, is in how it's presented, and this is worth a slow, languorous buildup. The music slows further, into a hypnotizing lullaby, and I feel the audience holding its breath. I dance to the other side of the table and bend to kiss Dante's forehead like a mother putting her child to sleep. I wave my hands slowly over the sleeping child in time to the music. Then I twirl to the front of the table and slowly lift the black coverlet over Dante's body. The audience can now see under and around the table.

Dancing to the end of the platform, I slowly, carefully, detach the end piece. It now looks as if half the table were floating in air. I gracefully wave my hand where the wood had been to show that there is nothing holding it up. Then I dance to the other end and remove that piece as well.

The audience gasps. I hear murmurs of surprise and shock. Picking up the silver hoop, I begin at Dante's feet and move it across so his body goes through the ring.

The audience goes crazy, whistling and clapping. I give a demure curtsy and then permit myself a moment to luxuriate in the sound. As I look into the audience, I see a man rise to his feet in the first row. I blush at the compliment, then freeze as I realize who it is.

Harry Houdini.

My heart bursts as the rest of the audience joins him in a standing ovation and for a moment I can't move. Then the music begins anew and I remember my routine. I put a trembling finger to my lips and then point at Dante, as if reminding the audience of the sleeping child. As soon as they are quiet, I gracefully put the table ends back on one at a time, fold the black velvet back off Dante's body, and help him off the table. He exits stage left and the music stops.

I look back out to where I'd spotted Houdini, but he isn't there. A magician always knows when to make his exit.

"And now, it's my mother's turn to amaze you!" The audience claps politely.

I pivot, triumph pounding in my chest. I'd nearly forgotten her during the end of my performance, and now I brace myself, waiting for her anger to hit me like a wave. But instead of anger, I feel hurt. She blinks at me, her eyes bottomless pools of bewildered hurt.

Mother falters for a moment, then pastes a smile on her face and moves on to her portion of the show. She leaves out the muscle-reading trick completely. Though she performs without a hitch, her heart isn't in it. Her movements are stiff and wooden, her voice flat. Her part in the show is anticlimactic, and everyone, especially my mother, knows it.

As we leave the stage I hear a few people yell my name. Mother walks a few feet ahead of me, her back ramrod straight.

The triumph I felt onstage ebbs, leaving my chest tight and empty. I follow her to the dressing room, even though I would rather be anywhere but there. But I knew when I planned my debut that this moment would come. Only a child would run away, and I'm no longer a child to be intimidated. I can take whatever she has to give.

Only she doesn't give me anything. She just goes to her dressing-room table and drinks down her wine in several long gulps. She doesn't speak. She doesn't look at me. Picking up her hairbrush, she runs it through her hair awkwardly, her movements lacking her normal catlike grace.

I bite my lip, wanting her to say something, anything, so I can defend myself. I want to let her know I'm different, that things have changed, but she remains silent. I begin to feel more and more like a child too naughty to be acknowledged.

The door opens behind me and Jacques comes in. He rushes to my mother, a frown on his face. "Magali, darling, are you all right?" He bends over my mother and she leans her head against him. "I could tell from your performance that you were not feeling right. Anna was brilliant, but you did not seem well at all. Is there anything I can do?"

His voice is creased with worry and concern. In the mirror, I can see that her eyes are closed, and I am struck by how drawn and tired she looks. Not like my mother at all.

Her hand snakes up and he reaches out to grasp it, bending down to put his lips against her hair.

Then, for the first time, Jacques's emotions transmit themselves to me strong and clear from across the room.

He's achingly in love with my mother.

Suddenly I feel as if I'm peeping in on something I shouldn't be seeing. Forgotten, I slip from the room, more alone than I've ever been.

TWENTY-FIVE

I stumble down the hall, looking for Dante and Mr. Darby, and instead find the short, compact figure of Harry Houdini waiting for me.

He smiles. "I couldn't leave without congratulating you on your performance. You really *are* a magician, Anna."

Tears prick at my eyes, but I blink them away. "Thank you, Mr. Houdini."

"And your mother. She is as lovely as I remember. Did she tell you that we knew each other long ago?"

His voice is mild, but his eyes are not. The look he levels at me burns right down to my soul. "Yes. She did," I answer simply.

"Ah. I thought she might." He pauses. "I must go. Please give my regards to your mother and again, congratulations on a fine performance."

He turns to leave, but I catch his sleeve. I may never get another chance to ask. "Are you a . . ." I catch myself and rephrase the question. "*Do* you have psychical powers, Mr. Houdini?"

He laughs, his eyes amused. "You must have been reading the ravings of my former friend, Sir Arthur Conan Doyle."

"Anna!"

I hear Mr. Darby calling from behind me, but I press on. "Do you?"

Houdini's face stills. "I've said it before and I will say it again. I do not. Now, you should go; your friend is calling for you."

Frantically, I send out a ribbon only to find it . . . blocked.

With another unreadable look, the great magician turns and walks down the hall.

I stand there looking after him, loss, grief, and desolation warring in my chest. Without another word, I turn to where Mr. Darby and Dante are waiting for me.

I accept their congratulations woodenly as we wheel the table to the waiting truck.

Cole is fidgeting outside when we come through the doorway. I stand slightly away from the group as the table is loaded into the back.

"Careful now." Mr. Darby grunts, gripping his end. "This thing is worth its weight in gold."

I don't tell him that I'm not sure I have the heart to use it again.

Ezio is waiting to take his son home. I can't tell which one is prouder, Dante or his father. I bend and give Dante a hug. "You were wonderful." I hand him a five-dollar bill, which he pockets.

"Anytime you need me, I'm your man!"

I watch them leave, the father's hand on his son's shoulder.

Without a word, Cole's arm folds around me. I tilt my head back to look into his eyes. He's hardly spoken to me for days, but he knows without a word how I'm feeling.

I give him a small half smile, liking the feeling of his arm across my shoulder. I shuffle closer, noticing Mr. Darby has already climbed into the truck to leave us alone. I want to tell Cole that I'm sad and confused and lonely. I want to tell him how much I love my mother and how much I hate her at the same time. I want to tell him how desperately I wish she loved me back the same way I love her. I want to tell him how I feel about Houdini, who may or may not be my father. "I forgot my coat," I say instead.

"Do you want me to go get it?"

I shake my head, thinking of the scene I just left. "No."

"You'll get cold," he objects.

I move even closer into the protective circle of his arm. "No, I won't."

Heat flares in the depths of his dark eyes and his arm tightens, but all he says is "We should get home, then. We need to get the table unloaded and return the truck. Besides"—he looks up at the sky—"I think it's going to snow."

The ride home is quiet. Cole keeps his arm around me and I'm grateful that he doesn't press me for answers to the questions I sense swirling in his mind.

The first flakes are falling as we unload the table. After we put it away, Mr. Darby leaves to take the truck back before the snow starts to accumulate.

"You want to tell me what happened?" Cole asks, handing me a cup of tea. We're sitting at the kitchen table, the fire from the stove warming my frozen limbs.

I stare at the steam coming off the tea as tears sting my eyes. Putting my head in the crook of my arms, I sob until I can't sob anymore. I hear Mr. Darby return, but he slips out as quietly as he came in.

I wipe my eyes and then tell Cole everything from the very beginning. I tell him about seeing the *Titanic* sink and the time I envisioned stacks of dead bodies in the street just before the Spanish flu made that vision a reality. I tell him about my fear of policemen and about all the menial jobs I took in order to research clients. I tell him about my mother's obsession with Harry Houdini and how badly I wanted to believe he was my real father.

I talk until I'm almost hoarse, and as the words pour out of me, I realize how much time I've spent alone, waiting for my mother to come home.

At some point during my monologue, Cole places his hand over mine. I become aware of his concern as I wind down with the scene in the dressing room. I don't tell him about talking to Houdini. It's too personal, and I don't know how I feel about it yet.

"Do you think your mother loves Jacques, too?" Cole asks.

I raise a shoulder. "I don't know if she's even capable of love."

"Everyone's capable of love, missy," Mr. Darby says from behind me.

He takes my untouched cup of tea and pours it down the sink, then adds water to the kettle and puts it back on the stove to heat. I wonder how much he's heard about my visions and decide I don't much care.

"Your mother did the best she could with the talent and beauty God gave her. She was a woman alone raising a child, and instead of giving you up, she kept you with her. You spent your life traveling, meeting new people, and seeing new things." He raises a hand when I try to speak. "No, what you saw wasn't always pretty. Sometimes it was ugly and hard. But life is both the pretty and the ugly. Sometimes you were alone and afraid and hungry. Lots of people are alone and hungry."

I sit silent, taking it in. Part of me wants to argue, but I'm too tired to find the words.

The kettle whistles and Mr. Darby makes me a fresh cup of tea. I notice for the first time that the sink is full of dishes and crumbs cover the counters. He sees me looking at the mess as he hands me my cup.

"The cleaning girl didn't show up today. It's so hard to find good help. Now drink this and you'll feel better."

I sip obediently.

"I don't want to be too hard on you. Your mother is a cold woman. But I bet in all that travel you had some real good times too, didn't you?"

I think of Swineguard, Kam Lee, and all the rest who went

out of their way to befriend me and teach me how to survive. I nod reluctantly. Parts of our journey have been wonderful.

"There you go," Mr. Darby says smugly.

"There I go what?" I'm irritated and exhausted and I hate being told that I'm wrong. It's another thing I have in common with my mother.

"I think what he means is that you take the good with the bad because you don't have a choice. That's what life is made up of." Cole gives my hand a gentle squeeze and I feel his sadness.

I wonder if he's talking about the war. About losing his father. It's no wonder he takes life so seriously. I squeeze his hand back.

Mr. Darby nods. "The question is, missy, what do you do now? You're an adult, or will be soon. No one says you have to headline with your mother for the rest of your life. Sounds to me like she's pushing you out of the nest, anyway. She has her work and a man who loves her. She's taken care of. What about you?"

I can't help it; I shoot a glance at Cole. His dark eyes are as calm and steady as they were the first time I met him. I glance away, not wanting him to see the confusion in mine.

What about me? I wonder as Cole escorts me upstairs. This time he doesn't put his arm around me. Instead, he surprises me by pulling me close. I rest my head against his chest and listen to the steady rhythm of his heart. Then I feel the block he always has up when he's around me quaking. "Anna," he murmurs, his hand rubbing gentle circles on my back. Suddenly a floodgate inside him opens, and a sea of warmth washes over me. Startled, I tilt my head back to find his dark eyes smoldering with something I've never seen, or felt, before. He bends his head and presses his lips gently against mine. I tremble and lean against him, letting our emotions swirl around us, merging and melding together, creating something altogether new. Too soon he lifts his head.

"Get some sleep," he murmurs softly. "You've had a long day. We can talk more tomorrow. There are some things I have to tell you."

I look up at him, my lips still burning, even though it had been merely a whisper of a kiss. "What things?"

Cole smiles and kisses me on the forehead. "Tomorrow."

He waits until I'm safely inside and the door is locked before he heads back down the stairs.

The apartment is dark and chilly after the warmth of Mr. Darby's kitchen. I flick on the lights and start up the heat, then I grab a throw and curl up on the sofa.

What am I going to do now? I know for certain that for whatever reason, Mother doesn't want me in the show anymore. Especially after tonight.

But what do I want?

For years, I just wanted to have a normal home—a normal, respectable home with a normal, respectable family. A home just like this one. But when I finally got it, I started following Harry Houdini around like a lost child. I wonder what he was doing at the show tonight. He usually leaves mentalists who perform onstage alone. He seems to think them harmless entertainment. It's the séances that he hates. If only I can convince Mother to give them up. At any rate, I won't be participating in any more of them. I may not know what I want, but I do know what I don't want. If we find ourselves out in the cold again, I'll do what other people do when they need money—

I'll get a job.

So if the great magician wasn't there to discredit my mother, why was he there? For me?

My pulse quickens as I remember how he asked if I knew that they had known each other.

What if everything my mother told me is true? What if Harry Houdini really is my father? What if I *did* get my abilities from him?

I sit up, pulling the blanket tighter around me as I consider the thought. What would change if that were true? Would I be a different person? He would never acknowledge the connection. He is utterly devoted to his wife. So what would change?

Nothing.

Whether or not Houdini is my father, whether or not my mother loves me, I would still be me. A girl who loves magic. A girl with strange abilities. I will never be a normal girl. But maybe, just maybe, that's all right.

Thinking about my abilities brings me back to my thoughts of Cole and I snuggle into the couch cushions, reliving the moment he kissed me. *I could love him,*

I think drowsily. My body relaxes and I let sleep over-come me.

It's the vision. I know as it's happening that it's not real, but I'm powerless to stop it. I'm being washed away on an ocean of distorted images. My mother, terrified. Her fear comes to me in waves of panic. My body, broken. I feel the warm stickiness of blood running down my face. He's coming for me. Helpless. I'm so helpless. She's screaming. I'm sorry, Mama. Then the vision shifts and I'm back in the water, my lungs burning for air. Then my mother's face, her eyes wide with terror and grief.

She thinks I'm dead. And in that moment, I know just how very much she loves me.

I wake myself up, screams ripping from my throat. Bolting upright, I blink several times, completely disoriented. I wait for my mother to call out to me, to ask if I'm all right. Nothing. My heart pounds painfully in my chest. This wasn't supposed to happen. With Mrs. Lindsay out of the picture, I wasn't supposed to have another vision. But I just did.

"Mama?" My heart plummets as I realize I'm still alone.

Kicking the blanket off my legs, I make my way awk-wardly down the hall to her bedroom, stiff from having spent the night on the sofa. "Mama?"

Her bedroom is empty, her bed still made.

There's a sudden banging on the door and I press myself against the wall, positive my abductors have come for me.

"Anna?" My legs nearly buckle with relief.

"Cole?" I race to the door, my heart pounding in my ears. I can't get the door unlocked quickly enough and then I'm in his arms.

"What's wrong? Are you all right?"

"Yes. No. It's my mother—something's happened."

Cole searches the hall, as if expecting whatever's happened to be right there in front of us.

"No." I pull him farther inside and shut the door. "She didn't come home last night and I had a vision."

His brows draw together. "She was with Jacques, correct? Perhaps she's still with him?"

His voice is stilted, and if I wasn't so frightened I might have laughed. As if I would be shocked by my mother's indiscretion.

I grasp at the suggestion.

"You call Jacques and I'll make coffee." He pushes me toward the phone.

I stand for a moment before dialing, overwhelmed with gratitude. Cole didn't have to question me about the dream. He didn't have to ask how I knew my mother was in trouble. He just knows me. "Did you hear me scream?" I ask suddenly. He stops in the kitchen doorway.

"No, I felt it."

We stare at each other, the space between us brimming with unspoken words.

I nod. "Thank you."

I hurry into the sitting room and call Jacques. He picks up on the fourth ring.

"Do you know what time it is?"

"Where's my mother?"

"Anna?"

"Are there any other daughters who would call you to find out the whereabouts of their mother?" I snap.

"Of course not. I just don't understand. Your mother, she is not with me. She went home. What time is it?"

"I don't know. Early."

"Hold on." I hear him fumbling about. "It is six a.m. She went home several hours ago. She stayed late, talking. You were not a nice girl, letting me think your mother knew about the addition to the show."

My stomach twists.

"Wait. She is not home?"

"No."

His response is immediate. "I'll be right there."

He hangs up before I can say anything else, and relief washes over me. If this had happened several months ago, I might have suspected Jacques, but now I realize that I have grown to trust him. At any rate, there is no doubt how he feels about my mother.

I set the phone on its hook and walk into the kitchen. The coffee is boiling on the stove and Cole looks up at me, his eyes full of questions.

I shake my head. "She left hours ago. He's on his way over."

Tears prick behind my eyes, but I hold them back. Crying won't solve anything. I learned that early on.

Cole holds out a chair for me and I sit gratefully.

"I shouldn't have done what I did yesterday. I was so angry with her, but instead of confronting her, I stole the spotlight. Why did I do that? Why can't we just talk like normal people?"

He shakes his head. "You don't think your mother ran off."

It isn't a question but a statement. I give him a small shake of my head. No, my mother has never run away from anything.

"Then don't make this your fault."

I swallow my tears and nod. Cole hands me a cup of hot coffee and I drink, not caring that it's scalding my tongue. The pain clears my head. Only one thought keeps spinning around and around: This wasn't supposed to happen with Mrs. Lindsay in jail. *And if Mrs. Lindsay isn't the culprit, who is?*

"We need to make a list of possibilities, but before Jacques arrives, tell me about your vision. How many times have you had it?"

"I'm not sure. Four or five times."

"Is it the same every time?"

I nod, grateful that he's here to help me sort this out, grateful to have someone to talk to who won't think I'm crazy.

"Do you always have repeat visions?"

I shake my head. "No, but then I've never had visions like this before. As I told you, usually they're about big events, such as the *Titanic*, or the Great Kanto Earthquake. Never about my own life."

I get him a paper and pencil and he takes notes as I describe what I've seen. When I'm done, he starts with the questions.

"Can you describe the place where they're holding your mother?"

I try to remember but can't get past the look on her face.

"I know this is hard, but try to replay it in your mind. Close your eyes and picture it. Is it a large room or small? Can you tell if it's day or night? What are the walls made out of? Brick? Wood? Is there a window? What is the man wearing—are you sure it's a man?"

"Wait." I take a deep breath and sharpen my focus. "It's a small room. My mother is tied up just out of my reach." I focus, and the vision begins to replay itself. My stomach tingles and I reach out blindly to Cole, who takes my hand. I relax as much as I can considering the pain in my head and let the vision take me. But this time I am in control of it.

"It's dark, and light is coming through cracks in the walls. It looks like a shed or closet or something." The man enters the vision and my pulse skips, frightened in spite of the fact that Cole is here with me and I know this isn't real. "He's in black. It's an overcoat."

My heart races as the man comes toward me and then the vision changes. "I'm underwater now. I can't breathe." I open my eyes, my breath coming quickly. "I'm afraid for my mother."

Cole's face is white. I glance at the paper and see not only notes, but also little sketches. Suddenly, I understand. "You saw it too?"

He nods. "As soon as I touched your hand."

I swallow and study the drawings. "You're quite good. They look just like what I saw."

He nods. "Drawing will be a useful asset in my training."

My forehead wrinkles. "For the Society for Psychical Research?"

He shakes his head and gives me a little smile. "Well, no. I'm going to attend Oxford to study law."

"You want to be a lawyer?"

"No. I want to be a detective with Scotland Yard and I figure law will give me a good foundation."

I give a surprised laugh. "A policeman?"

He shrugs, not meeting my eyes.

I shake my head. "That explains a lot."

"You're not upset? You've told me how you feel about officers of the law." His voice is tight and I squeeze the hand I'm still holding.

"It's too late now. I already like you." I pause. "To be honest, I'm more upset about you leaving than about your chosen profession."

A knock at the door interrupts us and Cole tucks away the notes. I get up to answer it, but Cole shakes his head.

"I don't want you doing anything on your own until we find your mother. Someone tried to snatch you once already. Let's not make you an easy target."

I nod, but I now know in my heart that it's futile to try and change my vision. This isn't a nightmare; this is a portent—something that is *going* to happen.

Jacques rushes in, his hair mussed and his overcoat buttoned crookedly. "Have you heard anything?"

I shake my head. "I was hoping you had."

We move back into the kitchen and Cole hands Jacques a cup of coffee.

We sit at the kitchen table. "What time did she leave last night?" Cole has started on a clean sheet of paper.

"I think it was close to three. We were up late talking." Jacques casts me a look of disapproval.

I ignore it. "You let her leave alone?"

His sits up, affronted. "Certainly not. I called a cab and waited with her in the lobby until it came."

I raise an eyebrow. "Lobby?"

He fidgets a bit. "Yes, I live in the Hotel Monaco, more or less permanently."

"More or less?" His eyes avoid mine, and I suddenly understand. "This is *your* apartment. You gave your apartment to us."

He nods.

"Why would you do that?" I wonder and then the answer flashes in my mind. "Because you thought it would be temporary. You had every intention of moving in here with my mother!"

Jacques has the grace to look uncomfortable but then lifts a shoulder in a supremely French way. "It appears she is far more skittish about marriage than I first thought."

My mouth drops. "Marriage? You asked her to marry you?"

"Only every day since I first met her in Chicago."

My mind whirls, everything I know about Jacques shuffling and changing. Some Sensitive I am. I didn't even know my manager was in love with my mother until just last night.

"She finally agreed to think about it. I believe she would have married me a long time ago if it hadn't been for her worry over you."

"Me?"

"Of course! She was terribly afraid you would follow in her footsteps. She did not want you to be alone."

My brow furrows. That doesn't sound like my mother at all. I wonder if Jacques knows my mother's penchant for stretching the truth. Well, he'll find out soon enough.

If we find my mother.

TWENTY-SIX

Cole clears his throat. "We should really concentrate on locating your mother right now. Does she have any enemies?"

Jacques raises an eyebrow at me at Cole's naiveté.

"Of course she has enemies," I answer. "She's a medium. It's part of the business."

"I know *you* have enemies," Cole says shortly. "Someone tried to abduct you. And we are no closer to finding out who it was than we were before."

"I'm sure it was someone I've met before," I clarify, thinking of Mrs. Lindsay. I guess I can rule her and Lisette out—in this case, at least. A lump rises in my throat. I thought we were safe. I thought it was *over*.

Jacques clears his throat. "You think the same person has your mother?"

I can't tell him about my vision, so I just nod. "I think we can assume that. What cab company picked her up?"

Jacques snaps his fingers. "Of course. We should call them, *oui?*"

Cole nods. "What did you two talk about last night? Was she upset?"

Jacques shoots me another disapproving glance. "She was quite angry with you. You knew that, yes? But I talked with her. She was calm by the time she left. We spoke of the future, and for the first time, she considered a future without the show. I told her we could run my management company together. She kissed me and promised to think about it."

"So she didn't leave angry?" My stomach clenches.

"No. The only time she got angry was when I suggested that you had the talent to have your own show."

My heart stops. "You told her that?"

"*Oui.*"

I can just imagine how that went over.

Jacques's mouth is pulled down in condemnation. "That is when she told me she did not want your life to mirror hers."

I close my eyes for a moment, my throat tightening. It never occured to me that my mother ever gave a thought to my future. I wonder how many more surprises I can take. Then I shake my head. I can ask her about these things next time I see her. But first we have to find her.

Jacques goes to call the taxi company while Cole continues asking me questions and taking notes.

"You said of course your mother has enemies? Why would someone like you have enemies?"

I shrug. "It's part of the business. Remember Mrs. Lindsay?"

He nods.

"Well, she also attacked me in the park and later at Lindy's."

Cole's jaw tightens. "You didn't tell me about that."

I lean back and shut my eyes for a moment. "It was just before I was abducted. So much has happened since then." Then I look down at my hands. "Besides, at the time I thought maybe you already knew something about it."

"Excuse me?"

"I saw you talking with her shortly after she attacked me in the park." I wince at the hurt in his eyes. I know he wouldn't hurt me or my mother. I *know* it. So why did it come out like that?

He lays his hand over mine. "Anna, I went for a walk and she was standing on the corner. I recognized her from the séance and remembered how unstable she felt. She looked like she was having a hard time, so I gave her some money. I only spoke to her for a few minutes. I had no idea she attacked you."

I look down. "I know. I'm just scared."

He gives my hand a squeeze as Jacques comes in, looking even more worried than before.

"The cabbie was at the garage. He said he dropped her off here shortly after picking her up."

"She was here? Right out front?" I shut my eyes, dizzy with fear and anger.

"What should we do? Call the police?"

Jacques and Cole look my way, both bowing to my right to make the decision.

A knock on the door freezes us all. Again, Cole takes the initiative with Jacques on his heels.

"There's no one there." Cole's voice is puzzled until Jacques reaches out and clutches his arm.

"*Regarde!*" He points to the floor. I rise up on my tip-toes in order to see but my view is blocked by two sets of shoulders. Suddenly Cole is gone, racing down the stairs. I hear the front door open and slam behind him. Before I can move, Jacques kneels and picks something up. Peering over his shoulder, I see him carefully holding an envelope between his thumb and forefinger.

He looks up at me, his face stricken. "It has your name on it, *chérie.*"

I swallow, staring at the heavy block letters. He hands the envelope to me just as the front door opens. I hear Cole coming up the stairs, breathing heavily. He shakes his head at Jacques. "They were long gone."

We all stare at the envelope. "You should open it," Cole suggests.

I slide my finger carefully under the flap and take out the folded paper inside. Both Jacques and Cole lean in to get a better look.

I have your mother. To ensure her safe return, I will need ten thousand dollars placed at a specific drop spot of my choice. Do not go to the police.

I will leave further instructions soon. If you have trouble coming up with the money, use your connections.

My hands shake and Cole leads me into the sitting room. The blanket is still lying on the floor. On the side table is a deck of cards and an ashtray overflowing with cigarettes. Nothing has changed, and yet nothing will ever be the same. The trembling starts in my hands, and by the time I take a seat, it's spread over my whole body.

Jacques stands in the doorway, still as stone, while Cole sits close to me, the note in his hands. Silence covers the room like a smothering blanket. I don't even know how to begin dealing with this. Whenever my mother and I have faced adversity before, we faced it together. Now it's just me.

"Use your connections? What does that mean?" Cole asks.

I startle as the words drop into the silence like pebbles in a pond. "What?"

He points a finger at the note. "It says use your connections to get the money. What connections?"

My breath leaves my body in a whoosh and I stare at him, my mouth dry. "My father. They're talking about my father."

"How common is that knowledge? I mean, how many people know about that relationship?"

I drag in a deep breath, trying to regulate my breathing before I pass out. "I'm not sure. I know Mother likes to tell select people to increase publicity, but I don't know who. Do you?" I turn to Jacques.

He spreads his hands out in an apologetic manner. "I'm not sure who she told, but I know the rumors are going around certain circles."

"Then that's no help." Cole looks disappointed and I reach out and squeeze his hand.

"What circles?" I want to know.

"The rich. Potential clients. Some of the mediums and mentalists have been whispering about it, but most of them think it's a publicity ploy."

"Which brings us back to Mrs. Lindsay, right?" Cole turns toward me. "Do we even know if that's her real name?"

I shake my head, despair settling over me. "No, that's a dead end. She was taken into custody after she attacked me at Lindy's."

Jacques raises an eyebrow and I fill him in.

"How do you know she was arrested?"

"Dr. Bennett told me." Now they both look at me with questions in their eyes. "Dr. Bennett is a lecturer at Cynthia's spiritualist church. He's a specialist in psychical phenomena. We were meeting him when he showed up with Mrs. Lindsay."

Cole turns toward me. "Wait. What was a lecturer doing with an insane medium?"

"He called her a colleague." I shiver, remembering the tortured look on Mrs. Lindsay's face. "She was as surprised to see me as I was her."

"I think the first thing we should do is make sure that Mrs. Lindsay is still in custody somewhere," Cole says. "If we just had some idea who had tried to abduct you . . ."

Jacques clears his throat. "Actually, your mother had me hire a private investigator to look into that."

"My mother?"

He nods. "Of course, she was worried about you."

I digest that. "What did you find out?"

"The detective and I were supposed to meet last week, but he had to go out of town suddenly. We were planning on meeting when he returned so he could give me an update."

Bowing my head, I rub my hands over my face. I must look like death. My blood chills at the metaphor. I can't just sit here. I have to do something.

"Can you meet with him?" I ask Jacques. "As soon as possible?"

"Of course."

My mind blanks. What else can I do? Cole gently squeezes my hand.

"Have you considered simply going to the police? I know the note says not to, but I think we need some help here. I'm sure they'd be discreet."

Jacques makes an angry noise deep in his throat and his black eyes snap. "*Non!* If the culprit is having Anna watched, they would be alerted instantly."

"Maybe one of us could do it?" Cole counters.

"The person who did this obviously knows Anna. You think he wouldn't recognize either one of us?"

"Then what would you have her do? Just sit here waiting for another note?"

They both look at me, and I want to hide under the sofa.

"We need to get the money together," Jacques says quietly. "Most of my money is tied up in investments, but I could probably get together about five thousand."

I stare up at him. I knew Jacques was rich, but not that rich. He sees my look and twitches a shoulder. "I invest. I have been very smart and very lucky."

A lump rises in my throat and I want to hug him. How could I have been so wrong about him? And if I've been that mistaken about Jacques, what else have I been wrong about? I give a nod and a wobbly smile, hoping he can see my gratitude.

"I could probably get the rest of the money, but I would have to wire London for it. It would take time."

I stare at Cole in shock. Is everyone around me rich? Then I remember what Cynthia said about him. That he had scads more money than Owen. Apparently, she's right. "I have about fifty-eight dollars." I begin to laugh and then it's cut off by a sob. "What am I going to do?"

"Could you go to your father?" Cole asks.

"No!" Somehow that would be the ultimate betrayal, and I've already betrayed my mother enough. "I think I know where I can get the money," I say slowly. I turn to Jacques. "Why don't you go make arrangements to meet the private investigator and get what money you can. I'll stay here and . . ." My voice falters and Cole cuts in.

"Wait for further contact from the kidnappers."

I nod. "And get the rest of the money together."

Jacques gives my shoulder a brief squeeze before leaving the apartment.

Cole reaches forward and takes my hand into his. My body leans toward him. It's hard to believe it's only been a month or so since I met him. So much has happened: meeting my father and taking control of my abilities. Now this, my mother kidnapped and taken God knows where. I meet his eyes, and they're so full of warmth and caring that my breath catches.

"Do you have any idea who this could be?" Cole asks me gently.

Pain radiates through my head in waves as I try to sort it all out. "When the visions started I tried to figure it out. I was sure it was the Lindsays." I start to giggle and then clap my hand over my mouth when it changes to a sob.

"The night you were followed, when I ran into you. Did you sense anything?"

I shake my head. "All I know is that I thought I recognized the voice of the woman in the van. But I can't really be sure."

Cole squeezes my hand. "Why don't you go get cleaned up and I'll get you something to eat? There's nothing you can do right now anyway."

I'm suddenly conscious that I'm wearing the same clothes I slept in. "I will. I just have to make a phone call first."

For a moment it looks as if he is going to ask me a question, but then he nods. "I'm going to go downstairs for a few minutes. Lock the door behind me."

I follow him to the door and make sure it's locked before

picking up the telephone. I hate what I'm about to do. It feels so fishy in a let's-be-friends; can-I-borrow-five-thousand-dollars? kind of way.

But what choice do I have?

A maid answers and tries to tell me it's too early to disturb Miss Cynthia. "This is an emergency," I tell her in my firmest voice. "If you don't get her right away, she will be furious with you."

There's a long pause. "One moment, please."

I smile. Chances are, the help knows *exactly* who Cynthia's family is.

"This better be good," Cynthia snaps, and my smile falters.

I take a deep breath to calm my nerves. "I'm in trouble. I need five thousand dollars as soon as possible."

"Hold on." I hear something cover the phone. "Gretchen, I need my coffee now!" she yells. "I'm back. I can't do anything without coffee. When do you need it by?"

I almost sob with relief. It'll serve Mother right if Cynthia's money ends up saving her. That will teach her to judge a book by its cover. "I'm not sure. Soon, I think."

"It'll take me a couple hours to get it together. Jack's off hunting, can you believe that? With foxes and hounds and everything. He and all his friends think they're English now." She snorts and then gets back on track. "I don't know how much I have in my personal account, but don't worry. Everything will be fine."

I clutch the phone, gratitude closing my throat.

"Can you tell me about it?" Her voice is soft and worried.

I shake my head before realizing she can't see me. "Not really."

"All right. Hold on. I'll be in touch soon."

"Thank you," I whisper into the phone before replacing the receiver.

I take a deep, shuddering breath, trying to clear my mind before heading to the bathroom to wash and change. The everyday ritual brings a bit of normalcy into my surreal morning and calms my screaming nerves. But nothing can stop the thoughts from spinning round and round in my head. What if my vision is coming true right now? What if my mother is sitting in that room at this very moment, waiting for someone to save her? Could I have stopped it? If I hadn't acted like such a spoiled child, she would have come home with me and been safe right now. Or would it have happened anyway? My mind keeps asking questions there are no answers for.

I finish cleaning up and find Cole in the kitchen, pouring yet another cup of coffee.

"I ran downstairs while you were in the bathroom. Your biggest fan sends his love and some breakfast." He waves his hand toward the table where two thick pieces of toast sit.

My eyes widen. "He fixed the toaster!"

Cole smiles. "No, he sent away for one."

I actually laugh at that and sit at the table, though I know I won't be able to eat anything.

Cole watches until I pick up the toast and take a bite. My stomach churns, but I bravely wash it down with a sip of coffee and give Cole a weak smile. He sits across from me and I'm struck by a thought.

"Last night you said you had something to tell me. What was it?"

Cole frowns. "It was about the letter. But I'm not sure if now is a good time. . . ."

"No, go ahead," I tell him, though part of me never wants to hear about the letter again. "I need something else to hear about or I'll go crazy."

"First I just want to say how sorry I am that I was so secretive. The Society demands it to protect the Sensitives. They take secrecy very seriously. But I should have trusted you."

He looks at me and I nod. Just like I should have trusted him.

He continues. "One of our researchers broke away from the Society. He was one of the ones who fought against teaching Sensitives how to control their powers, saying that it would skew the results of the tests. He didn't care if they went mad as long as they performed like he wanted. He tried to recruit me and he didn't take the rejection well. Part of the reason I came to the States was because my friends wanted me safely out of the way. He'd gone on an extended vacation and no one in our network could find anything about his whereabouts. Until the letter."

A thought comes to me. "In the letter it says you thrashed him. Is that what you mean when you said he didn't take the rejection well?"

Cole looks embarrassed. "I didn't really thrash him. My friend has a tendency for exaggeration. Dr. Boyle tried to stop me and I hit him."

I smile at the image of quiet, controlled Cole hitting anyone. "How do you think he found you?"

Cole shrugs. "I'm not sure he has. We kept my destination fairly secret and planted rumors that I was heading to Switzerland. One of the reasons I chose to stay with Mr. Darby is that the relationship is so distant. They didn't believe anyone could trace it."

"What do you think?"

It takes him a moment to answer. "I think Dr. Franklin Boyle is a very ambitious man who's capable of anything. There are more members on the board who are sympathetic to him and his plan than we'd thought."

"What is his plan?"

Cole shakes his head. "We're not sure. We do know he's recruiting untrained Sensitives. They don't know how brutal he can be when he wants something."

I remember what Dr. Bennett said about the Society and I nod. "That's what . . ." The ring of the telephone cuts me off, and Cole and I freeze, my breath trapped somewhere in the vicinity of my throat.

Cole's hand squeezes mine. "You have to answer," he whispers.

He rises to his feet, pulling me with him. Each ring of the phone travels down my spine as we hurry into the sitting room. With a nod from Cole I pick up the receiver and he leans close to hear the conversation. "Hello?"

"Anna! I spoke to Uncle Jacques. Are you all right?"

"It's just Owen," I mouth to Cole. He frowns but doesn't move away from the telephone.

"I'm fine. Cole is with me."

There's a pause. "Good. I'm glad you aren't alone. Do you need me to come over?"

"I'll be all right. I don't want to make the kidnappers suspicious."

"I can't believe this. Do you have any idea who it might be?"

"No. Not really. Your uncle hired a private investigator to look into my abduction. He's talking to him today as well as picking up half the money for my mother's release."

The pause goes on so long this time, I thought we'd been disconnected. "Owen?"

"Sorry. I'm just surprised. I didn't know Uncle J had that kind of money."

I slap my hand on my forehead. Maybe I shouldn't have said anything. Maybe there was a reason Jacques hadn't been in touch with his family for so long. I don't know how to fix my blunder, so I keep my mouth shut.

"I'll be over as soon as I can. I know you're not alone, but I really want to be there with you. I have a stop to make on my way, but I should be there within the hour."

He hangs up before I can protest. Somehow having him and Cole in the same room doesn't seem like a good idea to me. I can tell by the tightness of Cole's jaw that he doesn't think so either.

I set the receiver down. "There has to be something I can do. When we hand off the money, I'm following them."

He turns to me and catches both my hands in his. "I don't want to put you into that kind of danger. What if your vision comes true?"

I stare at him and then let out some air. "I don't want to be in that kind of danger either. But you don't understand. The reason my mother is in danger is because they couldn't hold me. It's because of what I did last night. There are a million choices I made that led to this. I have to help her."

"Maybe the best way to help your mother is to bring the police in?"

I shake my head. "I've read the newspapers. Most victims never return if you go to the police. I have to do something. And besides . . ." I bite my lip and stop.

"Besides what?"

"Nothing." I give him a slight smile.

I don't tell him that I know in my heart that my mother is waiting for me, just like always.

Waiting for me to come and bust her out.

TWENTY-SEVEN

I spend the next hour pacing, waiting for a knock on the door or the ring of the phone. When a knock finally sounds, I freeze, afraid to answer it. With a glance at me, Cole cautiously opens the door a crack.

"Who are you?" Cole's voice is as commanding as I've ever heard it, but the voice that answers is not only more commanding, but filled with frightening authority.

"I need to speak to Anna Van Housen. Cynthia sent me."

I know that voice . . . I hurry to the door and fling it open. Outside my door is Arnold Rothstein.

"Thank you so much for coming," I say, ushering him in and giving Cole a hard look. His brow furrows, baffled. I probably should have told him that I'd asked Cynthia for the rest of the money, but I had no way of knowing she was going to send her uncle over.

He takes a seat in the chair closest to the door. I sit on the corner of the settee while Cole remains standing in front of the hallway. After seeing Uncle Arnie's eyes slide twice toward him, I signal Cole with my eyes to come sit next to me. He complies, puzzlement still on his face, no doubt picking up on both my relief and my uneasiness.

Uncle Arnie relaxes and gets down to business. "So, Cynthia tells me you're having some trouble and need five big ones right away."

I nod, my eyes straying to the black doctor's bag he's carrying. Does it contain money or guns or . . .

"She also told me you wouldn't tell her why you needed the money. But you'll tell me, right?"

His shrewd black eyes are locked on my face, and I nod. Of course I will.

"My mother's been abducted. I'm not sure who's taken her, but they want a lot of money to get her back."

Reaching into his pocket, he takes out a cigar and raises an eyebrow. I nod. "Go ahead."

As if I would tell him no.

He lights it and I wait as he puffs it to life. "And you're going to pay up? Isn't that risky?" he finally says.

I turn to Cole. "Could you please get me a glass of water? With ice? There's some in the icebox. You can just chip some off."

Cole looks like he is going to argue, but after another look from me, he inclines his head and goes into the kitchen.

My guest waits patiently, puffing away on his cigar, as if we were just exchanging pleasantries. Except that he is without a doubt the most deeply alert man I've ever met.

"I'm not letting them just take the money," I tell him quietly. "I'm going in after her."

The only change of expression in his face is a slight narrowing of his eyes.

"Is that wise?"

For some reason, I know that his handing over of the money in that bag hinges on my response to that question. I lean forward. "No one is better qualified to bust my mother out. I can pick locks, sneak in and out of just about anyplace without detection, and I am very, very good with a knife."

He blinks, the only evidence of his surprise. He stands up as if something has been decided, and I stand as well. "I wish you luck," he says. "You're going to need it. But I have a few things to tell you."

Cole comes in just then with my water and I take it automatically without looking at him. My eyes are fixed on Uncle Arnie.

"My men checked the perimeter of your home. We didn't find anyone watching the place, but that doesn't mean someone won't be later. Also, the reason Cynthia didn't come is because I wouldn't let her. If something goes wrong, she is completely out of it and I never visited." His eyes bore into mine and I nod, tremors going up and down my spine.

"Well, good then. That's settled."

He moves to the door, leaving the black bag next to the chair.

"Excuse me, you've forgotten . . ." I grab Cole's arm to

shut him up and he stops, though I can feel his agitation loud and clear.

"Thank you so much, Mr. Rothstein." I open the door for him and he claps his hat back on his head and walks to the stairwell. "But you said you had a few things to tell me. You only mentioned two."

He turns and gives me a wide smile. "If you ever get tired of the magic racket, give me a call. You'd be a hell of an asset to my business."

He tips his hat and runs lightly down the stairs to where one of his men is waiting for him.

I shut the door and lean back against it, breathing rapidly.

"What was that?" Cole demands. "Who was that man, and why did he leave his bag behind?"

"That was Cynthia's uncle, and he's the boss of one of the biggest crime organizations in the country. That bag contains five thousand dollars."

Cole freezes, his eyes wide. I see him swallow a couple of times. "Very well, then."

That's what I thought. But I just nod and go back to pacing.

The phone rings. It's Jacques with the news that Joanna Lindsay has indeed been incarcerated. "They actually just moved her to Bellevue to be evaluated. Her daughter has been by her side the entire time."

"So that's a dead end, just like we thought." Even though I expected it, my heart still sinks. Now we have no leads on who it could be. "What else did the investigator say? Anything new on my abduction?"

"Apparently, the police found an abandoned milk truck down by the river near the store where you were found. It had been stolen from the delivery company, but no suspects."

Another dead end. "Anything else?"

"No, *chérie*. I'm very sorry. I am going to stop by the bank and then come back to the apartment. Be careful, *oui*?"

"I'll be careful," I promise, and hang up quickly.

There's a knock on the door and my heart pounds until I hear Owen's voice. "Anna, it's me."

I open the door, and he wraps me in a quick hug. "Do you have any word?"

Cole stiffens next to me, but I don't have time to worry about him right now. "No, nothing."

Owen gives me another hug and Cole clears his throat. "Didn't you say Jacques was on his way?" he asks.

I nod.

He looks over at Owen, his dark eyes unreadable. "I'm going to go downstairs and clean up. Can you stay with Anna until your uncle gets here?"

"I'm not going anywhere," Owen tells him.

Cole nods and leaves and I lock the door after him. "Would you like some coffee?" I ask Owen.

He nods. "You look like you could use some too."

We go in the kitchen and he indicates that I should sit, then he reheats the coffee Cole made earlier. A headache is blooming behind my eyes and I rub my temples. I accept the cup with a smile and Owen sits across from me, worry evident in his blue, blue eyes. Then I frown, noticing that Owen's tie is askew and his blond hair is mussed. My throat tightens with emotion. He must have run right over.

He takes a sip of his coffee. "I don't know what you see in that guy. What do we know about him anyway?"

I frown. Why does he always do that? The moment I feel warm and tender toward him he has to ruin it somehow. "Cole? I don't know what you're getting at but I trust him completely."

Owen sighs, his eyes remorseful. "I'm sorry; I'm just so jealous I can't see straight. I've been trying to let you know how I feel about you, but I'm such a dolt it never comes out right."

I shake my head. "I don't think this is the right time."

"Wait. Let me get it out before I lose my nerve. I think we would be amazing together. We could be real partners onstage and off. We could travel and . . ."

I shake my head and he reaches out and covers my hand with his. His agitation is clear. "I'm sorry," Owen continues, his blue eyes miserable. "I know my timing is off. We can talk about it later."

I shake my head again. I may be a novice at romance, but as handsome and funny as he is, I'm pretty sure that Owen and I will never be more than friends. I pull my hand away gently. "No, we can't. I'm sorry."

I'm hit hard by a charge of anger so sharp, I almost gasp out loud.

"It's the Limey, isn't it?" Owen's low voice vibrates with bitterness.

My hand trembles as I lift my coffee cup to my lips. I take a careful sip. "No. No. Of course not. I just . . ."

"You know what? Forget it. I shouldn't have said anything."

His emotions are fading, but they're still brushing across my skin like nettles.

I stand and move to the sink. I pour the coffee down the drain, my stomach churning. Uncomfortable silence stretches between us. I want to say something, but exhaustion and worry make it impossible.

A knock at the door saves me from having to try and I glance at Owen, who is still staring morosely into his coffee cup. I walk down the hall. "Who is it?"

"Jacques."

I let him in and he removes his overcoat, shaking off droplets of water. "It's pouring outside."

Owen comes up behind him and Jacques gives his nephew a nod.

"I have to go," Owen says stiffly. "I've got something I have to do, but I'll be back later."

"Thank you for coming . . ." I stop, puzzled by the jumbled pulses of emotion coming from him. I concentrate, sweat breaking out on my upper lip. Barely suppressed anger pulses back to me, but there's something else. A sense of . . . secrecy. My heart beats faster and cold rushes over me. Owen is *hiding* something.

Trembling, I send out another strand, trying to get a clearer sense of what Owen is feeling, but I can't focus, can't concentrate. His agitation is evident by the tightness of his jaw. Is he just angry about our conversation or is it something else?

He steps out the doorway and panic blooms in my chest. I have to find out what he knows, what he's up to! "Are you sure you don't want to wait with us?" I ask desperately.

"I'm sorry, Anna." For a moment I think I see real regret flicker across his handsome features, but then he shakes his head. "I'll be back as soon as I can."

And then he's gone, his feet tramping down the stairs. I step out after him, but it's too late; the front door has already shut behind him.

Mr. Darby's door opens and Cole steps out. He takes the steps two at a time as if sensing my distress.

Turning, I hurry into the apartment and pace the floor of the sitting room. Why did Owen call Jacques this morning of all mornings? Why was he so disheveled? *What was he hiding?* Cole and Jacques watch me. Jacques's dark eyes are immeasurably sad. Cole's are worried.

"What happened?" he finally asks, his voice tense.

I hesitate. How will Jacques feel about me accusing his nephew? Surely, there's no time now for hurt feelings. But how would I explain my suspicion without revealing my own secret?

"I think we should explore other avenues, since the Lindsays are out." I turn to Jacques. "How well do you know Owen?"

Oddly enough, Jacques doesn't bat an eye. "I knew him

as a child, of course, but not as an adult. My Boston visits were rare. Why?"

Cole glances at me, trying to figure out what I'm saying. "His behavior was odd today." It isn't much to go on, but neither man questions my assessment.

Jacques nods. "I called my sister several weeks ago. It seems my nephew has become, how do you say? The black sheep of the family. There was a scandal involving the boss's daughter and a great deal of debt, but my sister wouldn't speak of it. She only mentioned it because she was hoping I would be a good influence on him."

"And you didn't tell Anna this?" Cole asks.

"I told her mother. I thought she had told you."

I burn at that. No, Mother hadn't told me, but then there was a lot Mother hadn't told me. I shake my head. It doesn't matter. The important thing is to get her back.

I can tell her exactly what I think of her after she is safely home.

"What else do you know about him?" I ask, trying to keep my mind on the task at hand. "Has he mentioned any friends? Do you know where he lives?"

"After my sister called, I did a little checking. This grand bank job of his is a ruse. He's no more than a mail boy."

I continue pacing the room, trying to remember as much as I can of my conversations with Owen. I don't even remember the names of the friends I met the night of the Cotton Club. My face burns remembering our dance. He couldn't really be involved, could he? But his manner today was so suspicious.

I need to find out. Making up my mind, I walk to the phone and dial Cynthia's number.

"I need to get in touch with your uncle," I tell her. "I need a favor."

There's a pause. "You know that his favors might cost you," she finally says.

"I know."

"He'll be in touch," she says, hanging up the phone.

Jacques looks confused.

"Don't ask," Cole tells him. "You don't want to know."

The phone rings almost immediately. It isn't Cynthia's uncle but a man with a heavy accent. He asks me a few terse questions and I tell him all I know about Owen Winchester. After he hangs up, I turn to Cole and Jacques. "Now we wait."

The next hour passes slowly. Cole keeps trying to get me to eat, but I just shake my head and continue shuffling the cards I have in my hands. Jacques pretends to read yesterday's newspaper but never actually turns the pages. By the time the phone rings I'm ready to scream with nerves.

"Hello?"

"My men checked out that boyfriend of yours. He's a real winner."

I don't try to explain that Owen isn't my boyfriend. "I'm listening."

"First off, he's married. Did you know that?"

I close my eyes, remembering the times I smelled perfume. The woman at the Cotton Club. "No, but that makes sense."

"He seems to owe a lot of people money and has a reputation for not paying his debts. A very dangerous habit, if you ask me."

"Where does he live?"

Uncle Arnold gives me the address of Owen's building and I write it down. "If I had more time, I could probably tell you what kind of pomade he uses, but this is what I can do on such short notice."

"It's more than enough," I assure him before ringing off.

"I have the address," I tell Cole and Jacques. "We're going."

"Wait," Cole interjects, but I turn on him before he can say anything else.

"No, I'm tired of waiting! What if Owen really is behind this? We need to find out for sure." Don't they realize that my mother could be injured? The tiny wooden room plays just behind my eyes. She could be there right now, frightened and hurt.

Cole opens his mouth to argue with me, but the ringing of the phone cuts him off. We freeze for a moment before I rush to pick it up, thinking it's Uncle Arnold with more information.

"Hello?"

"Do you have the money?" I grip the phone in my hand as the room shifts and tilts.

"Yes," I say when I'm able to speak. "But how do I know you'll give me my mother once you have it?" I don't want to negotiate with my mother's captor, just keep him talking long enough to see if I recognize the voice.

"I guess you're just going to have to trust me." The voice is muffled, but I'm sure it's one of the men who abducted me.

Anger flares. "Trust a lowlife like you? If you want any money, you are going to have to send me proof that my mother is still"—I swallow as my stomach threatens to heave—"alive."

"If you don't leave the money at the assigned spot at the assigned time, she won't be."

"But I don't even know where that is, or when!"

"You will. Look outside your door."

"Wait!" A click tells me that it's too late and I close my eyes. I point to the door and Jacques rushes to it as Cole comes to me. I set the telephone down and lean against him, glad I'm not alone.

Jacques bends and picks up an envelope. This time, Cole doesn't bother running outside. It could have been left anytime during the phone call, and we know there won't be any trace of the person who left it.

The note is terse and to the point—where, when, and alone.

I look up from Jacques, whose eyes are full of pain, to Cole, whose eyes are full of worry.

It's time to go bring my mother home.

TWENTY-EIGHT

"What time is it?" I ask Jacques for the umpteenth time. He takes his pocket watch out again.

"Nine forty-five."

We're sitting in the backseat of his car a couple blocks from the meeting place. The plan is for me to walk there alone so the kidnapper won't know I'm being followed.

"Are you sure you want to do this?" Jacques asks.

I nod. What else can I do? Our only advantage is that we're pretty sure Owen is behind this, though it's hard for me to get my mind around a fop like Owen masterminding any kind of kidnapping plot. Apparently, he's a far better performer than anyone gave him credit for. But why would he do this? Money? Is showing his father some kind of success worth all this? I close my eyes, remembering being shoved into the van. He must have arranged the whole scenario, even to the point of taking a hit on the jaw. My stomach is twisted in a permanent knot and I wish again that Cole were with me. He's watching outside Owen's building and will follow him to wherever it is they are holding my mother. We know from my vision that she isn't being held in a regular apartment building. And this way, if Jacques loses me, Cole will be able to follow Owen straight to the source.

I glance at Jacques's profile and realize how little I know him. "Can I ask a question?"

He turns. "Of course."

"I saw you run out of our building a couple weeks back, yet you didn't go in to see my mother. Why?"

He looks ahead. "Your mother informed me that I was smothering her. So I always thought twice before coming to visit. That time, I decided not to press my luck."

I stared at his profile. "I'm sorry," I said softly.

He twitches a shoulder and I see the corner of his mustache rise as he smiles. "It is one of the many reasons I love her. She is always a challenge."

That's all right for him to say. It's harder to live with a challenge when you're her daughter. I close my eyes and take a deep breath.

"It's time," Jacques tells me.

I open my eyes and nod.

He reaches out and snatches up my hand. "Good luck, Anna. Bring her home to us."

I give his hand a squeeze. I'm really glad to have him in my corner, but part of me can't help but wonder as I slip from the car and start walking down the block: Does he really know what he's getting himself into by loving my mother?

There's no time to worry about that now. I hear car doors slam behind me and know Jacques is getting out of his car and into the taxicab he hired so Owen won't recognize him.

I turn the corner, clutching the duffel with the money in it tightly. I'm wearing a dark coat, cap, and, much to Jacques's unspoken disapproval, woolen trousers. Cole borrowed them from his uncle, agreeing that they made more sense than wearing a dress would. They'll keep me warmer and give me far more freedom of movement. They also give me a place to stash my knife and a picklock. I have another one pinned behind my ear, carefully hidden by my hair. We planned this rescue operation as cautiously as possible. All that's left is to pray we planned cautiously enough.

My steps are measured, but I can barely hear them over the thudding of my heart. The kidnapper knew what he or she was doing; the streets here are pretty much deserted. I'm almost to the drop site when a door creaks open in the alley next to me. My steps falter as I see a man shoving a woman out the door and hear her cries. She's smaller than I am, and her blond hair shines in the streetlamps. I know I need to move on with my mission but can't help asking "Are you all right?"

She turns toward me and her cries grow louder. "Help me." She slumps to the ground and I reach toward her.

Hands clasp around my waist and mouth. I'm being dragged sideways into the alley. I jab my elbow upward and feel it strike something just before being smashed forward into a brick wall. The pain stuns me and the last conscious thought I have is a prayer that these are the kidnappers and not some random thieves.

I awaken sometime later and it's my nightmare come to life. My cheek is pressed against a rough wooden plank and shadows play against the walls. One eye is swollen shut and my face and head throb with every beat of my heart. Ropes bite painfully into my wrists and ankles. The stench of garbage and decaying fish is so strong, it almost makes me wretch.

I hear a movement behind me and my breathing stops before I realize who it is.

Mother!

I try to move but sweat breaks out on my forehead and nausea overwhelms me. I close my eyes and swallow convulsively. "Mama?" The word takes me back to countless strange rooms as I whisper it in the dark, wondering, always wondering if she was there or not.

"Shhhhh. Keep your voice down. We don't want the guard to know you're awake."

I grit my teeth, fighting the whirling in my head and stomach as I inch myself into a sitting position against the wall. Sucking little breaths between my teeth, I calm myself until the world around me stops spinning. My eyes adjust to the dim light coming in through the wooden slats of the walls and I finally spot her, huddled in the corner opposite me.

"Are you all right?"

"Are you hurt?"

The corners of my mouth curl up briefly as I answer first. "I fought with a brick wall and lost, but I think I'll be all right."

"I'm cold, hungry, and furious, but other than that I'm fine." She pauses, then adds, "Owen won't be if I ever get hold of him."

So it is Owen. I suspected as much, but having it confirmed is still like a shock of icy water. Pain tightens around my heart and I realize how much I didn't want Owen to be involved. "Have you seen him?"

"Once. It's mostly his bitch of a wife who comes in here."

So his wife is involved, as well. I wonder if his wife knows that he asked me to be his partner. I'll play that card if I have to.

"Any guards besides the wife?"

"One. I conned him into giving me a blanket and some food and water."

I smile in the darkness. Of course she did.

"I saved some for you."

I frown, confused. "Some what?"

"Water."

My breath catches. "Then you knew . . ."

"That you would come for me? Of course."

I hear the smile in her voice and tears prick at my eyes. I want to tell her a million things—how much I love her, how angry I am at her, how wonderful she is, how selfish she is—but now isn't the time. I may have to wait years for the right moment, but if I don't get us out of here, that time will never come.

"Where is the guard? And do you have any idea where they're hiding us?"

"The guard is right out front. As far as I can tell, we're in an abandoned warehouse near the river. They blindfolded me, but I could smell the docks. We're in a storage room, I think."

Pride wells up inside. My mother had to have been terrified, but she still kept her composure enough to take notice of her surroundings. Our captors underestimated the Van Housen women.

"Is the door locked?" I ask.

"Yes."

"Are your hands and feet bound?"

"Yes. Rope."

"You tied to anything?"

"No."

I test the ropes that bind my wrists. Whoever tied them did a much better job this time. I might be able to release myself, but in the condition I'm in, it would take far too much effort and leave me unable to defend myself or my mother. "Can you come over to me?"

In answer, I hear the whisper of something scooting across the floor. "Owen was here earlier, but he left. I think it's just the guard now."

When she reaches my side, I lean closer. "My knife is tucked into the back of my trousers. We need to be back to back."

"You're wearing trousers?" is all she says as we move till

our backs are leaning against each other. It takes her several tries before she can pull the knife free. Thank God I wasn't searched while I was knocked out.

She places the knife in my fingers.

"Now lean away from me."

Without asking why, she leans her body away as I flick my balisong open. "Now lean back, but slowly." I want to cut the ropes, not her hands.

Feeling my way with my fingertips, I slip the knife in between the ropes and begin to saw. The rope isn't thick and I make short work of it.

The effort winds me, though, and I lean against the wall as my mother undoes the bindings on her feet.

Then she kneels in front of me, touching my face gently. "My God, you weren't kidding about the brick wall, were you?"

I shake my head and then wish I hadn't as my temples throb in response. Without another word, she loosens the rope around my wrists and ankles.

"Hold on." She stands up, stretching her cramped muscles carefully. "You need some water."

She brings me a small tin cup and I take cautious sips, not wanting to get sick. The room keeps spinning and fear clutches in my stomach. How am I supposed to get us out of here when I'm not even sure I can stand?

I hear a ripping sound and then she takes the cup away for a moment. After putting it back in my hands, she dabs my forehead and the side of my face with a cool, wet cloth. I close my eyes and try to steady my breathing. It seems to help.

"Now what?" she asks.

I take another deep, careful breath. "We have to get out."

"How?"

I'd smile, except my face is now hurting too badly. My mother doesn't dither or waste time moaning. She may be many things, some of them rotten, but Magali Moshe is, above all, a survivor.

"We go back to our places and pretend we're still bound. Divert his attention. Then we'll play it by ear."

She nods and scoots back to her corner, while I lie back down, careful to hide the ropes underneath me. I try not to think of all the things that could go wrong, if Owen is back or if the guard has a gun. Why didn't I think to ask my mother if he had a gun? Too late. My mother gives me a nod and begins to sob.

Showtime.

I hear her inhale. "Joseph! Hurry! Please!"

Her voice is frantic, fearful. Sometimes I forget what a good actress she actually is. There's a scraping sound of a key and then a squeak as the door opens. I blink against the sudden light.

A man in dark clothing comes through the door. "What are you whining about now?"

His voice is lightly accented and I recognize it as one of my abductors from the van.

"My daughter, I think she's dead. I don't think she was

supposed to die? How are you going to get any money from her father if she's dead?"

I almost startle but hold myself still. Of course, my mother would make it known that I am worth far more alive than not.

He turns toward me and my heart pounds. My mother's face is white and terrified behind him, but also determined. I wait until he's bending down toward me and then give her the signal with my outstretched hand, a fist and then three fingers, which always meant *now* in our shows.

In a silent flash she's across the room and a rope is wrapped around the guard's neck. I twist myself around and sideswipe his legs out from underneath him before he can react. Then I'm on top of him, my knife pressed to his throat.

"You say anything and I'll cut through your vocal cords," I whisper. "Understand?" He nods slightly and his eyes tell me he understands perfectly.

While Joseph and I are exchanging pleasantries, Mother is doing a neat job of tying him up.

Once he's tied, I take the knife from his throat.

"You won't get away," he snarls. "The boss will be right back."

Mother holds her hand out for the knife and I give it to her. Bending, she cuts a strip of material from her slip and balls it up. "You talk too much." She shoves it into his mouth. Before she turns away, she hauls her leg back and kicks him in the ribs with all her strength. "Goodbye, darling."

My eyes widen, but I say nothing, I'm too busy concentrating on staying upright.

"Can you walk?" Mother slips the knife into her pocket and puts her arm in mine.

"I think so."

We pause at the door, listening. Nothing. Stepping out into the next room, I quickly take stock of our surroundings. It looks as if we're in the office of an old warehouse. Several large desks dot the perimeter of the room and a long window runs down one wall, no doubt looking out onto the rest of the warehouse. A thick layer of dust covers everything.

"This way." I nod toward a door to our right. "That probably goes outside. The other one probably goes down inside the . . ." I stop my heart leaping into my throat as I hear noises from outside.

My mother grabs my arms and pulls me to the opposite door. We enter the darkness and nearly fall down the stairs. I cling to the wall on one side and follow my mother downward. We pause at the bottom, instinctively shying away from the vast darkness; but at the shouts above, we plunge forward, immediately blinded.

Slowed by our inability to see, we make our way forward, hands clasped, until we find a wall. Then we search slowly, carefully, for a door.

My heart is racing and my mouth is dry. If we can't find a way out, we're as trapped here as we were in the little room. My shin rams painfully into something hard and I freeze as something metal clatters to the floor.

Suddenly the door above swings open wider and Mother and I still.

"Come out, come out, wherever you are," Owen singsongs.

Suddenly an electric lamp goes on overhead, bathing us in a golden glow. Above us on the stairs is Owen, a gun aimed right at us.

"Grab the handcuffs," he orders someone behind him as he makes his way slowly down the stairs. "Let's see her get out of those."

When he reaches us, he doesn't reach for me but instead for my mother. He holds the pistol to her head, his mouth twisted into a smile. He knows I won't do anything as long as my mother is being threatened. I can't believe I ever found him charming.

"Hands above your head."

I slowly raise my hands, brushing my ear as I do so. With my hands on top of my head, I palm the picklock, never taking my eyes from Owen. My eyes widen as a woman with a gun runs downstairs. It's the girl who was working for Mr. Darby.

"Cuff her," Owen orders.

She grabs my arms and twists them behind me. "Oh, how the mighty have fallen."

"Shut up, Lorraine," Owen snaps, and I see her mouth tighten.

"Take her mother upstairs and lock her in the room with Joe. He'll like that."

"My pleasure."

I want to cry as Lorraine ties up my mother. *I'm sorry, Mama*, I think, trying to tell her with my eyes.

But my mother is coolly eyeing her captors, disdain written across every feature. "You'll never get away with this," she tells them. "You're both too damn dumb to pull it off."

Lorraine smacks my mother's face and I wince.

"Meet us at the boat," Owen orders, and turns toward the door only a few feet away from where my mother and I stand. So close.

Silently he opens it and pushes me through. The icy wind feels good on my swollen face. He leads me out onto a long dock as my mind races, trying to figure out anything that will stall him. Cole has to be coming. Or Jacques. Anyone! Then it flashes into my mind so hard, I stumble. *Cole!* I've never sent out a strand without something to connect it to, but I remember how Cole heard me screaming in his head after my nightmare. God, was it only this morning?

I frantically send out a strand but it's hard to visualize because I don't know where to send it. Maybe I should try something else. I quickly switch to imagining beams of light going in all directions, searching. As I concentrate, my steps slow, and Owen pokes me in the back with the gun.

"Hurry up."

I send out another wide sweep. *Please, Cole, please* . . . I have no idea if what I'm trying to do will even work.

"Why?" I ask reasonably. "Don't we have to wait for Lorraine? Unless you're going to double cross her."

He just pokes me with the gun again and I continue walking.

"What are you going to do with my mother?"

"That's none of your beeswax. Just keep moving."

Owen's voice is defensive and threaded with a regret that tugs on my heart. Why? Why would such a handsome, talented young man do something like this? Is it really about the money? Did he just get over his head? I push that out of my mind. I can't afford to feel any sympathy toward him. I have to find a way to save my mother. Besides, he doesn't deserve it. He made choices that led to this just as I did.

I concentrate on sending out more strands and suddenly something comes back at me. Cole! It's only for a second, but it's enough to keep me going. I know he's out there, somewhere.

"Owen? Why are you taking me with you? You have your money."

"It wasn't just the money." His voice is miserable but resolute. "I want you. Don't you see? I want the fame and fortune that Houdini's daughter can bring me."

"He doesn't even know he's my father!" I say desperately.

"That's what your mother said. Boy, she was sure surprised when I told her you'd snuck off to see him several times."

So he or his wife had also been following me. I'm surprised they didn't run into Mrs. Lindsay. We reach the end of the dock where a small boat is tied. My steps slow even further when I see the figure of a man step away from the shadows.

"Well done, Owen. Frankly, I wasn't convinced you could pull it off, but you are to be commended."

I freeze as a British accent floats to me on the breeze. I know who it is even before Owen says his name.

"Thank you, Franklin. I told you I could get her here."

TWENTY-NINE

Owen's self-importance barely registers as I focus on the man behind him.

"I had serious doubts after your first botched attempt."

The man comes closer. I sense, rather than see, his triumph. Why didn't I figure it out before this? Dr. Finneas Bennett—Dr. Franklin Boyle. It was so obvious! Threads of panic unravel at the edge of my mind. If only I had trusted Cole . . . I take a deep breath. "Dr. Bennett. Or should I say Dr. Boyle? What do you want with me?"

Dr. Boyle tips his hat. "You may call me Dr. Boyle. I only go by Dr. Bennett at The New Church. And no offense, Miss Van Housen, but at the beginning, you were just a means to an end."

Cole.

"If you had only stayed put in the milk truck, none of this would have happened. Franklin would have gotten the Limey and you would have been released," Owen says.

"You turned out to be more resourceful than expected," Dr. Boyle says, his voice surprised.

"So you kidnapped my mother to get to me to get to Cole? Isn't that a little excessive?" This cannot be happening. I shut my eyes for a moment, hoping that when I open them, this will all disappear.

It doesn't. Owen is still standing close to me, a gun in his hand, and Dr. Boyle is still waiting for Cole to show up.

"Young Owen here convinced me that Cole would never cooperate unless there was a very real threat to you."

"Owen convinced you?" I ask bitterly. "More like you convinced him. We both know just how *convincing* you can be. You probably mesmerized him!"

Dr. Boyle shrugs. "You give me too much credit. On the other hand, I don't think I've given you enough credit. Now that I know how very talented you are, I've decided to take you along as well."

I still, barely able to breathe. "I don't understand."

"I think you do, Miss Van Housen. Not only did I have the test to point me in your direction, but Mrs. Lindsay's reaction to you confirmed it. I had originally tried to recruit her for my project. I'd heard very good reports about her and she passed all my tests. Unfortunately, she was already too far gone, as we witnessed at Lindy's. But you, you not only have the talent, you are also very much in your right mind. You and Cole will be valuable assets to my organization. And remember, I did ask you to come of your own free will."

I start to tremble, remembering the letter and the young girl who went mad from Dr. Boyle's experiments. *That could be me. Or Cole.*

"That wasn't the deal, Franklin. When you first approached me, you said I could have her. You get Cole, I get Anna." Owen sounds like a petulant child whose favorite toy is being threatened in the sandbox, and I flush.

"You get me? Like I'm a carnival prize? And what makes you think you can hold on to me?" Power tingles down my arms, telling me Cole is nearby. *No!* I scream in my head, sending out a pulse so strong I'm surprised it doesn't light up the docks.

Dr. Boyle suddenly laughs. "She has a point. I don't think you could hold her for very long. It is best she comes with me. Having both of them would ensure their good behavior."

"Why are you doing this?" I ask to keep him talking. Anything to keep from getting on that boat with him.

"Let's just say I'm being a good patriot. When England goes to war again—and mark my words, we will—the government will be more than thankful for the services my stable of trained Sensitives can provide."

Fear shoots through me as I realize that the man is as insane in his way as Mrs. Lindsay. "For a price, of course."

Dr. Boyle twitches a shoulder. "Of course."

"Where does Cole come in?" *Keep him talking.*

"Cole is a very special man. If he wishes, he can detect Sensitives in a crowd of hundreds. Unfortunately, Cole is also a very moral, almost priggish, young man. But I now have the key to ensure his cooperation."

He smiles at me and my heart stops.

"No! She's mine!" Owen bursts out. He turns to me, pleading. "Think of it, Anna; we could be famous and rich. We could travel. We would be a huge success. I just know it."

I see the desperation in his face and remember how badly he wanted to return to Boston in triumph.

"You and I, we really have something. I should have never married Lorraine," he continues. "It was a huge mistake. . . ."

"You bastard!"

I turn to see Lorraine waving a gun at Owen. There's a sudden flash and searing pain reels me off the dock.

The icy black water swallows me immediately and stuns me senseless. There's no light, only the pain in my shoulder and the shock of the water. Is this the end? Was my vision showing me my own death? *Oh, God, what will happen to my mother? What will happen to Cole?* Kicking with my feet, I rise to the surface to take a deep breath before sinking again, the current dragging at my feet. My strength is depleted by injuries. Weakness and lassitude overcome me.

I wonder if my father ever thought he was going to die alone and underwater.

An image of Houdini springs to my mind and with it the picklock I'd palmed earlier. I yank it from where it's still caught in my woolen jacket. With fingers numb from cold, I carefully stick it in the lock. It's much more difficult trying to do so underwater while kicking my feet. I rise to take another deep breath, struggling against my growing panic. I sink again and wonder if it's for the last time. Gritting my teeth, I continue working the lock until it finally springs open. I free my arms and swim to the surface, letting the cuffs and picklock sink into the river.

Disoriented, I look around and realize I've drifted downriver. Someone's yelling my name, but it's faint. And I'm cold. So cold. My body shakes violently, shutting down. I can hardly tread water. If only I could get close enough to the bank to stand, if only I could yell.

One foot touches something and then the other. Mud, I'm in mud. I collapse in relief and swallow a mouthful of water. I have to make it to the shore. I have to.

Struggling with every bit of strength I have left, I paddle toward the bank, which is now outlined in the dark. I try to stand. Try to walk. My legs are numb. My mind is numb. I crawl in the frozen mud, trying to send a signal to Cole. But I have no energy left. I lurch forward and everything goes dark.

I have never been so cold.

"Is she alive?"

My mother's voice sounds far away. I try to answer, but my lips are frozen, just like everything else. Someone is rubbing my hands and feet and the pain is like icy fire shooting up my limbs. I try to tell them to stop, but I can't make my lips move.

"The doctor's here now. Let him through, let him through."

I know people are surrounding me and I want to tell them I'm alive, I'll be fine, but I can't. I can't even open my eyes.

"You're going to be fine, Anna." It's Cole's voice I hear, and then I feel his warm lips brush my icy mouth like a thousand sunlit kisses.

I feel him throw me a strand and my mind grabs at it, clinging to it as he is pushed away by doctors. I hold on to the ribbon that links me to him as the doctors work on me. The tiny spark of the strand warms me from the inside out and I let myself slip back into unconsciousness, knowing the people I love are safe.

I'm conscious of the passage of time. My life becomes a blur of bad-tasting medicine, scratchy cotton sheets, and ridiculous nurses' caps. The faces may change, but the caps, with their stiff, cambric crowns and wide, starched brims, stay the same.

"How long have I been here?" I remember asking one cap during a lucid moment. The cooling sponge being wiped across my face feels wonderful.

"About a week," the cap says.

"Am I sick?" I ask it.

"Yes."

The next time I awake there is no cap hovering over me. My mind feels clear of fog for the first time since I fell from the dock. *The dock!* Memories come flooding back and

I struggle to sit up, but a throbbing pain in my shoulder stops me.

"I wouldn't do that if I were you." My mother's voice comes from somewhere on my right. Peering through the gloom, I find her sitting in a chair in the corner of the room, working on a newspaper crossword puzzle. The only light in the room is coming from a small lamp next to her. "The bullet only nicked you, but they just changed the bandage so it'll be sore."

She sets the paper aside and walks over to my bed. I frown, trying to figure out why she looks so different. She's wearing a boxy, blue jacket and matching pleated skirt with low-heeled, black oxford pumps. Instead of her usual hodgepodge of costume jewelry, only a single strand of pearls adorns her neck.

Very conventional. This must be her I'm-visiting-my daughter-in-the-hospital outfit.

"How long have I been here?" I croak. My throat stings, and I clutch at it with my good arm.

My mother gives me a sip of water, then places it back on the bedside table. "Almost two weeks. You developed pneumonia. They didn't think you were going to make it. That'll teach you to swim in the Hudson in November."

Her words are light, but her hands are trembling. She clasps them in front of her and squeezes them together. Hard.

"What happened to Cole?"

"He's fine. I sent him home to get some sleep. Very stubborn young man. He's been here the whole time, even when

I told him it wasn't necessary." Her voice contains grudging respect and I hide a smile, imagining the conversations they must have had—Cole so quietly unmovable and my mother so charmingly insistent. "I think you have a suitor."

A suitor? I raise my brow at her old-fashioned choice of words. Then I remember something. "What about you and Jacques?"

"Oh, he told you, did he? I thought he might have. We're getting married on New Year's Day. He's another stubborn man."

Married? My mother's getting married? It's hard for me even to think about marriage and my mother in the same sentence. Another strange notion hits me. Jacques is going to be my stepfather. Suddenly I wonder if Harry Houdini knows I'm in the hospital, but that's not something I can ask my mother. My lids grow heavy, but I'm not done with her yet.

"What about the show?"

Her mouth tightens and I wonder if she is remembering the last time we did the show together. I want to tell her I'm sorry, but I'm not. I'm only sorry it hurt her.

"Jacques and I canceled the show."

I almost sit up again, but she pushes me back down. "Don't worry; it'll be fine. Jacques wants me to be his business partner."

But what about me? Anger flashes over me as I remember how she tried to maneuver me out of the show. So she finally got her wish. Then I remember all the things

Jacques told me about how she was afraid I would end up like her.

Her face takes on a carefully arranged blankness, which means that asking more questions about the show is useless. One of the most important things I've learned about my mother is that when she puts something behind her, it is dead and gone. Evidently, the life we've lived up until now is, in her mind at least, dead and gone.

She pats my shoulder and tucks the blankets around me. "It's all for the best, really. Now you can decide what it is you truly want to do with your life."

A cap interrupts us then to make me take more foul-tasting medicine and then insists that I rest. After the light is turned out and my brow kissed, I turn the question over and over in my mind, *What do I really want to do with my life?*

Our sitting room is filled with sweet-smelling hothouse flowers. I wonder how many flower shops are low on holiday bouquets because my mother, Jacques, and Cole keep buying them all up.

I've been home for three days now, and I feel stronger every morning. Right now, I'm lounging on the settee, my shoulder still taped, even though it's almost healed. Fortunately for me, Lorraine was as lousy a shot as she was a housekeeper.

"Checkmate!" Mr. Darby rubs his hands together across the board set up next to me. I barely resist the urge to sweep all the pieces to the floor.

"That's the last time I play you!"

"That's what you always say," Mother says from the doorway. "Then you always play him again. A glutton for punishment."

"I live with you, don't I?" I mutter under my breath.

"Don't strain yourself, darling," she says wickedly as she brings me a cup of tea.

My mother and I have come to an uneasy truce. I love her and she loves me, but we won't ever work together again. I'm so thankful the séances are over. Though Cynthia is practically inconsolable about having to find a new medium. She thinks I should strike out on my own and move in with her as her private spirit guide, but I gave her an unequivocal no to that dizzy idea. Personally, I think she's just bored and wants her best friend with her all the time. The largest bouquet in the room is from her.

Mr. Darby puts the chessboard away. "I'll come by and see you again, missy. Take care of yourself now."

I smile up at him as he pats my arm and takes his leave.

My mother fusses over me for a moment. "Cole will be up shortly to sit with you. I guess Macy's puts on some big parade, and Jacques is taking me to see it. When I get back, perhaps you'll be feeling well enough to go to Thanksgiving dinner."

I smile at her and she pauses at the door. "Are you sure you're up for the trial?"

I nod. "The lawyers say it's an open-and-shut case. You already gave your deposition. With my testimony, both Owen and Lorraine will be put away for a good long time."

A faint, cold smile flickers across my mother's mouth. "As is only fitting."

She leaves me to my thoughts and I settle back against the pillows, my shoulder aching. I'm so thankful Cole went against my wishes and brought the police in on the kidnapping at the last minute. They watched Owen's place until he and Lorraine left with their suitcases, then shadowed them to the warehouse. It was Cole who found me, though.

There was no trace of Dr. Boyle. He probably left when he realized the police had come along with Cole. The police had a description of him, but he's probably long gone. I shiver at the thought that he may be out there somewhere, plotting to kidnap more Sensitives. At least Owen won't be bothering us again.

Inside my chest my heart twinges. I still can't believe Owen took me in so easily, but then again, maybe he really had been under Dr. Boyle's influence. At any rate, it just proves that being a Sensitive doesn't mean you're immune to deception.

Glancing at the door, I reach down and pick out a small box from the stack of gifts next to me. Apparently, the newspapers published an article about my ordeal, and notes, gifts, and flowers had been arriving ever since. The box I'm holding had been delivered with a dozen yellow roses just after I arrived home. Because I've received so many presents, my mother has no reason to believe this one is any different. But it is.

I lift the lid and finger the solid silver handcuffs inside. I unfold the note and read,

Dear Anna the magician,

I hope this note finds you mending and the gift makes you smile. You will be receiving a visitor soon. His name is Martin Beck. I trust you will know the name. He is putting together a troupe going to England to perform in various theaters. He does this on occasion to "season" young acts so they can perfect their craft before performing in the States. After I told him of your potential, he agreed to come see you in order to gauge your interest. I believe it to be a good opportunity for you. Of course, you may not want to leave your mother. Please don't feel any obligation because of our relationship.

Thinking of you,
Harry Houdini

P.S. You were right. The secret lies in shortening the bolts.

Martin Beck is one of the most famous entertainment managers in the world. He'd built the Orpheum Theaters Empire, and even though he no longer owns them, he's still one of the most influential men in the entertainment world. Jacques is small-time compared to Beck. I'd received another note just this morning from Beck himself setting up a time to meet.

And I already knew what I would tell him—yes, a thousand times yes. Performing, astonishing people with the unexpected—*that* is what I want to do with my life. Plus this way, I'll not only get to do what I love, I'll be near Cole when he starts college.

I hear a tap on the door and Cole's professor voice reaches me from the hallway. He's still uncomfortable around my mother, but then again, my mother isn't a very comfortable person.

As I fold the note and stick it in the box, I realize it doesn't matter if Houdini is my real father or not—as long as I think of him this way he will always, in a way, be mine.

Smiling, I set the box aside, and my heart leaps as Cole opens the door and pokes his head around the corner. He's been with me almost continuously since I've come home, and every time we're together, our connection grows stronger. I can't wait to gallivant about London with him. I don't need a vision to know that it's going to be splendid.

He takes my hand and bends down to brush his lips across mine.

"How are you feeling?" he asks, carefully sitting next to me.

I look into those midnight-dark eyes and I can't help but smile. "Magical," I say, squeezing his hand. "I feel magical."

ACKNOWLEDGMENTS

Books don't happen out of thin air, and I know for a fact this one didn't. It started with an idea—a spark partially ignited and kept going by my teen coworker, Nicolas Braccioforte. Nic, a magic enthusiast, listened to my ideas and gave me invaluable feedback on the magic scenes. The spark was kept alive by my husband, Alan, my children, Ethan and Megan, and my mom and dad, Lyle and Carol Foreman, who always supported me, even when I was whining. Numerous critique partners and friends went over a gazillion drafts of my manuscript and gave me feedback and encouragement, including Kelly McClymer, Cyn Balog, Amy Danicic, Delilah Marvelle, Ann Friedrick, and Jessica Smith. A huge chunk of gratitude goes to my incomparable agent, Mollie Glick, who so completely believed in Anna's story that she worked with me for months to whip the manuscript into shape. Without her, I would not have found my amazing editor, Kristin Rens, who made delving into 1920s New York a joyous experience. And lastly, I would like to thank the one and only Harry Houdini, whose legendary life provided such juicy inspiration for my story and whose fame and mystique will live on forever.